KILL ME AGAIN

This Large Print Book carries the
Seal of Approval of N.A.V.H.

KILL ME AGAIN

MAGGIE SHAYNE

WHEELER PUBLISHING
A part of Gale, Cengage Learning

GALE
CENGAGE Learning

Detroit • New York • San Francisco • New Haven, Conn • Waterville, Maine • London

10. Dec14
Gale
3099(2634)

GALE
CENGAGE Learning

Copyright © 2010 by Margaret Benson.
A Secrets of Shadow Falls Novel #1.
Wheeler Publishing, a part of Gale, Cengage Learning.

LIBRARY OF CONGRESS CATALOGING-IN-PUBLICATION DATA

Shayne, Maggie.
    Kill me again / by Maggie Shayne.
      p. cm. — (Wheeler Publishing large print hardcover)
    ISBN-13: 978-1-4104-3093-9 (hardcover)
    ISBN-10: 1-4104-3093-6 (hardcover)
    1. Single women—Fiction. 2. Novelists—Fiction. 3.
Secrets—Fiction. 4. Vermont—Fiction. 5. Large type books. I.
Title.
PS3619.H399K54 2010b
813'.6—dc22   2010031114

Published in 2010 by arrangement with Harlequin Books S.A.

Printed in the United States of America
1 2 3 4 5 6 7 14 13 12 11 10

To Lance, my partner, my best friend,
my inspiration. You
understand my craziness,
you weather all my storms and
you are my constant,
steady, calm harbor.
I wrote you into countless
novels, never ever realizing
that one day you would
step off the pages and out
of my imagination to
sweep me into your strong arms.
But you did.
You've fulfilled my heart's
desire and made my
dreams come true. Thank you
for loving me.

1

Today was the day Olivia Dupree was going to meet the only man on the planet who saw life the way she did — as one long series of disappointments, as a perilous journey best navigated entirely solo — for the very first time, and she didn't have a thing to wear.

Not that what she wore really mattered. She wasn't *that* sort of fan. Not only didn't she think he would care what she looked like, but she would also be extremely disappointed if he did.

And yet she'd given in to the inner idiotic teenager that had *never* been her and stood on her bed, so she could gauge her appearance in the big mirror that was part of her dresser. She didn't own a full-length mirror. She'd never thought she needed one and still held that opinion. Her ordinary style was pretty basic. For work she wore skinny, knee-length pencil skirts with matching blazers when it was cool, and sensible pumps with two-inch heels. She kept her dark hair in a tight bun and applied her makeup in the same minimalist fashion every weekday. College English students didn't really care what their professor looked like, after all. And she wasn't out to capture the attention of anyone who might.

On weekends, she traded the suits for jeans, the bun for a ponytail and the makeup for sunscreen.

Now she needed something in between. Something relaxed but attractive. Not seductive, just attractive. She was *not* a doe-eyed, adoring fan. But she'd never met Aaron Westhaven before, and she wanted to make a good impression.

Nothing more.

Freddy, her very best friend in the entire world — and the *only* specimen of the male gender, canine or otherwise, she trusted with her heart — tipped his massive head from one side to the other as he watched her standing somewhat unsteadily on the mattress. Standing was not what the bed was for, he seemed to be thinking.

She glanced down at him. "It's okay, boy. I'll get down momentarily. And standing on the bed is still verboten when it comes to you, okay?"

He heaved a giant sigh and lowered his two-hundred-pound, brindle-patterned bulk to the floor. He was only average size for an adult male English mastiff, but even she had trouble believing how big he was, and she'd had him for three years.

She hoped Mr. Westhaven didn't have an aversion to dogs. He hadn't written dogs into any of his novels, so she couldn't be sure, but she suspected he would love Freddy. Because anyone with a heart would love Freddy, and Westhaven *certainly* had a heart.

She felt as if she knew him well. The reclusive author's heartbreakingly tragic novels lined her shelves and spoke to her soul. They were her own guilty little secret. But they so reflected the way she felt about life and love. You really couldn't depend on anyone but yourself. He seemed to understand that. God knew she did.

And now she was about to meet him — right here in Shadow Falls, Vermont.

She glanced at the combination she now wore, a pair of dressy black trousers and a lavender button-down blouse with a black blazer over it. Too stiff. She unbuttoned the blazer and thought she still looked too formal. Then she took it off and thought she looked too casual.

Frustrated, she threw the blazer down by her feet. Big mistake. Freddy saw that as an invitation, sprang upright and bounded onto the bed with a giant "woof" that reverberated through her chest. The mattress sank, the box springs squeaking in protest.

"I couldn't see anything from the waist down," she explained, as she tried to keep her balance. He bounced in response to her words, and the mattress tidal-waved beneath her. Laughing, she fell onto her butt among the rumpled covers, and Freddy moved over her, trying to lick her face as she laughed too hard to breathe. "You're a lug. Get down!"

He obeyed immediately, then stood there waiting for her to join him. She got down, traded the trousers for a skirt, slid her feet into a pair of sandals and looked at the clock on the nightstand, then at her wristwatch. "Gee, Freddy. Mr. Westhaven is late." She frowned as a little knot of worry tightened in her stomach.

"He's *really* late."

And she was concerned. Because though she admired him, she didn't entirely trust him, simply because he was male. The fact that he'd agreed to be the surprise guest speaker at the English Department's summer fundraiser had been nothing less than a stunner. She'd invited him with every expectation that he would decline, if he replied at all. The man *never* made public appearances. She'd been shocked — and a little bit suspicious — when he'd accepted the invitation.

But she'd chalked that up to her own man issues, and tried to count on him to show up as promised and not pull a no-show.

Maybe that had been a mistake.

Time would tell, she supposed. She brushed the dog hairs off her lavender blouse and exchanged it for a sleeveless silk shell in jade green. It would just have to do.

Samuel Overton wasn't supposed to be driving *at all* without his mom in the car, much less driving a big Ford Expedition that wasn't even theirs. But he was doing it anyway. He didn't really know how she expected him not to. It was the Funkmaster Flex Edition, not just *any* SUV. And it was freakin' *sweet.* Checkered flag design on the dashboard and console, unique black-and-red paint job, sound system to die for. Better yet, it had a 300 horsepower, 5.4-liter iron-block, 24-valve V-8 in it. Hell, this thing was a dream vehicle. Car-show worthy.

Besides, he didn't have any reason to think his mom would find out.

Kyle Becker, Sam's best friend, cranked up the music, and Sam shoved his hand away from the dial and turned it back down. "It's distracting."

"It's *Metallica.* You don't turn down Metallica."

"Then turn it off."

"No way. It'll do you good to get used to distractions," Kyle said, with the wisdom that came from being a licensed sixteen-year-old, and a whole six weeks older than Sam. "And while you're at it, you might want to go faster than thirty-five."

Sam pressed on the gas pedal, picked up speed and sent a cloud of dust up behind them. They'd taken a back road where there would be little traffic, so he could practice driving a car that had a little more guts than his mother's minivan.

He felt a little ping and knew he was throwing up pebbles in addition to the dust cloud. Shaking his head, he hit the brakes and pulled over. "This is stupid. This dirt road's no good for a cherry ride like this."

"I told you, we'll wash it before we take it back," Kyle insisted. "No one will ever know."

"Right, unless I end up dinging it or something. Professor Mallory will notice that when he comes back from Europe, even if Mom doesn't." Sam sighed, frustrated with himself as he slowly realized there was almost zero chance he was going to get away with this undetected. Mom *always* found out. "I must have been a moron to have let you talk me in to this."

"No, you weren't. You've got to practice on something, right? How are you going to pass your test next week if you don't? And you can't take your mother's minivan when she has it parked outside the damn hospital all day every day."

"Yeah, well, I can't keep taking Mallory's dream machine out, either. I mean, I shouldn't. He left it with Mom for safekeeping while he's away. I doubt this is what he had in mind."

"Why the hell not? You're not hurting it any. And he did ask your mom to drive it once in a while to keep it loose, right? You're *helping* him, dude."

"You wouldn't be saying that if it was *your* dream machine I was driving over a cow path," Sam said. "If Mom finds out, she'll have a freakin' breakdown."

"She's not gonna find out." Kyle said it as if he were offering his personal guarantee that it was true.

The dust was clearing, and Sam sighed. "Let's just go. We still have to gas it up and wash it, and hope to hell nobody sees us driving it back."

"Yeah," Kyle said. "We probably better get on that. But we can take it straight back to your mom's garage, bring the gas in a can and wash it right there, so we don't draw notice. You want me to drive it back?"

Sam nodded. "Just in case we meet a cop or something," he said. "Mom would be even more pissed if I got a ticket for driving on a learner's permit without a licensed over-eighteen driver along." He opened his door, getting out of the SUV to go around to the passenger side.

Kyle got out his own side, but then he just stood there, staring toward the side of the road a dozen or so yards ahead of them.

And then he went really tense all of a sudden, and his mouth opened.

"What?" Sam asked, trying to see what he was looking at.

Kyle lifted a finger and pointed. "Holy shit, is that a *body?*"

"No way!" Sam turned and spotted the lump that had caught his friend's attention. Something that, he had to admit, looked like a person lay in the deep grass at the bottom of a patch of a slope.

The two boys headed for the human-shaped lump of clothing. When they got as

14

close as they could without leaving the road, Kyle said, "Sure as shit, Sam, there's a *guy* down there. And he isn't moving."

Elbowing his friend, Sam said, "Go see if he's alive." Then he tugged his cell phone out of his shirt pocket.

"Screw you, *you* go see if he's alive!"

"Fine." Sam held out the phone. "You can call 911 . . . and my mom at the hospital."

Sighing, Kyle shook his head. "*I'm* not calling your mom. I'll go see if he's alive."

When her telephone finally rang, Olivia had all but given up on her special guest. He was known to be rabid about his privacy. She should have trusted the instinct that told her to distrust his promise to appear. But at the time she'd been convinced that the director of special events would never agree to Aaron Westhaven's terms anyway. No press, no announcement, no photographs, no hotel. But he had conceded to all of it. Westhaven had even accepted Olivia's offer to let him stay in her guestroom, allowing him to forego any of the far more public local inns or B and Bs. The fundraiser was by invitation only, so the invited guests had been told only that it would feature a "secret guest speaker" guaranteed to be worth their donations. The tickets had

15

sold out in record time.

And now it looked as if he wasn't even going to show up.

She never should have believed he would keep his word. People seldom did. Especially men.

When the phone rang, her hopes climbed in spite of her doom-and-gloom realism, though she scolded them back into place even as she snatched the receiver up so fast that she didn't even look at the caller ID first.

"Professor Dupree," she answered.

A female voice came from the other end. "Hi, Olivia. It's Carrie Overton. How are you?"

"Carrie?" It took her a moment to process the name, since she had been expecting her errant guest speaker to be calling with a huge apology and a fistful of excuses. Frowning, she held the phone away and looked at the ID screen. *Shadow Falls General Hosp,* it said, before it ran out of room. She lifted her brows and brought the phone back to her ear. "I'm fine, a little frustrated right now, but — is everything all right?"

Carrie was one of the few women she'd built something of a friendship with over the past sixteen years — and even then, only

16

a casual one. Olivia knew it didn't pay to let too many people get too close when you had as many secrets in your past as she did.

"I'm calling from —"

"The hospital, I know," Olivia said, a tiny kernel of concern beginning to form in her chest. Carrie had no earthly reason to be calling her today — especially not from her job, which she took very seriously. "What's going on?"

Carrie drew a breath. "Okay, it's — I have a patient here. Male, mid-thirties maybe. Dark hair and eyes. Six feet or so, pretty buff. No ID."

"Sounds like you're looking for a home for a stray, Carrie."

"Sort of. He had your business card in his pocket, so I thought you might be able to help us identify him."

Olivia closed her eyes slowly as her mind fit Tab A into Slot B. God, was it Aaron Westhaven? Was that why he was so late? "Is there anything written on the back of the card?" she asked.

"Yeah. Your home phone number. Address, too. *Do* you know who he is?"

"I think so," Olivia whispered. It was *him.* It had to be. She didn't give *anyone* her home address. *Ever.* But she'd made an exception for the semifamous recluse with

17

the direct line into her brain. "Is he all right? I mean how bad —"

"I really can't discuss that —"

"Right, right." Rules, regs, confidentiality. Carrie wasn't going to breech protocol and risk her medical license. Not over the phone, anyway.

"Can you come over here?" Carrie asked.

Olivia nodded hard, just as if Carrie could see the motion. "I'll be there in fifteen minutes," she said, then hung up the phone without another word. She headed for the door, the issue of what to wear entirely forgotten, and grabbed her handbag on the way.

Freddy ran ahead of her and waited by the door, tail wagging.

She crouched, but only a little, and cupped his great big, flappy jowled face between her palms. "You have to stay here, Fred. I'm going to the hospital, and they don't allow dogs there, so you have to stay here. But I promise I won't be long."

He sighed heavily and lowered his big head, just as if he understood every word.

She kept hold of him, though, and kissed him right on the snout. "Don't be sad. I'll be back."

He got up and plodded away, sinking onto his supersize doggy bed as if his heart was breaking.

Olivia took momentary pity on her best friend, and snapped on the TV, tuning it to Animal Planet. Freddy seemed marginally placated. Then she tossed the remote onto the highest shelf in the room to keep him from eating it and headed for her hybrid SUV.

Fifteen minutes later she was standing in front of the nurses' desk at Shadow Falls General, asking for Dr. Carrie Overton. A hand on her shoulder made her stop in midquestion, and she turned to see a face she knew, though not the one she'd been expecting. She stared up at the tall cop. "Bryan. I almost didn't recognize you in your uniform. Must seem good to have it back, hmm?"

"Better than you'd believe," Bryan Kendall said. "How have you been?"

"Good. Good."

"And that horse you call a dog?"

"Moping that he didn't get to ride along, but otherwise good. You and Dawn should stop by and visit him." Then she frowned and asked, "What are you doing here?"

"Same thing you are," he said.

That reply made her brows go up. "The police are involved in this?"

Bryan nodded, his face serious. "Yeah. I'll

19

explain what I can while we wait for Dr. Overton. Right now she's busy reaming out her kid for taking the car without permission." He nodded to the left, and Olivia saw the stunning redhead, wearing a white lab coat and a stethoscope, apparently in midlecture. Her audience consisted of two teenage boys with their heads hanging low.

Carrie glanced up, and Bryan beckoned her over. She pointed sternly, directing the boys to a pair of chairs, then called over her shoulder as she came through the glass door, "Do not leave that spot until I come back."

Then she took a breath, smoothed her fiery curls and approached them. "Thanks for coming, Olivia. Did you fill her in yet, Officer Kendall?"

Olivia shook her head as Bryan said, "No, not yet." Then, with a sympathetic look at the boys in the other room, he added, "You know Sam and Kyle probably saved the guy's life by finding him, right?"

"That's no excuse," Carrie said. She looked at Olivia again. "The mystery patient is this way. Will you take a look at him for me?"

"I don't know what good it will do," Olivia began, following as Carrie walked briskly down the hall, stopping outside a door with the number 206 on it.

"Why not?" Carrie asked.

There was a window beside the door, the blind open just enough to reveal the man in the bed. He lay on his back, staring at the ceiling, his head swathed in bandages. "Because I've never actually seen — Oh." Olivia lost her words somehow, and her breath with them, as her gaze slid from the white bandages on the man's head to his face. God, he was beautiful. She hadn't expected that.

"Do you know him?" Bryan asked.

"Not by sight," Olivia replied. She thought she ought to face Bryan while speaking to him, but she couldn't take her eyes off the man in the bed. His were open, and they were soft eyes. Their color was green or maybe brown. She couldn't tell from this distance. But they were dark and striking, as was the way they turned down slightly at the outside corners, giving him an inherently sad expression. And while his age surprised her — as did her instant reaction to his good looks — the pain and stoic, steadfast endurance expressed by those eyes didn't shock her in the least. She'd *expected* him to be strong, she realized.

"Olivia?" Bryan prompted.

She blinked and cleared her throat. "I've

21

never actually met him before. But I'm fairly certain I know who he is, and that he was on his way to see me."

Bryan tensed a little. He was one of the very few people who knew Olivia's secrets. And inviting a stranger to her home wasn't something he would expect her to do.

"It's a long story," she began.

"Just give us the digest version for now," he said.

She nodded. "He's a writer, an author, as well-known for being reclusive as for his work, which is, to put it mildly, brilliant. His name is Aaron Westhaven, although as closely as he guards his privacy, it's probably a pseudonym. He doesn't do public appearances, doesn't even allow himself to be photographed, and doesn't want anyone to know he's in town."

"Why was he coming to see you?" Bryan asked.

"I invited him to speak at a fundraiser at the university."

"And he agreed?" Looking more coplike than ever, Bryan was frowning now.

"Yes, he did," Olivia said. "I was stunned, really. But there were strict stipulations. We were doing this as a secret-guest, by-invitation-only thing. He insisted on no press, no publicity. Just a private lecture, with wine and cheese and him as the guest speaker. He was supposed to stay at my place — more private than a motel or an inn."

"And you agreed to that?"

She met Bryan's eyes, saw the disbelief in them. "It was my idea. And the university agreed to every condition. Getting him at all was a real coup, Bryan. He's special. His work . . . it's meant a lot to me. I even used to write to him. Not often. I mean, I'm not a drooling groupie or anything."

"I would never mistake you for a drooling groupie, Olivia," he said dryly.

She acknowledged that with a nod. "He never wrote back, probably never even saw my letters. But still, I felt —" She turned her gaze back to the man in the bed. "I felt as if I knew him in some small way, through his work. I felt we were on common ground about some things."

"Uh-huh," Bryan said, the way you say it when pretending you understand something you actually don't.

Olivia read his face, then frowned, turning to Carrie as what should have been an obvious question occurred to her. "He's conscious. Why aren't you asking *him* all these questions?"

Carrie lowered her head. "We *have* asked

him. But he can't give us any answers. He, um . . . well, he says he doesn't remember."

Olivia felt her eyes widen. "You're saying he has amnesia?"

Carrie bit her lower lip and nodded deeply.

"You think it's for real?" Bryan asked. "I thought that kind of thing only happened in daytime dramas."

"I don't have any reason not to believe him," Carrie said. "I'm sure it's temporary. I hope so, at least. Amnesia is rare, and *permanent* amnesia, really unusual. Then again, with a head injury like this, it's impossible to tell."

Olivia looked at him with his head all wrapped, and more obvious questions came to her, the first of which was, "What happened to him? Car accident?"

Bryan said, "He was shot."

Her head snapped to the side fast, and she searched Bryan's face.

"He was shot in the back of the head from fairly close range."

"Like . . . an execution?" Olivia whispered.

"If he didn't have a steel plate in the back of his skull, he'd be a dead man," Carrie explained. "As it is, there was remarkably little damage. It's amazing, really, how lucky he was."

24

"You can say that again," Bryan agreed. "And if your son hadn't been practicing his driving skills on that deserted back road, we might not have found him in time."

He was, Olivia thought, obviously trying to help the kid out. Not knowing Carrie Overton as well as she did, he wouldn't know how much she adored her son. He probably feared she would be too hard on him — which was, to Olivia, kind of funny. Or would have been under other circumstances. If anything, Carrie tended to let Sam off too easily.

Carrie rolled her blue, blue eyes. "He insists Kyle was driving."

"Well, he's not stupid, and he doesn't want a ticket," Bryan said. "Being that he's taking his driving test in — what did you tell me — a week? Yeah, I'm sure he was trying to get some practice in. But since I can't prove it, I'm not going to ticket him."

"That's quite all right, Officer," Carrie said. "Because *I* intend to *murder* him."

Or at least ground him for a weekend, Olivia thought.

"The question remains," Bryan said. "Is this man the reclusive author Olivia believes he is?"

"May I see the card you found on him?" Olivia asked.

Carrie pulled the business card from her breast pocket and handed it over. It was smudged with black.

"What's all over it?" Olivia asked, wrinkling her nose.

"I had to dust it," Bryan said. "No usable prints. It's useless to us."

Olivia flipped the smudged card over, saw her own handwriting on the back and nodded. "Well, this is the card I sent to Aaron Westhaven. I have no doubt about that." She looked into the room again, and this time found the man staring back at her, his expression curious now that he'd noticed the three of them looking at him as if he were a specimen in a zoo.

"Maybe he knew this could happen," Olivia said, very softly, almost speaking to herself. "Maybe that's why he's always been so private, because he knew someone might come after him if he were out in the open."

Bryan met her eyes, and they shared a silent exchange. He knew that was how *she* felt. He knew there was someone who would probably kill her if he ever found out she was still alive. He knew she wasn't even using her own name, and hadn't been for the past sixteen years. And he probably thought she was projecting.

She shook her head. "So what do I do but

convince him to come out into the open, and the minute he does, he gets shot. God, I feel terrible."

"You didn't *convince* him. You invited him. You didn't even expect him to accept. And he was free to say no," Bryan said.

Carrie nodded her agreement. "Will you talk to him, Olivia?" she asked. "He's completely in the dark here, and none too friendly — though I don't blame him, given his situation. Even if you've never met him, you know more about him than any of the rest of us do. It has to help a little."

"Of course I'll talk to him." Olivia held the man's steady gaze through the glass. "I've been waiting years for the chance to talk to him." His eyes were fixed on hers, and they were intense. A little chill whispered up her spine. She should have known he would be beautiful. Anyone who could write the way he did had to be beautiful inside and out.

"All right, you go talk to him, then," Bryan said. "Call me if anything comes up. Meanwhile, I'm going to get back to the station, make some calls, figure out who his publisher is, or his editor, or his whatever. There must be *someone,* somewhere, who knows this guy."

"Wait." Olivia turned to Bryan. "Am I

27

right in assuming you didn't catch the person who did this to him?"

Lowering his head, Bryan pushed a hand through his hair. "We don't have a clue. Not even a bullet casing. The bastard took it with him."

Olivia was worried by that. "Mr. Westhaven doesn't want publicity about his visit here. And I can't help but think it's pretty obvious now that he has good reason for that. Can we keep this quiet, at least for now?"

Bryan nodded. "I think that's probably best. I'll talk to the chief, but I expect he'll agree. Dr. Overton?"

"Confidentiality is what we do best around here, Officer Kendall. As far as I'm concerned, he's still Patient John Doe."

"Can I keep this?" Olivia asked, holding up the business card.

"Yeah. Go on in. I'll call you later," Bryan said.

"I'd like a word with you, Olivia, on your way out," Carrie said.

Olivia nodded and turned to the patient-room door. Her heart was lodged in her throat — because how was she supposed to anticipate her first conversation with someone she'd admired so much for so long, especially under these conditions? She was

28

nervous, not wanting to make things worse for him. But she supposed any information would be welcome, so she opened the door and walked into his room, then crossed to his bedside.

"Hi," she said. "My name is Olivia. And I'm pretty sure yours is Aaron."

2

Aaron.

He'd expected a rush of memory to flood into his brain once he knew his name. But it didn't. There wasn't even a mild sense of recognition. Not of the name she spoke. Not of the woman, either. And he didn't see how any conscious, breathing male could forget a woman who looked like she did.

She was a classic beauty. Dark brown eyes and thick black lashes. Sun-kissed skin, sable hair, even if it was all bundled up. She had a slender body and luscious, full lips. And best of all, she didn't even seem aware of her looks. She didn't dress to show them off, that was for sure.

Beyond that, though, she was the first person who'd walked into this room that he felt glad to see. He was actually interested in talking to her. The others had been boring. Not one of them had any useful information to share, but they'd all been full of questions he couldn't answer. Doctors, nurses, cops.

Damn, he hated cops.

He didn't know how he knew that, or why he hated them, but he knew it was true. It had to be true, as uncomfortable as he'd been with the one who'd been in here grilling him.

Someone had shot him. *Shot him.* He closed his eyes and thought, yeah, that sort of thing would tend to make a lot of people ask a lot of questions. Personally, it made him feel sick.

And now there was this . . . Olivia. She wasn't a medical professional — unless she was a shrink. And she wasn't a cop. He knew that for sure, though again, how he knew was a mystery.

"Olivia," he said, repeating her name and waiting to see how it felt on his tongue. Familiar? Sadly, no. "Are we . . . lovers?" he asked.

Her eyes widened, and the word *no* burst from her lips before she could give it any thought. A rush of heat suffused her cheeks, and she didn't meet his eyes.

He lowered his head as if disappointed, and said, "So we're just friends, then?"

She frowned at him, tipping her head to one side and searching his face as she finally caught on. "Are you *teasing* me? A man in your condition?"

"My condition isn't all that bad. Doc Redhead out there tells me I'm fine. Aside from the fact that the only thing in my head right now is a massive ache, I actually feel pretty good for a guy who just took a bullet. And no, I wasn't teasing. Not entirely. I was hoping to God they finally found someone who knows me. Intimately." He sighed heavily, told himself to quit with the self-pity and get on with this. "So how *do* you know me, Olivia?"

"I don't," she said. "I'm sorry, but we've never actually met."

Nodding, and trying not to literally deflate in disappointment, he said, "Figures. It's just about in keeping with the way my day's been going, I guess."

He pursed his lips and reminded himself that this poor woman wasn't the one who'd shot him. Then again, how could he even be sure of that much?

He looked at her again, and thought, no, she wasn't the kind to put a bullet in a man. Not like that — not in the back of his head. She was stiff, kind of wary, maybe a little repressed, but not mean. Not a killer.

"Why don't you sit down, Olivia, and tell me about myself?"

"I'll try." She moved to the chair beside the bed and adjusted it to a position she liked, a little closer, angled toward him so she could see his face. Then she sat down, her lithe frame folding itself into the chair in a smooth, easy motion. She crossed her legs at the ankles, leaned her knees to one side. "I didn't expect you to be so . . ."

"What? Grouchy? Sarcastic? Getting shot in the head will do that to a guy. Sorry I'm not pouring on the charm."

"I understand that," she said. "It's just that your books are so —"

"My *books?*"

She bit her lip, then nodded and shifted in the chair. "Maybe I'd better start at the beginning."

"Maybe you'd better." He sat up in the bed, though he'd been told not to.

"Okay." Smoothing her skirt over her nicely shaped thighs, she seemed to organize her thoughts. "Okay," she said again. "I'm Professor Olivia Dupree. I teach English over at the State University of Vermont's Shadow Falls campus. Shadow Falls — that's where you are now. I've been here for sixteen years, and I've been helping to plan this year's summer fundraiser series for —"

"Excuse me." He held up a hand, and she stopped speaking. "I really do want to know all about you at some point, Olivia, but right now, could you get to me?"

She held his gaze, and hers went stony. "Not if you keep interrupting."

So, she had a bit of a temper. Good. He liked that. She wasn't as tame as she appeared. Sighing, he felt around in the covers for the remote, then pressed a button to raise the bed so he could lean back without being entirely prone. His head felt loads better than when he'd been sitting upright, and he made a mental note that the redheaded doc had been right about that.

"Where was I?"

"Summer fundraiser for something or other," he said.

"Short-term memory is all right, then?"

He met her eyes, saw the sarcasm, figured he had it coming. "I'll try not to interrupt again."

She nodded. "It's all relevant, I promise."

He nodded at her to continue.

"I've been reading Aaron Westhaven for years. He's known to be very reclusive, very private. Still, I used to write to him once a year or so at a P.O. box that was listed in his first novel."

"And you think I'm him?" he asked.

She lowered her head and lifted her brows at the same time, sending him a look that

34

told him he'd interrupted her again.

"Sorry," he said. "Continue."

"I never heard back, and the address was missing from all the future books. But I kept writing. Every time a new book came out, I would read it and send a letter. I liked to think of him — you — getting my letters personally, not along with the piles through the publisher. I liked to think of . . . you reading them with the same eagerness I felt whenever I got the newest novel."

He was frowning as he watched her go on. Her eyes actually lit up as she talked about a man she'd never even met. Until now. Maybe.

"I guess I should say thank you," he said. "And, uh, maybe apologize for never writing back."

She shrugged. "Don't be silly. What celebrity answers his own fan mail?"

He shrugged. "A recluse can't, by definition, be a celebrity, can he?"

"Of course he can."

"Well, celebrity or not, it seems rude as hell to me."

She smiled a little. "If you *are* him, you can apologize to me later."

He was beginning to hope he was, so her doubt jabbed at him a little. "You're not sure I'm him, then?"

"I'm fairly certain," she said. "It's just that Westhaven is *so* reclusive. No public appearances, no known photographs, even —"

"Damn," he muttered, shaking his head.

"What?"

"Aaron Westhaven is an asshole, that's what."

Her eyes widened, and she'd risen from her chair before he'd stopped speaking. "He is — *you* are not!"

"If I'm him, I am. I mean, who do I think I am? Shakespeare? Where do I get off, anyway?"

"You are *not* an . . . an asshole," she said, stumbling a bit over a word he was certain she'd never uttered in her life. "If you'll let me finish my story, you'll begin to see that."

"Fine. Finish the story."

She smoothed her hands over the seat of her skirt, forcing his eyes to follow, and sat down the way he imagined royalty would.

"All right. So, despite . . . your . . . understandable reluctance to answer what must have seemed like fan mail, I decided to write again, asking *you* to come and speak at the annual summer fundraiser lecture series for the English department. To my surprise, I received a response this time. An acceptance."

"I said yes?" Then he rolled his eyes at his

own question. "I guess I must have. I'm here." Then he thought about it a bit further, because her explanation didn't make a lot of sense. He wondered what reason she might have to lie to him, then wondered what reason anyone would have to *execute* him. And then he wondered if the two things were related.

He looked her up and down slowly. No. She *really* wasn't the type.

"So if I'm famous and I agreed to come to town to speak, why didn't anyone know who I was?"

"Your terms were explicit and a little extreme," she said, averting her eyes. "We were only allowed to advertise a secret special guest speaker and had to promise not to tell anyone it was you. We had to make the event by invitation only, and we were told to invite only the top one hundred most generous contributors among our alumni. No more. So there's been no press announcement or publicity around this at all. With it being limited to invited guests only, advertising wasn't necessary."

He was watching her, and it occurred to him that he was looking for signs she was lying and not finding any. And that was an odd thing to catch himself doing, wasn't it? As if he was accustomed to being lied to, as if he knew what it looked like. "So I'm famous enough to get away with those kinds of bullshit demands?"

She shrugged. "The university agreed to all of it."

"So that's a yes, then."

"I sent you my business card, with my unlisted number and home address handwritten on the back," she said, pulling the card from her pocket and handing it to him.

"So you have my home address?" he asked quickly, a gusher of hope rising in his chest.

"No, I sent it to the P.O. box. That was the only return address on your reply to me. Sorry."

He felt the disappointment but tried not to let it show by focusing on the card she'd handed him, turning it over as he checked it out. "Did they find any prints on it?"

"How did you know that was fingerprint dust?"

He shrugged, handing the card back to her. "Isn't it?"

"Well, yes, but I didn't know that. Neither did Dr. Overton."

"The redhead?"

"Yes, the redhead," she said.

She sounded a little exasperated with him, and he found that mildly amusing. She was so staid and tucked in, he found he enjoyed ruffling her a little bit.

But she was staring at him, awaiting an answer. He sighed. "I don't know how I knew. I don't know anything. Remember?"

She nodded, taking the card from him and setting it on the table beside his bed. Then she snatched a few tissues from the box there and used them to wipe the black smudges from her fingertips.

"So you're sure that's the card you sent me."

"I certainly haven't sent anyone *else* that information," she replied.

That caught his attention, because it was such an *adamant* reply. As if it were ludicrous to think she might have given her personal info to anyone else.

Maybe it was. There was more to this woman than had been apparent at first, he thought.

She seemed to try to pull her focus back to the matter at hand. "To get back to the subject, Mr. Westhaven was due to arrive today."

"Arrive where?" he asked.

"My house. He — you — were going to use my guest room. But he never arrived. And my card, the one I sent to him, was on you when the boys found you."

"Along with the pocket watch and key ring

they found on me, it's the sum total of my worldly possessions at the moment."

"Still, that's why it's fairly obvious that you're him."

He nodded. "If I *am* him, I still say I sound like a pompous prima donna. Making you people jump through all those hoops just to get me to visit for an afternoon."

She shrugged, but her puzzled frown was genuine, he thought. "It seems clear that you have reasons to guard your privacy. *Big* reasons. Reasons that go way beyond just being a prima donna, Aaron."

It was odd, being called by a name that didn't feel like his own. It felt odder still, that her point sounded right on target.

"Most people who've heard of it probably think your reclusiveness is about privacy or shyness, or that it's just a publicity stunt, a big-time author being eccentric and arrogant and getting away with it."

She'd given this a lot of thought, he mused. She'd probably been justifying this ink-Nazi's egomania ever since she'd decided to worship him from afar. "Uh-huh. And what do *you* think?"

She shrugged. "The first time you stuck your head out in the open, someone tried to blow it off. I'd say you knew that could happen, and *that's* why you play the recluse. To keep yourself alive."

He nodded slowly. "You know, I think you just might have a point there. Now, would you do me a favor and grab my clothes from the closet?" As he spoke, he shoved his covers back.

She frowned at him. "Why? What are you going to do?"

"Leave."

She got up again. "You can't just leave," she said.

"No, what I *can't* do is just stay here. Hand me my stuff, will you?"

She nodded, the motion jerky, and turned to open the closet. She pulled out a suit and held it out, looking it over. "Too bad," she said.

"What?" He was reaching for the hanger, but she shook her head and put it back in the closet. "It's an Armani, but it's completely ruined. Blood, dirt. There's no saving it." Then she bent down. "Shoes look all right, though."

He let his head hit the pillow and sighed. "I can't stay here. It's not defensible."

"What do you mean?"

"I mean, someone just tried to take me out. I was shot in the back of the head, all my ID was taken and my body was dumped

41

in the middle of nowhere. That was a hit. A professional hit."

She stood very still for a long moment, and he watched her absorb that piece of information. Her only reaction was to close her eyes slowly, leave them that way for a few ticks and then open them just as slowly. "Some professional," she said, moving again to close the closet door. "Seeing as you're still alive."

"Yeah, clearly he wasn't Einstein, but a steel plate in the skull isn't something most people would even think of. Still, even an amateur would know enough to verify the kill." He smiled grimly.

"That was a mistake, but he won't make another." He looked at her, saw her looking at him as if for the first time. "What?" he asked. "Are you not getting it? The minute this guy figures out I'm in the hospital, he'll be coming by to finish the job."

"I thought of that already."

She had? He went stone silent.

"I asked Bryan — Officer Kendall — to try to keep this out of the press for now, and he agreed it was for the best. No word of a gunshot victim being found and taken to the hospital will appear in the local newspapers. I guarantee it. The hospital staff are cooperating, too."

He blinked at her, surprised she would have come up with that strategy on her own. "Thank you for that," he said.

She nodded. "You're welcome."

"Even so," he continued, "it won't stay a secret for long. People talk. The boys will say something. Wives will tell their husbands. Husbands will tell their best pals. Those best pals will tell *their* wives, and so on."

"It'll only have to hold for a day or two," she said. The odd way she'd been looking at him before — like a wary doe eyeing an armed hunter — had faded. "Bryan's going to contact your publisher to see if someone there can identify you, or if they know of someone who can. From there, we should be able to find out where you live, who your relatives are, all the things you must be so eager to learn. As frustrating as I know this must be, it won't take long to fill in the gaps. In the meantime, there's no reason to let the killer know he didn't succeed."

Did she know how much better she was making him feel? he wondered. To think he would have all the answers in a day or two . . .

"But . . . the shooter probably expects to see something in the papers about a *body* being found. That would be big news in a town this size, wouldn't it?"

She frowned at him. "How did you know Shadow Falls was a small town, not a city?"

He stopped short and wondered about that. "I don't know. Bits of conversations pinned together, combined with the view outside my window, I guess."

"Or because it's something you knew before, and the knowledge is still there, in your memory, right where you left it. I think it's a good sign, Aaron."

He felt his worry lighten just a little. "I hope you're right."

She nodded. "I'm sure I am. But to answer your question, you were found along a back road that leads through a state forest. It's dirt, not pavement, not even gravel. Just dirt, and hardly ever traveled. It's near one of the spots where the high school kids go to party and underage couples go to have sex, when they aren't out at the old abandoned Campbell farm or the vacant cheese factory. It's perfectly believable that a body dumped out there might not be found for a few days."

He frowned and looked her up and down yet again, taking in her pencil skirt, silky blouse and tightly wound hair. "You say you're an *English teacher?*"

"Why do you ask it like that?"

"Because you think like a cop. Or a criminal."

She looked away so quickly that he knew she had something to hide. Some deep, dark secrets of her own. And all of a sudden he was almost as curious about her past as he was about his own hidden history.

There was something fascinating about Professor Olivia Dupree, but the shadows in her eyes told him it wouldn't be easy finding out what it was. He didn't really believe she was a criminal, much less in league with a hit man. But there was definitely *something* hiding behind those intelligent brown eyes.

She met his curious gaze and stared right back. The tension, the attraction — oh, yeah, the feelings were there, and they were real — built. Finally, she looked away. "There's a policeman guarding your room," she told him. "That should reassure you."

"Yeah, I just *love* cops," he said, and he made his words as sarcastic as possible. "But having one outside the door is only going to make the gossip mill grind a little faster, isn't it?"

She nodded and licked her lips, the motion of her tongue, quick and slight though it was, grabbing him by the testosterone and not letting go.

"I'll phone Bryan," she said. "I can ask him to send a plainclothes officer instead. You're right, the uniform raises too many questions."

"A plainclothes cop will be just as obvious."

"To you and me, maybe. But not to anyone else." She moved closer to the bed, leaned over him just a little, and her face softened. "You really do need to spend the night, Aaron. Dr. Overton wants to be sure she hasn't missed anything, and you know how tricky head injuries can be. Your brain could swell later on and you could be dead —" she snapped her fingers "— just like that."

"Did you just come in, or did you somehow miss that I already could have been dead —" he snapped his fingers "— just like that? I don't like being in this hospital. I'm a sitting duck here."

"I don't think you have a choice."

"You don't know me very well, then."

She thinned her lips, looked at him steadily. "I think it would be a bad idea for you to leave, but you're an adult. You do what you want. I'm going to leave that card here." She bent over it, picked up the nearby pen and scribbled something. "I put Bryan's numbers on it, too. But I'm closer — only fifteen minutes away. If you need anything, feel free to call me, okay?"

"You're going, then?" He almost tried to snatch the words back and wondered if he could have managed to sound any more like a disappointed four-year-old.

Her chocolate eyes melted. "I'm going out to talk to Dr. Overton. But I'll come in and say goodbye before I leave."

"No need. You've told me all you know."

She moved close to the bed again, and for a second he thought she was going to touch him, put a hand on his shoulder or brow or some sappy thing like that. And while he didn't think he would mind her putting her hands on him in the right circumstances, he definitely didn't want it like that.

She didn't, though. She said, "Aaron, your work has seen me through some . . . difficult times. It's probably been more important to me than you can imagine. And if I can return the favor by helping you now, then that's what I want to do. So if you need anything, call me. Okay?"

He frowned at her, finding this whole thing very strange. She was a *fan*. He had a *fan*. Images from the film of Stephen King's *Misery* ran through his mind, along with a surge of frustration that he could recall old

47

movies but not a damn thing about his old life.

Still, he replied, "Okay," and let it go. He didn't want to need this woman's help. He wanted to think that all he really needed was his past.

"Okay," she said. "It was a real thrill meeting you, Aaron."

He nodded. "Wish I could say the same. But I don't feel like I have — met me yet, that is."

She sighed. "You're talented, gifted even. Special. You really are."

Hearing that from her made him feel kind of queasy inside, and then suddenly he was sucked into his own head, into what he thought must be his own past.

He saw himself, and thought he would have recognized his own body even if he hadn't spent several long minutes staring into a mirror when he'd first awakened.

He was standing on a sidewalk in the dark, in the pouring rain. Streetlights gleamed on slick pavement. He stood motionless; then, slowly, he raised his arm and looked down its length to the black handgun resting easily in his hand. The laser sight shot through the murky gloom and appeared as a tiny red spot on the chest of the man who stood farther along the broken sidewalk, laughing and talking to the person walking beside him.

He felt himself take a breath, release half of it, and squeeze the trigger. He heard the soft *pffft* of the silencer, felt the 9 millimeter buck in his hand. And then he saw the man — his victim — jerk stiffly, crumple to his knees and topple facefirst onto the sidewalk.

The victim's companion looked down for a moment, then glanced up and said, "He never saw it coming. You're a freakin' artist, Mr. Adams. An *artist.* You know that?"

"Yeah," he heard himself mutter. "I'm something, all right."

He blinked away the memory and was back in the hospital bed, looking at the woman who'd paused near the door to glance back at him.

"Are you all right?" she asked.

He gave his head a shake. "Yeah. Fine. Sorry, I'm tired. I guess I zoned out a little."

"You've had a rough day. Get some rest."

"Yeah. I will, thanks."

She smiled at him, a gentle, reassuring smile, and then she walked out of the room. Aaron stared at the ceiling and wondered what that vision had been about. He hoped to God it wasn't a memory and was scared to death that it had been. He didn't think he was a reclusive novelist anymore — if he'd ever believed it. He didn't think that was even *close* to what he did.

3

"It wasn't my car," Carrie Overton said softly.

Olivia had left Aaron, though she'd done so reluctantly. He certainly wasn't what she'd expected. But she was captivated — and eager to spend more time with him, even while rather disgusted with herself for feeling that way.

She was torn. He was a hero to her. Yet he was still a man. She didn't know what she'd expected him to be. Some kind of genderless word wizard, a spiritual, asexual guru, she supposed.

But he was one hundred percent male in every way that she'd been able to detect. So how did she reconcile the author she'd so admired, and the purity of the bond she'd felt with him through his work, with the gorgeous, sexy man in the hospital bed? The type who would normally send her running in the opposite direction.

She didn't know. And there were a hundred other things on her mind at the moment, things far beyond her questions about Aaron and who would want to kill him, and why he knew about fingerprint dust and hit men and defensible positions. She was also thinking about having to cancel tomorrow's fundraising event, telling the main office to refund money for the one hundred spots they'd sold, and the length of time she'd left Freddy home alone. Even though he had a doggy door and a fenced-in backyard, he didn't like being by himself for extended periods. She actually came home between classes to spend time with him most days.

So Carrie's statement wasn't translating in Olivia's brain just then. "What?"

Carrie held up a set of keys. "The car that my *brilliant* son and his best friend, Kyle *Einstein* Becker, decided to take out joyriding today — the car they were driving when they found our John Doe in there — it's not mine."

Olivia's eyes widened. "Are you saying they *stole* a car? *Sam stole a car?* Come on, Carrie, Sam wouldn't steal a Tic Tac."

Carrie nodded and jangled the keys. "I need you to take it, so he doesn't do this again."

"Excuse me?" Olivia was baffled. "How

52

can I take a stolen car?"

Carrie shoved the keys into Olivia's palm. "Sorry. I'm not explaining this very well. I feel guilty as hell for not being honest with the police, but I don't want Sammy ending up arrested for grand theft auto."

"What's going on? Whose car is it? Do they know it's missing? Are they pressing charges?"

"Not exactly." Carrie lowered her head, and her long red curls curtained her face. "Long story short, okay? I'm dating Karl Mallory."

"Professor Mallory — head of the math department? I had no idea he was dating again." Olivia thought Karl Mallory was a milquetoast dishrag without much of a spine or a hint of a personality, and that a beautiful, intelligent, successful woman like Carrie could do far better. "Seriously? Since when?"

Carrie nodded. "Two dates. It's very casual. But still — he's in Europe for the summer, and he left his gorgeous, prize-winning showpiece of an SUV in my garage until he gets back. *That's* the vehicle my son took out today."

"Oh," Olivia said. "Bryan didn't mention that."

"That's because I didn't tell him. I did

phone Karl. Told him what happened. He was upset, but willing to forgive and forget, thank God. I just want to move the thing elsewhere, anywhere, just to get it out of Sam's reach until Karl gets back in two weeks and can take it home."

"Mmm-hmm."

"He said I should ask you."

Olivia lifted her brows. She and Karl Mallory weren't close, but they were friendly enough. "I really don't think Sam would do it again, Carrie. Do you?"

"No. But his friends . . . that's another matter. Aside from his girlfriend, Sadie — that girl is a gem, I swear to God — the rest of the kids he hangs out with, I wouldn't trust as far as I could throw them. And they can be pretty persuasive — and you know about peer pressure." She closed her eyes. "I keep getting these nightmare images of what could have happened if they'd gotten there earlier — while the killer was still there, I mean." She said the final words in a whisper, even though they were alone at the nurses' desk for the moment.

"It won't do any good to think about that," Olivia said. "It didn't happen that way. He's okay, and he knows what he did was wrong. That's what matters. Besides, he saved the man's life. Bryan said so."

"That's no excuse." Carrie lowered her head, sighed. "Karl says you have a two-car garage with only one car in it. So will you do it? Take his SUV and keep it at your place for two weeks?"

Olivia shrugged. "Sure, why not? I have room."

"Are you sure? It's huge. A Ford Ex-something."

"It's fine. My garage is pretty big and nicely free of clutter. My SUV's a Ford, too. Escape Hybrid. How much bigger can it be?"

"Great. It's in the parking lot nearest the E.R. Red with black — the paint job jumps right out at you. Hard to miss."

"I'll take it home now and leave mine here overnight. I can get it tomorrow morning."

"Better leave your keys here, then. If it looks like it's in danger of being towed, I'll move it for you, and I'll leave those instructions for the night shift, as well."

"Thanks. It's white, by the way."

"Well, of course it is."

Olivia paused in the middle of handing her own keys to Carrie, about to ask just what that comment was supposed to mean, before thinking better of it. She was boring. Okay, everyone knew it. That was exactly how she wanted to be.

Carrie hung the keys on a peg beside the nurses' desk. "So what do you think about him?" she asked. "Do you think he's that writer?"

Bringing his face to mind, Olivia said, "I don't see how he could be anyone else." She looked at Carrie, bit her lip, then blurted out the question on her mind. "Is it just me, or is he gorgeous?"

"Oh, he's gorgeous, all right," Carrie told her.

"I thought so. Just didn't trust myself."

"Why not? You're that big a fan?"

"I've admired him so much for so long that . . . I don't know, I was afraid my brain might have interpreted him as gorgeous no matter what he looked like. Though I'll admit, I half expected a balding bookworm with Coke-bottle glasses and a pretentious goatee, or maybe a guru in white robes with a shaved head and a vow of celibacy or something."

"I guess I need to read some of his books," Carrie said. "But I think I'm happy for you. You got something far better than a guru or a goatee."

Olivia glanced up at her friend. "I didn't *get* anything."

"Come on. He's got amnesia. You're his lifeline. And he thinks you're hot. I can tell."

56

"He thinks *you're* hot, unless he's blind," Olivia said. *And he has it all over Karl Mallory,* she added silently.

"Yeah, well, he didn't look at me the way he looked at you, I'll tell you that much."

"We're cold, divvying up the poor guy like a leftover steak." Olivia made a face. "That's not like me. I don't usually even *like* men."

"You'll learn to like this one, I'll bet — if he stays in town long enough," Carrie said.

Olivia elbowed her lightly in the ribs and smiled, but the smile died quickly. "Carrie, how is he? Really?"

"I think he's fine. His head hurts. And head injuries can be sneaky. But so far, I don't see any sign there's going to be a problem."

"But you want to keep him overnight anyway."

"If his brain swells, he'll be in trouble. It's best he stays right here, just overnight. If there's no swelling, he can go home tomorrow. Which is just as well, since we don't even know where home is today."

"I guess so."

"So are you heading home now yourself?"

"Not yet. I told him I'd come back to say good-night before I left. Thought I'd run over to the vending machines and get him some junk food first."

Carrie stared at her for a moment, her head tipped to one side.

"What?"

"I don't know, you're . . . kind of perkier than usual, aren't you?"

"I am not." Olivia waved a hand dismissively and went to the vending machines, then headed back to Aaron's room with some chips, some cookies and a couple of cans of root beer.

He lifted his head when she came in, and his eyes warmed a little. She dumped her booty onto his tray table and said, "I figured this would get you through the night."

The smile in his eyes reached his lips then. "How do you know I even *like* junk food?" he asked.

She shrugged. "Gotta be better than hospital food," she said. "Besides, how do *you* know you *don't?*"

"Oh, I think I do. My mouth is watering at the sight of it."

"So your mouth doesn't have amnesia?"

"Apparently not." He tore open a bag of chips, ate one and held the bag out to her.

She took a chip and munched. Then she licked the salt from her lips and fingertips, and said, "You seem like a nice guy, Aaron. And you write beautiful, touching stories for a living. I just can't imagine anyone having any reason to want you dead. Can you?"

He averted his eyes, and the motion *felt* like an obvious sign of deception, but Olivia told herself that was just her overcautious mind reading into things. She knew she often saw suspicious motives in ordinary behavior. It came from being in hiding for so long, she supposed. Using a name that wasn't her own. Living a life that felt as frail and temporary as the puffy seeds of a dandelion. One stiff breeze and it could all blow away.

"I just wish I could remember more about my past," he said. "I must have *really* pissed someone off."

"*More* about your past? Then you've remembered some of it already?" she asked, eager to hear more.

"No, not really."

It was a lie. It not only felt like a lie, but it also looked and sounded like one, too. He *had* remembered something.

Okay, now she was being ridiculous, she told herself. What reason would he have to lie to her? He didn't even *know* her.

She shook her head slowly. "Most victims of violent crimes don't jump straight to the conclusion that it was somehow their own fault. Or if they do, they shouldn't. It could be something else. Mistaken identity, a jealous competitor —"

"Yeah. I hear the East Coast writers and the West Coast writers have a real grudge fest going on."

"I'm not sure I would joke about this, Aaron. Someone really did try to kill you, after all, and that means there has to be a reason."

He frowned as he studied her. "You seem to be pretty familiar with my . . . career. Have I been accused of anything in the press? Any violent episodes touted in the tabloids or something like that?"

She lowered her head and told herself to try to state the facts without sounding like a gushing fan. "I think if you knew who you really are right now, you wouldn't ask those sorts of things."

"And *you* know who I really am, is that what you're saying?" he asked.

She let her eyes sweep over him, head on the pillow, toes sticking out from beneath the white covers. "I don't know if I do or not. I know the man I think you are, based on the stories you tell. I'd like to think that man is for real."

"Well, don't keep me in suspense. Tell me. Who am I?"

She took a breath, choosing her words with care. She wasn't going to heap praise on him or pretend a relationship that didn't exist. She didn't see herself as a sappy fan, and she didn't want him to see her that way, either. "I like to think any writer puts something of themselves into their stories. Your protagonist, Harvey Trudeau, is the main character in every one of your novels, and it seems to me his personality is probably the best chance we have of unraveling yours. I could be entirely wrong, but that's my theory."

"Understood. So you're going to tell me about Harvey, and then time will tell whether the same things apply to his humble creator."

"Exactly."

"All right. So tell me about Harvey."

She shifted her eyes in thought, and then her gaze turned inward as she recalled the character she'd grown to love. "Harvey is a gentle human being. He's sensitive. He sees beauty in everything around him. There's not a violent bone in his body. He's sweet, and kind, and emotionally deep. He's also very in touch with who he is."

"Sounds perfect."

"Far from it. Harvey's got his flaws. He doesn't trust people easily, and they usually prove him right. But he misses out on a lot of good relationships because he paints everyone with the same brush. His logic is that it's better to be alone than to risk being hurt and disappointed by trusting someone not worth trusting. I understand that about him."

His intense eyes seemed to sharpen at those words. But he didn't interrupt.

"So as a result, I think . . . I think you're lonely."

"*I'm* lonely? Don't you mean that Harvey's lonely?"

"I think I mean both."

"And what makes you think that, Olivia?"

She thought that, she mused, because she was lonely, too, and for the very same reasons. She recognized it in him. Had done, even before she'd met him, just by reading his books. She had felt it coming through the pages. But she couldn't very well say so. "I guess it's because Harvey always ends up alone at the end of every book."

He nodded slowly. "What if I'm nothing like my books?" he asked.

She shook her head. "I suppose that's possible, but it just doesn't seem very likely. How could you write the way you do if you didn't feel it on some level?" Then she made herself stop, deciding it might be best if she left now, before she made a starstruck fool out of herself. "I should probably go. I'm starting to sound like a gushing fan, and I'm not that. If you need anything, call me, okay?"

He lifted his brows. "You said that before, but honestly, you've done enough already."

"No. I'm the one who agreed to take care of you while you were in town. And I intend to keep my promise, even though we have to cancel the fundraiser."

His lips thinned. "I'm really sorry about that."

"You were *shot*," she reminded him. "My card's on the nightstand. Call me if you need me. I mean it. And I'll be back in the morning." She got up and moved toward the door, then turned back once more. "Are you going to stay the night here?"

He looked at her a little strangely, but he nodded. "I'm going to try. If I start to feel too antsy, though, I'm going to trust my gut and check myself out."

She didn't want to leave him — it felt like abandoning a lost boy, somehow. But he wasn't a boy, and it would go beyond the bounds of their very brief acquaintance for her to stay. She forced herself to turn and walk out the door.

The house was dark when Olivia arrived

home. The Expedition's headlights illuminated the front entrance, probably burning through a layer of paint while they were at it. The thing was *huge,* and beyond macho. It screamed big, rugged, sporty, manly man, and it was the polar opposite of what she would have expected a bookish little man like Professor Mallory to own. She guessed you never could tell about people. She would need to move some things before putting the SUV in the garage, she realized. It would have to be okay outside for now.

The overbright headlights lit up the front steps with their wrought-iron railing. She'd rushed out in such a hurry that she hadn't bothered to turn on an outdoor light. No matter, she wasn't too worried with Freddy around.

She shut off the engine, which had a deep growl to it that she was unused to, and took the shopping bags she'd procured on the way home from the passenger seat, then slid out of the SUV to the pavement below, landing with a jarring thud. Then she ambled up the walk while fumbling in her bag for the house keys and thinking she ought to consider trading up. The thing had tons of room for Freddy in the back, and it was fun to drive.

After a successful search, she stuck the

key in the lock and, with the ease of long practice, stepped inside, flipping the light switch as she went.

"Freddy!" she called. "I'm home!"

He didn't answer. And that was not like him.

"Freddy?" She walked through the house, checking every room. It wasn't that big a place, so searching it was neither difficult nor time-consuming. The dining room and kitchen were one large, open room, separated only by a countertop, with French doors on the far side leading to the deck and fenced-in backyard.

She headed in that direction when there was no response from inside the house, turning on lights as she went along. She hated being in the dark. And she especially hated being alone in the dark. It was just too creepy.

There was a very large doggy door — she'd had to have one custom-made to accommodate Freddy's bulk — just to the side of the French doors. But it was very unlike him not to hear a car pulling in, and come bounding from wherever he might be to see who was at the door, much less come at her call. Something about this was off. And something about the house felt off, too.

An icy chill danced up her spine and along

the back of her neck. She shivered, and quickly unlocked and opened the French doors, eager to be with her dog, and feeling the earliest warning signs of impending panic. If anything ever happened to him . . .

"Freddy!" she shouted as she stepped out onto the redwood deck. "Freddy, come!"

She used her most commanding tone, but even to her own ears, there was a hint of fear wrapped within it. And then, quickly, fear was overshadowed by relief. Freddy came bounding toward her, appearing out of the darkness like a ghost from the very farthest part of the back lawn. His brindle markings made him all but invisible in the dark. But there he was, running toward her and chomping away on whatever was dangling from his jowls.

"What in the world? Freddy, what have you got? Give it to me. Give it to me, come on." She tried to wrestle the wet thing — a piece of meat, she realized — from his jaws, but he got a better grip and then swallowed it whole.

"Freddy! Was that a *steak?* Where on earth could you have gotten a steak?"

Freddy belched loudly, then jumped as if startled by the sound, and looked around him to locate the source of it.

"Where did you get that?" Olivia de-

manded. "Where, huh?"

Freddy sat, his tail thumping the wood.

"I swear, Freddy. You didn't kill something, did you?" It would be alien to him to harm anything, she thought. When he spotted wildlife, he wanted to play with it, not eat it. He was a gentle giant. Besides, it really had looked like a good cut of meat to her, not a mangled woodland creature.

This was just bizarre. She stepped back inside and reached for the little wine rack, where she kept a large flashlight, just because it fit so nicely there. Then she went back outside and across the deck, the flashlight's beam guiding her way. She'd turned on the outside lights now, and they helped, too, as she walked from the deck to the lawn, and then followed the fence all the way around the backyard. She didn't see anything. No meat lying around, and no sign that any small animals had been devoured.

Freddy circumnavigated the lawn right by her side, but he didn't give away a thing.

"Well, go figure, pal. Apparently you have yet another fan," she told him. She wasn't all that surprised. Freddy was something of a local celebrity. Everyone who met him loved him, and well-meaning neighbors sometimes left him treats, despite Olivia's softly spoken objections. Crouching, she set the light aside and took his face in her hands. "Don't you *ever* take candy from strangers, Frederick. Do you understand me?"

"Woof!" said Fred, and then he turned and galloped back toward the house, as if daring her to race him, his long ears flapping in the breeze.

Olivia declined the challenge and walked back more slowly. She took one more look around, but by then she was feeling a little sheepish about her case of nerves. Okay, a lot had happened today. A man had been shot. But that didn't mean that her own ghosts were going to come floating out of the distant past tonight. No one had tried to kill *her*. And Aaron's situation had nothing whatsoever to do with her own.

She locked the house up tight, took a quick shower and went to bed. But sleep didn't come easily. She kept thinking about Aaron, and how different he was from what she had expected. And she kept wondering if he was lying awake, frustrated and alone.

It wasn't like her to spend so much time thinking about any man. But she couldn't seem to help herself where he was concerned.

She'd spent most of her adult life in hiding from the violent man she'd narrowly escaped so many years ago. She'd avoided romantic relationships ever since. But she had allowed herself, in her weaker moments, an imaginary one in her mind, because it was harmless and next to impossible. Aaron Westhaven wasn't real to her. He was an ideal. He stood for the antithesis of violence. He was tender, sensitive, affectionate, wonderful. She knew he couldn't be as perfect a human being in real life as he had become in her own mind. But it hadn't mattered, because there had never been a chance she would meet him in real life anyway. And she had imagined that, if she did, he would be a huge disappointment.

But now she *had* met him. And he was *far* from disappointing. Something inside her seemed to have broken loose and started all kinds of silly chemical reactions. He wasn't what she'd expected him to be, personality-wise. But physically, he was far, *far* more. He was one of the most incredibly handsome men she'd ever set eyes on.

What if he *wasn't* too good to be real? What if he turned out to be all the things she had allowed herself to imagine he was? What then?

She sat up in the bed, scowling hard and

wondering just who the hell had taken over her brain. Professor Olivia Dupree was *not* a giggling sorority girl with a crush. And besides, no matter what the psychiatrists and anthropologists said, she firmly believed that human beings were *not* designed to fall in love. Romantic love was a made-up idea with no real basis. It was what people *wished* they could feel. But it wasn't real. She knew that. And Aaron knew it, too, depicted it powerfully and repeatedly in his novels. That was why she connected so strongly with his work. So what was wrong with her now?

She punched the pillow, lay back down and tried to sleep.

And she did begin to drift off — right up until she heard the unmistakable sound of the French doors swinging open with their telltale creak, followed by footsteps sneaking silently across her kitchen floor.

Aaron tossed and turned, and tried to sleep, but he didn't have any success at all. Every time someone passed in the hall beyond his closed hospital-room door, he came to attention, watching, listening, waiting, certain it was his assailant, back to finish the job.

It was worse when the passerby *did* pause near his door, and worst of all when they actually came inside. A nurse wanting to check his vitals or administer meds or adjust the IV or whatever. They came in what felt like fifteen-minute intervals, always advising him to relax and get some sleep when they left. Right.

He wished he could remember something. Anything besides the terrifying vision of committing cold-blooded murder. And he tried. He said his own name over and over in his mind. Aaron Westhaven. Aaron Westhaven. Aaron Westhaven. He tried to visualize his fingers racing over a keyboard, typing the words of some blockbuster. But none of it felt familiar.

None of it.

He drifted off once, only to see himself standing over a lifeless body, looking down at the bloodstained white shirt of a motionless corpse, the smoking gun in his hand, its gleaming barrel still warm. He could smell the gunpowder. The vision was that vivid, that real.

He came awake with a start that had him sitting upright in the bed. Memory? Or nightmare? That made twice now that his mind had filled itself with the image of killing someone. What the hell kind of man was he? Not the sensitive geek Olivia Dupree apparently thought he was, that was for *damn* sure.

He had to get to the bottom of this mess, and he had to do it now, tonight. He felt like a living, breathing target lying there, and dammit, he knew he was supposed to trust his instincts above all else, though he didn't know where that knowledge came from. Was it something he'd lived by, or something his injured brain had just made up to fill space?

Fed up, he kicked off the covers, climbed out of the bed and went into the little bathroom off his room, so he could use the mirror there to help him get the bandages off his head.

It still ached, but not as much without the too-tight mummy wrap. Creeping to the door and peering out, he watched the activity at the nurses' station for a while. Every so often the tall desk would be deserted as the nurses headed in different directions, tending to patients, answering their call buttons.

The place was clearly understaffed.

Good.

He spotted the key to Olivia's car hanging on a peg near the desk. He'd been at the door, listening intently to every second of the conversation between her and Dr. Overton earlier. He knew about the doc's kid joyriding in a borrowed SUV, about Olivia

72

leaving her own car there overnight to take the bigger one home. He'd seen the keys get hung up there, and knew what kind of car she drove.

He grabbed the zip-top bag holding his few belongings from the drawer beside the bed, tucked Olivia Dupree's business card inside it and waited. The stuff in the bag had been examined by the police and returned to him, and it consisted of a pocket watch, a key ring with a rearing stallion on it and bearing a single key with a *P* engraved on its face, and a packet of Big Red chewing gum. It wasn't much, but it was all he had to his name at the moment, and he wasn't leaving it behind.

The next time every nurse was way from the desk, Aaron slipped out of his room, padded along the hall and lifted Olivia's car key right off the rack. Then he turned and moved farther along the hallway, passing patients' rooms, peering inside until he spotted a man in a bed who looked to be in the vicinity of his own size and shape. The patient was sound asleep, no nurses hovering nearby. So Aaron ducked into the room, moved quietly to the closet, opened it and saw the man's clothes stored there just as his own had been.

Ducking into the bathroom, he donned

the clothes — jeans, a black T-shirt and a denim jacket — as fast as he could. The running shoes were two sizes too small, so he didn't bother exchanging his own scuffed but expensive-looking black ones with those. Then he had to watch and wait for the nurses to get busy again before he could slip out of the room, toward the door marked Stairs.

Once in the stairwell, he figured he was home free. He took that route all the way to the ground floor. No one noticed him as he headed toward the exit, or if they did, they didn't say anything. He didn't take any more time than necessary, looking as if he knew exactly where he was going, exuding confidence and purpose and probably a hint of impatience.

Finally he was passing through the exit doors, and into the parking lot. And only then did he breathe a huge sigh of relief, followed by a refreshing lungful of fresh, cool, summer night air. It tasted good here, he thought, and wondered if that was something new to him. Maybe he lived in a city.

It took him a few minutes of searching to find Olivia's car, but only a few. It was the only white hybrid SUV in the parking lot. He hit the unlock button, and it flashed its headlights at him in response.

Moments later he was pulling in to the scarce traffic of a Shadow Falls night.

He gave himself time to get a few blocks away before pulling over again. Then, feeling safe — or as safe as a man who knew someone with a gun was out there looking for him *could* feel — he took the time to turn on the dash-mounted GPS device. He touched the screen, chose Navigate To and then looked at his selections. Street Address, City Center, Point of Attraction, Home.

Smiling, he touched the word *Home.*

Olivia Dupree's address popped up onto the screen, and a female voice said, "Left turn ahead."

4

Olivia sat up slowly, her heart pounding so hard she would have sworn whoever was in her house could hear it as clearly as she did. "Freddy," she whispered harshly. "Freddy, where are you?"

But there was no reply.

He wasn't lying on the floor beside the bed, the way he usually did, so she could let her arm dangle over the side, and stroke his big head until he fell asleep. He wasn't lying *on* the bed, across her lower legs, or with his head on her chest, rendering her immobile or in danger of suffocation, either.

Where was her dog?

And who was creeping around in her kitchen?

Olivia reached for the telephone on the nightstand, pushed the talk button and heard nothing but dead air. No landline. Her blood went cold. Had the intruder cut the phone line?

And then her mind went to the place it would have gone sooner if she hadn't trained herself to avoid it. Her ex-lover, Tommy Skinner. Had he finally found out the truth? That she was still alive and in hiding, living a false life under a false name. A life that felt more real than any other one ever had. Had he finally come, sixteen years later, to exact revenge for what she'd done to him?

She had to get out of the house, she realized, no longer willing to downplay the fear that was trying to keep her alive.

But first she had to find her dog.

She slid from the bed, unconsciously smoothing her red flannel pajama bottoms and white lacy camisole top, and tiptoed to the bedroom door, which stood two inches ajar. She never shut it all the way, so that Freddy could come and go throughout the night. Her cell phone was in her purse, which was on a hook in the living-room closet. Dammit. She didn't have a gun, either. Not there in the house, anyway. She'd never thought she would *need* a gun with Freddy around.

She peered through the slightly open door into the living room, and saw Freddy, lying on his side on the hardwood floor. Asleep, she thought — and then the truth hit her. He was lying too still, not moving at all.

And he would have heard the sounds that had awakened her far sooner than she would have. She tensed in shock and fear, about to pull the door wider and run to him, but before she could, it crashed inward, hitting her in the head and sending her backward onto the floor. Her forehead screamed in pain, and she felt a trickle of blood there, even as she realized a man wearing a black ski mask was standing over her. Scrambling backward, crablike, she shielded her face with one arm, and went icy cold in terror when he lifted a gun and pointed it at her.

"Stay still!" he barked from behind the mask.

"What did you do to my dog?" She made no effort to keep her voice down.

"Quiet, dammit!" He worked the gun's action.

"All right, all right." She stayed still and bit her lip to keep from speaking again. She was shaking from head to toe, yet her mind kept on working. She tried to get a look at him in case she lived through this, so she could give a description later on. Her arm was still blocking her face. She couldn't seem to convince herself to lower it, so she peeked around it. Her assailant was lean and wiry, not overly tall, though he seemed it as she lay on her back on the floor, looking up into his gun barrel. "Please," she whispered, unable to keep her mouth shut, despite his threats. "Please tell me what's wrong with my dog. What did you do to him?"

"Shut up!"

She shut up but kept taking mental notes. He was wearing a ski mask, a black turtleneck, black jeans and black gloves. At first she wasn't even sure of his skin color, but then she glimpsed it through the eye holes of the mask. He was Caucasian. It was too dark to guess his eye color.

He went to her dresser and yanked open the drawers, raking his hands through her clothes, sending them flying in the process, all the while keeping the gun and one eye on her. He pulled one drawer all the way out and flung it to the floor when he was finished, then turned to her closet.

"What do you want?"

He turned sharply and stared at her. "I told you to shut up, bitch! Do you *want* to die like your dog?"

"Freddy! No!" She surged to her feet, ignoring him, his threats and his gun, and took one lunging step toward the bedroom door.

Her attacker caught her bodily around the

waist, flung her backward onto the bed and leaned over her. "The disks. I want the disks. Where are they, Sarah?"

"Sarah . . ." she whispered. God, no one had called her that in more than sixteen years. "No, I'm not Sarah. I'm Oliv—"

He swung his gun hand so suddenly that she couldn't anticipate the blow, and her position on the bed didn't leave room to duck it, anyway. The side of the handgun connected with her jaw, and her head snapped hard to one side. He straddled her on the bed as stars exploded behind her eyes and lifted the gun again.

But then something — no, some*one* — tackled him from the side, the momentum carrying him off the bed to the floor. Olivia scrambled off the bed herself, though her head was spinning. Stumbling toward the doorway, she managed to stay upright, to get through it with only one thought on her mind.

Freddy.

He was still there on the floor, and he hadn't moved. She staggered toward him, then fell half on top of him, hugging his big neck. "Oh, Freddy, come on, baby. Freddy? Freddy!"

The other two crashed into the living room, and she surged to her feet again, racing for the closet and the cell phone she'd left in her purse. The newcomer delivered a series of blows delivered so rapidly she couldn't have counted them. The intruder's head snapped back with each one, and she finally realized that her rescuer was none other than the man she had fallen asleep thinking about. Aaron Westhaven.

Even as she watched in stunned awe, he snapped the gun from the intruder's grasp, removed and pocketed the clip, then ejected the bullet in the chamber. And he did it all in about a half second, while she stood there with the cell phone in her hand. He met her eyes and gave her a subtle shake of his head, telling her no.

Then the intruder ran for it, blowing past her and out through the front door. Aaron ran after him, but she caught hold of his forearm just as he reached the doorway.

"Aaron, please don't!" she cried.

He stopped in his tracks in the doorway, turned to look at her. But she was focused on Freddy again. Releasing his arm, she returned to her beloved pet. She rubbed his giant head as tears spilled over her face. "Oh, God, oh, God, *oh, God!* Freddy."

She heard a motor roaring away, and then Aaron was kneeling beside her, his hands on her dog. "He's breathing. Hey, you hear me? He's okay."

She sniffled and lifted her eyes to his. "He's not dead?"

"No, he's breathing. His heart's beating strong. Feel." He closed one of his hands around hers, enveloping it entirely, and then he pressed it to Freddy's chest. She felt the powerful, steady throbbing of his massive heart against her palm.

Her mouth fell open, and her eyes closed. "He's alive! Freddy, come on boy, wake up. Wake up for me now." She bent and kissed his muzzle, then rubbed his face and ears, but he didn't respond.

Aaron sighed and then bent closer, running his hands over the dog's huge body in search of injuries, frowning the entire time as if puzzled. He laid his head on the dog's side, listening. Then he sat upright again, nodding. "I think he's fine. There's not a mark on him. My best guess is that he's probably been drugged."

"*Drugged?* Dammit, it was the steak."

He looked at her, brows raised.

"He was eating a piece of steak when I got home, and I couldn't get it away from him."

"So your burglar fed him some doped meat. Can't blame him. You don't break in to a house with a dog this size unless you

82

take some precautions, right? I think he'll be fine. Can you turn on a light?"

Sniffling, she got up and found a light switch.

Aaron was still looking at her dog, lifting his eyelids, looking at his eyes. "Yeah, he'll be fine. He's starting to come around already. It would take a huge dose to do any lasting harm to a dog this size. Hell, he's almost a pony." He glanced up at her, and his face changed. "Damn," he said, and he rose, coming to her, gripping her chin very gently, turning her face. "What did he hit you with?"

"First my bedroom door. Then his gun." She ran her fingertips over her hurting jaw. "What are you doing here, Aaron?"

"I was feeling like a sitting duck at the hospital. And I overheard you and the doc talking before, so I knew where to find your key and your car."

"So you just left?" She let him help her to her feet.

"I didn't think you'd mind."

"Mind? You probably just saved my life."

She let him lead her into the kitchen, though she hated to walk away from her dog. But he eased her into a chair that left her a clear line of sight to Fred's still-prone form. Then he turned on the water, located a washcloth and soaked it, then went to the fridge, where he filled the cloth with ice. "Here, hold this on your jaw."

"Thanks."

"It's not even close to enough to say how sorry I am, Olivia."

She frowned up at him. "Sorry? About what?"

"Bringing this to your doorstep." He returned to the fridge, this time in search of something to drink, and brought out two diet colas, opening both and setting one on the table in front of her. "Obviously this has something to do with me. Maybe the killer knew I was supposed to be staying with you, so when he found out I wasn't dead, he came looking for me here."

She met his eyes, saw the regret in them, and shook her head slowly. "This didn't have anything to do with you." She said it softly, warily, hoping not to have to tell him anything more.

"Yeah, right." He took the ice from her hand, repositioning it on her face, and then pressing her palm to it again. "You have killers after you, too, right?"

"I've been hiding from them for more than sixteen years," she said softly. His eyes shot to hers, and she held his gaze. "And no, I don't want to talk about it. But I have the feeling you can understand that, seeing as you've been doing the same thing."

"I have?"

She shrugged. "You do the math."

He nodded slowly. "So you think this guy was after *you?*"

"Yes."

He frowned. "I heard him call you Sarah. He asked about . . . disks."

She averted her eyes.

"Maybe if you just gave them to him —"

"I don't have them here."

"Just as well, because you can't stay here after this."

She looked up slowly.

"He'll be back until he gets what he wants, or until I render him incapable of unassisted breathing."

She smiled a little at what she hoped was sarcasm. Having seen him fight, though, she rather doubted it. Smiling hurt, and she winced.

"If I were you, I'd get whatever disks he's after, so that we at least have something to negotiate with when he returns."

"What do you mean 'we'?" she asked, lowering the ice even while raising her head to look into his eyes.

He shrugged. "Look, I'm not comfortable just sitting around doing nothing. I need to get busy figuring out who I am and what I'm doing here, and who the hell tried to kill me. But since I don't have a clue to go on, I might as well help you with your problem first."

She frowned as she searched his face. "Th-thank you. I think."

"Yeah, well, I'm not convinced these incidents aren't related."

"You're not?"

"It would be an awfully big coincidence, don't you think? I come to town to see you, someone tries to kill me, and only hours later, someone attacks you in your own home. You, the only person in this town with any kind of connection to me whatsoever."

"That we know of," she said.

He shook his head. "A sixteen-year-old back-story is a far less likely explanation than a connection to me, given what happened to land me in the hospital. There has to be a link."

She sighed, lowered her head, but couldn't for the life of her see how there could be. Freddy moaned then, and she shot out of her chair, every thought that wasn't about him grinding to a halt. Aaron joined her at the dog's side, got down on one knee and stroked his big head.

Freddy lay there with his eyes open only

slightly, looking miserable.

"Feelin' a little hungover, are you?" Aaron asked. "Yeah, I know. It'll pass, buddy."

Freddy lifted his head weakly, sniffed Aaron's neck, then lowered it again with an audible sigh. Olivia knelt beside him, too, petting him, nearly weak with the force of her relief.

"He's a helluva dog," Aaron said. "He doesn't look real, he's so big."

"He's the best dog in the whole entire world," she whispered back.

"I'll bet he is," Aaron said with a nervous smile. "I'll bet you are, Fred." But then he turned his focus to her again. "That guy's gonna be back, Olivia. I think we should get out of here, at least for the rest of the night."

"I should call Bryan."

"Bryan?"

"Officer Kendall."

He tipped his head slightly to one side as he studied her face, making her wonder just how badly bruised it was. She must look awful. Silly pajamas, bed-hair, tearstains and bruises to boot.

"Are you and he . . . ?"

"Oh, no. Just friends. Less than friends, really. We were held at gunpoint together a few weeks ago, along with his fiancée, Dawn."

His brows went up.

"Totally unrelated incident," she said.

"Busy little town, this Shadow Falls, isn't it?"

"Lately it has been. What scares me is the way they say these things happen in threes, right? So this makes two. What the hell could be next?"

"Maybe it's already three — if my killer and your intruder are two different people." He looked around the room. "I think we should keep this to ourselves for now."

"Why?"

"My instincts are telling me that I know what to do, and that keeping quiet is it. And I trust my instincts."

"What if *I* don't trust your instincts?" she asked. "What if I have some instincts of my own to follow?" And even as she said it, she knew what those instincts were telling her. Pack up the dog, grab her escape kit from the safe-deposit box in Burlington and run as fast and as far as she could. She had always known this day might come.

Aaron sank back, looking a little daunted. "All right, I'll try logic, then. We don't know how that guy found you. We don't know if he's related to what happened to me, or if he is, where he's getting his information. How did he know I was alive, or that I'd left the hospital, or that you were the only contact I had in town? How did he know to come looking for me here? If there's a leak, it's got to be either at the police department or at the hospital."

"I see the logic there, but I already told you, this has nothing to do with you."

"You can't be sure of that."

"I'm as sure as I need to be. The life I've built here is over, Aaron. I hoped I could help you, but I don't see how I can. I've got to disappear."

He lifted his brows, looking at her as if he'd never seen her before. "You've got a whole lot going on under the surface for an English teacher, lady."

"Maybe I do."

"Still, you agree that staying here tonight is a bad idea, right?"

"Staying here at all is a bad idea," she told him. "And you're right that I need to leave here tonight. But not with you. Just like Harvey Trudeau, I have to do it on my own."

He frowned as if he couldn't understand her. "The way I see it, we're in the same boat here. Someone's after you, and someone's after me. Maybe the same someone, maybe not. But dammit, we can help each other."

She looked at him, her eyes narrowing.

89

"Why would you want to help me?"

He held her gaze for a long moment, letting her look her fill, as if he truly had nothing to hide. "I don't know. I have a feeling I'm . . . *supposed* to."

She tipped her head sideways, the way Freddy did when he heard a sound and didn't know what it was.

"Look, you seem to like this life of yours pretty well," he said. "Why give it up for good if you don't have to? Isn't it worth at least trying to stay?"

She thought on that and finally nodded. "What do you suggest . . . we . . . do?" The word *we* felt foreign on her lips.

"Let's go somewhere else for what's left of the night. Tomorrow we'll pick up those disks you've got stashed off-site — a smart move on your part, by the way — and then . . . well, then we'll figure out our next move."

She searched her soul but couldn't trust what she found there. If this man were anyone else — *anyone* else besides Aaron Westhaven — she would tell him to take a hike, and then she would deal with her own problems on her own terms.

But this *was* Aaron Westhaven. And she wanted to trust him. "I don't know," she said softly.

"I just saved your life," he reminded her. "Remember?"

She pressed her lips tight and sighed.

"Go pack a bag, okay?"

"Okay," she said, conceding. She started to get up, then hesitated. "Aaron?"

"Yeah?" He was petting the dog again, watching his face, maybe counting his breaths. As if he really cared. And that, all by itself, was telling her just about all she needed to know about the man. When Freddy lifted a paw weakly and then placed it on top of Aaron's knee, it told her even more.

But Aaron was looking at her, awaiting her question. So She asked it. "How do you suppose you learned how to fight like that? Or . . . how to handle that gun the way you did? I mean, you took it apart as if you really knew what you were doing."

He nodded. "I know. I've been wondering about that myself. It sure doesn't seem like the kind of thing a reclusive writer would be all that good at, does it?"

"No," she said softly. "No, it really doesn't."

Aaron knew a handful of things as he watched her head into the bedroom to pack her bag. He knew that he had come to this town to see her. He had no doubt about that. That knowledge had become more and more fixed in his mind, and he considered the fact that he'd had her business card proof positive of it.

He knew another thing, too — though this one with far less certainty. He damn well didn't think he was this reclusive writer she seemed so convinced he was. He wasn't gentle or sensitive or lonely or any of those things she thought about him. And if he had created a character who *was* all those things, he sure as *hell* wouldn't have named him Harvey Trudeau.

He was pretty sure he had killed. He knew someone had tried to kill him. Maybe deservedly so. Maybe not. But he felt with everything in him that this woman — this mild-mannered, dog-loving, unknowingly gorgeous, buttoned-up, wary-as-hell English professor — was the key to his past.

He had to stay close to her until he figured the rest out. So he would help her with her little problem on the way to helping himself with his own.

And if it took letting her believe he was an eccentric bestselling author, then he would let her believe it. He wasn't even altogether sure she was wrong, but it sure *felt* like a lie.

Another thing was bugging him while she

packed a little overnight bag, too. He was attracted to her. In a big way. It had surprised him to acknowledge that, because he hadn't thought that a man in his condition would have much hope of focusing on anything else besides his own dire straits. And yet he'd felt the attraction growing in him since she'd walked into his hospital room.

But his instinct — that tiny voice he somehow knew he had to trust — told him that beginning even a mild flirtation with her would be a huge mistake. He would need to keep that in mind and himself in check.

He sat back, and finally relaxed his mind. A part of him wondered how he could trust any of the conclusions he'd been reaching. None of them were based on knowledge, because everything he knew was hidden from him. He was basing everything on gut feelings. On instinct. On intuition.

It was a scary way to deal with a life-and-death situation.

And yet it was all he had.

5

Olivia packed her only two pairs of jeans into an overnight bag, along with a few other essentials, all the while telling herself it was insane to take off in the dead of night with a stranger.

But it wasn't insane. It might have been for anyone else. But not for her. For sixteen years she'd been living with the knowledge that this day might come. And now it had. No one here knew about the diskettes. She'd taken them from Tommy as some kind of lame, poorly thought out insurance policy when she'd run away all those years ago. And no one knew her name was Sarah, either. No one from *this* incarnation, anyway. All that was coming from her past life — the one she'd left behind.

She had to run. And as for going with Aaron, well, he wasn't *really* a stranger to her. Besides, he needed her help.

Decision made, she zipped her bag and

returned to the living room to find Aaron and Freddy both missing.

Frowning, she looked around at the demolished room. Only it wasn't. Aaron had picked everything up, restored order while she'd been getting dressed and packing her things. She heard his voice outside and realized they hadn't gone far. She picked up Freddy's dog bed and opened the front door.

Aaron was standing at the back end of the dusty-but-impressive Expedition. The tailgate was open, and Freddy was standing with his front feet up on the carpeted floor of the cargo hold, and he wasn't budging. He was just looking at Aaron expectantly, as if he ought to know what came next.

"Um, Aaron, that's not my car."

He looked up as if startled. "I know. And you're a fast packer."

"It's going to be a short trip. I hope."

He nodded and returned his puzzled look to the dog. "Is there some kind of command you use to get him to jump the rest of the way in?"

"No. It's just that he's so big."

"And that matters why?"

"He'd have to get a running start to jump all the way in, and in my car he bangs his head on the roof. So he refuses." She eyed the Expedition. "He would probably never hit his head in this one."

"Would you believe that's why we're taking it?" he asked.

She sent him a look that told him she would not.

He shrugged. "I didn't think so. But I did overhear you talking to the redhead about this baby. No one knows you have it, right?"

"Only the redhead — er, Dr. Overton."

"Good. She'll never know we've taken it, and it'll take your cop friend longer to sound the alarm if your car is still here," he said.

"I should probably call her, though. She won't say anything if I ask her not to, but I don't want her to think I've been abducted by an amnesiac shooting victim —"

"You don't think that's what this is, do you? A kidnapping?"

She met his eyes. "If I did, I wouldn't be going. Besides, if you try anything with me, Freddy will eat you."

He shot the dog a quick look and nodded. "I bet he would. All right, good, then. You can call the doc later, though. We should get a move on before they figure out I'm not in the hospital. This is the first place they're going to come looking."

She nodded and set her overnight bag on

the floor of the backseat. Then she found the release and folded those seats forward, making even more room for Freddy.

Moving to the rear, she arranged Freddy's bed while he stood patiently, front feet still inside the SUV, watching her every move.

"I know, boy. I know." She got behind the dog and, bending, cupped her hands to give him a boost up. He lifted one hind foot into her cupped hands and pushed off as she lifted.

"Hey, no, let me —" Aaron began.

"I've got this." She put a little more effort into it, and Freddy got himself in, turned around three times and sank gratefully onto his bed with a sigh.

"Good Lord, woman, how much does he *weigh?*"

"Two hundred, give or take. Most of the time he gets in and out with a lot less help from me. Unless he's really tired or doesn't feel like going."

"Or he's under the influence of a tranquilizer," Aaron said. Then he held up a piece of plastic, with part of a label clinging to it. "I found this near the outside of the fence — right there." He pointed, and handed her the plastic.

She eyed it. "Ace-prome— huh?"

"Acepromazine. It's a tranquilizer, commonly used in veterinary offices. It would take a big dose for a dog this size, hit him within an hour, and probably last for three or four. That timing fit with what happened here tonight?"

"Like a glove," she said. "How do you know about veterinary tranquilizers?"

He shrugged. "Damned if I know. House all locked up?"

"I need to run back in for a couple more things."

"I should pull your car into the garage. It'll make everything look more normal."

"You still have my car keys?" she asked.

"Left them in it — got distracted when I heard you cry out."

"Okay. Grab some dog food from the bag out there while you're at it, will you?"

"I'll just bring the bag. In case we need to be gone longer than anticipated."

A little shiver worked up her spine as the voice of doubt — the one she'd been actively suppressing — whispered a bit more insistently. What if, just *what if,* this man wasn't what he seemed? "Maybe I should let Carrie know now that —"

"Let's just get going, okay?"

She tipped her head to one side, suddenly less sure about him than she'd been before. "Maybe I should give this a little more thought, Aaron."

He glanced at her, frowning, but then his frown eased and his face softened. "Hey, I don't blame you. You don't even know me."

But she felt as if she did. And yet . . . something wasn't quite right about all this.

"Then again, neither do I, at the moment," he went on. "But, Olivia, someone tried to hurt you tonight. And it wasn't me. Someone tried to hurt me, too. If the two incidents are related, then we have a common enemy. Even if they're not, we both have someone after us, and we both want to find out who it is and make it stop so we can get back to our respective lives."

She thought about that for a moment. It did make sense.

"Aside from the fact that someone else came after you, if I wanted to hurt you, I could have done it by now, couldn't I? With Freddy tripping out on acepromazine and the phones dead? I could have taken either vehicle and been long gone before anyone even found your body."

Her eyes flew wider as she shot him a look. "You don't need to be so graphic."

"I'm not your enemy. I may not know who I am, but . . . I know that." He shook his head. "Look, I need to get out of here. I feel that right to my gut. I need to get somewhere safe, so I can stay alive long enough to figure this mess out. And I really don't want to leave you here alone with some crazed lunatic still out to get you. But I will, if that's what you want."

Her throat was dry. She lowered her eyes, her mind whirling, as she realized she didn't know what the hell to do. Trust him? Or stay home?

But the thing was, she *couldn't* stay home as if nothing had happened. The new life she'd created, the new identity she'd claimed, the way she'd been living for the past sixteen-plus years — it was gone now. All of it. Someone knew her secret. So it wasn't a secret anymore. Even if she let Aaron go without her, after the attack she'd already reached the conclusion that she would have to take off.

And she was rapidly reaching another one. She needed to face Tommy and get things over with once and for all. But she wasn't so sure she could take him on all by herself and live to tell the tale. At least with Aaron at her side she would have one ally. For a little while, anyway. And while she hated to drag him into her mess, she supposed she could repay him for his help by helping him solve his own mysteries.

Aaron sighed, glancing nervously at the

road, as if expecting someone to show up at any moment. The police? The killer? The intruder? She didn't know. Maybe he didn't, either.

"All right, stay here then, Olivia," he said at length. "I'll leave you the gun. You can tell your friend the cop I stole the car." He leaned in. "Come on, Freddy, ride's off."

"No." She said it quickly, her decision made. "No, I'm coming with you. I'll go get what I need and lock up."

He seemed relieved. Turning, he closed the liftgate as Olivia drew a deep breath and headed back into the house. She closed the door behind her, set her jaw and walked calmly to the telephone stand for a notepad and pen. Then she scribbled a simple note for Bryan.

Dropping out of sight for a few days. Past lives catching up to me. Everything's okay so far. Just need some time. I'll call you in a few days, and that's a promise. If I don't — things have gone very wrong.

Best, Olivia.

She left the note on the coffee table, with a paperweight on top to keep it from drifting off. Bryan would find it if he decided to

101

come looking for her. He would understand what she meant. "Past lives" — he would know that meant Tommy. He would know to come looking for her if he didn't hear from her. He would know what to do.

She'd worked too hard to stay alive all this time to just put her hard-won life into the hands of any man now — even if that man *was* Aaron Westhaven. She needed to take some precautions of her own, and she didn't particularly care if her favorite writer liked it or not.

She hurried to the kitchen to lock the back door and secure the dog door. Back in the living room, she grabbed her handbag and jacket from the closet, then headed out the front, locking the door behind her.

She paused on the step, looking through the darkest of nights at the sleeping town where she'd built her new life. Shadow Falls had been her salvation. She hoped to God she would be alive to return and reclaim her life there. But she had a terrible feeling in the pit of her stomach that nothing was ever going to be the same again.

Aaron. As he drove, he couldn't get his head around thinking of himself by that name. It didn't feel any more familiar to him than Jack or Joe or a hundred other names he

102

could think of. Then again, he'd spent a lot of time in his hospital room running through every male name he could think of, and none of them had sent any sparks of recognition sizzling through his head. None of them.

Still, he was worried. "Aaron" didn't seem to fit. The persona of a novel-scribbling loner felt like a suit that was a couple of sizes too tight. And the dreams or flashbacks or visions he'd had of himself with a gun in his hand and a body at his feet certainly didn't seem to reflect the life of a reclusive novelist.

And now he had a sidekick.

Bringing Olivia with him probably hadn't been the brightest idea he'd ever had. She was bound to be a problem. Oh, she might seem like a staid, boring, highly intelligent professor, but she was clearly something else entirely. She had her own baggage, her own secrets — big, deadly secrets — hiding in her eyes, not to mention lurking in the shadows of her home last night. He'd heard her attacker call her Sarah and demand that she give him "the disks." What the hell was that about? Was the reserved intellectual actually leading a double life? Who was she really? And why had he come to Shadow Falls to see her?

It had to be related to what had happened to him. *She* had to be involved somehow. And sticking with her was the only way to find out how. Staying alive while he did it was imperative, so hitting the road was the only solution.

Before they'd traveled ten miles, however, she was digging her cell phone out of her oversize handbag.

"Turn that thing off."

She shot him a quick look, probably startled by his deep voice breaking the nighttime silence. "But I have to let the university know I won't be in for a few days. I'll just tell them I'm sick. And I have to call Carrie, too."

"It's 3:00 a.m., Olivia."

"I was just going to leave messages."

"Not yet."

She turned off the phone, but she frowned at him, and he knew she was going to argue. He could see her gearing up for it in the way her jaw got a little tighter and her eyes a little more intense. He thought she might be about to lose her temper with him. And he found himself looking forward to it.

But then she licked her lips, took a breath and let it out slowly. "I'm not going to tell anyone where we are or what we're doing," she said, calmly and rationally. "But if I wanted to do that, and I thought it would be best for me, I'd do it. You need to know that about me."

Logical. Straightforward. The closest she'd come to losing it had been when she'd thought her dog had been dead on her living-room floor. Threats to her own life seemed to have far less emotional impact on her.

"You wouldn't have to tell anyone where you are. You wouldn't even have to make a call. With your cell phone on, anyone with the know-how can track you."

Her brows went up, and she stared at him, the stubborn intellectual gone. There was worry in her eyes now. Maybe even fear. He decided he preferred the stubbornness. He knew what had instigated the change, though. She must be wondering how he'd come by the knowledge he'd just imparted. She had to be, because he was wondering the same thing.

"I must have done a lot of research — for my writing," he said, attempting to answer her question before she could ask it. But it rang false to him. It *felt* like a lie.

"You never wrote any crime thrillers, Aaron."

"Now how can you be so sure about that?"

She averted her eyes. That was telling, that

little thing. Looking away, as if embarrassed or ashamed or lying right back at him. She cleared her throat, lifted her chin a little. "I've read everything you've written," she said.

"Oh." He fell silent for a moment, trying to come up with an answer that would reassure her. This wasn't going to work if she was going to turn suspicious of him at every turn.

What wasn't going to work? his mind asked him. *You don't even know what the hell you're doing, pal.*

But he felt as if he knew *exactly* what he was doing. As if this kind of thing was second nature to him. Running, hiding, going off the radar to get his shit together. To regroup. To strategize.

He gripped the wheel a little tighter and came up with what he hoped was a reasonable answer. "You've read everything I've *published,*" he said. "I could be an aspiring thriller writer with *stacks* of unpublishable crime novels under my desk, for all you know — or for all I know."

Her head came back around, eyes interested, brows raised, fear erased. "That's true, you might." And then she smiled, sighed as if in relief, and shook her head in a self-deprecating way. "That's *got* to be it.

You know all of the things you do because of research you've done."

"Or books I've read," he said. "Maybe I'm a big thriller fan, even though I write . . . what would you call it? Sappy, emotional melodrama?"

"I would never call it that, and you shouldn't, either. It's not sappy. It *is* emotional, but not in that way. It's . . . emotional realism."

From the back, Freddy released a loud, long snore that sounded like some cartoon sound effect more than a real dog.

"He'll sleep for at least an hour now," she said. "Maybe more, given the tranquilizer."

But he was still focused on the earlier conversation. "You've read *everything*? You really *are* a fan, aren't you?"

She lifted her gaze again. It was a little bit soft, as if he were seeing behind the mask she wore. "I'm more than a fan."

Alarm bells went off. Was she an obsessed fan? A stalker type? God, that would be an added complication, wouldn't it? She didn't seem like that kind, though. "How do you mean?" he asked, his tone cautious.

She shrugged. "If you really feel the way your character Harvey does about life and love and loneliness, then I feel more like a . . . a kindred spirit, I guess."

"And if I don't?"

"Then I guess I'm only a kindred spirit to Harvey. Either way, you must understand him. Identify with him."

"So it stands to reason I would understand and identify with you." He nodded. "I've *got* to read some of my books."

"I anticipated that, brought some of them along. We can take turns driving if you want to read a little." She blinked then, as if she'd just thought of something. "You didn't forget how to drive."

"I didn't even think about that." He looked at his hands on the wheel and nodded. "It was kind of automatic, getting into the driver's seat. It didn't even occur to me that I might not know how." He felt himself smiling and realized it was the first time since waking up without a past.

"Maybe everything you ever knew is still right there, inside your mind," Olivia said. "Maybe it just hasn't quite surfaced."

He nodded. "I hope you're right about that."

"So . . . when do you think it would be safe for me to make those calls? Not that I'm asking permission, of course."

"Of course. My *suggestion*," he said, "would be to wait until we can pick up a new phone or two. The prepaid ones would be harder to trace."

"So we need to stop somewhere."

He nodded. "Once it's daylight. And only if we can get access to some cash. If we use plastic, they'll trace us."

"Well, even I knew that much," she said. "But I think you might be a little overly cautious here, Aaron. It's highly unlikely anyone is even looking for us yet."

"Oh, trust me. They're looking. Those nurses are pretty diligent about waking up patients every hour or so. Mostly to tell them to get some sleep."

She smiled a little at that.

"Besides, we already know *someone* is looking. Maybe not the police, not yet. But my shooter's looking for me, and your housebreaker is looking for you. There's no question about that. And we don't know how sophisticated these men are — assuming they're not the same man."

"Or how sophisticated the guys who hired them are."

He frowned. "You think someone hired that man to break in to your house, don't you? And you have a good idea who."

Her face went serious, and she gave a nod. "I can get us plenty of cash."

"ATM?"

She frowned at him. "Wouldn't *they,*

whoever *they* are, pick up on that faster than they would be able to track a cell phone?" she asked, and he wasn't sure if it was just him, or if she was starting to sound a little impatient. "And wouldn't it look fairly suspicious if I took a big chunk of cash out of the bank on the same night *you* went missing?"

"See? Even you've read a few thrillers."

"I read widely. I'm an English professor, after all." And then the stuffy facade wavered a little. "And I watch the occasional episode of *Law and Order.*"

He glanced over at her, caught her sheepish expression as she admitted to what had to be a guilty pleasure, and for just an instant he got caught up in the way her thick black lashes framed her chocolate-brown eyes. A few crow's-feet appeared at their outer corners when she smiled, but he got the feeling she hadn't smiled a lot in her life. Then he forced his gaze back to the road, a feeling in the pit of his stomach telling him he had just been looking at the biggest potential complication of all.

She was gorgeous. And he was attracted to her. He *had* to stop letting those facts catch him by surprise.

"Once people realize that you vanished on the same night I did, there's going to be plenty of cause for suspicion, believe me," he said, getting his head back on topic.

"Maybe not. I can be convincing on the phone, and I left a note at the house for Bryan in case he shows up and —"

He hit the brake pedal, jerked the wheel and brought the SUV to a stop on the shoulder, raising a cloud of dust behind them and sending Freddy sliding. "You left a *note?*"

Her brown eyes went slightly wider, and she clenched her jaw so tightly he thought her teeth must be grinding against each other. She nodded once, as if she'd just reached a firm decision, and closed her hand around the door handle as if she were getting ready to calmly step from the SUV in the middle of nowhere.

He drew a slow breath. "What did you write in the note?"

"None of your business."

"It *is* my business, since my life is on the line here, too." But her jaw was still firm, and she wasn't meeting his eyes. Her nostrils flared just a little, and he thought of a skittish horse getting ready to run flat out. He drew a deep, slow breath, calmed his tone ˥ spoke to her the way he imagined ᵒ would need to speak to that horse. ˩ldn't be snapping at you. Up to now you've helped me a lot. And I've helped *you,* too. But I need you to know that I'm scared, Olivia. I'm scared that guy who tried to kill me will find us and try again, and maybe succeed this time. And dammit, I don't know what kind of life I'd be leaving behind, but I don't think I'm ready to die before I even find out."

Her face softened just a little. She blinked, and her hand relaxed its grip on the door. "I didn't give anything away in the note. I'm not an idiot," she said.

"No one would mistake you for an idiot, Olivia. But . . . just to ease my mind, would you please tell me what you wrote? Word for word? Please?"

She blinked twice as she remembered. "I think . . . 'Dropping out of sight for a few days. Everything's okay. Just need some time. I'll call you in a few days.' "

He sighed, nodded and put the SUV back into gear as he wondered if she was leaving anything out. He sensed she was. That gut instinct again. He hoped it wasn't leading him on a wild-goose chase.

"So it didn't give anything away, just like I said. No harm done."

"Except that he'll call out the National Guard if he doesn't hear from you in a few days."

"That was the entire point," she said. "It's the bad guys we're running from, remember?"

He thinned his lips, realizing that kindred spirit or not, this woman didn't trust him. Maybe she didn't trust anyone.

He put the SUV into motion again. "Look, we're in this together. Could you maybe tell me what you're doing next time?"

"I'm not used to answering to anyone. I'm not sure I want to be."

She sounded pissed off. He glanced at her and knew he'd hit on a touchy subject, having a man trying to control her. He needed to come off much less alpha male than he was currently managing. She wanted a reclusive bookworm; maybe he ought to try to give her one. "I probably overreacted," he said. "I'm tense and frustrated, and I know you are, too. I didn't mean to scare you."

She nodded. "Just don't let it happen again, Aaron."

The words were delivered with a cold firmness he hadn't even glimpsed in her until then. He looked at her.

"I mean it," she said. "I *won't* be around a violent man."

"*Violent?* I didn't lay a hand —"

"A hot temper is a hot temper. Your reaction was violent. I do not tolerate violence in any man, Aaron. I won't." She lowered her head, shaking it slowly. "Not ever again."

If she'd punched him in the face, he wouldn't have felt more thoroughly put in his place — or shocked. Clearly she'd been subjected to violence at the hands of a man before. He disagreed that barking a question and bringing the SUV to a sudden halt were evidence of violence, but she clearly thought otherwise. And he felt a touch of remorse at making her think he was capable of violence, then thought that was a surprising thing for him to feel.

She was as flighty as a hunted animal — admittedly with good reason. But she had a core in her that had to be solid steel. He'd seen it in her eyes just then.

"I won't let it happen again," he said.

She nodded. "If you do, it'll be the last conversation we ever have."

After several minutes of driving in silence, he decided he didn't like the tension that had sprouted between them. It was of no use to him. In fact, it would work against him. He had to put her at ease again. He decided to try to divert her attention to a different subject.

"So if you're not going to an ATM, where is this cash coming from?"

"I have an . . . emergency fund."

He thinned his lips. "Now you sound like the one with an uncanny knowledge of how to disappear."

She shrugged but didn't explain why she had such a fund, or why she didn't keep it at home, which made him even more curious.

"I have a safe-deposit box in Burlington," she said. "It's an hour from here. Take the next right, then get on the highway."

"All right."

"And now that you've pissed me off, I'll add that if you want to stop me from calling Carrie Overton, you're going to have to use that gun you took from my attacker."

He shot her a look, blinking.

"Besides, if you think they're not going to call Carrie when they find you missing from the hospital, you'd better think again. At the very least, she'll be talking to Bryan the minute she gets to work in the morning, and believe me, Carrie Overton's workday begins way earlier than we can get into a bank, empty my safe-deposit box and go buy prepaid cell phones."

He kept on driving, trying not to show his surprise.

"She'll tell them I've got Professor Mallory's car, Aaron. Unless I talk to her first."

Dammit, she was right.

At length he glanced her way, gave her a nod. "It shouldn't matter. We haven't gone very far yet, anyway. Go ahead and leave her a message. Keep it short, and turn the phone off after you finish, okay? Please?"

She nodded once, then dialed as he drove, and he thought again that there was a lot more to this woman than he had first imagined. She might look like a mild-mannered English teacher with a boring life and a dog as her closest companion. An introverted, probably repressed woman who kept the world at bay and her hair in a tight bun.

But all of that had peeled back a little further just now, and he'd glimpsed a frightened tigress hiding underneath, crouched and ready to spring. He'd unintentionally poked that cat with a stick and gotten a taste of her temper for his trouble. If cornered, he thought, she would come at him with claws and teeth bared, fan of his alleged work or not.

He wasn't worried that she posed any real threat to him. But he knew for sure it would be easier to deal with the bookworm than the beast, so he intended to do whatever was necessary to ensure that the beast stayed caged.

116

6

Police Officer Bryan Kendall arrived at Shadow Falls General Hospital at 3:32 a.m. It had been three quarters of an hour since a nurse had phoned him at home, waking him from a restless sleep to tell him that the mystery patient had vanished from his bed.

He went straight to the nurses' desk, where a blonde who looked too young to be in charge of much of anything greeted him. Her tag read Kathy Curry, R.N.

"Officer Kendall," she said. "I'm sorry to wake you at home, but I was told to call you directly if anything happened."

"That's what I asked for," he said. "And fortunately, my fiancée is very understanding. So what happened?"

"We don't know. I checked him at two, and everything was fine, but —"

"You personally?" he interjected.

"Yes. I've been the only one taking care of him this shift. But when I went in to get his

3:00 a.m. vitals, he was . . . gone."

"Has someone searched the hospital?"

"Security has been all through the place. Still checking, but so far there's no sign of him." She came around the desk and walked briskly toward the missing patient's room, leaving Bryan to try to keep up. Nurses, he thought. They walked like they were doing time trials for the Indy 500 or something.

He caught up to her at the door, and they both went inside. Bryan took a quick look around. "Did anyone report seeing anything suspicious? Did he have any visitors?"

"No, Officer Kendall, nothing like that."

"Did they check the parking lot?"

She nodded.

"Has Dr. Overton been notified?"

"Not yet. I thought I should talk to you before deciding whether to wake her."

"Okay. Look, I want this room closed off. No one in or out until I get a forensics team in to go over it. Got that?"

She nodded.

He pulled out his cell phone, then paused. "Is it okay to use this in here?"

"Yeah. The cell companies finally made it into the twenty-first century. Cell phones don't interfere with pacemakers anymore."

"Took them long enough." He put in a call, waking Chief MacNamara, though he

118

hated to. The man was a bear when he didn't get enough sleep.

"Kendall," the chief growled when he picked up. "What?"

"Sorry, Chief. I'm at the hospital. Our shooting victim has vanished. I figured you'd be madder if I didn't call than if I did."

"Hmmph. You figured right. So did he leave on his own, or was he taken?"

It was the first question Bryan had asked himself, as well. "I don't know for sure, but it looks like he left on his own. No one saw anyone hanging around his room. No visitors since the professor left him. His clothes are still in the closet. Shoes are missing, though. Window's locked from the inside. Hospital's being searched, but so far, no sign of him."

"You get a positive ID on him yet?"

"I have a call in to the publisher, but it's the weekend. Doubt I'll hear back until Monday."

The chief sighed. "What's your plan, Kendall?"

"Get some guys out here to dust the room for prints, check for traces of blood, gunpowder residue."

"It's a hospital room. There'll be prints everywhere. Traces of blood, too."

"They keep them pretty clean, Chief."

"Still . . ."

"They're going to close off the room until we clear it. Meanwhile, I want to head out to Olivia Dupree's place."

"Why?"

"Because she's the only person we know of with any connection to him, and the last visitor he had before he vanished."

"A damn flimsy connection," Chief Mac replied.

"But the only one we have."

With a slow sigh, the chief said, "Okay, go ahead. Order a team to go over the room, and check with Dupree personally. Keep me posted."

"Done." Bryan disconnected and clipped the phone to his belt, then turned to Nurse Kathy, but she'd vanished. Heading into the hallway, he met her coming toward him, her steps rapid and silent, her hands bearing a large manila envelope.

He pulled the door closed, touching the edge of the wood, not the knob. "Put up a sign or something until I can get a team in there, okay?"

She nodded. "I thought you might be able to use this," she said, holding the envelope a little higher.

"What is it?"

"His head shot. Come with me."

He followed her into an empty room, and she pulled the X-ray from the envelope and slapped it onto a panel on the wall, then flipped a switch to turn on the backlight.

"How's this going to help?" he asked with a frown, staring at the illuminated human skull.

"The steel plate. You can see the serial number. Right here," she said, pointing it out for his untrained eye.

"And . . . ?"

"It'll be in a database. We can get a positive identification with this."

He lifted his brows and took a second look at the nurse, his opinion of her rising. She might be young and pretty, and she might walk as if her feet were on fire, but she was sharp, too. Smart, quick, efficient. Probably all good qualities in an R.N. He squinted at the numbers, which were so blurry he could barely make them out, then looked at her again. "Is there a way to enhance this?"

"Not here. But maybe you have something in your . . . crime lab, or its Shadow Falls equivalent."

"There is no Shadow Falls equivalent. But I can send it out. Can I keep this?"

"Yes. In fact, I made this copy for you." She took the X-ray down, slid it back into its envelope and handed it to him. "Should I call Dr. Overton?"

He shook his head. "Why wake her? There's not a damn thing she can do here that can't wait a few more hours. I'll be in touch. Thanks for this. You've been a big help."

"You're welcome."

"Remember, we're still keeping this quiet."

"It won't stay quiet for long. Not with a forensics squad dusting the room for prints," she said.

He sighed, lowered his head. "As quiet as possible, then."

She made a zipping motion across her lips.

Bryan tucked the envelope under his arm and headed for the elevators.

He drove straight out to Olivia Dupree's place. The house was dark, and the doors were locked up tight. Her car was in the garage. Nothing looked out of place or suspicious. And he hated to wake her in the dead of night, but he was worried. Olivia had a past she'd been dodging for sixteen years. He and his fiancée, Dawn, were the only people in this town who knew the truth about that past and the dangers it posed to her present — hell, to her *life* — if it ever became common knowledge.

And no one knew for sure who this missing patient was. Admittedly, it looked as if he was probably the reclusive author Olivia had been expecting. But Bryan didn't think authors were generally targeted by professional killers. Better to wake Olivia for nothing and be safe than wait for morning and be sorry, he thought.

Besides, she would want to know the guy was missing.

He went to the front door, rang the bell and waited. When there was no response, he rang it again. After the third try, he started getting that feeling he got when something was wrong. Even if Olivia were out cold, Freddy would have been at the door the second he heard the chimes. So he tugged his cell phone off his belt and dialed her number.

He couldn't hear the telephone ringing beyond the front door. No ringing. Nothing.

He now had probable cause to think she might be in danger. And he didn't think Olivia was likely to mind too much, anyway, if he went inside uninvited. He went around back, through the gate into the fenced-in yard, and then crossed the deck to the French doors in back. Much easier to break in that way.

It took some doing, but he managed to

break the security latch on the dog door, and then he crawled inside.

"Olivia?" he called. "Olivia, it's Bryan!"

No answer.

"Freddy! Freddy, come here, boy!"

Nothing. No heavy paws tromping toward him. Not even a plaintive whine or playful snort.

He went through the house quickly, his heart in his throat as he entered her bedroom, praying he wasn't going to find her body lying on the mattress. Echoes of ghosts past whispered up and down his spine as he scanned the room.

His prayers were answered. No body in the bed. Olivia wasn't there. She wasn't anywhere.

Returning to the kitchen, he resecured the dog door from inside, then went to the living room, so he could leave through the front and lock up behind him. But he paused when he saw the note on the coffee table, held in place by a clear acrylic paperweight with a sunflower inside it. He read it, but it only worried him more. A few days away. Past catching up with her. It was worded so that he would know what she was talking about but no one else would. Not unless they knew the entire story. She wouldn't have written it that way if she'd been forced to leave a note. At least, he hoped not.

Still, this wasn't feeling good at all. "Where the hell are you, Olivia?"

Olivia directed Aaron to the First Community Bank of Burlington, Vermont, and he pulled into the parking lot in the rear, found a spot and killed the engine. She dug through her handbag to find the safe-deposit key, then turned in her seat to stroke Freddy, promising to come back soon. She didn't even object when Aaron got out of the car and walked with her.

They followed a well-kept sidewalk around to the front of the brown brick building. The bank was surrounded by yellow-and-gold floral explosions. Marigolds, daisies and other flowers she couldn't name blossomed in abundance, and she felt the same twinge she always felt upon seeing a beautiful garden. Jealousy. She'd always wished she could have a green thumb. For her, plants tended to just . . . die.

Aaron opened the heavy glass door and held it for her. She went inside and up to the counter. The bank had only just opened for the day. To kill time before it did, the two of them had pulled onto the shoulder of a secluded side road and taken a nap right in their seats, then driven on to the city. And, she thought, she used the term *city* loosely.

She hadn't expected to be able to sleep when they stopped, and she'd been right. She'd drifted off a few times, only to wake with a gasp and a start within a few minutes. She guessed her adrenal glands were still pumping that fight-or-flight response through her veins. She'd taken pity on her poor canine, since she couldn't sleep anyway, and let him get out and romp in a nearby meadow while she sat in the tall grass and watched him. After a while she'd joined him in his running and jumping. She found a good-size branch on the ground and threw it to give him something to chase and shake and, eventually, chew into smaller pieces.

Freddy had still been restless in the SUV, even after an hour's playtime. Which Aaron had slept straight through, she'd noted. He'd been through a lot, probably needed the rest.

Now, at the bank, Olivia felt sorry for leaving Freddy in the SUV again so soon and vowed not to take too long.

A smiling woman at the counter greeted her with an overly cheerful, "Good morning! How can I help you today?"

"I need to get some things from my safe-deposit box," Olivia said. Then she wondered if she looked as grouchy as she sounded, and tried to paste a semipleasant expression on her face.

"Number?"

"Three-seventy-two."

The woman vanished from behind the counter, then reappeared a moment later and opened a half door, motioning Olivia to follow her.

Olivia went through the door, Aaron following her. She'd wondered if he would. They accompanied the teller into a room with a wall of locked drawers, a table and a couple of chairs. Olivia inserted her key into her box.

The teller inserted her own key into the second slot, then pulled the box partway out. "There are complimentary sacks on the wall there." She nodded at a hook on the wall, where plastic drawstring bags with the bank's logo on them hung at the ready. "Help yourself if you need one."

"Thanks."

The teller left the room. Olivia lifted the hinged metal lid and looked inside the drawer. Then she turned to meet Aaron's eyes. He stood behind her — no view of the box's contents from there. She said, "Would you get me one of those 'complimentary sacks,' please?"

He smiled a little at her use of the cheerful clerk's terminology and turned to get the bag.

Olivia set the box on the table, sank into a chair and reached inside, touching items she hadn't handled in more than sixteen years. Her driver's license was in there. Faded and long expired. God, had she really been that young? The round-cheeked face staring up at her, the name Sarah H. Quinlan underneath it, barely resembled the woman she was now. She moved the license aside and found her birth certificate underneath. Below that, her Social Security card, a passport and several banded stacks of cash, each one holding five grand. And underneath all of that, a stack of three-by-five floppy disks and a little black .38 special with a box of bullets beside it.

In a flash she was back in Chicago on the day it all went down. She remembered the timing — how close it had been.

Tommy had had a rough day on the job, and came home with beer on his breath and coffee stains on the shirt with the Chicago P.D. emblem over his heart. She knew right then it was going to be a bad night.

And it had been. The worst one yet. She

128

remembered hoping she hadn't waited one day too long to put her escape plan into action. It wasn't ten minutes before he'd lost his temper and found some excuse to start hitting her. She tried to remember what infraction she'd committed to set him off that last time. Right, right. She'd left the outdoor light on all day.

She'd been pretty sure her life was over that night. That all her plotting had been for nothing, because he'd kept on punching even her after she'd gone down, and he didn't usually do that.

But then the police were pounding on the front door. She'd heard the noise through a haze of pain and thought, *Thank God. I'm still alive. They're here, and I'm still alive.*

His own colleagues kicked in the front door of a home no rookie cop should have been able to afford and presented him with a search warrant. When he demanded to know what the hell this was about, they told him they were acting on a tip. And of course they found pounds of marijuana and hash right where their anonymous informant had told them to look, hidden above a ceiling panel in the master bedroom closet.

She remembered the look Tommy had sent her as they'd cuffed him and dragged him out the door. It had been murderous.

And his words couldn't compare with that icy hatred she saw in his eyes, even though her own were beginning to swell by then.

"You did this, didn't you, Sarah? *Didn't you?*"

She'd shaken her head no, backing even farther away from him, bumping into a cop she knew. One she'd tried to tell about the beatings before, but who hadn't believed her. His eyes said he was sorry. "We need to get you to a hospital," he said aloud. "Did he do this to you?"

She licked her lips and held Tommy's murderous gaze. "I fell," she said. "And I'm fine. No hospital." They wouldn't help her before, and she sure as hell didn't need their help now. She was doing this on her own.

She'd had two choices, the way she saw it. Kill him, or send him to prison. Leaving him without doing one or the other first would only have ensured her own demise. And staying wasn't an option. She wasn't the kind of woman who would tolerate being abused. She'd been planning her escape since the first time he'd laid a hand on her — and planning it in a way that wasn't going to get her killed.

At least not right away. But when he got out, if he ever found her . . .

"I'll kill you for this, Sarah," Tommy

promised as he was shoved out the door in handcuffs. "I'll fuckin' *kill* you."

The cops told her she would have to leave the house until they'd finished processing it. She'd been more than happy to comply. She'd already taken the stack of three-by-five floppies Tommy had taken such pride in. Records of his clients, their names, addresses, how much they bought from him, how much they paid for it. There were photos of many of the transactions, too. Invaluable information, Tommy always said. Priceless. So she'd taken them all, and then she'd removed the hard drive from his computer. With the drugs in the house, the police wouldn't need that information to convict him. And she saw no point in causing trouble for his customers. Besides, as closely as he guarded those files, she thought he might want them back someday. He might even *need* them back. So she could use them to bargain with — maybe for her life — if he ever found her.

She'd taken the disks, all her important papers and as many of her clothes as she could reasonably carry. Everything was in the trunk of the car she'd managed to borrow from the wife of one of Tommy's best customers. A woman who'd seen her bruises and guessed their cause. She'd taken the piles of money from his stash in the basement. Not all of it, but a lot. A hell of a lot. And she'd taken one of his guns and a supply of bullets to go with it.

Tommy was going to jail. And while he was away, unable to get to her, she was going to escape. By the time he got out, she hoped to have a whole new life under way. But as things had turned out, it ended up being an even more complete change than she had ever imagined.

"Your bag," Aaron said, startling her back to the present. She'd forgotten he was in the room. Hell, she'd forgotten *she* was. She looked up to see him standing behind her, looking over her shoulder, all the items in the box clearly visible.

He whistled soft and low.

She pursed her lips, not looking at him. "Don't ask."

"Uh . . . I'm pretty sure I have to."

"No, you don't." She scooped out the banded stacks of money, the gun, the bullets, the diskettes, the ID, all of it, and dropped everything into the bag. Then she closed the lid, got to her feet and slid the box back into its drawer. She held the bag in one hand, hiked her purse onto her shoulder with the other and turned to walk out of the bank.

They crossed the highly polished tile floor in silence, but the second they were outside, he said, "Seriously, Olivia, what the hell kind of mild-mannered professor are you, anyway?"

She kept right on walking. "Look, you have amnesia, right?"

"Yes."

"So I can't ask you any questions about your past. About anything, really. Correct?"

"Yes, you know that's correct, and *I* know where you're going with this, but —"

"Then you know I'm going to suggest we keep things fair and even. I can't ask about your past, so you can't ask about mine."

"I don't think that's fair and even at all," he said. "I *can't* tell you about my past."

"And I *won't* tell you about mine."

"Fine." He unlocked the car and got in, slamming the door.

"Fine," she said, and got in her side, slamming her own door.

Freddy sat up in the back, his head touching the ceiling, turning to look from one of them to the other.

Aaron started the vehicle. "You don't need to tell me, anyway. I can put it together pretty much on my own."

"Oh, really?" she asked, looking at him and wondering if he really could. And then she realized she was acting as if he were her enemy. Probably just because he was male. So she tried to soften her expression, tried to remind herself that he was on her side.

At least, all indications pointed to him being on her side. So far. And he was, after all, the writer she'd admired, the kindred spirit she'd sensed, not a drug-dealing abusive thug.

She lifted her brows and tried to inject a teasing note into her tone. "All right, then, if you're so smart, go for it. Try."

He tilted his head slightly to the side, his face confident, his impatience fading. "I know you've been beaten up on by a man. You let that slip earlier."

"Did I?" She didn't confirm or deny it.

"Now, if I put that together with the fake ID — or maybe it's the real ID and your current one is fake — and the stash of money and the gun, I'd say you must have run away from an abusive husband or lover. You're always ready to run again at a moment's notice, if he should find you. The contents of that box is how you make sure you always can."

She stared at him, unblinking, and silently amazed that he'd pieced together as much as he had.

"What I don't get is that little stack of

disks. Clearly that's what the guy in your house was after. What's on them?"

"They're . . . my insurance policy."

He sighed. "You're not going to tell me, are you?"

"I haven't decided yet."

He was silent for a long moment. "But they *are* the disks I heard that bastard in your house demanding from you, right?"

"Yes."

He waited for her to elaborate. When she didn't, he sighed and said, "All right, where to next?"

"Let's drive a while. I don't want to get too far from Shadow Falls just yet. But we do need to find a place to just . . . chill. Freddy needs to get out of this car, and frankly, so do I. We can pick up some of those prepaid phones on the way."

"And then?"

"And then . . . and then I think I'm going to ask you to place a call to my ex for me."

He lifted his brows. "You sure?"

She nodded. "I'm sure he's found me. There's no question. The things the burglar said —"

"He called you Sarah."

"Yeah."

"Is that your real name, then? Sarah Quinlan? Like on that Illinois driver's license?"

God, he didn't miss a thing, did he? She shook her head slowly, and sat in silence for a time as he maneuvered the big SUV through Burlington and back to the highway. She was debating how much to tell him, if anything. He'd probably given up on getting any answer at all by the time she finally spoke.

"It was my name once. But Sarah Quinlan died. Tommy beat her to death that final night. When I ran, I ran away from who I was as much as I did from him. And when I became Olivia Dupree, I was reborn. My life began that day." She blinked, thinking how sad it still made her that another life had had to end to enable her own new one to start. "I don't think of myself as Sarah anymore. I haven't in a long, long time. So I'd appreciate it if you wouldn't, either. I'm Olivia."

"Okay." He reached across and slid his hand over hers.

The touch startled her, and she almost jerked her hand away, but she stopped herself and just stared at his large, male hand covering hers. It felt strong and warm and dangerous, all at the same time.

"I'm not the enemy, Olivia. I'm on your side. Remember that."

She met his eyes, and she saw kindness

there. Not anger. And she felt herself relax a little in response to no more than the warmth of his hand on hers and the matching warmth in his eyes. "I'll try," she promised, and she meant it.

Aaron drove until they were near, but not too near, Shadow Falls, and he worried while he did. He was way more intrigued by this woman than he ought to be. It was a bad idea. He was sure of that. It was one of many things that had just seemed to show up in his head automatically. He believed it, too. His gut hadn't led him wrong so far.

And yet, *damn,* she got to him.

He wanted her, he realized. It was getting worse with every hour he spent in her company. If she'd stayed a boring professor and not revealed the complex woman inside, he might have done all right. But . . . *damn.*

The growing attraction wasn't the thing making him feel so nervous about her, though. He'd been attracted to her from his first glance — which, given the other issues on his mind, had to be saying something. No, it wasn't that he wanted her. It was that he wanted to *know* her. Everything about her. Her secrets. Her moods. Her . . . appetites. The sounds she would make when —

This was a very bad idea.

They stopped at an electronics store for prepaid phones, one for each of them, and started off again, phones in hand. Olivia looked at him, lifting her brows. "I'm beginning to feel like an actual fugitive."

"Haven't you always been?"

The smile fled her face, and he regretted his words. She'd been teasing, even a little bit playful, and he'd brought reality down on her like a smack in the head.

Settling back in her seat, her eyes serious, she focused on her untraceable phone and punched in a number. He reached over and took the phone from her, depressed the speaker symbol and handed it back.

She lifted her brows, her eyes questioning him, as a phone rang on the other end.

"You don't mind, do you?" he asked. "I mean, we're in this together, right?"

She blinked, and he knew he wasn't fooling her a bit with that line. She knew he didn't trust her and wanted to hear both ends of her phone call. Well, too bad. He *didn't* trust her, couldn't afford to. And he didn't even know why. But he needed her to trust him, so he had to be careful.

"Dr. Carrie Overton." He'd heard the doctor's voice before and would have recognized it even if she hadn't identified herself.

"Carrie, hey. It's me, Olivia."

"It's about time! I got your message as soon as I turned on my phone this morning, and not five minutes later Bryan Kendall was grilling me as to your whereabouts."

"Did you tell him I had the professor's SUV?"

"Of course I didn't. You asked me not to. But I have to tell you, I don't like this."

"What's not to like? I'm fine."

"Are you with *him*?"

"Who?" Olivia replied.

"The amnesia guy. The hot one? He disappeared, you know."

"No, I didn't know that," Olivia said. "So obviously I'm not with him."

"Then why are you hiding from the police?"

"I'm not hiding from anyone. I just want to be left alone for a few days. Is that so hard to believe?"

"Yeah, actually, it is." Carrie sighed. "But it's none of my business."

"Thank you, Carrie."

"If I get the feeling you're in trouble, I'll spill my guts."

"And I'll be glad you did," Olivia said. "But in the meantime, tell me. Did they find out who the mystery patient is yet?"

"They're trying to get an ID from the serial number on the steel plate in his head. Actually, they already tried once and came up with the name of some guy who died years ago. But the numbers were blurry in the X-ray, so they must have gotten one or more of them wrong. Anyway, the police expect to hear from Westhaven's publisher by tomorrow, so that ought to tell them once and for all if it's really him."

"Makes sense."

Aaron watched Olivia's face as she spoke. Mostly she was intent on the phone, or her gaze was turned inward. But just then she looked up and met his eyes, gauging his reactions to what was being said.

"Olivia, I have to ask just once more, why don't you want Officer Kendall to know where you are?"

"I don't want *anyone* to know where I am."

"Why not?"

Her eyes met his again, and he held her gaze. She didn't blink or look away as she said, "Because it's a small town, Carrie. If one person knows I'm off on a romantic weekend with a handsome stranger I picked up in a bar, then the whole town will know it by the time I get back."

"Handsome stranger? Olivia, you don't *go* to bars."

140

"Trust me, I do now. I've gotta go, Carrie. But just remember, not a word about the SUV to Bryan. I'll make it right with Professor Mallory later, I promise. I just don't want my getaway messed up because of this amnesia guy."

"All right, Olivia," Carrie said at length. "All right. Have fun."

"Oh, I intend to."

She said it as if she meant it, he thought, and she kept her eyes glued to his the whole time. Her lips were pulled very slightly upward at the corners. And her eyes seemed a cross between bravado and nervousness.

She disconnected, then set the phone on the dashboard. "Happy?" she asked.

"Deliriously. Now . . . are you going to tell me the rest of your story or not?" he asked.

She crossed her arms over her chest and nodded. "Yes. I think I am."

7

"He was a dealer," Olivia began.

They'd grabbed fast food from a drive-through window and driven to a boat launch on the Winooski River for a break from the car. They sat in the grass, eating, while Freddy splashed in the water, bobbing for river stones and coming up soaked.

"I assume you don't mean used cars," Aaron said.

She nodded. "Nothing major — weed, hash, strictly small-time. But he was a cop, too, so . . ."

"Your ex-husband — the guy who beat you up — he was a cop?"

She nodded. "I never married him, by the way. We lived together. But, yes, he was a cop. That's why I couldn't just get him for assault the first time it happened. No one believed me. He'd set it up, though I didn't know that at the time. He'd talked about me at work, made me seem flighty, unstable.

So when I started asking for help, it was almost as if they'd been expecting it. No one in authority took me seriously. But I wasn't about to stay and put up with being abused. It's just not in me, so I had to find another way out. I figured the cops might be able to ignore me, but they couldn't ignore a few dozen pounds of illegal substances." She lowered her head, shaking it slowly. "All I needed was time to get away. I just needed him locked up long enough for me to put a safe distance between us."

He nodded. "I get that. And the disks?"

She drew a deep breath, stared at him, and he wondered what she was looking for in his eyes. He tried to show sincerity and concern. He didn't know if he was pulling it off. He just knew something was telling him to find out the answers to the question of who she was, so he was doing it. Trusting his gut. He had a feeling it had been important to him . . . before.

"Names, dates, amount purchased, amount paid, photographs of the transactions."

"Photos?"

She nodded. "Tommy got photos of every sale, whenever he could manage it. Usually toked up a little with the customers, just so he could. He used to have cameras set up all over the damned house. Hidden in plants and stuff, and no one ever knew the difference. I asked him why, once. He said it was an investment, said those photos would increase in value over time. That they might even be worth a fortune someday." She shrugged. "I figured if he ever found me, maybe I could use the disks to, you know, pay him off."

"In exchange for him not killing you," he said, as if he already knew.

She nodded jerkily. "It was probably a stupid idea. But it felt like something at the time."

"Hey, something's better than nothing."

"Yeah."

Freddy came trotting up to her just then, dripping wet, and dropped a big round stone in front of her.

"Thank you," she said with all the enthusiasm she would have used had the rock been a diamond in the rough. "That's a really nice rock you have there. What do you want for it?"

"Rrrrrrruff!" said Freddy.

"Oh, okay, then." She broke a piece of her sandwich off and fed it to him. Then she threw the rock, and he bounded off after it, but he went suddenly still and alert as a rowboat went by on the river. The guy inside

144

wasn't even rowing, just floating and smiling.

"You know, I'm going to do that someday," Olivia said. And she sounded a little wistful.

"What, go down the river in a rowboat?"

She lowered her head as if embarrassed. "Sounds dull, doesn't it? I don't know, it's nothing special, but I've never done it, and it seems like it would be — kind of soothing. Maybe even a little spiritual."

Aaron watched her, and he couldn't help but like her even more than he had before. She talked to her dog as if he were human, and the gargantuan beast actually seemed to understand and hang on every word. And she was embarrassed that her idea of an exciting new thing to do would be to go floating down a lazy stretch of river. Hell, it didn't sound bad at all to him.

She really did love that dog, though. They were quite a pair. Stunning.

Both of them.

Okay, okay, he was getting distracted. Back on topic. "So you want me to call this ex of yours, you said."

She nodded. "I need to find out for sure if he's the one who sent that guy after me. So I'm going to have you feel him out about it. I just haven't quite figured out how yet."

She tilted her head to one side. "What do you think?"

"I think you're overlooking the obvious."

"What's that?"

"The disks. When's the last time you looked at them?"

"When I was copying them, sixteen . . . almost seventeen years ago."

"So don't you think you should take another look, and then decide what to do?"

She nodded slowly. "Yes, that's a really good idea." Then she lifted her head. "Assuming we can find a computer with a floppy drive, much less an operating system that'll read something this old."

"We'll find one. But not until after lunch. Freddy seems to be really enjoying his break."

After their lunch break, they found just what they needed with the help of the built-in GPS system and a 411 call. Smart-Biz was open 24/7, had 13 branches in Vermont and purported to be the most complete business center in the Northeast. There's Nothing You Need That We Don't Have! the cheerful slogan beneath its logo bragged.

"We're about to find out, Smart-Biz," Olivia said, when they pulled into the lot.

Freddy was napping off his midday swim,

making the car's interior smell a lot like wet dog as a result. The lady professor who wasn't what she seemed was going to need to have it detailed before it was returned to its rightful owner, Aaron thought.

They went inside together, leaving the SUV running with the AC on for the dog. Aaron took note of the surveillance cameras as they entered and was surprised that he could tell by looking that they fed into a computer system, not a VCR.

More research, right, guy?

He sighed, brushed the thought away and watched the smiling twenty-something guy on the other side of the counter flash a high-beam smile at Olivia, while pretending not to check out her breasts.

"Can I help you?" the kid asked.

"Oh, I hope so." She held up a disk. "Got anything that'll still read this?"

He didn't even flinch. "You know the software?"

"Probably Word. I don't know the version anymore, but it's about sixteen years old."

He nodded. "No problem. Come on back."

Olivia shot Aaron a happy look that made him smile a little. And the way the younger man watched her butt as she walked past him reminded him again of his own attraction to her. Instead of dwelling on that, he denied himself the pleasure of watching her hips swing subtly as he followed her into a room in the back that was lined with computers, each one with a chair in front of it.

"Third one on the right ought to have just what you need," the clerk said. "If you need copies, the CDs are on that wall over there, a buck apiece. Printouts —" he pointed to the bank of printers back in the main room of the shop "— come out of number five. Twenty cents a page. Thirty-five for color. Copy machine is over there, prices are listed. Fax —"

"Okay, okay. We've got it. Thanks, pal." Aaron patted the kid on the shoulder while moving him back in the direction he'd come from.

The clerk stopped talking, looked perplexed; then light dawned, and he got the message. "Oh. Well, I'll leave you to it, then."

"Thanks." Aaron watched the kid until he'd gone back into the shop. Then he turned to Olivia.

She was looking at him with her brows raised. "What?" he asked.

"You were unnecessarily rude to him, don't you think?"

"We *do* have urgent business and a need

148

for privacy, don't we?"

She nodded, then sat down, took out a diskette and slid it into the floppy drive, which whirred and buzzed. In moments a no-doubt ancient version of Word opened up, showing the list of the documents on the disk.

They were named according to a meaningless alphanumeric code, probably generated at random by the computer Tommy had used to create the file.

And then she opened the first one, a chart with names, dates, column after column of personal information and records of drugs bought in years gone by.

Olivia scrolled down the list, reading name after name after name.

And then she came to a stop at one that was very familiar. "Oh, my God."

Aaron leaned closer. "Phil Gainsboro," he whispered out loud. "Is that *Senator* Phillip Gainsboro?"

"We'll have to look at the photos to be sure. But if it is . . ."

"They say he's planning a presidential run. He's the pundits' current top pick to win the Republican nomination in the next primary," Aaron said.

"That's who he is now. We don't know who he was seventeen years ago. But if this

149

is him, he was buying weed from my boy-friend. Inordinate amounts of weed, as a matter of fact."

"He wasn't just using," Aaron said softly. "He was dealing." He licked his lips. "And if he knew you had this information, there's no doubt in my mind he would have the resources and the connections to send a hit man after you."

"So it was either him or Tommy."

"Don't be too sure just yet, Olivia." Aaron nodded at the screen. "He's not the *only* name on this list. There might be others with just as much to lose. We're going to need a printout."

"I agree. But go stand by the printer so no one else sees any of this."

He looked at her quickly. "There's no one else in here."

"It's open to the public. Anyone could walk in at any time. Do you really want to draw attention to what we're doing by running across the room to beat some curious snoop to the printers?"

He just looked at her. "You know," he said at length, "if you don't want me ordering *you* around, maybe —"

"You're absolutely right. I keep forgetting that I don't hate you."

"Huh?"

"I'm sorry. Please, go out by the printers? I'd feel better if you did."

"Sure. No problem." He crooked a brow at her. "That wasn't so hard, was it?" Then he headed out to the printers.

By the time he returned, Olivia had inserted each of the five floppy diskettes and hit the "print all" command for each of them. And she'd been opening and looking at the files on the computer as she did. Some of them were downright amusing.

She had also secretly burned the contents of all five disks onto one DVD, then made three more copies of that DVD and buried them all in the bottom of her handbag. As she did, she felt the handgun resting in the bottom and shivered a little.

She didn't think she needed to protect herself from Aaron Westhaven. More, she didn't *want* to think it. But life had taught her that you took precautions anyway. He was carrying a weapon, so she was, as well. She'd taken it from the bank sack and tucked it into her purse without Aaron's knowledge. Her attacker could try for her again. It paid to be prepared.

So that was what she was doing. Being prepared. If Aaron tried to steal the diskettes from her, now that he knew how valuable they were, she would have copies. If she were forced to turn them over to Tommy or Senator Gainsboro, she would have copies. If either of them seemed likely to kill her for what she knew, she would tell them she'd left copies with someone who would send them to the press or the U.S. attorney general if she vanished. She didn't know what good any of that might do her, but she would have those copies, just in case having them could save her life.

She felt guilty, keeping secrets from Aaron. But she shouldn't. She didn't *really* know him. He wasn't *really* the long-lost friend he sometimes felt like. Almost as often, he felt like a complete stranger to her.

A stranger, yes. But one she wanted to know better. Much better.

She closed her eyes briefly as that thought flashed through her mind. What was she doing, allowing herself to feel . . . *that way* . . . about a man she didn't even know? A man she might not be able to trust? Was she falling into the pattern she thought she'd banished long ago? Was she letting herself be drawn to another man who would hurt her in the end?

Aaron rejoined her with a stack of printouts, some of them on photo paper, all contained in a blue Smart-Biz file folder.

"Ready?"

"Ready." She removed the final floppy from the drive and returned it to the bag. "Were you *looking* at those photos as they came off the printer?" she asked.

He grinned at her. "Did you see the one of the chick sucking on that five-foot bong?"

She nodded. "It looks pretty bad, doesn't it?"

"Yeah, but not bad enough to kill for."

"I swear I knew her," she said. "But I'm damned if I can remember any details."

"Hey, join the club." He grinned. "So where do we go from here?"

"You're asking me?"

"You're running this show," he said.

Her brows rose. "Since when?"

"Since we decided to deal with your disks, burglar and mysterious past first, and my hit man, identity and even more mysterious past second. Hell, I've got nothing to go on but a pocket watch and a key, after all." His eyes were warm when they met hers. "Besides, I'm starting to want to find your answers almost as badly as I want to find my own."

She frowned and tried not to let her heart turn to mush at the casually spoken declaration. "Why?"

"I don't know. I guess I'm getting into the

mystery. And maybe starting to like you a little." He lifted a hand, and touched her hair, then pushed it gently off her forehead. "You've got bruises from that asshole last night. And I keep thinking about that other asshole, from your past. Hurting you back then. Maybe trying to hurt you again now. And I gotta tell you, professor, it bugs the hell out of me."

She smiled a little. "Probably just your chivalrous nature leaking out," she said.

"I think it might be more about you than me. But either way, I don't like it. If I can help make it stop, I want to. And I mean that."

She thought he really did.

"But if you're looking for input as to where we go from here," he went on, "I'd really like to find a haven of some kind. Someplace where we can just rest and go over what we've got here, figure out our next move."

She smiled slowly, her guilt over being less than honest with him leaving a sour taste in her throat. "Okay. Let's go find a haven, then. One that accepts dogs." She hefted her handbag higher on her shoulder. He took the bank bag from her, adding the file folder to its contents, and they went up to the register.

The young clerk sent Olivia a big smile and began tapping keys. "Okay, let's see then, you had twenty-two black and white, two dozen color —"

"We know what we had, hon," Olivia said quickly, silencing him before he got to the DVDs she'd used and blew her secret wide open. As well as they were getting along, she would hate to piss off Aaron now. "Just give us the total." She pulled out her wallet, removing some of the cash she'd transferred into it from the bundles in the safe-deposit box. And then she said, "As a matter of fact, don't. Here." She handed him a pair of twenties. "You just keep the change, okay?"

"Oh. Uh, sure. You want your receipt?"

The bell above the door jingled, and a chill went down her spine. She saw Aaron from the corner of her eye as he turned to glance over his shoulder. As if in slow motion, she saw his expression turn tense. He recognized the man who'd just come in. She saw it. His hand moved to the back of his jeans, and she knew he was going for the gun he'd taken from her attacker.

She drove her fist to the bottom of her purse, gripping her .38 and pulling it out. As one unit, the two of them spun around, leveling their weapons at the man who'd come into the store.

The guy in the doorway didn't seem too upset. He smirked, but lifted both hands. "I don't want any trouble," he said.

"Then you shouldn't have been beating up on a woman or drugging an innocent dog, should you, pal?" Aaron asked calmly.

"Don't know what you're talkin' about . . . pal. Must have me mixed up with someone else."

Olivia glanced sideways at Aaron. "It's him," she said. "I recognize his voice."

"Voice. Great. I recognized his shoes."

She looked down at the ordinary shoes the man wore, seeing nothing special about them. Aaron really didn't miss a thing, did he?

"Don't you try anything, either, kid," Aaron said to the clerk. "This isn't about you. Just stay out of it and you'll stay alive, okay?"

"I'm not doin' shit, mister."

"Keep it that way." Aaron moved closer to the man in the doorway. "Keep your hands up. Liv, keep your gun on him."

"Oh, believe me, I am. He twitches and I'm going to dot his third eye for him."

Aaron patted the man down with one hand.

"I'm unarmed," the guy said.

"Bullshit. Where are your car keys?"

"Right jacket pocket."

Aaron reached in and pulled out a key ring. "What are you driving?"

The man held Aaron's eyes. "Blazer. Red."

"Let's go."

"If you were gonna call the police once we leave," the man said, addressing the kid at the counter as he opened the door, "don't bother. I've got this."

Olivia turned to face the young man and lifted her hair, revealing the still-purple bruise there, then angling her jaw toward him to expose another. "He did that to me, not to mention he nearly killed my dog," she said. "He's a criminal. We're the good guys. We just need to make sure he doesn't keep following us. Promise."

The kid nodded, but he looked scared out of his wits.

"Come on, pal. Let's go." Aaron reached behind him. "Give me the sack, Liv."

She hurried forward, picked up the sack he'd dropped to the floor when he'd gone for his gun and handed it to him. Aaron stuffed his weapon into the bag but kept hold of it, pointing it at the other man as they moved out the door. Olivia tucked her gun into the back of her trousers and wished for more casual clothing. She untucked her silk blouse and let it hang out, more or less hiding the gun, but it didn't have much of a tail, and she was sure someone would glimpse the weapon.

She walked behind the two men. Out of the building, to the left, then down the sidewalk. The man, who looked like a weasel to her, with his pinched-up face and too-close-together eyes, began to whistle an off-key, unrecognizable tune.

"Stop it," Aaron barked.

They'd reached the end of the building when *something* from the alley came out of nowhere, right down onto Aaron's head.

He hit the sidewalk like a ton of lead, the bag and his weapon falling from his hands. The first weasel bent to grab his keys from Aaron's limp hand, while the other went for the sack. Olivia sprang forward like a shot, so automatically that she didn't even think about it first. She was reaching for her gun as she lunged.

"Back off!" She landed with one foot on the bag, the other one kicking the car keys out of reach. They plunked right through a drain grate, into the sewer. Her stance was wide, her aim steady, as she pointed the weapon at the two men, moving it constantly from one to the other.

The bastard who'd drugged her dog whirled and set off at a dead run. The other one stood there, hands up, rapidly shuffling backward.

"Who do you work for?" she demanded. He moved faster. "Wait, dammit. Who sent you?"

He just shook his head and, having backed up enough to feel brave, turned and ran after his cohort. He was out of sight behind the building in a second, and she heard his footsteps only a few seconds longer.

When she was sure he was gone, Olivia returned the gun to her pants and bent over Aaron, all the while keeping an eye out around them.

"Aaron? Are you okay?"

He lifted his head, blinking her into focus.

"You're bleeding," she said, her fingers parting his hair to reveal a gash in his forehead. A tire iron lay on the sidewalk nearby. No wonder he was bleeding. "Your head again. God, I think you're going to need stitches."

"I'm fine," he said. "Did they get the disks?"

"No, but they did get away." She tore her eyes from him and looked around again. "We're going to have a crowd around us in a minute, though. You need to get up, Aaron."

He braced his arms on the sidewalk. She

159

reached down to help him, even while keeping her eyes busy, watching the cars moving by on the street and the onlookers, a few of whom were starting to venture closer. She held up a hand at the closest one. "We're fine, thanks. We're fine."

The kid was in the doorway of the store. No doubt he'd hit the alarm button by now. Aaron was on his feet. She held his arm, her purse and the bag, and made her way across the street to where they'd left the SUV. As fast as she could, she opened the passenger door, kept hold of Aaron while he got inside and then ran around to the driver's side. Leaning in, she tossed the bank-logo bag in the back, then she got into the driver's seat, putting her handbag on the floor beside her feet.

Freddy was agitated, standing on all fours in the back, moving as close to the front as he could and leaning over the seat to try to lick Aaron's gashed head. She pushed the dog back — a little pressure from the palm of her hand to the front of his chest and the word *back* was all it took. She couldn't have actually *pushed* him if she'd wanted to. Then she handed Aaron the little packet of tissues she kept in her purse and set the SUV in motion.

She would have sworn she didn't breathe

again until several blocks later. "I don't think we're being followed."

"We weren't being followed all day. But they found us anyway." He pressed a wad of tissues to his bleeding head. At least this injury was in the front, not the already wounded back of his skull. "We need supplies," he said.

"What you need are stitches."

"They know what we're driving," he went on. "They tracked us here. But how? They weren't in sight. I would've spotted a tail."

"Right. Authors always know how to spot a tail," she muttered.

"Wait a minute."

"I'm not waiting a minute, I'm driving. We're either going to a clinic or an E.R."

"Drugstore. You can patch me up as well as they can. But first you'd better pull this damn vehicle over so I can search it."

She shook her head firmly. "You can search it while I go buy first-aid supplies. Maybe they have kits specifically designed for men who get lots of holes in their heads."

He sent her a look, but when their eyes met, his warmed, and that made her feel warm inside, too. "You did all right back there," he said. "Pulling the gun, keeping those guys off me. I wouldn't have expected an English professor to handle herself that way."

"There's still a lot you don't know about me, Aaron."

"A lot I want to know," he said softly.

She had to avert her eyes. "Are you really okay?" she asked him.

"Yeah. But really, you need to stop."

"Do you think it's safe? Do you think they'll come after us? I mean, I kicked their keys into the sewer, but —"

"I missed that. You're like Jane Bond or something."

"So you don't think they're . . . in pursuit?"

"Not without a car, they aren't. If they show up again, I'm shooting first and asking questions later."

She looked at him, and her fear must have shown in her eyes, because he put a hand on her shoulder and gave a slight squeeze. "I think we have time. Even if they have a spare set of keys somewhere, they'll want to regroup, make a new plan. Just pull over."

"I am. Right here." She nodded at the sign towering above the drugstore and pulled into the lot, then drove around to the back, where the semis parked to unload their inventory. Out of sight. "I'm going to run in and get some stuff to patch you up. You search to your heart's content while I'm in there, but keep an eye out, okay?"

"Don't be long, Olivia. In case I'm wrong about them needing to regroup before making another try."

"I'll hurry. But you haven't been wrong about much so far." She turned around, patted Freddy on the head. "Keep an eye on him for me, boy."

She got out, and so did Aaron, still holding the tissues to his forehead. Olivia hurried into the drugstore, moving so rapidly that she attracted a few odd looks. Bandages, gauze, antibiotic ointment, butterfly tape for holding the edges of the wound together, a small pair of scissors. It took her about two minutes to locate everything she thought she might need, and another five for the cashier to ring the items up and bag them, despite the fact that she was willing the girl to move faster than your average snail.

Finally she was done. Olivia grabbed the bag without waiting for the receipt and ran to the exit. The SUV was sitting right there, Aaron at the wheel, the engine running, Freddy looking as eager to get moving as Olivia was. He obviously sensed the excitement going on around him. He always knew when things weren't right, and things were definitely not right at the moment.

Aaron reached across to open her door, and the moment she hopped in, he took off — fast.

"Okay, so it's safe to assume you found whatever you were looking for?" she asked, as she tugged the seat belt around her.

"Yeah. There was a tracking device hidden in the wheel well."

She felt her eyes widen. "You mean someone has been tracking us, everywhere we go?"

"Yeah." He sounded disgusted, as if it were his fault. "I took care of it. But they had time to track us here before that, so we need to move."

She nodded and held on as he accelerated. "I can't very well patch up your head while we're speeding."

"We're not speeding. That would attract attention. We're going the speed limit. This won't take long."

Sighing, she held on as he drove through town. She found herself keeping a close eye on every vehicle they passed, scanning the interior of each one in search of the weasel and his partner, who she'd dubbed the pig. She didn't see them, but that didn't mean they weren't around. The police were probably at the business center by now, asking questions. Had the kid gotten a good look at their car? Would the cops set up roadblocks before she and Aaron managed to get out of town?

Her stomach was in knots.

Aaron touched her leg just above the knee, a comforting touch, not a sexual one. "Don't look so frightened. They can't follow us now. I bought us some time."

"How?"

"There was an unattended semi back there, so I slapped the device on the bottom of the fuel tank."

She turned to stare at him in amazement. "That was . . . that was pretty smart for a guy with two holes in his head. But . . . what if they shoot the poor truck driver?" she asked.

"They're pros who were paid to get those disks. Pros are not going to shoot first and ask questions later, or they won't get the disks, and if they don't get the disks, they don't get paid by whoever hired them."

She stared at him, brows raised. He seemed to feel her eyes on him, and he glanced back at her. "What?" he asked. "Writers *know* these things."

"Yeah, so I've been told."

He shrugged, but the joke did make her feel a little easier.

"So now what?" she asked. "You've got blood running down your face, you ought to be in the hospital from that earlier head wound and you probably shouldn't even be driving."

"Let's put some miles between us and them," he said.

"Miles. I'd like to put something a lot deadlier than miles between us and them."

He frowned at her. "You're angry."

"Of course I'm angry. You know, it's one thing for Tommy to send his thugs after me. I knew that was a risk I'd have to spend the rest of my life living with, and I chose to take it. But when he starts drugging my dog and hurting people I care about, then that's —" She bit her lip to shut herself up.

He was silent for a moment, too, and then he said, "You care about me."

He didn't make it a question.

She shrugged. "You saved my life last night. And . . . Freddy likes you."

It wasn't really an answer, but it was going to have to do.

"Is it because you're convinced I'm your favorite writer?"

She shrugged. "I don't know." She looked at him. "You say that as if you're *not* convinced of it."

And then it was his turn not to answer.

Instead he said, "Once we get far enough away, we need to find a store. A *big* store."

"Those supplies you keep whining about. Do you have a list somewhere, Aaron? Because I really don't know what we need besides a room for the night."

He glanced her way and lifted one brow. "No room is going to be safe. We need a tent. Sleeping bags. A lantern —"

"Are you saying what I think you're saying?" she asked, and she searched his face, but he refused to look back at her.

"Oh, come on," she said when he didn't reply. "I mean, really, come on. We're *not . . .* camping."

"Yeah," he said softly. "We are. And now I have one more thing to ask about, before I stop driving and let you try patching up my head."

"What's that?" she asked.

He looked at her. " 'I'll dot your third eye'?" he said slowly. "What the hell kind of a taunt is that?"

"I don't know. It just . . . came out."

"It was *terrible!*"

"I know," she said, and her voice was oddly pitched, because she was trying so hard not to laugh. She held it in until he grinned widely and said the line again, this time in a falsetto voice that was supposed to be hers.

"I'll dot your third eye for you, bucko!"

She burst out laughing, then, and so did he. "I never said bucko!"

"It was in your tone. There was definitely bucko in that tone."

She had tears brimming in her eyes, unable to figure out how he could make her laugh at a time like this. He was laughing almost as hard as she was, and dabbing at his own eyes. "I almost lost it right there," he said.

"I'm surprised the bad guys didn't." She drew a breath, released it with a sigh. "That felt good. Laughing like that."

"Yeah." He looked at her. "You needed it. Been a while?"

"I don't think I've . . . ever laughed that hard."

"You should," he told her. "You deserve to."

She tipped her head a little. "You can't know that."

"Maybe not. But I trust my instincts."

"So you keep telling me."

8

The oversize "Super Center" had everything they could have wanted and more, and thanks to his companion's deep pockets, Aaron thought, they were able to pick up most of the items on his mental list. Tent. Sleeping bags. Lanterns and fuel, and a big blue metal coffeepot and saucepan.

While he was loading a cart with camping gear, Olivia had wandered off with her own plan in mind. And when they met again at the register, he noticed the things she'd picked up. Practical clothes, which included a warm jacket, an extra pair of jeans, some thick socks, a pair of suede hiking boots and some rubber flip-flops. Smart purchases, every last one of them.

He saw her noticing his purchases, too, which by then included food, a big cooler and a bag of ice. "You need clothes," she said. "Who knows how long it'll be before we find out where you live, where all your stuff is?"

"Good point." So he bought clothes. Jeans, T-shirts, a hooded sweatshirt, everything else he thought of that he might need.

The total came to three hundred and change, but she didn't so much as bat an eye. Maybe she saw the necessity as much as he did. The girl behind the register looked out from behind big glasses at his bandaged forehead and Olivia's bruised face, and smiled a little. "Maybe you guys need a safer sport than camping," she said.

He smiled. "Camping *is* the safer sport. We got this way rock climbing."

"You fall?" she asked, eyes widening.

"Only forty feet," Olivia told her. "It's really not as bad as it looks."

She met his eyes, a flash of mischief in hers.

Hell, he was beginning to really *like* this woman.

An hour later they were driving again, in search of a wilderness area close enough to Shadow Falls for them to keep an eye on things, far enough away to be safe, where they could pitch their tent. He drove, and she played with the GPS system.

Eventually she said, "Got it. This thing will find all the campgrounds in whatever area we choose."

"Try a fifty-mile radius from Shadow Falls," he suggested. "We'll be a little more off the beaten path."

"Okay."

"We want the most remote area we can find."

"Most remote is a difficult thing to tell from a GPS, but let's see . . ."

She played with the thing for a moment longer, then nodded. "I've got lots of campgrounds within fifty miles of us. Some of them seem like they're privately owned, though."

"Those are always small and crowded. Look for state parks."

She adjusted her search parameters and tried again. "Okay. Niquette Bay State Park." She paused, moving her fingers over the screen. "It's forty-five minutes away. Looks like nice and big, too."

"Sounds like it's worth a try."

"You're sure we can't just go to a hotel?"

"I wouldn't have wasted an hour shopping for camping gear if I wasn't." He glanced at her. "I'm trying to keep us alive here, Liv. You know that, right?"

She sighed, nodding. "Of course I know that."

"So navigate, navigator."

"Head for the highway. We're going west."

"All right."

"And we're in sad need of some music, I think."

"I hear that," he said.

She flipped on the radio, looked at the menu, then looked again. "Oh, my. Professor Mallory does have his priorities in order."

"Why?" he asked, but he was more interested in the expression on her face than in what she had to say. When she smiled . . . God, she was something else when she smiled.

"Satellite radio," she explained. "What kind of music do you like?"

He opened his mouth, then closed it again and sent her a glance — a quick one, as he was driving — and shook his head. "I don't know. Isn't that a bitch? I don't even know what kind of music I like."

"It's not — it's not even a problem." She cranked up the volume a bit. "I'll browse, and you tell me when you hear something you feel like you could get into. In just a few minutes you'll know exactly what kind of music you like. Now how is that a problem?"

He slid his eyes toward her. "You're displaying a decidedly more optimistic attitude than usual here, Olivia. Is that your

172

normal attitude and it's just finally return-ing to you, or is it something new?"

She tipped her head to one side, thinking about it. "It's new. I'm usually pretty realis-tic. Some people call that pessimistic, but I've never thought it was. I just like to see things as they are, then call them as I see them."

"Um-hmm. And how do you see our cur-rent reality?" he asked, because he was honestly curious. The woman looked . . . alive. More color in her cheeks. More sparkle in her eyes than when he'd first met her. She was animated, talkative, though not cheerful. Of course, she would have to be an idiot to be cheerful, given the situation. But she was definitely . . . present in the moment, he thought.

"Our current reality?" she asked. "Well, obviously it's pretty bad. We don't know who you are. We *do* know someone wants you dead, and also that someone is after me, looking to take the disks and either kill me or mess me up in the process. And they don't mind messing with my dog while they're at it, which is the ultimate sign of a truly evil person."

"Someone who'd mess with a dog."

"Yes."

"Not someone who'd club a woman upside the head with a Glock?"

"Not as much."

He glanced behind him. Freddy had sat up, as if he knew they were talking about him, and was looking from one of them to the other, mouth agape, a thin strand of drool hanging from each floppy jowl.

Aaron had to smile. You couldn't look at that dog and not smile.

"He's going to love camping way more than being in a motel," Olivia said softly.

"And how about you?"

She shrugged. "I'll feel safer in the woods than in a hotel room. I didn't think I would at first, but the more I think about it, the more I realize I was wrong." She shrugged. "Actually, it might be kind of fun."

"Fun?" He frowned at her then. "Your mood really *is* lighter. I don't get it. Things just got a whole lot worse back there, didn't they? What am I missing?"

She shrugged. "I don't know, Aaron. I'm feeling oddly . . . relieved, I think."

He thought about that for a moment. "You've been hiding from this ex for a long time, now. Living in fear of him finding you. If he finally has, that fear is over. It's happened. You don't have to dread it anymore."

"*Yes,* exactly. Now I have no choice. I can't run and hide anymore. He's forcing me to finally deal with him once and for all. And if I survive, I'll never have to be afraid again." She shook her head slowly. "Maybe I should have confronted him a long time ago."

"At least we know the reason your mood seems to have improved so radically," he said.

She looked at him, then looked away. "Frankly, the company might have something to do with it, as well."

The compliment was so unexpected that his reaction was unguarded and immediate. He felt a warm rush of pleasure surge through his chest, and a big smile flashed to life on his face.

She met it with one of her own and switched the radio dial. The soft strains that came from the speakers caught hold of him, and he held up a hand to tell her to stop right there.

Listening, she nodded. "That's Sammy Gold. You've got good taste in music. He's a country music legend."

"That much I remember," he said softly.

"It'll come back, Aaron. It'll all come back." And with the tender certainty in her smile, he found himself believing her.

Ninety minutes later they stood in the middle of a hardwood forest on the shore of a glistening Lake Champlain bay, a tent spread out on the ground between them and a giant brindle mastiff standing smack in the middle of it, refusing to budge. There were tent poles lying every which way, like a giant game of pick-up-sticks gone terribly wrong.

Olivia held the instruction sheet, unfolded, flipping and flapping with the breeze coming in off the bay. "I think the long ones go in first," she said. Then she pointed. "Front left to back right, front right to back left, crossing in the middle. Come on, Freddy. Get off the tent. Come here now!"

The beast obeyed her, sitting so close to her side that he was touching her from ankle to hip.

Not that Aaron particularly blamed him. He was feeling a compelling urge to get a little closer himself.

Instead, though, he knelt by the confusion of poles, and began sliding them through the loops and pockets of the tent. Soon they had a large X in front of them.

"Now," she said, peering at the sheet in front of her, "we put the bottom of each pole into the pocket at the corner." She dropped the instructions to the ground, placing a round rock on top to keep them from blowing away, then she started sticking poles into their designated pockets.

He grabbed the far end of one and said, "I have the feeling camping wasn't one of my hobbies."

"I know it's never been one of mine," she said. "But we'll get by. Come on."

They moved, maneuvered, shoved, bowed and, finally, got the poles situated where they belonged, and the little dome tent was suddenly up and tight and even quite roomy-looking.

"Okay, now we insert the side poles, the rain fly, stake it down and we're good," she said, consulting the instructions once again.

She looked at the SUV, the back open, supplies piled inside. He followed her gaze and winced. Poor Freddy had been crowded on this latest leg of their insane journey.

"You know what?" she said. "This part looks fairly simple. I think Freddy and I can handle it, if you want to start unloading the rest of the, uh . . . survival gear."

"You sure?"

"Yeah. Go ahead."

"All right." He went to the SUV and left her to it, thinking she was pretty damn handy. Not a helpless female. Not a needy one. Then again, her life would have been considerably shorter if she'd been either of those things. She'd had to stand on her own, take care of herself. And she'd done it in spades.

He had to wonder, though, what would happen to the happy life she'd created for herself if her secret ever got out. Just whose identity had she stolen? Where was that person now? She might even end up facing charges — fraud, that sort of thing — depending on what she'd had to do to pull off her identity switch and keep it intact for so long.

He unloaded a pair of folding camp chairs and removed them from their canvas storage bags, placing them near a tiny stone circle that was obviously a fire pit. There was a metal grill leaning up against a pine tree nearby, for cooking over the fire, and a wobbly warped picnic table off to one side. Outhouses and showers were a mile up the twisting dirt road. They should have complete privacy here.

They'd signed in under false names, Jeff and Judy Jones. Just cute enough to be believable, he'd thought. And they'd paid in cash. He'd even altered the license plate number of the SUV when he'd written it in the register. Only one digit off, just in case.

By the time Olivia finished setting up the tent — she'd even unrolled the sleeping bags and placed their respective bundles of clothing inside — he had unloaded the SUV, gathered enough deadfall and limbs to feed the flames through the night, and had a cheerful fire burning in the stone fire pit. A little pot of water was on the grill, and two boil-in-the-bag camp meals were cooking. He had a tin cup ready for her when she took the vacant camp chair beside his own.

Night had fallen. Crickets and bullfrogs were chorusing so loudly that the noise could, he imagined, keep some people awake. Not him. It was going to sing him right to sleep. Particularly given the contents of his own tin cup.

She reached for hers, frowning.

He smiled, dropping one hand to the ground beside his chair and picking up the bottle he'd left there. "Found this in the Expedition," he said. "Your Professor Mallory has good taste."

She read the label. "Imported Caribbean rum." She picked up her cup, took a short drink, then another. "I really do like it better with Coke."

"Well, we didn't buy any Coke." He shrugged. "We can pick some up tomorrow."

"Oh, this will be gone by tomorrow."

He lifted his brows. *"Professor!"* he said in

mock surprise.

She shrugged. "It's been a rough day, okay?" She slugged some more of the rum, then held her cup out to him for more.

"Uh, yeah, but . . ." He poured a large shot into her mug and then splashed some more into his own. "Just hold up for a second, would you?"

"No." She took another drink. "I think I've been on hold my entire life — the last sixteen years of it, anyway. So what's for dinner?"

"Beef stew. But I think we ought to discuss the, uh — well, you know, the sleeping arrangements. Before you get too . . . you know . . . smashed."

She smiled slowly at him, then leaned back in her chair and stared up at the stars, drained the rum and refilled the cup herself. "You better talk fast, then."

She was in an odd mood, he thought. "What do you mean about your life being on hold?"

She sipped, watched the fire. "I mean . . . I was so afraid he'd kill me, I did everything I did in order to stay alive. And then I didn't live at all. You know?"

"No."

"I mean . . . here I am, sixteen years later. No kids. No man in my life. Just my job and my dog. Don't get me wrong. I love my dog. And I like my job pretty well, too. But I haven't been . . . living."

She drained the cup again, leaned forward to set it on the ground and paused, still bent. "Whoa, that's some potent rum."

"Yeah."

Freddy lifted his head from his paws and sent her an adoring look, then sighed and lowered it again.

"This is nice out here," she said, tipping the bottle to her cup before sitting up straight again. "It's beautiful. And we're safe."

"For the moment," he said.

"I should have been doing this all along."

"Running from a hit man or drinking rum?"

"Camping. With Freddy. And . . . you. Or some nice guy somewhere."

"Oh. So you haven't dated much, huh?"

"Not at all. I've spent my whole life hating men. Not trusting them, you know? Even though I know, in the practical part of my brain, that not all men are jerks like Tommy. I work with lots of decent men. But I keep my distance. A loooong distance. Do you know how long it's been since I've had sex with a man?"

He felt his throat go dry. "I, uh . . . no."

"Years."

"Oh." He wasn't quite sure what she was saying. But he was interested enough to want to find out — and fast. "So are you saying you . . . want to?"

She sipped again. "I'm saying, if it happens to happen — happens to happen. That's funny." She paused to laugh at her own joke. "Where was I?"

"If it happens to happen," he prompted.

She laughed again. "If it happens to happen, I won't be upset about it." She tilted her head to one side. "You?"

"I . . . No. I wouldn't be upset about it, either."

"Cool. So we'll just enjoy the night and the stars and the fresh air and the rum, and see what happens."

He swallowed hard, because in the back of his mind warnings were going off as loudly as the red-alert siren on the Starship *Enterprise.* Something was wrong. Something was very wrong with the notion of having sex with this woman. Even beyond the fact that she was too drunk to know what she wanted, it felt wrong. It felt as if it would be some kind of violation, as if it would be breaking a rule that was carved in stone.

What could account for that?

He frowned and looked at his hands, spreading out his fingers.

"What?" she asked. "What are you thinking? You looked really pens — pens — *thoughtful* just now."

He shrugged. "I was just wondering if I'm married or . . . you know, in a relationship with someone in the life I can't remember."

She frowned. "I really don't think that's the case, Aaron."

He met her eyes, then rolled his. "You don't even know me. How can you have an opinion?"

She drew back slightly, letting him know his reaction had hurt her feelings. But she covered quickly with a nonchalant shrug. "Because anyone who writes about relationships the way you do can't possibly be in one."

"*If* I really am Aaron Westhaven — and I'm not convinced I am — but *if* I am, then I'm a fiction writer. Do you really think every author writes what he lives? I mean, do you think mystery writers are into committing murders, or even solving them? I don't. So you shouldn't think a guy who writes the stuff I do is living his own life of . . . of —"

"Unfulfilled yearning," she interjected. Only *unfulfilled* came out sounding as if she'd forgotten to include any vowels.

"Yeah, that."

"I suppose you have a point." She looked at his hands, then shrugged. "Still, no wedding band."

"Doesn't mean there isn't someone in my life."

She studied him in the darkness, with the campfire popping and snapping, its flames making her skin all orange and amber and dancing their reflection in her eyes. Her hair had come loose from its bun, and was falling all around her face and dangling over her nape. She was beautiful.

"Why is this just occurring to you now?" she asked softly. "Why didn't you wonder about it sooner?"

He shrugged. "I suppose because you brought up sex."

"And?"

"And it felt . . . as if it would be wrong, somehow. On some kind of gut level. I can't explain it any better than that."

"Oh." She frowned. "Yeah, okay. That . . . that really does seem as if there must be a reason."

"That's what I'm saying."

She stared at the fire, then heaved a big sigh and lifted her cup in the air in surrender, rum sloshing over the sides. "Fine, no sex, then. Is that stew about ready?"

Bryan Kendall was sitting on the wrong side of a table in his own police department's interrogation room. It was after hours on a Sunday night. The Fed, a wiry little assistant director by the name of Bruce Modine, sat in what should have been Bryan's chair, with a big open file folder and a notebook. No tape recorder. Bryan didn't know if that was a good sign or a bad one.

He'd been summoned from home by Chief Mac an hour ago, with a request he get to the station ASAP and he'd shown up to find this suit waiting to "talk to" him.

"Okay, for the record," the A.D. said, "you are police officer Bryan Kendall of the Shadow Falls P.D., is that correct?"

"Why the formality, Modine? You're not taping this. And you know who I am."

"So that's a yes, then." Modine made a mark on his notepad with his pencil. The way his balding head remained upright, even as he bent over the notepad, made Bryan think of a German shepherd on alert. "Your record isn't exactly immaculate, is it?"

"Is yours?"

"You were suspended after shooting a suspect in a hostage standoff —"

"Suspension during the investigation is standard in any shooting. But I don't have to tell you that. I was cleared of any wrong-doing and returned to active duty. But I don't imagine I have to tell you *that,* either."

"You were cleared," Modine agreed, glancing down at his notes. "After several weeks in therapy for PTSD."

"To rule it out, not to treat it. And it *was* ruled out." Bryan tipped his head to one side. "Are you deliberately trying to rile me, Modine?"

"Just reviewing the facts. Now, as I understand it, right before you were supposed to return to duty, you became the lead suspect in several murders, didn't you?"

"I was being set up. The real killer was exposed, and he's dead."

"Yes, your, uh — well, I guess *mentor* is the word, right?"

"Yes, that's the word. Nick and I were good friends, too. Or I thought we were. But again, I was exonerated. Completely."

The man looked up, skewering Bryan with his pale blue eyes. He was sitting back in his chair, one ankle propped on the opposite knee. He dropped his gaze and pored over the file folder for a moment. "He's dead. Makes it a little hard to know anything for sure."

"Doesn't matter. I've been cleared. It's all in the file."

"Mmm-hmm. Okay, so what do you know about Professor Olivia Dupree?"

Bryan lifted his eyes. "You're here about Olivia?"

Assistant Director Modine lifted his head and met Bryan's eyes again, his own curious.

"It's just that the chief said this was about the gunshot victim we brought in yesterday."

The Fed nodded. "Yes, but since she's the only person in this town with whom he had any sort of connection, naturally we want to learn all we can about her. And I was frankly surprised at how much there was to learn. So how well do you know her?"

Bryan didn't flinch as he held the man's gaze. "Barely at all."

"And yet you refer to her by her first name."

Bryan shrugged. "We were in a tense situation together a few weeks ago. Nick Di-Marco tried to kill both of us. We survived. That tends to bond people."

"So you have a bond. But you barely know her. Is that what you're sticking with, then?"

"That's the truth."

"I see." Modine made a note. "So you didn't know, then, that Olivia Dupree is not her real name?"

Bryan blinked, saying nothing.

"Her real name is Sarah Quinlan," the other man went on. "She ran away from her abusive live-in lover in Chicago almost seventeen years ago, after buying herself some time to get away by turning him in for dealing marijuana. Took off with a pile of his cash and some pretty valuable documents."

"Why would she do that?" Bryan asked.

Modine shrugged. "Probably figured he'd kill her if he caught her. She lucked out, though. Moved up here where she didn't know a soul. Got herself a roommate who wound up murdered, and with a whole lot of help from a cop with powerful connections, switched identities with the dead girl."

"How do you know about all this?"

"It wasn't hard. She'd never have kept her secret this long if anyone had ever had a reason to take a closer look at her. But no one has. She's led a quiet, uneventful, even boring, life here."

Bryan shrugged. "Maybe it would be best to let her keep on living it."

Modine frowned at him. "Except that she's missing. And so is our guy."

"Yeah, *your* guy. Do you mind if we talk about him a little more? 'Cause I'd really like to know who he is and why the Feds are so interested in him."

The A.D. shifted his pale eyes back to the notebook, too smart to risk giving away a thing via his expression. "I'm not at liberty to give you any details on that."

"Is he this Aaron Westhaven, then?"

"I'm sorry, I can't say. But let's get back on topic. This Dupree woman, do you know anything about her that might help us track her down?"

"Believe me, there's not a damn thing I can tell you about her that you don't already know."

Modine frowned. Bryan thought maybe the man had noticed the way he was choosing his words, giving away nothing without lying outright. He was worried about Olivia. Her secret was out — unless the Feds decided for some reason to keep it in.

"So Professor Dupree's ex thinks she's dead, then?" Bryan asked.

"He did. We believe he might know the truth now."

"What makes you believe that?"

"I'm not at —"

"— liberty to say. I got it."

"Sorry."

No, he wasn't, Bryan thought. "Tell me this, Agent Modine. If Olivia is with this guy, is she in danger?"

"It's *Assistant Director* Modine. And, yes, she's in some pretty deep shit if she's running with our amnesiac shooting victim. So if you have any way of tracking her down, please don't keep it to yourself."

Bryan nodded and felt his stomach twist itself into a hard knot. He wanted more information, and this bastard was about as generous with it as Shadow Falls's grouchiest miser, Nate Kelly, was with a dollar.

"You know, I'm going to know who he is soon anyway," Bryan said. Hell, it was worth a try.

The man looked at him, brows raised. "You mean because of the X-ray you sent off to the crime lab? The one showing the serial number on the steel plate in his head?"

Bryan frowned, a little alarm sounding in his mind. This guy was way ahead of him. "Yeah, as soon as we enhance the image a little better, we just go to a Web site, key in the number and it spits out an ID."

"Yeah. Well, you keep working on that." The Fed flipped a card out of his shirt pocket like a magic trick and snapped it down on the table. "You call me if you think of anything, learn anything or hear anything from your pal Olivia."

Bryan didn't bother adding another useless denial. "I will," he said, lying outright for the very first time.

"Great." Modine got to his feet, closing his file folder, tucking it under his arm. "In the meantime, I've instructed your Chief MacNamara to continue the press blackout. I don't want word of any of this leaking *at all,* if it can be helped." He turned and headed for the door. "I'll be in touch."

Oh, goodie, Bryan thought. He got up and went to the door, too, pausing there to watch Assistant Director Modine stride purposefully through the bullpen and out the far end.

Chief Mac was huffing toward the interrogation room before the department's exit doors swung closed behind Modine.

"Tell me you held your own, didn't incriminate yourself and didn't piss him off, Kendall."

"I did, I didn't, and I might have."

"What did he say?"

"Didn't give away a damn thing." Bryan met the chief's eyes, shook his head slowly. "We need to get an ID on our John Doe, Chief. I think we've got a bigger fish on our hands than we thought. How is the crime lab coming with that head X-ray?"

Chief Mac's bushy white brows arched,

making his forehead look like ripples in a pond. "Didn't he tell you?"

"Tell me what?" Bryan was afraid he knew what was coming next. And he wasn't wrong.

"Modine confiscated the film. Even went to Dr. Overton and got the copy she had."

Bryan looked at the floor and shook his head slowly. Then he looked up, feeling a little more optimistic as he thought of one more option. "We'll hear from Aaron Westhaven's publisher tomorrow. At least we can find out if that's who this guy is."

"If it is, he's a lot more than just some reclusive writer," the chief said. "So what did the bald bastard pump you about?"

"Olivia Dupree." Bryan drew a deep breath and knew it might be time for him to tell the chief what he knew about the professor. He was constructing his words in his mind. They would have to go into the chief's office to talk privately, and he would have to explain why he'd kept Olivia's secret between himself, his fiancée and the notorious serial killer who had been a cop and his mentor. And why he had *not* told his boss, the Shadow Falls chief of police.

It wasn't going to be an easy thing to explain.

And maybe that was why he decided to

keep it to himself for just a little bit longer. He didn't know if the Feds would give it away or not. But until they did, as long as it wasn't hurting anyone, he decided he was going to do his best to keep Olivia's secret. Her life here would be over if it came out, so as long as there was a chance it wouldn't, no matter how small that chance might be, he would keep his mouth shut.

"What did you tell him?" Chief Mac asked.

"What *could I?* He already knows more about her than I do." He sighed. "Look, Chief, why don't we both go home and try to get some sleep, huh? I'm beat."

The chief nodded slowly. "Yeah. Yeah, that's probably the best idea. I'll see you back here in the morning, Kendall. Don't be late."

"Yes, sir."

9

They ate their stew as Freddy munched his own evening meal nearby. Olivia thought the tension seemed to melt away from her companion as the evening wore on. She couldn't quite believe she had been as forward with him as she had. It wasn't like her. Or maybe it was. God knew she'd kept her interactions with attractive males to a minimum. She'd been so badly burned by her relationship with Tommy Skinner that she'd never found the courage to trust a man again. She'd never had the desire to, either.

Until now.

The scars and the fear, it seemed, didn't apply to this man. Oh, she knew how ridiculous it seemed, but she felt as if she *knew* Aaron Westhaven. She knew his soul, because it came through in his words. In his work. He wrote with such grace, such a deep understanding of the human heart. He wrote about the heartbreak of unrequited love, of love gone wrong, of love lost forever, in a way that no one had equaled since the Bard had penned *Romeo and Juliet.* She *knew* this man. Even if the man she was getting to know now seemed to have a lot more going on inside than the one she had thought she'd known. Being with him, spending time with him — it was a revelation. He wasn't what she'd expected.

He was more. Better.

And she was drunk.

Obviously Aaron didn't have the same lack of inhibitions where she was concerned, but then again, he didn't have any way of knowing her the way she knew him. He hadn't read her words over and over again.

Unless . . . unless he'd actually read the letters she had sent him years ago. She'd shown a little bit of her heart to him in those. Not all of it. But there had been pieces there.

Still, even if he had read those letters, he had no memory of them now. Might not have remembered them even without the amnesia. He must get thousands of letters from admiring readers.

At any rate, the idea of sex with her had made him get tense all over. It showed in his face, came through in his voice. She had felt it wafting from his body in waves. So she decided to defuse the situation, to put him at ease, as he dished up more stew, handed her a bowl and sat down beside her once again.

"You know, I've never been camping in my life," she said. "Not even when I was a kid."

"No?"

"Nope. Chicago wasn't exactly a camping kind of place, you know?"

"I can imagine."

She shrugged, then slapped a mosquito just as it landed on her forearm. "Never thought I was missing anything. But now I see I was. Bugs. And campfire smoke." She moved her camp chair a foot to the left to elude the ribbon of smoke that had decided to aim for her face. Freddy stopped eating to look up when she moved. He wasn't going to let her get far from him. Seeing her settled in her chair, he relaxed and resumed his munching.

"Funny thing about campfire smoke," Aaron said. "It'll pick one person and follow them around the fire all night long. You no sooner move your chair than the smoke changes direction to find you."

As soon as he said it, the gray stream shifted and wafted right into her face again.

She waved a hand and blinked her burning eyes. "Sheesh, I think it hates me!" She got up to move her chair again.

Then she stopped in midmotion, just clear of the smoke but still standing up. "Hey, you said you didn't think you'd gone camping a lot. But you *have* gone. You *remembered* that, didn't you? That bit about campfires and smoke and —"

He met her eyes, his own animated. "I did. In fact, I remember tents, and a water hole with a rope over it. I remember s'mores and ghost stories, and a bunch of other guys in uniforms of some sort."

"You were a Boy Scout. You must have been." She sat back down.

"I guess . . ." He shrugged. "How do you like your boil-in-the-bag beef stew?"

"I think it's delicious." She scooped another bite from her bowl and didn't speak again until it was scraped clean, then got up and took his bowl with her to the nearby lake, rinsed them thoroughly and wiped them dry. Freddy abandoned his dish to go with her, but when he went to get into the water, she held up a hand, and said, "No, Freddy. Leave it alone."

He obeyed, but he whined about it.

Aaron remained by the fire, but she felt him watching her every move as she cleaned the dishes.

When she came back, he was still staring at her, and he kept on looking as she went to the tent to put the bowls away.

When she came out, he was standing halfway between the fire and the tent, as if he'd been about to join her inside and then changed his mind.

"I, um . . . I'm going to wash up and get ready for bed," she told him. "We have a big day tomorrow."

"Do we?"

"Yeah. We're going to try to make a deal with the devil himself."

"This ex of yours, you mean? You still want to do that?"

"Yes. But he *is* dangerous, Aaron. I ran for my life. That's how bad he is. So if you'd rather I did this on my own, I'll understand."

"I'm not running out on you, Liv. You don't need to worry about that."

She smiled a little. "No one calls me 'Liv.' "

"No? Do you mind?" he asked.

"No. I like it when you do it." She shrugged, then turned and walked back to the lake, toting the little mesh bag of supplies she'd bought at the store. Freddy fell right into step beside her.

"Be careful in the water. Don't forget, you've been drinking."

"I will, don't worry." She paused, eyeing her dog. "Do you think you could keep Freddy with you? I don't want a wet dog curling up with us in the tent tonight."

"Sure, if you think he'll stay. C'm'ere, Freddy. Come on, boy."

Freddy tilted his head to one side, then the other, looking first at Olivia and then at Aaron.

"Say, 'Freddy, come,' " she told him. "And say it like you mean it."

"Freddy, *come*."

Freddy obeyed immediately, and she felt her chest swell a little with pride. He was *such* a good dog. And Aaron was telling him so, too. So she continued walking, confident that he could keep Freddy out of the lake.

Part of her wondered if Aaron was still watching as she stripped bare in the star-sprinkled darkness and stepped into the lake to begin her chilly bath. And all of her hoped he was.

She didn't know, though, and thought she probably never would, as she emerged from the cool water far more awake and a little more sober than she had been when she'd gone in. She toweled off, shivering, and pulled on her nightshirt, knowing full well she was going to need a whole lot more to keep warm tonight. She scrambled to gather up her things, and then scurried barefoot back to the tent, shooting inside fast and heading for her sleeping bag.

Two seconds and she was inside, burrowing and pulling it tight around her as she curled up to half her normal size.

"Colder than you thought?" Aaron asked.

She opened her eyes, to see him sitting in the corner, watching her with thinly veiled amusement coloring his eyes. He'd traded the large white bandage on his forehead for a smaller square adhesive strip that was all but invisible behind his dark hair. Freddy was stretched out on the floor, his head in Aaron's lap, even though his own bed was two feet away.

"Pretty cold, once I got out and the night air hit me." Then she frowned. "Where did you find a sleeping bag this big?"

"I zipped two together to make one bigger one. It'll be warmer."

She lifted her brows and peered out at him. "I thought you didn't want to have sex?"

"I . . . never actually *said* that."

"So you do, then?"

"I didn't say *that,* either. I just want us both to be warm. If you're not comfortable with that, then —"

"I'm *fine* with that." She noticed he had something in his hand, something round and gold. He was turning it over and over. "What have you got there?"

"Pocket watch," he told her. "I had it on me when they found me. Cops checked it out and returned it to me. Said it didn't tell them anything."

She nodded and sat up for a better look.

He slid closer without getting up. The roof was too low for standing upright, anyway. She held out a hand, and he gave her the watch.

Sighing, Freddy got up, too, wandered to his bed and pawed at it as if to smooth it out before lying down — for the night, she hoped.

Olivia drew the watch closer, examining it with care. It was engraved with a pattern of Celtic knots, a shamrock in their center. "Seems to suggest you might be Irish."

"There's something else."

"What?" She looked up at him, her brows furrowed as her fingers felt for the catch, found it and opened the watch up so she could see its face. "I don't see anything else."

"I don't, either. But I *feel* it."

She inhaled, turned the thing over, looked

and looked at it, but for the life of her, she didn't feel a clue coming on. "I don't see anything that *could* be useful — unless the knotwork spells out a secret message or something." She strained her eyes, but no matter how she tried, she couldn't make a single letter of the alphabet out of those swirling patterns.

Shaking her head, she handed it back to him. "Maybe it'll come back to you. Other things have."

"Yeah." His tone was on the dark side. "Yeah, but I have to tell you, nothing that's come back to me has anything to do with writing or books or . . ."

"What has? Besides how to drive and what camping is like, I mean?"

He licked his lips, and his gaze turned inward. "That's about it."

She knew it was a lie. His tone was deeper, and he didn't meet her eyes as he said it. "Wait a minute," she said softly, sitting up fully and probing his face. "You *have* remembered something else, haven't you?"

"I just told you what I've remembered."

"And you were lying."

"And you're an expert on that?"

"Either that or you're a terrible liar."

He shook his head. "Get some sleep, Liv. Disconnect the sleeping bags if you want to.

I'm going to go take my turn in the lake."

"Okay." He went, and she set the pocket watch on top of his pile of clothes, and curled back into the sleeping bag to get warm and await his return. She would have to ask him again what he had remembered. She was certain there was something he wasn't telling her.

She thought she knew what was going on, though. He hadn't been happy in his former life. Bestsellerdom must not be worth much if it meant living life alone, in hiding. With no one to be . . . a partner. An ally. Everyone needed someone like that in their lives, she thought. One person who would be there no matter what. Without judgment, without reservation, without even a second thought.

She'd seen that kind of love and devotion. Not often, and never without a pang of jealousy for what those few rare couples had. A connection that went beyond marriage or sex or parenthood, or whatever other things they shared. Lots of people got married. Very few of them seemed to have the sort of bond that made it seem as if they were . . . extensions of each other's soul.

But some did. She'd seen it. And secretly, she'd longed for it for most of her life. But she'd also spent most of that time knowing she could never have it. Because she couldn't get that close to anyone, not another living soul. You couldn't be that close to someone and keep secrets from them at the same time. Big secrets. Like who you really were. She'd often wondered how she could have a romantic relationship with a man when she couldn't even tell him her real name.

And her answer to that was, she couldn't. Not ever. And so she hadn't. She'd resigned herself to living without love, but she'd never fallen asleep one single night, nor wakened to greet a solitary sunrise, without regretting its absence to the depths of her being.

He must feel that way, too. And maybe deep down, on some subconscious level, he knew that was the life he had forgotten. And so now he didn't want to return to that lonely life again. He wanted to be someone else, someone different. That was why he was denying who he was, finding reasons to doubt he could possibly be the man she knew him to be.

He would rather believe himself to be someone else. Anyone else. That had to be why he was so doubtful.

But if that were the case, if human contact and a deep connection with someone was what he'd been missing in life, then why was he so averse to the notion of having sex with her?

She supposed figuring out the mind of any man was beyond the ability generated by her limited experience, and figuring out the mind of a reclusive genius author was probably beyond anyone's.

She rolled over, sliding one arm out from beneath the covers now that the chill had eased from her bones. It was a beautiful night. The screen was zipped closed, but the outer flap was tied open, so she had a breathtaking view of the night. Trees surrounded the tent, pines with their delicious tangy aroma that seemed to stimulate all her senses. And above, the stars that dotted the sky were like flawless diamonds, illuminated from within and scattered across a swatch of black velvet. Her eyelids felt heavy as crickets played a raucous symphony, singing her to sleep. And when she woke again, sensing that time had passed but having no idea how much, it was to find Aaron lying on his side next to her, his eyes on her face.

She was on her side, too, facing him, as she sleepily became aware. She smiled very slightly, unsure of herself now. Not sure she was brave enough to try again, after he'd rejected her once — or was it twice? —

already. And so she lay there, waiting for the courage to arise within her, or for him to make the offer this time.

He didn't. He just stared at her, his eyes deep and contemplative, making her wish she could see inside his mind, hear the thoughts that must be racing around in there.

She couldn't. And he wasn't going to share them. But his hand rose, and his fingertips moved along the side of her face, sliding to push a lock of hair behind one ear.

She held his eyes. Everything in her wanted to look away, but she forced herself to hold them. And then he leaned a little closer, and he kissed her lips. He parted his a little, just before they made contact, so that when he pressed closer, he was tugging at her lips with his, teasing them apart.

She sighed at the surge of wanting that shot through her at that sweet contact, and he swallowed her breath with a shudder of his own. His arms slid around her, and he rolled onto his back, pulling her onto his chest as he continued to kiss her. And the moment her lips parted in a silent plea for more he complied, his tongue entering her, tasting her, sliding in and out of her mouth in a mocking imitation of the lovemaking she was sure would follow.

Only it didn't.

He broke the kiss, his eyes blazing, and even though she could feel his erection pressing into her thigh, he gently eased her off his chest and rolled onto his side again, so they were lying just as they had been at the beginning.

Softly, he said, "Good night, Olivia."

"Good night," she said back, because she didn't really know what else to say. He was clearly not going to make love to her tonight. And she didn't know why, but she was frustrated to the point of almost feeling angry about it. That kiss had been . . . electric.

She rolled onto her opposite side, putting her back to him so he wouldn't see the tears of anger and confusion that were burning, ridiculously, in her eyes. And she thought she might need another few shots of that rum if she hoped to get any sleep.

He slept, and he dreamed, and he twisted and turned in his sleep, trying to wake up but unable to. It felt as if he knew where the dream was going, but he couldn't stop it. It was as if he were a passenger aboard a runaway train, with no way to control it or slow it down, much less to jump off, even though he knew the tracks ahead were missing, the bridge was out and a gaping chasm waited to swallow it whole. And him along with it.

So he held on, dreading what was to come as the dream unfolded. He saw himself, and he saw another man, saw him clearly. Saw his skin, which was sun-kissed and healthy. He had a horseshoe of close-cropped black hair surrounding his suntanned bald head. He wore wire-rimmed glasses over his brown eyes, and he had thick dark lashes. Full lips. Lean, trim physique, and a white button-down shirt and tie that covered what he knew to be a powerful chest and ripped arms.

"Why don't you just shave the rest of your hair, pal?" he asked, in the dream. "You'd look a lot tougher."

"Looking tough isn't the goal, son," the balding man said. "*Being* tough is. And let's face it, if you don't look it, you have an advantage."

"I get it."

"So you think you can handle one last job for us?"

He felt himself nodding, knowing, understanding what the "job" was — then. He didn't now, though, and he couldn't access the knowledge that lay just beyond his reach.

"They're offering a million. Half up front. Half when it's done."

"A million?" He looked at the balding man. "She must have pissed off someone important."

"Majorly important, but you don't need to know who. You're going to meet with the bag man tonight. He'll have five hundred grand in cash and a dossier on the mark. But as always, we're way ahead of the client." He handed Aaron a manila envelope.

Aaron opened it and slid out an eight-by-ten glossy color photograph. A photo of Olivia Dupree. As he stared at it, he felt a tightness in his chest, a closing off of his airways, that made no sense. He hadn't met the woman. Had no reason to feel anything at all about her one way or the other.

The man took the photo away from him, slid it back into the envelope and set it on the nearby table, where a .44 Magnum with a laser scope and a silencer lay, partially dismantled, surrounded by various brushes and rags and gun oil. He'd been in the middle of cleaning it when Bruce had shown up.

Bruce. The other man's name was Bruce.

"Meet the guy tonight. Take the job and

take the money," Bruce said. "Then go to Vermont and make this Professor Dupree disappear for good, Adam."

"Adam?" he said.

Awakened by the sound of his own voice, he blinked out of the dream, and into the present. He was in a tent, inside a sleeping bag, beside a beautiful woman.

A beautiful woman he was very, *very* afraid he had been sent to Vermont to kill.

10

By the time Olivia woke, Aaron was up, dressed and ready for the day. When he called her name — repeatedly, insistently — she growled deep in her throat, rolled onto her back and parted her eyelids, only to slam them closed against the bright yellow sunlight pouring into the tent around his dark silhouette in the doorway.

"Close the flap!"

"Nope. Open your eyes, sweetheart, it's time to be up and moving."

"What time would that be?" she moaned.

"It's already past seven." He said it as if substituting "noon" for "seven." She tried using her vision again, squinting at him and shielding her eyes with one hand. "Okay, okay. Just give me fifteen minutes."

He held out a blue tin cup with white speckles, and Olivia's nose twitched as she caught a hint of the aroma. "Is that . . . ?"

"Coffee," he said. "Fresh brewed and piping hot. This one's mine, but I have a cup out here waiting for you."

"Okay, *five* minutes, then," she said. "And don't let that coffee get cold."

He grinned at her and, nodding, backed away from the tent, letting the flap fall closed and plunging her back into blessed dimness.

Groaning in protest, she wrestled her way out of the sleeping bag. Her fantasy of making love with her favorite writer in that little downy nest was long gone. She supposed it was a dumb idea anyway. He wasn't a rock star and she wasn't a worshipful teenager girl, and writers didn't have groupies.

He probably thought she was an idiot.

She got dressed in the semidarkness of the tent. The fabric allowed enough light to pass through for her to see by, but not enough that it had disturbed her exhausted, rum-aided sleep. Emotional exhaustion, she thought, but exhaustion all the same. Tired was tired, and she was none too happy at being awakened so early.

Dressed, she dragged a brush through her hair, tied it into a high ponytail and fished in her bag for a pair of sunglasses before emerging into the full force of the summer sun.

He was standing there, waiting, her coffee

cup in his hand. Freddy stood beside him, eager, tail wagging, tongue lolling happily. There was a campfire blazing a few yards away, and balanced precariously on a nearby tree stump, a plate of food big enough to feed three of her.

"Breakfast," he said, when he saw her staring at the food.

"Are we having guests?"

He rolled his eyes and returned to his folding canvas chair, retrieved his own overflowing plate of food from a nearby boulder and dug in.

Sighing, she went to grab her plate and took the other chair. After a few bites of a concoction that included scrambled eggs, bacon and who knew what else all blended together, she paused long enough for another slug of coffee and to ask, "How did you manage all this in the middle of the forest?"

"We're not in the middle. We're on the edge. And it was easy. One pan, quick cleanup, minimal fuss and lots of protein. We'll need it. Eat up."

She tilted her head, studying him, her belly full though her plate still was, too. "You really have done this before."

"I must have. And despite what I said yesterday, often, I think. It feels as natural as breathing."

She rose, set her plate on the ground and said, "Come and get it, Freddy."

The dog would have smiled if he could. Instead he just hurried to the plate and cleaned it in about three seconds and two gulps. Olivia returned to her seat to sip her coffee. And as she did, she studied Aaron. He seemed to be avoiding her eyes this morning as he tucked into his breakfast with relish and apparent haste.

"So what's the plan?" she asked.

He paused to look at her as he took time to swallow his most recent bite. "You still think your ex sent that guy to your house?"

"I do."

"Even though there are other names and faces on those disks?"

She nodded. "None of those others would know I had the disks, much less where to find me. Of course, I still don't know how Tommy figured that out, either." She lowered her eyes then. "I don't like thinking about him."

"I don't imagine you do. But if he's found you, and he's sent someone to kill you —"

Her head shot up fast and she interrupted. "*Kill me?* We don't know that. Maybe he just sent that guy to get the disks. We can't be sure he was going to do any more than that." She blinked. "Can we?"

He hesitated a moment, his eyes holding hers, probing them. Then he looked away as he said, "No, probably not."

"So we're going to call him. He always has one listed number."

"Uh-huh, and what are *we* going to say to him?"

"*I'm* not saying anything. You're going to talk to him."

"Yeah, you said that. I'm just not sure what I'm supposed to say when I do."

"I've been thinking about that," Olivia said. "The thing is, we *don't* know for sure it was him who sent that guy. So what if it wasn't? It's a slim chance, yes, but a chance all the same. So what if it wasn't him? Maybe he doesn't know I'm alive. If I call him, I give that away, and that's the last thing I want to do."

"Okay, that makes sense."

"So you call, you feel him out, try to figure out how much he knows about me."

"Yes, you said that, too. What I don't know is how. What do I say to him?"

"Tell him you're . . . working for someone who has some disks that belong to him, and that you want to return them. See what he says."

"And . . . if he already knows you're alive?"

215

She lowered her head. "I'm fairly sure he does. I feel it in my bones that he's behind all of this. Maybe if he does know, he'll agree to leave me in peace in exchange for those damn disks."

She looked at Aaron, waiting for his reaction. He seemed deep in thought, but finally, he said, "And you expect a man like him to keep his word?"

"I could always tell when he was lying."

He shook his head. "It's a lousy plan."

"It's the only plan we've got," she said. "So it'll have to be good enough. Unless you have a better one."

"I don't." He sighed, looked into his cup, then tossed the remaining coffee into the fire. "All right, then. Let's break camp, pack up our gear and get out of here."

She frowned. "But where will we stay tonight?"

"Not here. Never the same place twice, Olivia. Not if you don't want to be found."

"Oh." She watched him as he rinsed his now-empty plate and mug in a bucket of water he must have brought up from the lake. He emptied and cleaned the coffeepot, too, then packed everything away. Taking the hint, she finished her coffee and got to work helping him.

An hour later, the tent, the sleeping bags,

the folding chairs, the pan and the lantern were stowed away, as well, all rolled into impossibly small bundles and tied onto the rack on top of the SUV, leaving plenty of room for Freddy in the back.

As Aaron drove, he handed Olivia one of the cell phones they'd purchased. Prepaid, untraceable. He'd said that they would use one for a day or two, then toss it and use the other one. She figured she would be able to check on things at home that way, too. She really wanted to call Bryan and find out how the investigation was going. Had they figured out yet who had tried to kill Aaron, and why? Would it be safe for him to return with her to Shadow Falls once she got Tommy off her back?

Or was someone still lurking, waiting to end his life?

She looked at the phone, licked her dry lips, felt her stomach churn.

"As soon as you get a signal," Aaron said, "go ahead and try to find your ex's number. Then we'll place that call."

She nodded jerkily and watched for the telltale bars to appear on the phone's tiny screen. As soon as they did, she dialed, her heart in her throat. It felt as if she were standing face-to-face with the most terrify-ing part of her past. Tommy Skinner loomed in her vision like a giant monster, even though she knew she herself had built him up into that beast in her mind over time. She'd allowed her fear of him to give him power over her. And that fear, she realized now, had never gone away. It had been lurking, living and growing inside her, getting bigger all the time she'd been living her quiet, anonymous lie of a life. It had kept her from *really* living just as surely as Tommy himself had tried to. It had been waiting, that fear. Waiting for this very moment, this very day. In her soul, Tommy was Godzilla, and she didn't stand a chance against him.

She never really had.

But maybe, just maybe, with Aaron's help, she would find that she could beat him at last. Maybe she could conquer the monster of her nightmares. She was finally going to face Tommy Skinner once and for all.

She just hoped she would be alive when it was all over.

Bryan had phoned the publishing house three times before 9:00 a.m. His calls were returned at 9:15, finally, and he thought he would shout in relief when he answered the phone on his desk and heard a voice say, "This is Cynthia Rayne, executive editor at

Obsidian Press, for Officer Bryan Kendall."

"This is Kendall," he said quickly. "Thank you for returning my calls, Ms. Rayne. We've had a . . . an incident here in Shadow Falls, Vermont, that I believe involves one of your authors. However, we have yet to verify his identity."

The woman was silent for a long moment. Then she said, "Are you saying one of my authors is *dead?*"

Bryan could have kicked himself. "No, no. Just that he has no ID and a head injury that has . . . impacted his memory. However, since he was due to speak here in town, scheduled to arrive the very day he was, uh, injured, we're fairly sure who he is. We just need to be certain."

The woman said, "I see," but she didn't sound as if she saw at all. "So who do you *think* he is?"

"Aaron Westhaven."

There was a sound on the other end. Kind of a choking sputter, as if the woman had been drinking something and had just spewed it all over the phone.

"Ms. Rayne, are you all right?"

She cleared her throat. "Describe this author, would you?"

"Sure. He's about six-one, very fit, as if he works out regularly, dark hair and eyes, no beard or —"

"It's not Aaron Westhaven," she said. "I'm sorry, but it's not."

"How can you be so sure? I mean, I could fax you a photo or —"

"Officer Kendall, I can't tell you why I'm so sure, but I am."

"Ma'am, I'm sorry to be pushy, but this is a police investigation. This man was shot, so — I'm afraid you're going to have to tell me how you can be so sure he's not Aaron Westhaven."

She sighed. He heard fingernails drumming near the phone. Then she said, "I need your vow that you will never repeat it to anyone. *Ever.* Can you guarantee me that?"

He thinned his lips. "Of course I can," he lied, knowing full well he would have to share whatever information she imparted with Chief Mac, and possibly with Olivia, as well. The Feds — well, fuck them. They weren't sharing with him, so he wasn't going to share with them. Besides, they probably already knew.

"Aaron Westhaven is really *Erin* Westhaven," she said. "*E-R-I-N. She* is a woman."

"What?"

The editor on the other end of the phone sighed heavily. "It's our most well-guarded secret, Officer Kendall. It's why Westhaven

220

never does public appearances anywhere, and why she never would have agreed to speak in some small town in Vermont. Someone has been playing you people."

"But . . . I don't understand. Why?" Inside his mind, though, his brain was telling him that it didn't freaking matter why. The guy wasn't Westhaven. And whoever he was, he was with Olivia, and that wasn't good. It *couldn't* be good.

And so as the woman on the phone started going on about the different ways in which the general public and book critics the world over viewed emotional novels written by men versus those written by women, he tuned out almost entirely, managing to thank her when she broke off for a breath, assuring her the information was safe in his hands and hanging up.

And then he put his head in his hands, and whispered, "I've got to find Olivia. I've got to find a way to warn her."

Adam. He was experimenting with thinking of himself by the name "Bruce" had called him.

He'd half hoped it would feel as foreign as "Aaron" had. Unfortunately, it felt right. It felt familiar, comfortable. It fit him to a *T,* like an old, worn-to-butter-soft baseball mitt. And that made him nervous — hell, it scared him to death — because he didn't *want* to be Adam. Not if Adam was some kind of professional killer. And that was what he was starting to believe.

He'd had flashbacks. Visions. Snippets like a montage of clips from a faded old black-and-white film. He'd seen himself holding a gun. Firing a gun. He'd seen victims falling to the ground. He'd seen himself approaching their prone bodies as calmly and coolly as if he were taking a walk along the shore on a sunny afternoon.

And now this dream, in which he was being paid a million — *a freaking million* — to make Olivia Dupree disappear. Permanently.

He did not like where all this was leading, and though he tried to think of another explanation, he thought any logical person would draw the same conclusions he had. Though he wasn't sure of that, and he would have loved to run it by Olivia and get her opinion. That, however, would mean admitting he might very well have been hired to murder her. And she probably wouldn't react well to news like that. Particularly since she seemed to be harboring a bad case of hero worship for him.

Scratch that. Hero worship for the man

she *thought* he was. The man he almost certainly was *not.*

She also had a serious case of the hots for the guy she believed him to be. At least, she did while under the influence.

And that, he thought as he drove and watched her gnawing her plump lower lip and watching her cell phone as if it were a time bomb, was the problem. It wasn't that he didn't want her. He did. Big-time. Probably had his first impure thought about her the first time he'd looked up and seen her standing over his hospital bed.

But he would be damned before he'd have sex with a woman who only wanted him because she thought he was someone else.

And that felt like a familiar mantra of his. Something he'd decided long ago. Maybe in his line of work he often went around pretending to be someone else. Like, not a killer, for instance.

"I've got a signal," she said.

He pulled the car over in a safe spot. They were in the hills that overlooked Shadow Falls, probably too close for safety. He couldn't see the village, but he had a clear view of the giant neon triple-scoop sign at Alley's Ice Cream Parlour out on Old Route Six, which marked the "outskirts," in his estimation. He really didn't want to get too far away from town just yet. He needed answers, and those answers seemed to be there, in Shadow Falls.

"Okay, go ahead and place the call."

Olivia met his eyes. Hers were full of fear. He recognized it and, instantly, a barrage of visions surged through his mind, as if a metaphorical floodgate had been opened. Countless sets of eyes, staring at him, all of them filled with that same look of fear. She feared her ex the way others feared him.

Damn. He'd been right not to sleep with her. It only would have blown up in his face later.

Not to mention that it would have made it harder than hell to do the job, dumb-ass.

The voice in his head was his own, and yet not. As Olivia dialed Information to ask if there was a listing for Thomas Skinner in Chicago, Adam analyzed what that voice had just said. As if there were any chance in hell he was actually going to kill the woman. He wasn't. Hell, he *couldn't.* He didn't feel capable of putting a bullet into any innocent person, much less this one. And yet, that was what he'd done for a living up until someone had put a bullet into *him.*

Maybe not. Maybe there was some small chance he had this all wrong. Because damn, he didn't feel capable of murder. He just didn't.

And even if he had been once, he told himself, he wasn't anymore. And there was no way on earth he was going to hurt Olivia Dupree. Even if his memory returned full-force tomorrow. Even if he found out that his worst suspicions about himself were true. Even if it turned out he was working for the worthless pile of garbage she'd run away from long ago. He wouldn't — couldn't — go back to that. He had . . . changed.

"I'm scared," she said softly, lowering the phone from her ear.

She hadn't written anything down, he noted. "Did you get the number?"

She nodded. "What if this goes badly, Aaron?" she asked, speaking softly, looking at him with huge eyes full of trust. "What if there's no way to stop this chain of events until I'm dead?"

Tears welled up in her eyes as she voiced the question.

He ran a hand over her hair, then cupped her cheek. "I'm not going to let that happen, okay?"

She thinned her lips, lowered her eyes. Freddy leaned forward and licked the cheek Adam wasn't touching, and that made Olivia smile. But when she lifted her eyes

225

again, her face looked stricken. "Who'd take care of Freddy?"

"You will," he said.

"But what if I'm not here?"

He started to tell her she would be, but she interrupted. "No, I don't need re-assurances that I'll live through this, Aaron. We both know you can't promise me that — if you did, it would be a lie, and I don't ever want you to lie to me, okay? I just need to know Freddy will be okay if I don't make it. Would you . . . would you take him? He really likes you."

He stared at her for a long moment, and for some reason he couldn't say yes. This was a promise he couldn't make lightly. Something inside wouldn't let him. Her words — about never wanting him to lie to her — burned like battery acid in his soul. He looked back at the giant of a dog, drew a deep breath.

"I don't even know where I live. What if it's an apartment in the city or something?"

"You live on a former Christmas tree farm somewhere in Washington State," she told him. "Everyone knows that."

"Yeah, well, what if I don't?" He swallowed hard. "What if I'm not Aaron West-haven after all?" She looked alarmed at that, so he went on quickly. "Or what if the

226

charming Christmas tree farm in Washington is just a cover story I tell to keep the clamoring fans at bay?"

Her expression relaxed a little. "If it turns out you live in an apartment, I trust you to find a more suitable place to raise my dog. Or at the very least — and only if you have no choice — find someone else who would love him the way I do. I can't bear the thought of Freddy ever being mistreated. Or even shouted at."

He rolled his eyes. "Or even given a dirty look."

"That, too," she agreed.

He sighed, looking at the dog again. Freddy was staring back at him with his "eyebrows" raised and his brown eyes more pleading than he'd ever seen them. As if he knew exactly what was being discussed. The dog was practically a person.

"All right," he said. "I'll do it."

She seemed surprised. "You will?"

"Yes. Now, will you please dial the number before you forget it?"

She pressed the numbers with her thumb and handed the phone to him before it even rang.

Adam held it to his ear, heard the voice mail's generic recorded greeting, waited for the beep and then spoke. "I'm trying to reach Thomas Skinner," he said. "He can call me back at this number for the next four hours. No longer. It's in regard to several computer disks he lost sixteen years ago. I've found them and want to make arrangements for their return, under certain conditions. If he doesn't return my call by noon today, they'll go to the next highest bidder. Have a nice day."

He clicked off and turned to see Olivia staring at him, wide-eyed.

"What?"

"You . . . you just sounded . . . different."

"How?" he asked.

"I don't know. Scary. Intimidating. And really confident, as if you have reason to be."

"That's pretty much the only way to approach a man like your ex, Olivia. He's not going to respond to good manners and conversational chitchat. He deals with problems by sending someone to beat the hell out of people — or worse — not by talking them out."

"It just . . ."

"It just what?"

She shook her head, staring at her hands in her lap. "I understand all the reasons for wanting to sound the way you did. I just didn't expect it to be so . . . convincing.

So . . . real."

He sighed. Because she was right. It had come naturally to him. As naturally as disarming the burglar in her house. As naturally as taking steps to evade detection. As naturally as "never sleep with a mark," the refrain that kept playing through his brain over and over again.

And that was what she was. He was surer of it every minute. A mark. Even if he had no intention of playing out that scenario. He couldn't hurt her. He knew it right to his soul.

And maybe he'd decided that before he'd been shot. Hell, maybe it was the *reason* he'd been shot.

The phone rang, and Olivia almost jumped out of her seat. He would have sworn her head hit the ceiling.

"Easy," he said. "It's okay." He picked up the phone, saw Private Caller on the screen and figured that was about what he'd expected. Then he hit the speakerphone button and answered with, "That was prompt."

"I'm a prompt kind of a guy," a man's voice said, and Adam knew it had to be Skinner, just by the tone of his voice. "So you'll understand that I don't want to waste any more time before you tell me just who the fuck you are, and how you got your hands on my property."

"Wasting time is *all* you're doing, pal. Those questions are irrelevant and off the table. I've got the disks. You want the disks. What are they worth to you?"

"She's with you, isn't she?"

He shot a sideways look at Olivia. She was sitting motionless in her seat, tense and straight, eyes riveted to the phone. She was as frozen as a cornered rabbit.

"When you asked about your property, I thought you were referring to the disks," Adam said. "I don't know anything about any 'she.' "

"Liar. Is she there with you now?"

"I'm alone."

"Put her on the fucking phone."

"I'm alone."

There was a long pause. Then, "You're a liar. So what do you want?"

"I want to know if you've sent someone after the disks. Or to harm the person who had them in his possession."

"You mean *her* possession, don't you?" The man cleared his throat long and loud, as if he was getting ready to spit. "I'll tell you what. I'll give you a hundred K for the disks."

"And your promise that the person who's had them will never hear from or be harmed in any way by you or any of your . . . people . . . ever again."

"I've known she was alive since two years after she supposedly died, buddy. Believe me, if I'd wanted to hurt her, I'd have done it by now."

"I'm supposed to believe that?"

"You're willing to take my word that I'll leave her alone but not that I haven't already tried?" The man heaved a disgusted sigh. "I know who it might have been, though."

"Then telling me that is part of the deal, too," Adam said, hating this bastard more with every breath he drew, every word he was forced to listen to. He suspected that his hatred had a lot to do with the look on Olivia's face right then. She looked as if she was about to puke her insides out.

"I'll tell you. And I'll pay you. *And* I'll promise she won't be harassed by me or anyone in my employ. But I've got a few conditions of my own."

"And what would those be?" Adam asked.

"You meet me to trade the disks for the money. You bring every copy you've made. And I mean *every* copy. And you bring *her* to the meeting with you."

"Why?"

There was another long pause. "I just

231

wanna see her again. See what I missed out on. Or escaped from. Those are the conditions. You don't meet them, not only do you get nothing, I'll do the opposite of what I just promised. Agreed?"

Adam sighed, then looked at Olivia, telling her with his eyes that this was entirely her call.

She leaned close to the phone in his hand and said, "When and where, Tommy?"

11

"Sarah. I should have killed your sorry ass sixteen years ago."

Everything inside her turned cold as he spoke to her. Her stomach knotted up tight, just like it used to do when she would hear his car pulling into the driveway at night. Especially if it had been a few hours since his shift had ended, because that would mean he'd been at the local pub, slamming beer or, worse, whiskey.

"Sarah!"

He barked her name because she hadn't answered, and she jerked away reflexively, her back pressing into the corner between the edge of the seat and the car door.

From the back of the SUV, Freddy growled deep in his throat, his eyes on the phone.

"Shit," Aaron muttered.

Olivia saw him looking at her, and she was mortified that she'd shown such fear of nothing more than a voice on the phone. She straightened, shifted back to the center of her seat, lifted her chin. But it was too late. She'd revealed her terror of the man. There was no taking it back.

"Fine, don't talk, then," Tommy said. "I will. Be in Chicago a week from tomorrow at —"

"Fuck you, Tommy." She licked her lips, her eyes glued to the phone, her brain reminding her that he couldn't hurt her from a thousand miles away, and reminding her, too, that she wasn't a frightened, inexperienced young girl anymore. "I'm not coming to Chicago. You want the disks, you come and get them."

"I thought you wanted to live through this, bitch?"

Aaron clicked a button to shut off the speaker feature and put the device to his ear. "You're going to have to come to Vermont, Skinner. That's the only way this is going down." Then he paused, covered the phone with one hand and mouthed "Where?" at her.

Olivia scrambled for her handbag, dug out a crumpled drugstore receipt and a pen, and jotted an address, then handed the scrap of paper to him. It was the address of the abandoned Campbell farm, where the local teens went to party when they didn't want to be in found. Secluded and private.

"You'll need to fly into Burlington and rent a car," Aaron said. "Tonight. Text me your cell number, and I'll text you back with the address and time, so there are no mistakes." He paused, then, "Yes. Tonight." Another pause. "No, that's unacceptable. I'll be there alone, and I'll have the disks."

She leaned closer, trying to listen in, though she already knew what Tommy wanted. He wanted her.

"No," Aaron said again. "No, that's a deal-breaker."

"He's insisting I be at the meeting, isn't he?" she whispered, putting a hand on his.

Aaron met her eyes, nodded once.

She firmed her jaw. "I'll do it. Tell him I'll be there."

He shook his head. She could hear Tommy loudly making his own demands in Aaron's ear.

"I have to face him, Aaron. I really think I do."

Again he shook his head. "She's not coming. You can deal with me, or the diskettes are going to the media. You understand?"

Tommy's voice went silent.

"I'll see you tonight," Aaron said, and then he disconnected.

It felt as if a storm cloud left the SUV the minute the connection was severed. Even Freddy heaved a giant sigh.

"Done." Aaron seemed inordinately pleased with himself.

Olivia nodded. "Thanks for being so protective. But, um . . . you know this is my problem. I should solve it myself."

"You've been solving it yourself for sixteen years. Doesn't seem to be working out so well, does it?"

That angered her. "It was working out just fine until you showed up. Seems all this trouble came right in on your coattails, Aaron. Before that I was fine. Living a great life, having a great career, cozy in my pretty little house with my dog and my friends and my backyard. Everything was just perfect until you blew into town."

"Yeah, gee, sorry my getting shot in the head messed up your routine. Or I would be, if I knew you weren't lying through your teeth. You weren't so enamored of the life you've been living last night. Said you hadn't been living at all, the way I remember it. Or was that just the rum talking?"

She dropped her head into her hands and blew all the air from her lungs in one frustrated, infuriated whoosh.

His hand cupped the back of her head.

"I'm not the enemy, Liv. He is."

"I know. I know. I'm sorry."

"It's okay. I know that was hard for you, hearing his voice again. God, he beat the hell out of you, didn't he?"

"I don't want to talk about it."

"But you want to face him."

She nodded.

"Why?"

She sniffled and lifted her head, glancing over her shoulder at Freddy, who was lying in the back, head on his paws, tirelessly patient. "Need a walk, Fred? Hmm? Need a walk?"

His head came up, and he woofed at her.

Olivia got out, then went around and opened the tailgate. Freddy leaped out and stood on the shoulder beside her. She rubbed him all over, bent to kiss his nose and then started walking up the side of the winding dirt road.

She heard the car door close and knew Aaron was coming after her.

"I sent the text. The meeting's on for midnight."

"Good."

"What's at that address?" he asked.

"The old Campbell farm. One of three party spots the kids in town frequent. It's out past Sugar Tree, Nate Kelly's ski lodge.

Should be pretty private this time of year, especially on a Monday night."

He nodded. "Tell me why you want to see him," he said. And then he added, "And then tell me why you're not using a leash."

"What good is a leash going to do? He'll either stay with me because he wants to, or he won't. A leash wouldn't matter a bit to a two-hundred-pound dog. It's all about training. He won't run off."

"Not even if a rabbit or a deer goes shooting past him?"

"Not even."

"He's a good dog."

"He's the *best* dog. He does whatever I tell him — mostly."

"Hmm. Now if you could only train him not to eat meat laced with acepromazine."

"I won't have to. Twenty bucks says he won't fall for that trick again."

He lifted his brows. "He's that smart?"

"He's smarter than you."

He looked offended. "Okay, I'll reserve the right to debate that later. How about answering my other question?"

She stopped walking. Freddy, a few feet away, sniffed at a roadside weed, then watered it liberally. Olivia looked into Aaron's eyes. "I shouldn't have snapped at you. I'm scared. I'm not ashamed to admit that. I just — you were right before. What's to stop Tommy from taking the disks and killing me anyway?"

"That's why I want you to stay the hell clear of this meeting," he began. "That way —"

"That way he'll have to track me down and kill me later," she said. "No. We just don't have any way to be sure he'll keep his promise to leave me alone from now on. We have nothing to hold over his head. No power to enforce the deal." She sighed. "At least if I see him, I'll know. I'll know, the minute I look at him, whether he intends to let me live or not. And it's something I need to know. I don't want to live like this anymore. Looking over my shoulder, never quite sure I won't come home to find . . . exactly what I did the other night. I'm done with it. I need to see his face. I need to know."

Aaron sighed, lowering his head. And then he said, "There's another way, you know."

She frowned and studied his eyes, which had gone suddenly hard and cold. "No, I don't know. What other way?"

He averted his gaze, stared at the ground. "I go to the meeting as planned, and then I . . . kill him."

At first she thought he was kidding, but

the look on his face was dead serious. Slowly her heart turned to ice, and then the chill spread outward from that freezing center, filling her body. It was a sense of emotionless revulsion. She literally took a step back, away from him. Instantly Freddy was in front of her, placing himself between them and leaning heavily against Aaron's thighs, causing him to stagger a couple of steps backward.

He frowned down at the dog.

"Mastiffs don't generally attack people the way other dogs do," she told him. "They don't need to. They use their weight to intimidate and overpower anyone they feel is a threat to their person."

"Freddy doesn't see me as a threat to you."

"No. But I did, just now, and he picked up on that. I don't like feeling that way, Aaron."

"Stop calling me that."

She frowned. "Why?"

"I'm just . . . I'm just not sure that's who I am."

Tipping her head to one side, she studied him. "Who do you think you are, then?"

"I don't know. But that name — it just doesn't feel right."

"And that has something to do with you

wanting to commit murder for me?"

"No. Maybe. I don't know." He turned and paced away from her. "Look, the guy's a criminal. He's a threat to you. He's dangerous. And there's no real way to defuse him. I just — I guess I was trying out the notion. Seeing how it felt."

"And how did it feel, Aaron?"

He seemed to search inwardly. "Logical. Like a logical and entirely plausible plan."

She shook her head slowly. "But how did it *feel?*"

He sighed. "Necessary, I guess."

"Emotions, Aaron, I'm asking you to describe your emotions."

He frowned at her, and then he nodded. "It didn't feel good. Not like something I would *want* to do."

"But something you *could* do?" she asked.

He looked at her. "If I thought the guy was going to kill you otherwise? Yeah, I think I could."

Olivia lowered her head. "I don't think I like this side of you."

"I don't know if I do, either. But it doesn't seem like the kind of idea that would occur to a reclusive novelist, does it?"

"Not unless he was a thriller writer."

He nodded and looked down at the dog, who was now sitting in front of Olivia, his rump warming her feet, he was so close. She stroked his head, loving him even more than she already had, which was saying something.

"I'd never hurt *you,* Liv," Aaron — who didn't think he was Aaron anymore — told her. "Please believe that. I'm just . . . I'm just confused, I guess."

"Okay."

He nodded.

"But I *am* going to be at this meeting," she said. "And you're not going to even *think* about killing Tommy Skinner."

He licked his lips, lowered his eyes. "You must think I'm as bad as he is, to have something like that even occur to me."

She started walking toward the car again. Freddy stayed right beside her, walking in between the two humans. She was silent for a long moment. "I don't like violence," she said at length. "Probably because I was the victim of it myself. I don't like violent men, probably because I've suffered at the hands of one. But I love my dog. And I don't have any doubt *he* would kill to protect me."

He looked at her as they walked, his face puzzled. "I'm not sure what that means."

"Neither am I. But I will tell you my darkest secret. I've thought about killing Tommy myself. I thought about doing it before I left him, because I knew he would kill me if he caught me trying to get away. I thought about doing it after I left him, because I was unhappy living in fear he would find me one day. And I thought about showing up for this meeting and just shooting him full of holes. Just for an instant. I thought it. You thought it. You said it out loud and I didn't, is all. But . . . but the difference between us and men like Tommy Skinner is that we don't act on every thought that crosses our minds. We know that some of them need to be reined in, crossed off, controlled. We're human beings, not loyal dogs. We don't just go around killing what threatens us. If we did, we'd be no better than animals."

He nodded slowly. "I get that."

"Good." She closed her eyes, wondering what he was thinking, feeling, what he had remembered that had put the shadows in his eyes. It had to be something that had come to him last night. He was different this morning. And he was handling that pocket watch as they walked, turning it over and over in his palm.

"What do you suggest we do between now and midnight?" she asked. "We have all day to kill." She made a face. "Sorry. The pun was unintended."

"Killing time isn't illegal," he said. "Or inhuman. At least, not that I remember."

"Now *you're* delivering sorry one-liners." She shifted her eyes to the watch in his hand. "Why don't we find some tiny tools and take that watch apart?"

His brows creased just slightly, right in the center of his forehead.

"You said there was something more to the watch, but you just couldn't remember what. And you're constantly handling it, feeling it, looking at it, as if it's got some secret to tell you that you just haven't managed to access yet." She tipped her head to one side. "Why don't we open it up and see what's inside, just in case?"

He looked down at the watch in his hand and then up at her again. "I think you're onto something."

She stopped at the back of the SUV and opened it up. "We also need a home base. I'm sick of being in this SUV all the time, and it's going to drive poor Freddy insane."

"I don't really see what we can do about that."

"I do. I want to go home."

He looked as if he understood and sympathized. "I know you do. But not just yet, okay? It wouldn't be safe yet."

"Why not? Tommy says he didn't send

244

that guy after me. Plus I'm going to him tonight, and he knows it, no matter what you told him. And Bryan will protect us from whoever came after me, as well as whoever's after you."

"And who's going to protect us from Bryan?"

She frowned. "No one. No one needs to."

"He's a cop."

It was her turn to arch her brows in surprise. "Cops are the good guys."

"Right. This from a woman who got beaten down by one on a regular basis for . . . how long was it, again?"

"A year."

"A year," he said.

"Only because it took me that long to make and carry out a plan to get away alive," she said, feeling a little defensive. "He was a bad man. And a bad cop. The exception, not the rule. Even I know the difference." She frowned as she closed the hatch behind Freddy and moved to the driver's-side door. She got in behind the wheel because she was sick of being a passenger and wanted a turn as the driver. "Do you think maybe you have a bad experience with a cop lurking in your history somewhere, too?"

"I don't know."

He seemed to be searching his mind, and she had a twinge of sympathy for how hard that must be, how frustrating to try over and over, only to find a gaping chasm where his past ought to be.

She thought it might be time to change the subject, but she was beginning to realize just how little she knew about this man. She still believed he was Aaron Westhaven. Who else would have shown up in her little town, with her card on him, on the day Aaron was due? And if he wasn't Aaron, then the real author should have arrived or at least phoned her to explain why not.

No, there was no question. He was Westhaven. But maybe the stories he wrote didn't reflect his real personality as much as she had always assumed they did. Talking about murder, knowing how to fight, how to evade, how to hide, knowing all about weapons and having an inherent distrust of police . . . No, those things didn't reflect the man at all. At least, not the man she'd been coming to know.

"Could we maybe just drive past my place? See what's going on?"

He glanced at her. "It would be too risky."

"Why? No one is looking for this vehicle," she said.

"Unless someone got a look at it after our

copy shop incident."

"How would they connect it to us?"

"It's too flashy, Liv. We'd attract attention. Just be patient a little longer, okay?"

She sighed, but she promised to try.

They bought a tool kit made for repairing eyeglasses at a drugstore in a nearby town, and then she drove while Aaron tinkered with the pocket watch. She was itching to use her cell phone one more time. She'd had the brilliant realization that she could check her messages, and she intended to do so, just as soon as she could get away from him long enough.

And maybe that was being stupid, overly suspicious, even paranoid. Or maybe it was that she wanted to keep believing in him for as long as possible, and if he didn't want her checking her messages, it was going to be very hard for her to go on trusting him. And maybe, deep down inside, she already knew he wasn't the man she wanted him to be. He might be Aaron Westhaven or he might not, but either way, he wasn't the man she'd thought he was. That man wasn't real. She'd realized that at some point in getting to know him. That man was a creation of her own mind. He didn't exist.

This man did, and now that she was

finally clear on who he wasn't, she was eager to find out who he was. Eager, and a little bit afraid. And for some reason, every bit as attracted as she'd been before. Maybe even more so.

"I want to sleep in a bed tonight," she announced as she drove back toward Shadow Falls, certain he planned to spend another night in some other part of the forest.

"I don't think that's smart."

"I don't care if it's smart. I'm going to face my deepest fears tonight, and I want to do it from someplace that has indoor plumbing, a hot shower and a bed to come back to if I manage to come back at all. Is that really so much to ask?"

He held her eyes for a long moment, and there was something unexpected there. Some spark, a playfulness and a hint of . . . was that desire?

"No," he said. "You're right, you are risking your life tonight. You ought to have what you want. We'll drive forty minutes in any direction you want, and we'll get a motel room for the night. You can have your hot shower and a decent meal before the meeting. We can leave the guns locked in the car and relax. No one's coming after us today. How's that sound?"

She smiled widely. "Almost as good as going home would. Thanks, Aaron."

"You're wel—" He stopped there, as the back of the watch popped open at last. He'd been prying — way too gently — at the thing for the entire duration of the ride. He turned it over, peering into the opening, and a tiny piece of paper fluttered out and landed in his lap.

"I knew it," he whispered. Blinking, he looked over at her. "I did, didn't I?"

"You did," she said. "You said there was something more about that watch." She knew he needed reassurance. "You must have remembered that, Aaron. That means it's all coming back." She was having trouble focusing on driving at all. "Well? Aren't you going to look at it?"

He smiled slightly, but it was a nervous smile, not a happy one. "I'm almost afraid to."

"Just do it, before I stop the car and do it myself."

He met her eyes briefly, then, nodding, picked up the paper and unfolded it. He read it, with a deepening frown.

"Well? What is it?" she asked.

"It's an address. In Philadelphia."

"That's all?"

He looked at her and nodded. "That's all. Five-two-eight-one Sycamore Lane, Apartment P." He lifted his brows. "And . . ." He patted himself down, finally removing a key from a pocket. "There's also a P on this key."

She took it from him, hitting the brakes at the same time. He looked behind them, nervous of being rear-ended, but she was busy staring at the embossing on the gold toned key. It said P, all right. Lowering the key, she resumed driving. "Maybe you live in a penthouse apartment. That would mean you're wealthy enough to be Aaron Westhaven."

"You said he lives on a Christmas tree farm in Washington State."

"So that's just a cover story, just like you said. Or maybe you have several homes, like a lot of wealthy people do."

"Or maybe I'm not him."

"I think you hope you're not him. In fact, I'm developing a theory about it. I think you harbor some kind of fantasy of being an adventurer, writing those kinds of novels and living the lifestyle that goes with them. And I think this amnesia is a chance at recreating yourself. If you admit you're Aaron Westhaven, you become him again. But you want to be someone else."

He seemed to be mulling that over for a long, long moment, and then he looked at her, and said again, "Or maybe I'm not him."

She sighed. "Maybe." Then she looked at her watch. "I'm hungry. We need to get some lunch."

"Let's wait for the motel, see what's near it. We shouldn't be seen this close to Shadow Falls." He looked around. "Where are we, by the way?"

"Maple Valley," she said. "This is mainly ski country, and it's way off-season. So far off season I'll bet we can get the best suite to be had. Hot tub and all."

"I said *motel*, Olivia. We can't use our plastic. We have to pay cash. They're not going to —"

"Sure they are. We have enough cash to give them whatever security deposit they need. We'll let them think we're having an affair, can't risk the spouses finding out, something like that."

As she spoke she pulled into the parking area of a giant log cabin with an archway above the entrance that looked like the top half of a giant wagon wheel, each spoke an entire log. Within that spoke, spelled out in carved maple leaves, were the words *Sugar-Shack Lodge* and underneath, in smaller letters, *Rooms and Private Cabins Available.*

"This is not at all what I had in mind," he

251

muttered.

"Look, you. I'm facing my —"

"Deepest fears tonight. I've got it."

"Good. So shut up and play along." She chose a parking spot, gave her face the once-over in the rearview mirror, and realized her hair was down and loose. Then she looked at her shirt with the top few buttons undone and the blue jeans that fit her like a glove. And looked good on her, too, she thought. Surprisingly good. Lifting her eyes again, she thought that the woman looking back at her from the rearview mirror could have passed for one of her students.

Huh. Go figure.

"Liv?"

"I'll be right back." She got out, slammed the door and left him with Freddy in the car.

She was damn good at getting what she wanted, he thought. Because an hour later they were ensconced in a private cabin at the base of a beautiful mountain, with a stream bubbling nearby. She'd ordered food from one of the local restaurants, and it was due at the door any minute. And the way she was eyeballing the hot tub on the deck out back, he figured she would be in that sucker as soon as she finished her lunch.

She sure was going to make the most of the afternoon. That made him wonder if she really did believe that this might be the final one of her all-too-abbreviated life. Was she *that* scared?

Someone knocked. She was busy filling a large bowl with food for the horse she called a dog, so he answered it.

"Money's in my bag, on the table there," she called.

"Okay." He grabbed the wallet from her bag and glimpsed the little black handgun inside. His blood chilled at the sight of it. It reminded him just how afraid she really was of the man they were going to face tonight. The man he might have been working for.

Tommy Skinner. The name wasn't familiar to him, but that didn't mean much. The thug hadn't seemed to recognize his voice on the phone, though. That was a plus. But would he recognize his *face* tonight? Would he tell Olivia that her Aaron was really Adam, a hired killer he'd sent to end her life?

He took some bills out of the wallet and went to the door. The kid at the door handed over several white paper bags, took the bills and handed him back some change. Adam tipped him, then watched him go before closing the door and turning the lock. He carried the bags to the round wooden table and handed her the change.

She tucked it back into her wallet, then watched him unloading the bags. She'd ordered an old-fashioned roast chicken dinner, complete with mashed potatoes and gravy, warm rolls and soft butter, stuffing and baby peas, and a hot apple pie for dessert.

He shot a meaningful look at her purse as she set it back down on the table.

"Look, I forgot the gun was even in there, okay?"

"Whatever," he said. He was taking dishes down from the cupboard now. The kitchenette was stocked with everything except food. There were even a clean dishcloth and bottle of dishwashing liquid under the sink.

"I didn't bring it inside because I was afraid of you or anything like that," she said. "It just — I just thought it best to keep it close, given the circumstances."

"Makes perfect sense." He put the plates on the table and laid silverware beside each one.

"I don't like guns. I've been in conflict with myself over carrying it at all."

"It's all right, Olivia. I'm not angry. I *am* hungry, though." He pulled out a chair, sat down and began filling his plate.

She sat and did likewise. He watched her taking a little bit of everything. "You were upset. I saw your face."

"I don't think you know me well enough to judge how I feel."

She shrugged. "I've seen you angry before. When you confronted that burglar in my house. When you spoke to Tommy on the phone."

"And I seemed like that?"

Her lips thinned. She had to know he hadn't acted the same way at all. "Not exactly. You were just quiet, and your eyes went all cold, the way they do sometimes."

He shrugged. "Maybe I was a little bothered at the reminder of how afraid you are of that bastard. But not angry about a woman whose life is on the line taking precautions to protect herself." His plate was full, and he picked up his fork. "If you'd told me how you felt, I'd have told you to keep the gun close." Then he leaned over and sniffed the food as his stomach rumbled. "And for the record, Olivia, if I *had* been angry, this meal probably would have calmed me right down."

She smiled then, relaxing a little more. And that was what he wanted. No one should go out to face possible death without a smile and a good meal inside them. And though he had no intention of letting her get herself killed, he knew that in her mind, the risk was there. It was real to her.

"I just didn't want you to think I was keeping it close because I didn't trust you or anything. That's all."

He looked at her. "But you *don't* trust me. Not entirely. And you'd be a fool if you did, Liv."

She lowered her eyes.

"Look, we never said we were going to tell each other everything. But maybe, given our circumstances, it might be reassuring — for both of us — if we can agree to be as open and honest with each other as we can be."

"About . . . ?" she asked.

"About everything."

Olivia averted her eyes, and for the slightest moment he got the feeling there was guilt lurking behind them. Was she keeping something from him? And if so, what?

Then again, could he blame her? He hadn't told her about those dreams of his — about the snippets of memory that seemed to suggest he was a paid killer. But he had good reason, he told himself, to keep that information from her. Because if it were true, then the second she found out, she would be history. He would never see her again, and he needed her. He needed her to help him get his life back. Where would he be if she abandoned him right now? No car, no money, no clue who he was, nothing but an address on a slip of paper in the back of an old pocket watch. A voice from somewhere deep within him whispered, *It's more than that, and you know it.*

And she was going to find out sooner or later. He had no doubt her friend the cop had a line on who he was by now. He was itching to give Bryan Kendall a call himself, to ask what he knew. But it was too risky.

Still, eventually she was going to find out all the stuff he hadn't told her — and then some. He hoped to at least get her to take him to the Philadelphia address before that happened. Which meant he had to keep her on his side until then.

He shook his head as he contemplated his situation and his dependency on a mild-mannered English professor who wasn't really so mild-mannered after all. And okay, he might as well admit, at least to himself, that never seeing her again bothered him far more than not having a ride to Philly.

"Is there . . . anything you're kind of . . . keeping to yourself?" he asked.

She lifted her gaze, locked it with his across the table. There was something; he saw it there. But then she nodded and drew a breath. "I haven't told you where I got my name," she said.

"No, you haven't. And I have to admit, I've been wondering."

"I never knew my real family. I was abandoned at birth, and being a pretty sickly child, I was never adopted."

"What was wrong with you?"

"Asthma and severe allergies. It was so bad they couldn't even say for sure I'd survive. By the time I outgrew everything and my health was solid, I was older and — You know what, it doesn't matter. Digest version is that I was in and out of foster homes, and had no family I knew of. The real Olivia Dupree was a girl I met in one of those foster homes, and she didn't have anyone, either. We sort of . . . bonded."

"I can see how you would." He was rapt. He never would have guessed she had been an orphan.

"We were only together a couple of months before we were both moved again. But years later, when I came to Vermont, I answered an advertisement for a roommate, and it was her. I moved in. Two weeks later, I came home and found her in her bed. She'd been strangled."

"Holy God." He sure as hell hadn't seen *that* coming.

"I thought it was Tommy. I thought he'd sent someone after me who'd killed her by mistake. I told the police officer all of that." She shook her head. "He took pity on me, told me I ought to just let Tommy go on believing he'd killed me. And once he knew my situation, and hers — you know, no relatives, new in town — he suggested I take her identity. Let the world think Sarah Quinlan was the murder victim. Call myself Olivia Dupree. Never have to worry about Tommy again."

He nodded slowly. "It is kind of brilliant."

"He helped me pull it off. I had to bleach my hair for a while. But eventually I just let it go, said this was my natural color. I thought no harm was done. But it was wrong, what I did, and it caused problems I couldn't have known about."

"How?"

"Well, for starters, the cop who helped me turned out to be the real murderer. He killed a lot more women before he was caught. Maybe he had some connection to his first victim that no one knew about because of me. They were looking for a connection to the wrong person, you know?"

"That's reaching."

"Yeah, still . . . And then I learned — only a few weeks ago — that she'd had a baby.

The autopsy said she'd given birth about six weeks before she died. A month before I got into town. I never would have guessed that. And no one knows what happened to that child."

"She never told you?"

"No. The police looked for a while, but they were looking for Sarah Quinlan's missing baby, not Olivia Dupree's. It might have made a difference, sixteen years ago. Now it's a cold trail."

He was literally stunned. He'd had no idea how much the woman had been through in her life. Good God. And to think that after all of that, she'd somehow survived. Thrived. Gotten an education, built a career, made a home, a life.

She was about fifty times the woman he'd thought she was. And he'd already begun to think she was something pretty amazing. He just hadn't had a clue *how* amazing.

"Anyway, if it's all the same to you, I'd prefer not to talk about it anymore. It's . . . it's another bad memory."

"That's one thing I don't have to worry about," he said. "Bad memories."

She smiled a little and tried to make light of it. "I also haven't told you that I love roasted chicken with potatoes and gravy and stuffing."

He returned her smile, even though the secret he suspected she was still keeping worried him. "I kind of guessed that when you chose it for this particular meal."

Her smile faltered. Tears welled up in her eyes, and he sensed she'd been battling them for quite a while now. He reached across the table, covered her hand with his. "It's not your last one, you know."

"Neither of us can be sure of that."

"No, you're wrong," he said. "I *am* sure."

She sniffled, then ate a little, so he did, too. And then she said, "Tell me why you're sure." She might as well have said, "Convince me that I'm not going to die tonight. Take this horrible fear away." And more than anything, in that moment, that was all he wanted to do. He didn't examine his reasons too closely, maybe because there weren't any — none that made sense, at least.

"I was just thinking, Liv. You know, after we get tonight out of the way, we can drive down to Philly, check out that address, figure out my history."

"We haven't gotten through tonight yet."

"But we will. And you can rest assured, I'm highly motivated to keep you alive and well. Otherwise, I lose my ride." He smiled at her when he said it.

She rolled her eyes, leaned back in her chair and folded her arms over her chest. "Gee, thanks."

He shrugged. "And my only friend."

"Ohhhh," she said softly, as if she'd just spotted a cuddly kitten. "That's really sweet, Aaron."

"It's the truth. Look, you've got doubts about me. You'd be nuts not to. And it's true that I don't have much more of a clue than you do right now about who I am, much less what kind of man I might be. But right now, today, you really are the only friend I have in this world. And you're my ride. You're also my only source of cash. You're my confidante, my advisor and my companion. Not to mention my only ally in all of this. That means a lot. And I know I haven't said so, Liv, but I'm grateful."

She relaxed into her chair as if her bones had all gone soft. Her face softened. Her lips relaxed, and her eyes seemed easier.

"Thanks for that," she said.

"You're welcome. Now, why don't we try to forget what we're facing and just enjoy this meal? In fact, let's enjoy the rest of the day as if we're just two ordinary people out to have a good time together. What do you think?"

"I think it would be kind of hard to forget

what we're facing."

"Then we're going to have to try *really hard* to have fun."

Her smile was slow, but building, and the playful anticipation in her eyes was something he hadn't seen before. There was a sparkle there now that hadn't been there before, and it appealed to him on a gut-deep level that took him by surprise.

He liked this woman, he realized. He liked her a lot. The physical part of his attraction to her had just been kicked up a few more notches, and it had been pretty high to begin with.

"So what will we do?"

"I don't know yet, but I do know that I think better on a full stomach. So quit talking, woman, and let a man eat already."

And with that her transformation was complete. She dug in to her meal with relish, and her eyes, every time they met his, had something new dancing around in their melted chocolate depths. Excitement. She was looking forward to spending the afternoon with him, acting like two ordinary people. He guessed he'd better deliver and show her a really good time.

But from the looks she was sending him, the sidelong ones he just caught glimpses of, the ones she ended as soon as he caught her looking, he had a feeling she had a little bit more in mind.

Those looks made him nervous. There was another kind of anticipation in her eyes, or at least he thought there was. Sexual anticipation. And he hadn't promised that.

On the other hand, if she thought it was likely to be the last day of her life, he probably shouldn't be surprised she was letting her mind stray in that direction again.

And he wasn't all that sure he was going to have the willpower to turn her down a second time.

12

Olivia wondered if Aaron could tell she was keeping something from him. The way he'd been looking at her when he'd asked if she was keeping a secret, the way he'd told her, in so many words, that they needed to be open and honest with each other, when the entire time she'd just been waiting for him to leave the room long enough for her to check her messages, suggested that he did.

She was away from him now, taking that long hot shower she'd been so craving, but she couldn't very well take the second and only working cell phone into the bathroom with her.

She was tempted to make a call or two, as well, once the opportunity presented itself. To Bryan, to find out how the case was progressing and whether he'd caught whoever had shot Aaron in the head and left him for dead. And to Carrie, to make sure she still hadn't told Bryan about the borrowed Expedition. She also wanted to talk to her about Aaron, get her opinion on the things he'd remembered and ask her how much longer it might take for his memory to be fully restored.

She couldn't do those things, though. She wouldn't. She'd made a promise to Aaron, and she knew he wasn't overreacting or being paranoid about any of this. Someone had tried to kill him, after all. There was no question about that.

But she didn't see how it could hurt them in the least if she checked her messages. It was starting to make her nervous and jumpy, being so out of touch with her life. It was a small thing, but it would make her feel better.

Problem was, he showed no sign of wanting to leave her side, and in fact, he was turning out to be pretty good company.

Their meal was complete, and the leftovers, which would serve as dinner later on, were stored in the full-size fridge. They'd cleaned the dishes and put them away. And her hot shower was now a fait accompli, she thought, as she stepped out of the tub.

She had been trying hard not to think about tonight. Trying really hard, while she enjoyed a steamy shower and took her time drying her hair. But she hadn't had much luck. It was on her mind, no matter what.

"Ah, there you are." He was waiting in the only bedroom when she emerged from the bathroom, wrapped in a towel. He spoke from where he was sitting on the edge of the bed, and then he seemed to get stuck looking at her.

She should duck back into the bathroom, she thought. Or ask him to leave so she could get dressed. Funny, how her sexual bravado vanished without any rum in her veins. But she didn't do either of those things. She stood there, and he looked his fill, his eyes taking their time moving from her head down over her towel-wrapped body to her toes. It would have been insolent, his long, slow look, except that the expression he wore was bordering on rapturous.

She lowered her eyes. "Maybe I should get dressed."

"Maybe I should get *undressed*," he suggested.

Her gaze shot up again and met his.

"Sorry. That was obnoxious. I didn't mean it to be, it's just that you're . . . you're beautiful. I haven't told you that before, have I?"

She shook her head, her power to speak temporarily missing.

"And you're even more beautiful without clothes on," he added.

She rolled her eyes. "I'm wearing a blanket-size towel."

"Towel. Feedbag. Doesn't matter."

She closed her eyes slowly, then opened them again and strode to her dresser. She'd claimed the left side of the oversize chest of drawers, and had unpacked just as soon as they'd arrived, wanting the room to be neat and feel homey if she happened to get back tonight.

She opened the drawer to decide on the clothes she was going to wear for her meeting with Tommy. Then she frowned, holding a pair of jeans in one hand and her skirt, which was badly in need of laundering, in the other.

"The jeans," Aaron said.

She looked up, blinking, totally lost in her own thoughts, and pretending to have forgotten the sexual innuendo of only moments ago. "What?"

"The jeans. It's an easy choice, Liv. You want to wear something you can move in if you need to — or fight in, if it comes to that."

She shook her head slowly. "I want to look as if I've thrived without him. I want him to look at me and see a sophisticated, accomplished, intelligent, beautiful woman."

Aaron frowned. "That's what he will see. Olivia, that's what you *are.*"

She felt her brows rise. "Thank you for saying that."

"It's the truth. How can he see anything else but what you are?"

She looked at the jeans, narrowed her gaze. "In these, he'll probably see an older version of the girl who ran for her life to get away from him."

Aaron shook his head. "No, Olivia. No way. And frankly, I think you're wrong about even that part of it. He might have thought of you as a helpless little mouse he could beat up on at will. That's what you think, isn't it?" She nodded. "Yeah, I figured. Maybe he did. But you can bet your ass — which looks particularly luscious in jeans, by the way — that when he found himself behind bars and realized you had put him there, his opinion of you underwent a radical change."

She blinked. "Yeah. I became the evil bitch he wanted to kill."

"No. You became a woman who refused to stick around and be his victim. You became a fighter, and you fought him and won. You stuck it to him. He had no choice but to see you as a worthy adversary, not a helpless mouse. Not after that."

She lifted her head a bit. "I never thought of it that way."

"You shouldn't think of it at all. What he thinks of you shouldn't matter to you any more than the price of kitty litter in Altoona."

She blinked out of the haze that had sucked her back into her past, into seeing herself as that woman she had once been. The victim. Sarah Quinlan.

"I'm not that girl anymore."

"No one could possibly mistake you for that girl anymore," Aaron told her. "I mean it."

"Thanks." She looked at the clothes again. "So . . . the jeans?"

"The jeans." He sighed. "If you insist on clothes. We could always reconsider my first suggestion."

She met his eyes, lifted her brow. "You're the one who turned me down, remember?"

"It seemed like the right thing to do at the time. Still does, but I'm also human. Any possibility I'll get a second chance?"

"I'll let you know after you tell me how we're going to spend the next few hours. You promised me a fun afternoon, and here we are talking about . . . things we aren't going to talk about again until we have to."

He smiled slowly and said, "You're right. And I made a plan while you were in the shower. I promise, you're going to love this."

"What? What are we doing?"

"I'm not telling. Keep in mind, I had to think of something that didn't include exposing us to the general population. So that pretty much ruled out any of the usual date-night choices."

"Date? So this is a *date?*"

"Fortunately, I'm a creative guy," he said, choosing to ignore her question.

"You are, are you?"

"I am. I just discovered it, and I'm pretty pleased about it, to tell you the truth."

"I'll *bet* you are." She loved this side of him, she thought as she stood there in a towel, batting words back and forth. The humor. The relaxed teasing. The twinkle in his eyes. This was different from the Aaron she'd been seeing so far. It felt as if he was gradually getting more comfortable in his own skin, as if his true personality was seeping from his subconscious to the surface. It was like watching him slowly become himself again.

"Can Freddy come?" she asked.

"It wouldn't be any fun without him."

She smiled a little, wondering what he had up his sleeve. "Okay, I guess I'm game if

271

you are."

"Great. Get dressed, then."

Smiling, she clutched her jeans closer, snagged the blouse and undergarments she'd tossed onto the bed before her shower and hurried into the bathroom.

Three hours later they were in a rowboat, floating on a slow-moving river that meandered past the Sugar Shack's grounds and out into the wilds of rural Vermont. Olivia sat on the barely cushioned seat in the stern, while Aaron, on the bench seat facing her, was rowing.

Freddy sat on the floor behind her, in the very back of the boat, watching the waves fall away behind them and wearing the biggest dog smile Olivia had ever seen.

She smiled, too, and tipped her face up to the late-evening sun. It would be setting soon. And all too soon after that, it would be time to meet Tommy. She realized just then that it was the first time she'd thought of tonight's plans all afternoon. They'd been on the river for most of it, and it had been just as delightful as Aaron had promised.

They'd talked about everything from television shows to favorite foods, and she'd noticed that even though his name still escaped him, his memory was better the further back it went. It was more recent history that seemed to be taking the longest to come back.

"I was an only child," he told her. "I remember growing up in the 'burbs, riding my bike, skateboarding some."

"Do you remember how you got the steel plate in your head?" she asked.

"Yeah. Yeah, I do!" He seemed surprised. It was odd how he didn't know how much he remembered until she asked him. "I was ten, sledding with friends. We got the bright idea to pour water over the snow on this steep hill to make the sleds go faster."

She put her head in one hand and said, "Oh, no."

"Yeah. We formed a bucket brigade up the hill and kept pouring water, and it froze just as fast as we dumped it. So pretty soon we had this ice-trail. I volunteered to be the first test pilot."

She made a face.

He nodded in agreement with her horrified expression. "It was great at first. I mean, I *flew* down that hill. Problem came when I wanted to stop and couldn't. Couldn't steer around the maple tree, either."

"Oh, gosh. You're lucky you're alive."

He met her eyes. "Yes, I am."

And that made her smile. "So your friends had to scrape you off the tree and get you some help?"

"One ran for help while the others stood around trying to wake me up, or so I'm told. I was unconscious at the time, so I wouldn't know. By the time I came around it was three days later, and I had a shaved head that ached like hell."

She smiled harder and said, "Thanks for this, Aaron. I feel more relaxed than I think I've ever felt before. This was nice."

"It wasn't all that original," he said. "There was a brochure in the cabin. Said the lodge offered boat rentals, and had a map of the places where we can drop off the boat and catch a shuttle back to the lodge."

"It wasn't original at all. I mentioned wanting to do this the other day. And you remembered."

He shrugged and averted his eyes. Maybe he didn't want to admit that he'd taken her words to heart the way he had. Maybe it didn't mean to him what it did to her. Because it meant a lot to her.

"Have you got that map they gave you?" Olivia asked, to change the subject.

He nodded. "Breast pocket, under the jacket."

She had to dig hard to get beyond the requisite life jacket to the pocket of the shirt beneath it. But she did it and quickly unfolded the brochure to the map.

Tracing a finger along the blue line that represented the river, she said, "Right around this next bend, there should be a drop-off point."

"Really? Already?" he asked.

"We've been out here for hours, Aaron. God knows how long it'll take this shuttle to get us back to the cabin, and we have . . . that meeting tonight."

He met her eyes, and he seemed to know she didn't want to say Tommy's name out loud and ruin the afternoon they'd just shared. Then he turned away to look behind him, past the boat's nose in the direction they were heading. "That big bend up ahead?"

"Yes, the landing should be just past it."

"All right." He began to steer closer to the starboard riverbank as the current swept them around the bend, and then he nodded. "I see it." He frowned as they moved nearer. "I don't see any signs of life. How old is that flyer, anyway?"

"I don't know. Just put in, maybe there's a sign posted or something."

"Okay."

The oar blades slipped silently through the water. In fact, the only sound came from the droplets raining from the edges of the blades when he lifted the oars. Freddy stood up on all fours as he saw they were nearing the shore, and Olivia stroked him. "Easy, Freddy. Sit. Wait."

He sat, but he stood back up again as soon as his butt hit the floor. It was more a bounce than a sit.

"Freddy," she warned.

He sat again, leaving his butt down for two seconds this time, before jumping up again. He stared at the shore, and when they got close, he suddenly lunged into the water, one back leg getting temporarily hung up on the side.

"Freddy!" The boat tilted, but Olivia quickly eased the dog's leg the rest of the way over, and the rowboat righted again as Freddy paddled to shore. He trotted out of the water and shook himself mightily from his giant head to the tip of his tail. Water sprayed all over both of them as Aaron rowed nearer the wet canine.

Olivia looked at the plank building on the riverbank. It was little more than a lean-to with a shingled roof. It was utterly silent, aside from the whir of insects.

"I don't think anyone's around," Aaron

whispered.

She nodded in agreement, her eyes scanning the area. There was a pay phone on a pole, and numerous kayaks, canoes and rowboats on racks nearby. There was also a redwood dock stretching out into the water, and Aaron eased the boat so that it turned and floated alongside perfectly.

"I think you've done this before," she said.

"That's what it felt like when I saw the flyer. So I figured, why not try it, see if it's familiar."

"And?"

He met her eyes and smiled. A real smile. "Yeah. I remember doing this when I was a kid, too. And I remember the Scout troop and the camping in detail now."

"It's coming back, Aaron."

"I think so, yeah. All but my adult life. I remember my parents from when I was a kid, and I know my father died when I was in fifth grade. Heart failure."

"I'm so sorry."

"I don't know about my mother, though. You know, where she is now. But that, the more recent parts of my life — it just feels like a word that's right on the tip of my tongue. It's closer than ever. Maybe within reach."

"I'm so glad."

"Me, too," he said. "It's the first time I've felt sure it would return at all."

He moved to the bow and used the rope coiled there to tie the little boat to the dock. She turned and did the same with the rope in the stern, looping it around one of the upright dock supports.

Freddy had moved from the shore to the head of the dock when he saw Aaron maneuvering the boat that way, but he wouldn't step onto it. Just kept lifting one paw, putting it onto the wood, then removing it again.

"Right," Aaron said to him. "The big brave dog will ride in the boat, jump overboard, swim to shore, soak the captain — but he's too scared to walk out onto the dock."

"Woof!"

"You're a big baby!"

Freddy replied again, but this time it sounded as if he were trying to talk. "Row-ow-ow-mow." More or less.

"Don't get mouthy with me," Aaron said.

He climbed out of the boat, onto the dock, and reached a hand down to Olivia. She stretched hers up to him, still smiling from his exchange with the dog, and he closed his around it. So big, his hand. Strong.

When he pulled her up, she saw the sinews clearly in his powerful forearm, and she bit her lip against the surge of reaction.

Too late, though. He'd already seen it. It was in his eyes when they met hers again. He steadied her as she pulled herself up onto the dock, and she felt the pull of him, like a powerful magnet she could not resist. His hand on her waist, then on her hip . . . it was delicious. Almost forbidden. And she found her own hand settling on his shoulder, because she didn't know what else to do with it. It must have looked as if they were dancing without music, still in their life jackets. She smiled at how silly that image was, and then the look in his eyes stunned her, caught her and held her.

He was going to kiss her.

"I . . . um . . . gosh, this is starting to chafe. I need to get it off," she said, pulling free of him to mess with the buckles of her life vest.

"Yeah. Me, too."

In seconds he was sliding his off, while she was still on buckle number one.

"I'll go over to the building, see if there's — Yeah, there's a sign. I can see it from here."

He kept walking, and she finally found the magic catch and freed herself from what had been beginning to feel like a giant squid wrapped around her. Then she hurried to join him, shrugging the vest off on the way.

DRAG BOAT OUT OF WATER, ONTO SHORE, WELL AWAY FROM WATER'S EDGE, LEAVING OARS/PADDLES INSIDE. HANG LIFE VESTS ON RACK. USE PHONE TO CALL HOTEL. SHUTTLE WILL BE DISPATCHED. ESTIMATED WAIT TIME, 30 MINUTES.

"I see," he said. "And what if you didn't have a quarter in your pocket for the phone?"

She tipped her head to one side and pointed. *Phone is Free* was handwritten on lined paper and affixed to the top of the phone with silver duct tape.

"Oh."

"So are you going to call them?" she asked.

"Let's grab the boat first."

"Okay." She turned and headed back down to the dock, trotting all the way to the far end, where she'd tied off the stern. She began unlooping the rope from the pylon, as Aaron, who'd followed her, began untying the bow.

280

"Ready?" he called.

"Ready."

He began walking forward, towing the boat. She started following, then felt something odd on her ankle. She looked down, startled, to see the rope tightening around her leg.

"Aaron, wait! I —"

But that was all she got out before the rope pulled her leg right out from under her and her arms began flailing as she fell headfirst into the water.

She came up spluttering, pushing the water from her face with her hands. It was only about chest deep, but it was cold.

Aaron looked down at her from the dock, his face alarmed. "Liv! God, are you all right?"

He was on his knees, reaching down to her. She reached up to grab his hand. "I guess." She sniffled, choked, even threw in a shiver.

"Come on, I've got you." He closed his hand around hers, and she gave one mighty tug, yanking him headfirst into the water beside her.

When his head popped back up, she was laughing out loud. Big, full belly laughs that threatened to split her sides. And she couldn't seem to stop. God, she didn't think she'd *ever* laughed like that.

"Very funny," he said.

But she was still laughing, so he started laughing, too, and then he wrapped his arms around her waist and tugged her hard against him, pressing his laughing mouth to hers.

And then the laughter stopped. It probably fled due to the heat. She opened her mouth, welcomed his tongue with her own, as the two twisted and twined around each other. His hand lowered to cup her buttocks, tugging her hips hard against him. She arched even closer, wanting him, wanting this, and refusing to think of all the reasons why it was a bad idea.

He'd saved her life, that night in her home. He'd been by her side ever since. He'd considered killing a man he didn't even know to protect her. He loved her dog. If she couldn't trust him, who *could* she trust? The old Olivia would have answered, "No one." But this woman she was becoming since she'd been with him — the one who'd found her passion for life and laughter and the courage to face down any adversary — *that* Olivia disagreed.

His other hand slid down her back as his mouth plundered hers. He tasted her sweetness like a hummingbird at a lily. Both hands cupping her butt, he jerked her harder to him, and she felt his erection, even in the cool water, pressing against her. Then his hands slid lower, down the backs of her thighs, to where her knees bent, and he pulled them forward and up, wrapping her legs around his waist. Turning, he carried her through the water and up onto the shore.

She locked her ankles around his back, and he bent slightly to grab the rope on the bow of the little boat as they walked past it, barely breaking his stride. He pulled the boat up out of the water, releasing the rope when he estimated it was far enough ashore to be safe, and kept right on walking with her wrapped around him, still kissing her as if his life depended on it.

She certainly felt as if hers did. If he stopped, she was sure she would die.

He set her on the ground, then leaned forward, pressing her down onto her back in a soft mat of wildflowers and sweet grasses. Lowering himself on top of her, he broke his kiss to trail his mouth over her jaw, down to her neck. There he paused to nibble and suck and bite.

Every sensation imaginable shot through her, leaving her entire body tingling, with the hardest shocks of all reverberating deep in her center. She was no longer aware of exactly what was happening. There were his hands pulling at her clothes. There was the delicious instant when his mouth first covered her bare nipple and she thought her head would explode. She screamed in pleasure, and he sucked even harder.

After that there was more tugging, more pulling off clothes, until her jeans were gone and she lay naked in the grass. He was naked, too, and kneeling over her. She let her gaze move over his body, from his broad, defined chest to his sexy-as-sin abs, to the erection that seemed to her like the ultimate compliment.

His eyes were moving over her body, as well, and she hoped he liked what he saw. She was no gym rat, but she hadn't let herself go. And the slight smile on his lips told her it was appreciated.

And then he put his hand between her legs, touched her, parted and probed her, even slipped two fingers inside.

"Unh." Her head tipped back and her eyes slammed closed, so she could focus on sensation and only sensation. "I need you inside me, Aaron," she whispered.

Then, finally, he was entering her. Lowering his body on top of hers, sliding his shaft into her, smooth and deep and without pause.

She felt her body being stretched to allow him entry, and when he slid back and entered again, the wet friction was so good she whimpered.

"Okay?" he asked.

"Yeah. *Hell* yeah."

His smile was quick and bright, and it made her hotter than ever to see it. He moved in and out, entering with more force every time, quickening his pace even as her body twisted into tight tiny knots that seemed unbearable. And still kept tightening . . .

. . . until everything in her dissolved under an onslaught of sensation. Her entire body vibrated, trembled, pulsed. Tiny bursts of sound exploded from her lips, driving from the very core of her, and her body was coated in sweat as her skin became hypersensitive.

Wave after wave of pleasure hit her. She was oblivious to anything else.

And then, slowly, as her body unclenched, relaxed utterly, and she blinked her eyes open, she was aware that he must have achieved bliss, as well, because his body was boneless, draped over hers.

She stroked his hair slowly, repeatedly,

dragging her fingernails lightly over his scalp.

"I don't remember ever feeling anything like that before," he said softly.

"Oh, gee, thanks, Mr. Amnesia."

"No. No, I wasn't being a smart-ass. I honestly think I would. If it had been like that, I mean. I think I would have remembered."

She smiled. "It was . . . that good for you, too?"

He lifted his head from her chest and looked into her eyes. "I'm really glad it was mutual, Liv, because, yeah. Yeah, it was that good for me, too."

"I never —" she began. But then she bit her lip, shook her head. "As great as this is, we really have to get moving. I hate to, but . . . the meeting, you know."

He nodded. "I know. Timing sucks, doesn't it?"

She smiled, shook her head. "The timing was perfect. Everything about this was perfect."

His own smile was tender, and he kissed her once again. Then he sighed. "You're right, though. We need to get going. I need a shower before we leave for that meeting." He rolled off her and onto his back, sitting up as he did. Then he began dressing. "And while I wouldn't mind a stiff drink to bolster my courage, I want to be sharp as a razor for this, so . . . not this time."

"Call it a victory drink, then, and I'll join you when it's all over," she said, amazed to find herself thinking she might make it safely back after all. "And for what it's worth," she added softly, "I think you've just bolstered the hell out of my courage."

He laughed, then sat there in the grass and watched her every move as she dressed. It made her feel pushed just beyond the limits of her comfort level, but she didn't turn away, and that was something of an unexpected rush.

When she finished dressing he got to his feet and quickly threw on his own clothes, then reached out to take her hand. Together, they walked to the payphone, and he dialed the number for the shuttle.

13

Back at the cabin, Aaron hit the shower, giving her the opportunity she'd been waiting for. As soon as she heard the water running, she dug the cell phone out of the bag he'd been carrying and started pressing buttons, cringing with every barely audible tone.

The automated phone-system voice answered, and she followed the prompts, keying in her home phone number and pass code, and then she paced the room in quick, agitated strides while she waited for the way-too-talkative robot to finish its spiel and let her listen to her messages. And then, *finally* . . .

"Olivia, it's Carrie. I'm worried to death. I haven't said anything about what we talked about, and I won't — unless it looks like I have no choice — but damn, girl, check in, would you? Be safe, okay?"

She deleted that message and went to the next.

"Professor Dupree, this is Dean Cranshaw. I understand there was a last-minute cancellation of this fundraiser with barely any explanation, and that from a third party."

She wondered who had phoned in to try to save her butt. Carrie? Bryan, maybe?

"Naturally I assume there is a good explanation, but I'm baffled by your failure to contact anyone to explain yourself. Please call me as soon as possible."

She deleted that one, as well, thanking her stars she had tenure and a damn good reason for bailing out on the university the way she had. Maybe she would still have a job, if she survived this. Then the third message played, and her body tensed when she heard Bryan's voice.

Would this give her the answers she was seeking? She glanced nervously toward the bathroom door. The shower was still running. Good.

"Olivia, it's Bryan. I can't tell you how I know this, but the man you are with is *not* Aaron Westhaven. I repeat, he's not Westhaven. And the serial number of the steel plate in his head traces back to a guy who died during Desert Storm. Probably we got one of the digits wrong, but, the point is, he's not Westhaven, and we don't know who he is, and you could be in danger. Whatever this is, Olivia, it's big. The FBI are involved. So just . . . watch your back, okay? Watch your back — and if you did take off with this joker, then ditch him and come home just as fast as you can. At this point, I don't think I can keep this under wraps much longer if I don't hear from you, and I'm not even sure if I should. Please, for God's sake, call me."

She deleted the message and sat there, staring at the phone in stunned silence. Only very gradually, as her mind expanded to include the space around her again, did she realize the shower had stopped running and Freddy was nuzzling her hand, trying to get her attention. God, how long had she been reeling in shock?

She went into the cell's call log and deleted the entry for the phone call she had just made, then turned off the phone and dashed across the room to cram it back into the depths of Aaron's bag.

She straightened just as the bathroom door opened, and struck a casual pose, pretending to study an imaginary chip in her fingernail.

"Liv?"

She looked up as if startled. "You can't be done already."

"No, but I need my shaving kit. There's a little bag inside the big one. Would you mind . . . ?"

She turned quickly, her body between him and the bag, and moved her hand as if unzipping it, even though it was already unzipped. She found the shaving kit and left the bag open, so he wouldn't notice that it made a sound closing that it had not made when allegedly opening. Then she took the shaving kit to the bathroom door and handed it to him.

His eyes caressed her face.

She recalled the phone call and shivered in fear. Because she knew all too well that if he wasn't Aaron Westhaven, he could be anyone. Even someone sent to kill her. Why else would he have come to town, looking for her? And with her card in his pocket, the card she'd sent to the real Aaron.

God, she thought, the real Aaron had never arrived. Had this man done something to him? And if so, what?

She faked a smile, but he frowned in reply, as if he could see that something in her eyes had changed. She smiled harder and shoved the shaving kit at him. "Hurry up, will you? I miss you out here."

His worried expression relaxed. And the way he looked at her then made her heart hurt. God, she wanted to stop wondering about him. She wanted to *know*. She wanted the rest of this over with. Maybe there was a chance for that tonight, she realized, an idea taking shape in her mind.

"I won't be long," Aaron said, then backed inside and closed the door.

She leaned closer and called, "I'm going to take Freddy for a quick walk while you finish up."

"Okay."

She ran to the bag and grabbed the phone again. Dialing rapidly, even as she dashed through the cabin, she quietly opened the front door and stepped outside. She didn't even have to call Freddy. He romped out beside her, happy as could be. She pulled the door closed behind her.

It was dark outside — and it being the middle of summer, that meant it was late. She would have to face Tommy all too soon. God, she was nervous. And now she wasn't even sure about her only ally.

The phone at the other end rang and rang, but finally a familiar voice answered. "Kendall."

"Hey," she said. "It's me. Olivia. I got your message. You really think he's —"

292

"I don't know what he is. Are you with him? Please, tell me you're not with him."

"I am, but I'm fine. Look, there's something you don't know. A man broke into my house the other night, after I came to the hospital. He drugged Freddy —"

"No! Are you okay?"

"Yes, fine."

"And Fred? What about Fred?"

"Freddy's fine, too. But still, this guy was demanding something I took for insurance when I left Tommy. And at the very least, I don't think he cared if he had to hurt me, Bryan. But Aaron — I mean, whoever he is — showed up. He beat the guy up, disarmed him, probably saved my life."

"Yeah, ten to one it was the same guy who tried to kill him in the first place. Look, I know you don't want to think about this, but what if whoever sent your amnesiac also sent someone after him when he didn't do the job?"

"To kill him?"

"These guys play hardball, Olivia."

"Yeah, but to *kill* him? Besides, that theory doesn't hold any water at all. How could he have failed to do the job when he only arrived in town that day? He hadn't even met me yet. No, there's something more going on here."

"You need to come in, Olivia."

"I agree. I also need my life back. We're meeting Tommy tonight to trade the disks I stole from him sixteen years ago for his word that he won't come after me."

"That's insane, Olivia. To trust his word —"

"I *don't* trust his word."

"Why on earth are you going, then?"

"Because I want to end this. Listen, here's what I'm thinking. Tommy will have weapons, and he *will* try to hurt me. I *know* he will. So I want you to show up before us, set up an ambush."

"Tommy's a two-time loser," Bryan said slowly.

"That's right, and this will be his third strike. Automatic life sentence. And then I'll never have to worry about him again."

"I think you're brilliant, Professor."

"Well, that's sort of my job, isn't it?"

"You realize I'll have to take your . . . friend in, too."

"He's done nothing illegal, Bryan."

"Nothing we know of."

"You can't arrest a man for doing something you don't know of."

He sighed. "He's wanted by the Feds, Olivia. I don't have any say in the matter. It's out of my hands."

"Not if you don't tell them what we're doing. Look, if you want to talk to him, talk to him. But don't hand him over to anyone else. Or the deal's off."

He was silent for a long moment. "I'll talk to him first. And I'll do the best I can about the rest. I promise. Now when and where is this meeting taking place?"

"Midnight, tonight. The old Campbell farm."

"We'll be there. You be safe in the meantime, Olivia."

"I will. Thanks, Bryan. And . . . look, I like this man. I think he's a good man. And whatever he was before, well, maybe that gunshot changed him somehow."

"You can't know what will happen when his memory returns, though."

"I know. I know. I just . . . Go easy with him, okay?"

"Olivia? You're not —"

"Gotta go before he gets suspicious. Thanks, Bryan." She disconnected quickly, before Bryan could ask the question he was clearly about to.

And she didn't want to think about it any further, nor about how she would have answered.

Instead, she headed back into the cabin, deleted the number from the call log and replaced the phone, zipping the bag closed this time.

She felt terribly guilty for betraying the man she'd just made love with, but she knew — too well — what happened when you trusted a violent man. A ruthless man. An unethical man.

It had nearly cost her her life once. And while she didn't want to think Aaron — or whatever his name was — was a man who deserved any of those labels, she had to take precautions when it came to her own life. She'd fought too hard for it to do otherwise.

They arrived early, and Olivia was stunned to find that the place she had chosen was not as abandoned as she had expected. Instead, there were several cars parked in an untended field, one with music blasting from its sound system. A bonfire was visible in the distance, and a dozen or so partying teenagers stood around it.

The place had been a dairy farm years ago. But the house was long gone, taken out by a freak twister in '95. The family had left, never to return. The farm had been claimed by the county for back taxes a few years later. The barn and outbuildings were sagging as the elements worked steadily, slowly, patiently to reclaim what was left of them. You could almost see it happening, as the vines and bushes rose up along the walls, their fingers reaching out to embrace the wood and creep even onto the rusted metal rooftops, as the moss crept up behind.

There were no longer any driveways, but you could tell where they had once been, because the grass and weeds grew thinner in those areas. One path curved inward toward the largest of the barns, then looped back out again. Another path forked off from it and went around to the side, to where the barn bridge, a now crumbling, earthen ramp, led to the hayloft above. Another ghost of a driveway showed in front of the house, and still another took a twisting course through the field to the pond a few hundred feet from the main road and the foundation that showed where a house had once stood. The kids and their bonfire were out near the pond.

The meeting with Tommy was to take place closer to the road, near the barn.

Olivia hoped the kids were far enough away to be safe. Tommy wouldn't miss their presence and might think it was some kind of a trap. The bonfire was leaping high as its flames reached for the night sky. Their reflection danced on the surface of the water, like some kind of eerie optical illusion. The whole scene looked surreal. "Aaron" parked the SUV at the edge of the path nearest the road, farthest from the pond and the party, and sat there taking it all in. Then he looked at her and nodded. "I thought you said no one would be here? Or did you actually pick this spot because there would be people here? Witnesses."

"No. God, I'd never put kids at risk like that. It's a weeknight, for heaven's sake. I had no idea they'd be here."

"It's still summer vacation," he reminded her. "Weeknights no longer apply."

"I should have thought of that." She was tense, worried, and already regretting her choice to tip off Bryan about this meeting. But Bryan was her friend. Or, like Carrie, as close to a friend as anyone in Shadow Falls was to her. He was a good man and a great cop. Nothing bad would happen to Aaron. Not unless he really was some kind of a criminal and had it coming to him. Still, this was going to be hard. He would be hurt when he learned she'd talked to Bryan behind his back.

Olivia lifted her chin. She had to look out for herself first. She couldn't put her life at risk just because she was falling for this man.

God, she was, wasn't she? She was falling

for him — falling for a man she didn't even know, despite the fact that it felt as if she knew him better than anyone ever could. The truth was, she didn't even know his name.

Then why does keeping things from him feel so wrong?

"Do you think the kids will be at risk?" she whispered.

He nodded. "Your risk goes down by them being here. Theirs goes up. It's a trade-off."

"Forget it, then. Let's leave, let's call Tommy and —"

He put a hand on her thigh. "Easy, babe."

Babe? Lord, he *was* reading a lot into the sex they'd had, wasn't he? Could he really be starting to have . . . feelings for her, too?

"He's not likely to try anything with that many witnesses," he said, keeping his voice low. "He couldn't kill them all, and that's what he would have to do to make it worth his while to kill any of them, *or* either of *us*. You made a good call, choosing this spot. Come on."

"What?"

"Time to get you out of sight."

"Already? It's still early —"

"Trust me, it's time."

"But I told you — he has to know I would insist on coming."

"Yeah, and I'm going to tell him I refused to bring you and see if he'll make the deal anyway. You can get what you wanted. You can see his face — but from some safe vantage point."

She shook her head slowly as she opened the passenger door. "He'll never go for it. And he'll know I'm here."

"Then you'll come out and face him. But only if there's no other choice. Agreed?"

She nodded. "God, my stomach is churning. It feels like an acid factory in there."

"It'll be over soon." He opened his door and got out. She got out, as well, then leaned back in and stroked Freddy. "I'm sorry, boy. It might not be safe. Will you be okay?"

He pawed at the door and whined.

She kissed his nose and put the window down about halfway. Too small an opening for Freddy to get through, but plenty wide enough for him to stick his head out and fresh air to go wafting in for him. "We won't be long, I promise." She took a deep, steadying breath. "I hope."

She took the disks out of the glove compartment, where they were stored in a plastic zipper bag, then straightened, closed the car door and handed them to her mystery lover. "You'll need these."

He took them and nodded toward the barn, which was about halfway between the Expedition and the pond, where the partying kids were beginning to send curious looks in their direction. "Hide just inside the barn, but be careful. It looks like it could come down any minute. Just get out of sight. Don't poke around in there."

"Okay."

She held his eyes and hesitated. God, she felt bad. Had she made a terrible mistake in talking to Bryan?

"Go on. He could be here any minute."

"Okay." Impulsively, she leaned up and pressed her mouth to his. He was stiff at first, barely reacting, but then, just as she started to pull away, his arms snapped around her waist and he bent over her, deepening the kiss, turning it into something . . . incredible. Something that belonged at the end of a Bogie and Bacall flick.

When he lifted his head, she was breathless, her heart was racing, and her eyes were filling with hot tears. Dammit.

He slid the gun he'd taken from her purse into the back of her jeans. He already had his own in the same spot.

Turning, she ran to the crumbling barn and found a suitable hiding place just beyond its broken door. She ducked inside and was immediately startled by motion. Silent flight — something huge. She crouched low as it soared over her head, her mind imagining a giant vampire bat or something equally awful, but it landed on a beam, and she peered up at it. The ghost-face of a barn owl blinked back at her, startlingly creepy-looking, but in truth, perfectly harmless.

She sighed in relief and crouched near the door again, peering outside into the night. She had a perfect view of Aaron — she had to stop thinking of him by that name, dammit. She wondered if she should tell him that he wasn't Aaron Westhaven. He had a right to know.

But she had a feeling he already did. He'd been saying so from the start, hadn't he?

He'd walked away from the SUV and was sitting on a tree stump a few yards off the trail toward the barn. By going to the other wall and ducking down to look out through a gap between the boards, she could also see the party going on several hundred feet to the left.

A few minutes later a black Lincoln Navigator pulled in from the road. It bumped over the path and stopped right beside the barn. All four of its doors opened, and men spilled out. She held her breath as she counted them. Four, including Tommy. They were almost an hour early. And at least three of them had guns.

"Holy shit!"

She jumped and ran to the side wall, bending to look out through the broken boards. She saw two teenagers hunkered down behind a gnarled apple tree whose limbs curved upward and then bowed nearly to the ground, partially concealing them. It was heavy with tiny green apples and thick with leaves. Good cover as they hid from the men outside, but her oughtview of them was unobstructed. And she knew one of them.

Sam Overton, Carrie's son. And his companion was Kyle, the same boy who'd been joyriding with him that fateful day in Professor Mallory's SUV.

"They have guns," she heard Sam say.

"Yeah, and that other car, that's old man Mallory's! Didn't your mom have Prof Dupree take it to her place?"

"Mmm-hmm, and I heard she's been sorta missing ever since. So's that dude we found in the ditch. Mom's worried. The cops are, too."

"Yeah, well, I don't see her. But I think that's the guy right there."

"Yeah, that's him, all right," Sam confirmed. "But who are those other guys?"

"Looks like the freakin' Mafia."

"Something's going down here, dude."

"Think we oughtta call the cops?" Kyle asked.

"Again? My mother's going to have a stroke this time." Sam lowered his head, shook it. "Let's get a closer look."

"Dude, they've got *guns*."

"*Ssshhh!* They're talking!"

Olivia moved to the front of the barn again, sliding the gun from the back of her jeans, and crouched there to watch and listen — and pray.

"Thomas Skinner, I presume?" Adam, who was growing more and more used to thinking of himself by that name, spoke to the only newcomer who was not wielding a handgun. Though he had no doubt the bastard had one on him. Or more than one.

"That's right. Where is she?"

He was a big guy, but not in a good way, Adam thought. He was bulky, and a lot of it was muscle, but there was excess fat, too, and he had that puffy, pasty-skinned look of a man who drank too much, smoked too much and ate too much. His hair was dirty-blond and brush-cut. He had a scar on his chin, and pale blue eyes that didn't look normal or natural in any way. And his raspy voice and yellow-stained teeth gave away his nicotine addiction as much as the smoky smell that clung to him like an aura.

"I decided not to bring her."

"Oh, *you* decided? And you have that kind of pull with her?"

"I don't have any pull with her at all," Adam said, deciding not to antagonize the man. "I've only known her a couple of days. I'm just helping out here."

"You're not helping a damn thing. I came here hoping you'd see my point of view and figuring she'd show anyway. No Sarah, no deal."

Adam shrugged. "Fine. I'll send the disks to CNN or something."

"No skin off my ass, pal." Tommy turned to walk a few steps away, then stopped and bellowed, "Sarah! You'd best get your ass out here, bitch, or I'm gonna have my guys kill your boyfriend."

Adam rolled his eyes, turning and pretending he was about to walk back to his SUV. But as he did, he passed near one of the thugs and easily swung behind the man, gripping him in a solid headlock with one arm and using his free hand to press his gun to the man's temple. "Drop your weapon, and I'm not asking twice."

The other two men leveled their guns at him, but no one fired. They couldn't, not without hitting their cohort. The thug in Adam's grasp dropped his piece. It thudded to the grass. Adam nodded at the other two henchmen. "Now you. Come on, give 'em up or he gets it."

"Do you think they care?" Skinner asked.

"Good point." Adam aimed his gun at the boss, still using the henchman as a shield. "Give them up or *he* gets it," he said.

Skinner held his gaze. The man was trying to read him, Adam knew. He kept his face expressionless, cold as ice, holding the other man's eyes without flinching or blinking. Let this bastard see that he meant business here.

"Okay," Skinner said. "Okay, take it easy."

"We agreed to meet. You and me," Adam said.

"And Sarah," Tommy countered.

"No, we never agreed to that. And these three weren't part of the deal, either. Lose 'em or I walk. And if I walk, you never see those disks."

Tommy slanted a look at his men, then nodded, and they dropped their guns. Then Tommy looked back at Adam. "Now what?"

Adam let go of the man he held and gave him a shove toward the others. "You three, take the Lincoln and go for a ride. You can pick up your boss in twenty minutes. Come back a minute early and I'll shoot him."

The three looked at their boss.

He nodded. "Do it."

They bent, reaching for their weapons.

"Uh-uh-uh," Adam warned. "Leave 'em where they are and just go. You can get 'em when you come back."

Eyes narrowed, they straightened and backed toward the car. Adam wondered if they had other guns in there. Maybe. Probably. But would they risk getting their employer shot? He didn't think so.

He felt a huge surge of relief when they started the Lincoln and drove away, but he tried real hard not to let it show. When they were out of sight, he faced Skinner again, but he still held a gun on the man. "How about you put your guns on the ground, as well? I know you've got some on you."

"How about you just give me my fucking disks and show me where you've got her hidden? Huh?"

"Guns."

"No." Tommy turned. "Is she in the barn? Hey, Sarah, are you in there? I'm coming in. You might as well face me, woman, because this isn't happening until you do."

Adam cocked his gun.

The other man stopped and turned to face him. "I *will* see her."

"Tell me to my face. Did you send the thug who tore up her house?"

"Not directly, no."

"Indirectly, then?"

Tommy tipped his head to one side, gave a noncommittal shrug.

"Explain," Adam said.

The man sighed, clearly unused to being told what to do. But somehow Adam knew how to deal with his kind. It felt as if he'd done it before. Often. It was as familiar as breathing or combing his hair.

"Look, I didn't even care she took those disks in the beginning, you know? She only did it to protect the assholes who were on them."

"Right. She knew the police would take your computer and disks when they searched the place. And she didn't see any reason to put your customers in jail along with you."

Tommy nodded. "She trashed my hard drive, ripped it right out of the damn PC, and took all the disks I had for backup. But I didn't give a shit about that. I didn't need that information anyway."

"Then why are you so desperate for it now?"

308

Tommy lifted his brows. "Have you seen who's on it?"

Adam shook his head, even though it was a bald-faced lie. "No."

"Well, I'll tell you, there are some heavyweights on there. Maybe they were nobodies when they were buying weed from me back in the day. But some of them have risen pretty damn high over the years. Public faces. If the info on those diskettes gets made public, their careers would, you'll pardon the pun, go up in smoke." He laughed softly.

"So you want the disks so you can blackmail people?"

"Oh, I've already *been* blackmailing them."

"How?" Adam asked. "How can you get people to pay for something you don't even have?"

"I don't. I get them to pay me to tell them who *does* have it."

Adam shook his head slowly.

"I tell the rich bastards the disks exist. Then I tell them if they want to know where to find them, they'll have to pay for the information. They pay, and I give them fictional little Professor Dupree's home address."

Adam felt the wind leave his sails. "So

you've known about Olivia for how long?"

"My people tracked her down within two years after she supposedly died. She switched identities with her murdered roomie only a few weeks after she arrived in that hole-in-the-wall town. Did you know that?"

"No," Adam lied. Why tell the man something he didn't already know? he thought.

"I couldn't do anything about it at the time, being incarcerated. By the time I got out, I no longer cared about revenge."

"Bullshit. You've been taking revenge right along, just doing it in a roundabout way," Adam said. "How many people did you tell about her?"

Tommy shrugged. "Three or four."

"How long ago?" Adam demanded.

"All within the last few months," Tommy said, then shrugged. "I needed the money. The economic crunch hit me, too, you know."

Not as hard as Adam would have liked to hit him, though. "Which of them sent that thug to her house?"

"How would I know?"

"I think you know. I think you know exactly who it was."

Skinner shrugged. "Give me my disks and I guarantee it won't be a problem anymore."

"No? You can guarantee me no one is going to try to harass her, hurt her, kill her? No one's going to go after her?"

"I can't guarantee you that. But if I let them know I'm the one with the goods on them — that she doesn't have the disks anymore — why would they bother?"

"In case she looked at the disks. They could kill her just for knowing what's on there."

Skinner lifted his hands, palms up. "Nothin' I can do about that, though, is there? That's out of my hands. Hell, for all you or I know, there might be dozens of people jonesing to murder the traitorous bitch. Way beyond the handful I set onto her trail. Probably every guy she's ever fucked over."

"You know what I'm asking you," Adam said.

The other man sighed. "I'll make sure those who've been told she has the disks know that I have them now. And I won't mention her in any future dealings. Is that good enough?"

"And you won't go after her, either," Adam added. "Or reveal her secret to anyone else — ever."

Tommy shrugged. "I might agree to every last one of those terms — *if* she would show her freaking face and ask me herself."

"That's not going to happen."

The man shook his head slowly. "No Sarah, no deal."

"I'm right here," Olivia said, stepping slowly out of the barn. She met Adam's eyes briefly, sending some kind of message, but one he couldn't read. It seemed to be one of urgency. As if there were some reason to hurry things up.

"Sarah," Skinner muttered. He looked her up and down, blatantly and thoroughly. "Well, you don't look much like a backstabbing whore, even now."

"No? You look *exactly* like a lowlife scumbag, though. I guess I'm better at camouflage than you are, huh?"

"You always were," he said.

She lowered her head briefly, took a few steps closer, stood just beyond what Adam figured was arm's reach from Skinner, then met his eyes again. "I think you and I both know I didn't have any choice but to do what I did to you, Tommy."

"You had a choice."

"Yeah? And if I'd told you I was leaving you, what would you have done?"

He shrugged.

"Come on, Tommy, you broke my arm for burning your toast. You remember that?"

He had enough shame to look away. Briefly, quickly, then he was glaring and belligerent again.

"You'd have killed me. And you know it. I didn't have a choice."

"The choice," Tommy said, "was to stay. Show some fucking loyalty for fuck's sake."

She shook her head. "And let you beat the hell out of me at will? What kind of a life would that have been? Would *you* live like that, Tommy? If some son of a bitch broke your arm for burning the toast, what would you do?"

"I'd kill the bastard," he said. "But I'm a man. It's different."

"Not so different." She lowered her eyes, and her voice as well. "Not so different at all. I got the gun, loaded it. I stood over you while you slept off a drunk one night, and I put the barrel right up to your temple, almost touching, but not quite. I put my finger on the trigger, and I'm telling you, Tommy, I almost did it. I almost shot you. I thought it was the only way."

His eyes widened, and his skin seemed to pale a little in the darkness. He looked as if the wind had been knocked out of him. He said, "I don't fucking believe it," but it was clear that he did.

"Believe it. You'd be dead, and I'd probably be in prison right now if I hadn't been interrupted. I was ready to do it, Tommy. That's how badly I wanted to get away from you. I was going to put a bullet in your head. But just then someone pulled in, one of your regulars, looking to score an ounce. And that's when I got the idea to talk to the cops instead. Not about your abuse. I'd tried that before, and they never listened. You were one of them. You'd spent too long telling them about your half-lunatic girlfriend and her delusions. They didn't believe me. But I could give them evidence of your dealing. I could *prove* that. They *had* to listen to me then, Tommy."

"You're even worse than I ever imagined," he told her.

"And you ought to be on your knees thanking God for that prison sentence," she said. "It's the only reason you're still alive." She moved a step closer, on a roll now.

It seemed to Adam that once she started laying down the law to this bastard, it was like the floodgates opened, and everything that had been churning up her insides came pouring out all at once. "And I'll tell you right now, Tommy, if you start fucking with my life again, I won't make the same call. I *will* kill you this time. I swear to God, I will."

He stared at her as if stunned, as if he'd

never seen her before. "It's almost funny, you threatening me, you know that? Do you really think you're scaring me, Sarah?"

She leaned a little closer. "You just try me, you son of bitch, and I'll scare you plenty."

In one fast move he grabbed her, jerked her right up against him, mashing her face to his chest. Adam reacted, raising his weapon and aiming it, but Skinner quickly spun Olivia around, still holding her hard. He had a fistful of her hair, and he used it to yank her head up and back, so it covered the bulk of his face. Adam couldn't even take a head shot at the bastard.

"Now," Tommy said. "Let's quit with the melodramatic bullshit and get this over with. Give me my motherfuckin' disks."

Suddenly Adam was feeling a panic he didn't think he'd ever felt before. The man could kill her. He could end her life at any second. He had to do something, had to find a way to take the shot. And yet Olivia held his eyes, silently telling him *no*.

"Whoa, whoa, easy now, Skinner. You know damn well I didn't bring them here. You wouldn't have, would you?"

"If you didn't, then *Olivia* is going to cease to exist. Not that she ever really did."

Adam kept the gun on him, holding up

the other hand. "That's not how any sane person would do this and you know it."

"It's how any amateur would have done it, though," Skinner said. "But you're no amateur, are you? No, you're a pro. What did you do, Sarah, find yourself an outlaw a little badder than your ex? Hmm? Did you think he could protect you from me? How much is he milking you for this, anyway?"

She tried to shake her head, but she could barely move it with the gun pressed to her temple as it was. "I didn't hire him. He's not a criminal, not a pro. He's nothing like you."

"Bullshit. I've seen the prick in action, hon. Hell, I'd hire him myself if the situation was different." He met Adam's eyes. "So you figured we'd make a deal and do what? Agree on a location for the drop?"

Adam nodded. "Yeah, that's what I figured."

"Well, you figured wrong." Tommy looked down at Olivia, and his smile was slow and chilled Adam's blood. "Dead wrong. This is *way* overdue. So long, baby." He pressed a kiss to the top of her head, then moved his finger very slightly, but Adam saw it and knew what he was doing. He was going to do it. He was going to kill her!

Adam had to take a head shot, even at the

316

risk of killing her himself. He had no choice. He had to do it now. He leveled the gun, looked down the barrel, lined up the site with Skinner's forehead.

Olivia met his eyes, gave a nearly imperceptible nod and mouthed the words, *"Do it."*

14

Olivia held Aaron's eyes and thought they would be the last thing she ever saw. And as much as she was unsure about him, she knew right then. She *knew*. No matter who or what he was, he was sickened at the thought of Tommy putting a bullet into her skull. His skin had gone white. And his eyes — God, there was so much going on in his eyes. And yet his hand holding that gun was as steady as a rock.

Maybe he could do it. Maybe he could shoot Tommy between the eyes and not hurt her. Maybe he could even do it in time. Because he was her only hope. It was still only a little past eleven-thirty. The cops wouldn't be here until close to midnight.

And then she saw someone — and for some reason she was sure it was Bryan — crouching in the woods between the barn and the road. She wouldn't have seen him if he hadn't moved. He emerged slightly and lifted his gun, and his stance said he was about to spring the trap.

And then she was hit by something that felt like a football tackle. Someone slammed into her from the left, sending her and Tommy both crashing to the ground. Tommy's hand hit the dirt and the gun went off, even as it went flying out of his grip to land in the deep grass, instantly invisible.

She scrambled away from the bastard, moving instinctively toward Aaron, realizing that one of the boys was picking himself up off the ground. Sam Overton. God, he'd saved her life! His friend, Kyle, was lying on his belly, still in the bushes, watching it all with wide eyes.

"Freeze! Police!" Bryan shouted, his voice deep and commanding. "Don't you fucking move a muscle, Skinner. You're completely surrounded."

Tommy froze where he was, still lying in the grass. Sam and his pal went still, too. Olivia didn't. She kept moving, every cell in her body pushing her toward Aaron. He was moving toward her, too, and in seconds his arms came around her and he was holding her, pulling her with him as he ran, even as she struggled to break free so she could check on the boys.

The other cops came out of the night,

dark shapes emerging from the deeper darkness, weapons leveled as they closed in around the little group.

Aaron backed up slowly, his arms tight around Olivia, saying, "Thank God you guys are here," as he did, and with a few steps he and Olivia were *outside* the ever-shrinking circle of peace officers and still moving.

"Aaron, what are we doing?" she whispered.

"Getting the fuck out of here. They're occupied. We're running."

"But we don't have to —"

Suddenly gunshots rang out. Aaron grabbed her around the waist and pushed her to the ground, landing on top of her, one hand covering her head. She tried to peer up to see what was happening as weapons exploded all around her. "What's going on?"

"Skinner's men are back," he whispered harshly. "They were probably hiding somewhere, watching, the whole damn time! I should have figured. Stay down!" As the shots increased in frequency, he pushed her head down harder. She jerked free of him so she could see what was happening, terrified as she saw Sam Overton still lying on the ground, curled around himself, clutching one shoulder, his shirt stained dark with his own blood.

"Sam! Oh, God, Sam's hurt!"

"Come on. Come with me," Aaron said, trying to draw her away.

"That's Carrie's *son!*" she cried. Aaron anchored his arm around her waist and dragged her with him as he crawled, belly to the ground, away from the shootout toward the road.

"We can't just leave them!"

"I'm sure your buddy Kendall has already called for backup by now. They have the thugs outnumbered, anyway, and —"

"There are people hurt! That boy who saved my life just now is the same one who found you in the ditch and saved yours! He's Carrie's son, Aaron, and he's *bleeding!*"

"I saw that. Shoulder wound. He'll be fine."

They were near the Expedition now, swallowed up by the darkness. She heard Freddy barking in a way she'd never heard him bark before. He'd squeezed his huge body as far through the partially open window as he could and was fighting to get farther. No one back by the barn could see them. The shots were coming less frequently as Aaron pulled her to her feet.

"We don't have to keep running now," she rasped, breathless. "I mean, assuming the good guys won back there. We don't have to keep hiding."

"I do." He met her eyes. "You stay. You'll be fine. But I . . . can't."

She blinked up at him, glancing quickly toward Bryan and his men. Even in the darkness, she could tell that some of the cops were cuffing suspects and tending the wounded, while others provided protection by aiming into the bushes where Skinner's remaining men were still hiding and laying down covering fire.

She drew a deep breath, knowing she had to decide fast. But when she tried to think of reasons to go and reasons not to, she could only remember one thing. The look in his eyes when Tommy had held that gun to her head. It had told her all she needed to know. She trusted him.

Amazing, that. She hadn't trusted a man in more than sixteen years. She'd even had her doubts about Bryan.

But she trusted this man — this man whose name she didn't even know. She trusted him completely.

"I'm going with you," she said.

He nodded once. "Then let's go."

■ ■ ■

Adam drove the SUV about a half mile, while Olivia leaned over the back of her seat, hugging her dog around the neck and trying to calm him. He'd done a number on the interior of the car door.

He drove to where he spotted the big black Lincoln Navigator parked on the side of the road. And then he pulled over.

"Why are we stopping?" she asked.

The woman was as tense as a bowstring. And no wonder, having just escaped what had probably been her first shootout. It hadn't been his. He knew it hadn't. It hadn't felt all that shocking or even terribly unusual. He'd known exactly what to do, found himself able to name the weapons being fired by make, model and caliber, been able to spot the shooters by looking for muzzle flashes in the darkness. More than that, it had felt familiar to him. He'd been comfortable and confident. He'd felt at ease. Hell, he'd felt *at home.*

"Why are we stopping, Aaron?" she asked again, then bit her lip, as if wishing she were anywhere but here. Maybe she was finally starting to get that he was no sensitive reclusive novelist.

"The police saw this vehicle," he said. "They'll have the plate number. They'll set up roadblocks, put the word out, and we'll be stopped before we get ten miles. So we're taking the Navigator."

She frowned. "The one Tommy was driving?"

He nodded.

"But won't that just give him another reason to come after me?"

"You think he *needs* another reason? Besides, at this point he's either dead or in custody, so who the hell cares?" He opened the door and got out, hurrying around to the rear to open the liftgate. "Come on, Freddy."

Freddy got out, but he was agitated, pacing and sniffing, scanning the trees all around them. Adam glanced over at the passenger door, gratified to see it opening. Freddy ran over as Olivia started to get out, but when she tried to stand, her knees buckled. She gripped the dog's neck as she sank toward the ground.

Adam lunged forward, grabbing her underneath her arms, hefting her upward again as Freddy danced nervously, so close Adam was almost tripping over him. Olivia leaned against his chest, her arms twisting around his neck. He felt her shaking.

"It's okay. We're all right. And Tommy is going to do some serious time for this. They caught him holding a gun to the head of an innocent woman. He fired his weapon at police officers. His guns can't be legal. And he crossed state lines with them so he could do all of that. You don't have to worry about him anymore, Liv. Not for a long, long time, anyway — if ever."

She nodded stiffly. Then she lifted her chin, tipping her head up to look at him. "What about Sammy? He was shot. I saw him on the ground, and he was bleeding."

"Yeah, and I told you, it looked like a shoulder wound. He's going to be fine."

"I have to be sure."

He nodded. "Let's get out of here first." Shifting her to his side, he kept one arm around her shoulders, steadying her and walking as fast as he dared to the Lincoln. He opened the passenger door and helped her in. "Buckle up."

"You think they left the keys?"

He nodded. "I don't think it, I *know* it. Just like I knew it would be unlocked."

"How?" she asked.

He shrugged. "Suppose the guy with the keys in his pocket gets shot? Suppose they have to make a fast escape? What are they gonna do? No, guys like these don't take those kinds of chances. Trust me, there's a key." He closed her door, went to the rear and opened the hatch. Freddy was standing a few yards away now, having found a good tree for his purposes, apparently feeling his owner was safe for the moment. That was reassuring.

"Hurry it up, Fred. We've got to move."

The dog responded as if he knew exactly what Adam had said and came loping over. Adam patted the floor of the cargo hold and said, "Come on, Freddy. Get in."

The dog looked at him, his head slowly tilting to one side.

"Freddy, up!" Olivia said, her voice deep, even if trembling.

Freddy instantly put his front feet up onto the car.

Bending, Adam cupped his hands, slid them under one of the dog's hind feet and lifted. Freddy pushed off with his help and, after a slip or two, managed to get inside. Adam was stunned all over again by how damned *big* the dog was. "You're a monster, you know that?" He patted the dog on the head. "Lie down now. Everything's fine."

Freddy began sniffing his new digs as Adam closed the hatch and moved to the driver's side, running his hand under the edge of the wheel wells as he went and finding a magnetic key holder under the front fender.

He pulled it out, snapped it open and took out the key. "Told you," he said, leaning in to show her his prize. "We'll go in a minute. I just need to hide the Expedition before we go."

"We don't have time to —"

"If the cops find it abandoned, they'll know we took something else. And how hard will it be to figure out that the only other vehicle around would have been whatever Tommy and his boys arrived in? And how fast do you think Tommy will tell them the make, model and plate number?"

"You're right. I'm glad you thought of that."

He nodded at her, then smiled a little. "Okay, wait right here."

He quickly drove the Expedition as deeply into the woods as he could get it before his way was blocked by densely growing trees. Then he ran back to the Lincoln, hearing sirens as he got in.

"Duck," he said, as he cupped the back of her head and pushed her forward. He bent low beside her. "Freddy, lie down!" he called, using the same firm tone she did when giving commands.

He heard the dog move, knew he had

obeyed, and waited. Within seconds a parade of emergency vehicles screamed past, bathing them in strobes of red and blue, and stabbing at their ears with their sirens. Police cars. Lots of them. Ambulances, too.

"They'll have roadblocks set up before we know it," he said, sitting up as soon as the din passed them by. "We need to move, and we need to be smart about it." He put the vehicle into gear and drove. "Look around, see if you can find a road map."

He could manage without one, but the hunt gave her something to do. And he knew she was practically holding her breath, just as he was, as they navigated their way out of the mountains. She found a map, opened it and directed him toward the nearest highway, skipping from one back road to another. They didn't encounter anyone along the way, because they avoided the roads that connected the mess they'd left behind to the local cops.

When they finally hit the highway, he headed south, and she looked over at him. "Philly, then?" she asked.

He nodded.

"Yeah. I'll relax once we get out of Vermont. A little bit, anyway."

"How far before you think we're in the clear?"

"I don't know, but we should be safe, so long as we're quick." He looked more thoroughly around the vehicle and pointed. "This thing has a GPS."

"I think it's pretty standard in high-end cars these days," she said.

"What was the address we found inside the watch, again?"

She frowned as she tried to remember, then shook her head. "You have the paper?"

"Yeah." He dug into a pocket and found it, handed it to her. She inputted the information and watched the screen for a second or two, then nodded. "It's only seven hours and twenty minutes from here. We'll be there by morning."

"Then settle in and relax, hon. We're on our way."

She sighed, leaning back in her seat and closing her eyes, then sitting up straight again. "I can't relax. Not until I get some things off my chest. But first I have to ask — why are you still running?"

He lowered his head briefly. "I still don't know who I am, what I did. I need to find that out before . . . anything else."

"I can accept that." She lifted her chin and stared straight ahead, not meeting his eyes. "I checked my messages while you were in the shower."

He felt his eyebrows rise. "And?"

"There was one from Bryan."

He had a good idea what was coming next, so he spoke before she could. "He found out who I am, didn't he?"

"No. But he found out who you aren't. He said he knew for sure that you aren't Aaron Westhaven. He said the serial number from the plate in your head belongs to a man who was killed in Desert Storm. He thought they misread one of the digits or something, but he's having trouble finding out more, because the FBI has taken over the case."

He looked at her slowly. "The FBI."

She nodded. "And if you aren't Aaron, then I can only think of one reason why a stranger would show up in town looking for me."

He blinked, but it wasn't anything he hadn't considered himself. "You thought I was working for Tommy Skinner."

She nodded. "I had to consider the possibility."

"It would explain my . . . unusual skill set."

"Yes, it would. But Tommy didn't know you."

"No. He didn't recognize me, that's true. But he claimed he wasn't out to get you, that it was someone on those disks."

She nodded. "The senator?"

"Or someone else who's wealthy and powerful, but maybe not famous enough for us to recognize the name. Or maybe someone we haven't gotten to yet. Someone who hired me to do his dirty work."

Sighing, she said, "I don't believe it. I don't believe you were sent to Shadow Falls to hurt me. I just don't. I *know* you."

He felt sick to his stomach with guilt, because he *did* believe it.

"But I did consider it at first," she went on. "So I told Bryan about the meeting. I thought . . . I thought he would arrest Tommy and take you back to Shadow Falls, and maybe I could finally figure out the truth." She didn't look at him as she lowered her head, bit her bottom lip. "I'm sorry. I'm so sorry."

He nodded as he took everything in. Then he said, "I wasn't entirely honest with you, either."

"You weren't?"

"No. I, um . . . I didn't trust you any more than you trusted me, Liv. I told you the meeting was set for midnight, but it wasn't. Skinner wasn't early, he was right on time. I set it for eleven-thirty, then told you twelve. It was almost automatic, but partly, I wasn't sure you wouldn't do just what you did, or even try to go without me and handle the whole thing yourself."

She sighed, and it sounded like a sigh of relief. He looked her way, and she did look easier. "I guess we've both messed up a little bit. And it nearly got us killed."

He nodded.

"There's nothing else," she said. "I've got no more secrets from you."

"That's good to know."

She said nothing, waiting, he knew, for him to reciprocate in kind. But he couldn't. The dreams, the snippets of memory, his belief that he was some kind of a hit man . . . those were things he still couldn't bring himself to tell her. She believed in him. She *wanted* to believe in him. And he found himself in a quandary, because he wanted her to believe in him, too. It mattered to him what she thought of him.

She was asking him to open up, to tell her everything. But he had to hold back, just for a little bit longer. Just until he was sure.

Something had changed in him, back there at that abandoned old farm. When Skinner had been holding her, hurting her, pressing that gun to her head, when he'd thought she might not leave that starlit midnight meadow alive, something inside him had altered irreversibly, he thought. Every thought, every instinct, every skill, every *molecule,* in him had joined in one goal, and one goal only. To keep her alive. To protect her. To save her.

He hadn't spoken a word, and minutes had ticked past. Finally she nudged him. "Is there anything you haven't told me?"

He nodded.

"Are you going to?"

"Yes. Yes, I am. But for now, just the one thing. I think my name is Adam, because I had a dream, and in the dream, a man was calling me by that name."

"Does it *feel* like your name?" she asked.

"Yeah. It does."

"Adam. That's nice."

"Thanks." He drove, saying no more.

"Was there anything else to the dream? Any other revelations?"

"No."

She tipped her head to one side, and when he glanced at her, she looked worried. She said, "You know what I find fascinating, Adam?"

"No, what?"

"That we've only known each other for a short time, but I can already tell when you're lying."

She drew a deep breath, sighed and

reached down beside her seat. A moment later she apparently found what she sought, because her seat reclined slowly, and she leaned back, closing her eyes.

"Are you okay?" he asked softly. "After all that — ?"

She opened her eyes. "I'm . . . I'm relieved." Then she sat up a little. "Tommy's going to be locked up. He can't hurt me anymore. I faced him down, and I won. And maybe someone is still after me, or maybe Tommy will try to hurt me from behind bars, and maybe my secrets will be revealed to the whole world. But I feel like I can face anything now. I'm going to be okay." She smiled. "I've got my life back. *You* gave me my life back. Thank you for that . . . Adam."

She leaned her head back and closed her eyes again. Adam kept driving. The FBI was looking for him. He'd evaded the police. He had a steel plate in his head that belonged to a dead man. And he didn't know who the hell he was — or what. Only that he was accustomed to violence, to evasion, to deception, to weaponry, to combat, to escape — and to killing.

He was scared to death of what he would find when he got to that address in Philadelphia. There would be no more hiding the truth from her — or from himself — then.

■ ■ ■ ■

She felt the car come to a stop, the cessation of movement making its way through her sleepy brain and into her consciousness. Then the sound of the motor died, too, giving way to a silence broken only by a soft whine from Freddy.

She opened her eyes, picked up her head and turned toward Aaron — no, Adam. She had to get used to that. "Are we there?"

"No. I found a pet-friendly motel. I can't drive any farther without a few hours' sleep."

She nodded, surprised that she had fallen asleep, with all that had happened. And she'd obviously slept for a while, too. Beyond him, the sky was growing pale with the approach of dawn. "What time is it? Where are we?"

"We only have a couple of hours to go. I just thought — we don't know. The Feds might be watching the place, if they have the address, too."

"Then wouldn't it be better to arrive in the dark?"

"We'd never spot them in the dark. They have the advantage if they're surveilling the place, waiting for us to show. So we go by in the daylight, surveil it ourselves a little, see if it's being watched before we go inside."

She narrowed her eyes on him. "You say that with a lot of confidence."

He glanced at her quickly. "Yeah. I've told you. I trust my instincts," he said. "They haven't led us wrong so far."

"Oh. I was wondering if it might be because you've remembered something more."

"It's not."

She nodded, but she still looked at him *hard,* as if she could see the truth seeping from his pores. It made him want to avert his face.

"Do you, though? Remember more?"

"No." A dream wasn't exactly a memory, was it? So he wasn't really lying to her. Just leaving out some things. "I'll book us a room. We'll keep paying cash."

"We've got plenty," she said.

He nodded and reached for his door handle. But her hand on his shoulder stopped him, made him turn back to face her again.

"I'm putting a lot of trust in you . . . Adam."

"I know." He held her eyes for a long moment. "And I know what a huge thing that is for you, to trust a man. I don't take it lightly."

She nodded. "Get two rooms," she told him. "But only if they have an adjoining door."

He guessed her trust in him only went so far. She must have no interest in any further sex with him now that she knew he wasn't her favorite writer. He lost a little bit of respect for her, knowing that. Wasn't he the same guy he'd been before she knew? Hadn't he just saved her life, gotten her out of a hellish situation without a scratch on her smooth, copper-kissed skin?

He got out of the car and went inside, feeling insulted and a little bit pissed off. But he made the request she'd asked him to, and returned with two room keys, marked 3 and 4. He slapped them onto the dash and drove to the parking spot in front of Room 3.

"You're tired," she said.

Like she cared. "Yeah, I'm tired." Did that sound a little sarcastic? A little snippy?

She frowned at him, but when he didn't even return her gaze, she shrugged as if in helplessness, grabbed a key off the dash and opened her door. Then she went to the back and opened Freddy's. "Come on, boy. You poor thing, cooped up in there all this time.

Come on, baby. Come on."

Freddy rose, stretched and stepped down from the rear. He looked around, and so did Olivia. But there was nothing to see but the blacktopped parking lot and the sidewalk that ran in front of the rooms. Every other room had a tree growing in front of it from a circular hole in the otherwise unbroken pavement. There were flowers surrounding each tree. Pansies and petunias in thick, lush bunches, so thick you couldn't see the ground beneath them, their purples and yellows soothing somehow.

"That's really pretty the way they — Oh." She stopped speaking as Freddy walked purposefully up to the flowers and lifted his leg to water them.

She grinned, shaking her head, and looked at Adam.

He didn't share her private amusement, though. He just unlocked the door to *his* room, then walked back to the Lincoln to grab their luggage — and then realized they didn't have any. It was all still in the Expedition.

Freddy came running back to Olivia at her call, and the two went inside through the door Adam had just opened.

He shook his head and followed.

"Look, Adam, there's a dog bed — and

dishes, too!"

"Yeah." He glanced at the padded doggy bed on the floor. Brown plush, thick and cozy, and he thought it would only hold about half of Freddy's massive body. Fred preferred to be in bed beside his doting owner, though, so it probably didn't matter.

"And a back door. I need to see if . . ." She crossed the room toward the door in question as she spoke, flinging it open and looking outside. "Oh, this is perfect, I didn't realize. Freddy, come!"

The dog loped to her side and peeked out, and she stretched out her arm and pointed. "Go outside. Run, Freddy, run!"

With a happy "woof," Freddy bolted.

Curious to see that what had made the dog so happy, Adam opened the door to the second room, a twin of the one they were in, and joined her in the doorway. Behind the motel, a grassy lawn stretched out in either direction, completely surrounded by a shiny new chain-link fence. A wooden stand in a far corner held a trash can, a few scoopers and a sign that read Clean Up After Your Pet.

Freddy was running from one end of the lawn to the other, pausing to sniff at places where other dogs had left their scents, then spinning around and galloping off again so fast he nearly tripped over his own legs.

Adam couldn't help but smile at the dog's antics. His attitude relaxed a little, and he turned to look at Olivia. She was leaning in the doorway, watching her dog with the most loving expression on her face.

Imagine her looking at me that way.

Whoa, where the hell had that come from?

He shook himself, blinking, not sure what had come over him.

"I guess that second room and adjoining door were unnecessary after all," she said softly. "Freddy will be happy right out there."

He frowned. "The second room was for *Freddy?*"

She looked up into his face, her brown eyes dancing. "Oh, hell. You thought I wanted it for me, didn't you?"

He nodded.

She smiled a soft, romantic smile that was designed, he was sure, to make him turn to mush. He was not, he told himself, a mushy-turning kind of a guy.

"You thought I only slept with you because I believed you were my favorite writer. And that now that I know better, I wouldn't want to be with you again. Which would make me a pretty lousy person. Is that what you think of me, Adam?"

Her hand had curled around his nape, her fingers moving lightly over his skin, and he was fighting the urge to close his eyes, tip his head back and moan softly.

"I don't know what I was thinking. Just that it wasn't me you wanted. It was him."

"It was you." She stared into his eyes to emphasize the words, then went on. "Freddy's been cooped up for days now. I just thought with two connected rooms, he'd at least have a little room to romp. And a bed of his own, since we left his in the other SUV. That's all." She leaned up a little, brushed his mouth with her lips. "And I have to admit, I thought the notion of giving the big lug a bed all to himself would give us a little more room for . . . whatever."

His lips curved into a smile that felt a little crooked and a little goofy, but he didn't care. He stopped arguing with himself about what was wise and slid his arms right around her waist, pulling her close. And then he bent his head and kissed her, long and deep. She opened her mouth to him and their tongues mated, and he knew she still wanted him, maybe more than before. He could tell by the way she arched her hips against him. He was hard before the first kiss melded into the next.

He reached out to close the door. She

caught his hand and stopped him, muttering an explanation between kisses. "I want him to be able to get back in when he's ready."

"He'll be fine."

She shook her head beneath his mouth. "It's a new place. He'll be scared."

The notion of a two-hundred-pound mastiff getting scared almost made him laugh, but he didn't want to ruin the mood. Whatever Olivia wanted was perfectly fine with him, as long as she was going to give him another taste of her glorious body and another round of her enthusiastic passion.

Turning her toward the bed, he shuffle-walked with her, never breaking the contact of their lips. At the bed, she fell backward, pulling him down on top of her, and they made out like a pair of horny teenagers.

Twenty minutes later Freddy came loping through the door and right up to the bed, where he paused, staring at them. He lifted one paw, set it on the mattress and waited, a question in his eyes, brows crooked as if he were human.

"Go lie down, Freddy," Olivia said, pointing toward the second room as she grabbed a pillow and threw it at the back door. It connected, and the door closed with a bang. Freddy jumped, barked once at the noise,

342

then calmed again. With a giant sigh, he plodded into the adjoining room, and a moment later Adam heard the bedsprings creak beneath his weight.

About ten seconds after that, the sound of his chain-sawlike snoring filled both rooms.

Adam laughed in midkiss. She was laughing, too, and he realized this was something he was sure he'd never done before, even without his memory. Laughing while making love. They'd laughed the first time, too. It felt different. More intimate, somehow, than the sex act itself.

The outside door was closed now, the dog settled. No more reason to extend the pregame show, although he had to admit he was enjoying the hell out of it. But already she was squirming out of her clothes and tugging at his. So he helped, and with a bit more wiggling they were both naked and twined around each other again. He found her wet and eager, and sliding inside her, he felt a rush of sensation that was almost beyond endurance. And it was more than physical, dammit — though he told himself that realization would have to wait until later to scare the hell out of him.

And it would. He knew damn well it would.

But right at that moment, he didn't particularly care.

15

She lay curled in his arms, her head on his chest, his heartbeat thrumming in her ear. And she felt things she didn't think she ought to be feeling. She'd only known him such a short time. And to be honest, she'd been experiencing this onslaught of tenderness toward him from the beginning. But she'd written it off to empathy for his plight, to identifying with his situation — feeling hunted, having to hide. Those were things she understood all too well. Anything beyond that . . . she'd written off those emotions, as well. She'd told herself it was normal to feel so close to the man who wrote the novels that had fed her lonely soul for so long.

But none of those things explained the level to which her feelings had soared tonight. She knew he wasn't the author of the books she loved. She knew he might very well be more perpetrator than victim in whatever had befallen him. And yet there was this softness in the very center of her heart — a place that had been, she was certain, hard and numb before. What had been like the pit of a barely ripe peach had become the soft, warm, gooey middle of a fine chocolate truffle, and she could tell there would be no going back ever again.

She lay there on his chest feeling warm all over, one leg over his so she could rub her smooth calf over his hairy shin and enjoy the delicious contact.

He squeezed her a little closer, his arm around her shoulders, and she sighed. Then the sigh formed words, and the words were, *"I love you."*

She bit her lip, and her eyes popped open wide. She felt him tense beneath her and wished she could suck the words back, but there was no way. She'd said it. She didn't even know for sure if she meant it, but she'd said it. There was no taking it back now.

"You know that's not really possible, right?" he asked, after a moment of what had to be stunned silence.

"I didn't mean to say it. Really, I didn't. It was some kind of a . . . a . . . tic. A spasm."

"A spasm," he repeated.

"Like when you get a muscle twitch."

"Right, or a hiccup."

"Exactly. Just treat it like a hiccup and forget it."

"Not such an easy thing to forget. But like I said, pretty much impossible. I mean, you don't know me. Hell, *I* don't know me."

She swallowed hard and lifted her head to stare into his eyes. "I know you," she whispered.

He held her gaze for a long moment, but she said nothing more. It was the truth. She *did* know him. Not the minutiae of his life. Not the stats, the history, the details. *Him.*

He was a good man. An honest man. A brave one, and yes, perhaps a violent one, too, when it was called for. And skilled at it. But she didn't think he was the kind who would wield that skill against an innocent. He certainly hadn't done anything but watch out for and protect her.

And Freddy loved him.

Really, that said it all. He couldn't be dangerous to her, not in any way, or Freddy would know and wouldn't have tolerated him coming anywhere near her.

Then again, she thought with a little chill, Freddy wouldn't know if he posed a threat to her heart. That kind of danger wouldn't be so easy for her best friend to sense. And it wasn't the kind of thing he could protect her from, either.

She snuggled closer. Adam hadn't bolted from the bed at her impulsive declaration, and she took that as a good sign. She hadn't scared him too badly. Then again, he didn't scare easily.

"Get some sleep, if you can," he said at length.

She interpreted. "You mean you don't want to talk about emotional stuff anymore tonight. That it was just sex, and I shouldn't read anything more into it. And that you need a whole lot more time to process that stupid declaration I just made before you can even begin to know how to respond."

He rolled onto his side and stared into her eyes for one long, silent moment. "No. I meant what I said. You should get some sleep if you can. We have a big day tomorrow, and we can't stay here long before we need to get going again."

She blinked at him. "So you really don't want to talk about . . . this?"

"I don't know what there is to talk about. We had sex. It was great. Aside from that —"

"Oh, is that how it is?"

"Is *what* how it is? What do you want me to say? I don't even know who I am, Liv. Or what I do, or where I live, or if I'm married with six kids, for God's sake."

"What does any of that have to do with how you feel?"

"It has to do with where I'm coming from."

"But how do you *feel?*"

She was pushing, she knew it, and she didn't like it, and yet something was driving her. Some irrational part of her she felt she barely knew was pushing her to push him.

He shook his head. "I feel good. Satisfied. Relaxed."

"About me," she persisted.

He drew a deep breath, then let it out slowly. "I like you. I think you're beautiful and smart and very brave. And I think you've been hiding in a self-created shell for a long time, and that this is the first time you've allowed yourself to be coaxed out of it. I think you're living for the first time in a long time — really living. And parts of it aren't so good. Guns and killers and shoot-outs. And other parts are very good. Attraction and sex and excitement. And I think that this is like a thrill ride to you, and I think you're going to want to settle back down into the mundane life of a college professor in a small New England town when it's over."

She listened, nodding slowly, and when he finished, she said, "But how do *you* feel about *me?*"

He rolled his eyes. "Go to sleep, Olivia. And hold off on being too sure about those feelings of yours, at least until we find out who and what I really am. For your own good. Okay?"

"I'm not sure I have much of a choice in the matter, to be completely frank. I mean, it's not like I analyzed the situation and *decided* to fall in love with you, you know."

He frowned at her as if she were speaking some unknown dialect, then shook his head as if giving up on her completely and rolled onto his side, facing her. He hooked an arm around her and closed his eyes.

Ten minutes later he was snoring almost as heavily as Freddy was. And she lay there wondering if any of what she'd said tonight had made any sense at all. Because he didn't seem to think it did. And she wasn't so sure herself.

At 5:00 a.m. he was still awake. He hadn't really slept, only pretended to, so she would stop with the talk about *feelings.* Once Olivia had finally fallen asleep, he'd alternated between lying on his back, staring through the darkness at the ceiling, and lying on his side, staring at her face. Both objects of his attention gave him equal amounts of clarity. Zip.

How did a woman swear off men for sixteen years to keep herself safe, then fall in love with a complete stranger? How did she hold everyone she knew at arm's length, and fall for the first guy she let herself get close to? How did she stop trusting males so completely, only to give her trust to the guy who was probably less deserving of it than anyone she knew?

Was she that self-destructive?

And why was it bothering him so much? He ought to just write it off to female insanity and let it go. If she was fool enough to think she loved a man she didn't know, then she deserved whatever she got, right? Including a broken heart.

So then why was he so damn nervous about what they were going to find in Philadelphia? It wasn't that he was afraid of learning the truth. Whatever it was, he would deal with it. It would be better than not knowing.

He was actually obsessing, he realized, about what *her* reaction to the truth about him would be.

And as much as the potential outcomes wanted to take turns racing through his mind, he knew there was only one way to find out, and that was to get on with it.

They'd solved her biggest problem: Tommy Skinner. Maybe someone else was after her, and maybe not, but he knew he could keep her safe as long as she was with him. So now it was time to solve his biggest problem — he just hoped it wasn't going to unleash a whole passel of new ones.

He slid out of bed, careful not to wake her, and she rolled onto her side, stretching one arm and one leg out from beneath the covers in a pose worthy of a centerfold before settling more deeply into sleep again. He stood beside the bed looking down at her and thinking he wanted to climb right back in, kiss her awake and have another round of incredible sex.

Unfortunately, that would likely result in her wanting him to talk about his feelings some more, and he didn't want to hear it. Not now, not when he still thought he might be a hired gun sent to kill her.

Freddy bumped him in the hip with his giant head, and he looked down to see the dog staring at him with a look of impatience in his eyes. He could have been thinking Adam was an idiot not to declare his undying love just to keep this smart, beautiful, sexy woman by his side for as long as possible. But it was more likely, Adam thought, that the dog just needed to go outside.

He opened the door to let him, and then he hit the shower.

Two hours later, they were on their way.

He'd intended to be under way much sooner, but she'd had other ideas. She'd lingered in the shower, then insisted on buying fresh meat for Freddy as a special treat, and after feeding him, she'd spent forty-five minutes romping through a vacant field with him. When that was done, she'd started chirping about needing coffee until they stopped at a Dunkin' Donuts for a vat-size mugful and a breakfast sandwich.

And then, *finally,* they drove the last hundred miles into Philadelphia, the GPS directing them in its calm, steady voice. Something in Adam's mind seemed to perk up as they ate up the distance to their destination.

"It feels familiar, doesn't it?" she asked.

He nodded, barely hearing her through the rush of sensations swirling through his mind. The neat sidewalks, the buildings, the smells. He nodded. "This is where I live." And then he felt a smile pull at his lips. "There's a bar around that corner — Paulie's Pub."

He turned the corner, pointing, and she spotted the name on the sign. "Oh, my God, you're right," she breathed. "You're remembering!"

"I don't know. I mean, I know it's there. And that I've been there. And I know I like it because people mind their own business there. But I don't remember anything specific."

"No? What's it like on the inside?" she asked.

As soon as she asked the question, he could see the inside of Paulie's. The round amber globes over the low-hanging ceiling lights that gave the place a quiet ambience. He saw the bar stools, burgundy leather upholstery and antique-looking gold-toned tacks holding it in place. He saw the horseshoe-shaped bar and the mirrored wall behind it, the racks on that wall filled with bottles and glasses.

But before he could relate any of it to her, the GPS was interrupting. "You have reached your destination."

He blinked, his eyes shooting first to the dashboard and then to the buildings around him. One stood out. It wasn't redbrick like everything else on the block. It was reddish-tinted concrete, with a pair of matching cement lions guarding the double doors. The circular drive was brick, though, curving around a giant fountain that stood between the building and the street.

"That's it," he said. "That's where I live."

She lifted her brows. "It looks like a hotel."

"Condos. And I own the penthouse."

She stared at him, blinking.

He swallowed hard. "I can almost see inside it."

"You can *actually* see inside it," she said. "You have the key, remember?"

He nodded, cruising slowly past the building, tearing his eyes from it to look at the other vehicles on the street. He saw no sign of surveillance. No FBI types seemed to be watching. There wasn't much traffic, and anyone parked, or just sitting or standing, nearby and trying to look inconspicuous would be easily spotted. There was no one.

"I don't see anyone suspicious," she muttered, her eyes wide, taking in everything, watchful. Her body had gone tense.

"No, I don't, either. Nothing that looks like an unmarked car. No one pretending to read a newspaper on the bus stop bench. No one just standing around looking bored."

"But what if they're inside?" she asked. "In the building across the street or something?"

He looked up at the windows near the tops of the buildings but didn't see anyone looking back at him. "I don't know if there's any way we can be sure of that. But I have a feeling no one knows where I live."

"No one?" She frowned at him. "Why would you think that?"

He shrugged. "If everyone knows where you live, you probably don't feel any pressing need to write your address down and hide it in the back of a pocket watch for ID."

She nodded slowly. "I guess not."

"I think it's a rule I have. Keep your home address to yourself. Tell no one." Just like the other rule he'd remembered. Never get involved with a mark. Hell.

She watched him drive as he circled the block. "Okay, there's the underground garage. I'm not going to park in there just yet. Too vulnerable." Instead, he pulled the oversize SUV into an open spot in front of a meter a block away from the building. He dug around in the glove compartment, found a bandana and tied it around his head. He also found a pair of sunglasses and slid them onto his face. Then he looked at her. "Ready?"

"I guess so." She searched the console between the seats and helped herself to a handful of the quarters lying in one of the cupholders. "Let's go."

They got out, and she went to the back to

356

let Freddy out, as well. Adam felt as if his stomach was digesting itself. His past was right there, right at the tip of his memory, about to burst forth full-blown. He felt it, sensed it, didn't doubt it. And yet he also dreaded it as he stood there, waiting while Olivia fed the meter. Then, to his surprise, she came up beside him and closed her hand around his. Freddy trotted over to take up a position on his other side. He realized he was flanked by a woman and a dog who both loved him, and it was the most foreign thing he'd ever felt.

Maybe he was more like that fictional Harvey what's-his-name than he'd known, he thought. Maybe he was used to living his life alone.

"It's going to be okay," Olivia said. "I know it is."

"I hope so." He let himself squeeze her hand as they walked back down the block to his building. Freddy stayed right by his side, despite the absence of a leash and all the exciting new scents around him.

He went to the door, wondering how the hell he was going to get in, looking for a keypad or a magnetic key reader or something he would be unable to access. But before he could even finish his assessment, the doors were opening, and a uniformed doorman greeted him with a smile.

"Mr. Adams, welcome home. I trust you had a good trip?"

He blinked at the man. God, what kind of man gave his own doorman a phony name? "It was . . . eventful."

The doorman frowned. "I'm sure you're glad to be back." Then he nodded at Olivia. "Ma'am. That's one beautiful dog you have there."

"I hope it's all right to bring him inside," she said. "He's very well behaved."

"I can see that," the doorman said. "And around here, anything Mr. Adams wants is all right with us." He sent Adam a wink, as if he should have known that was the case.

She nodded and smiled, then spotted the elevators and let Adam know with a single swift look. He followed her cue and saw that one of them was marked Private.

She beamed at the doorman again. "I swear, his manners sometimes . . . I'm Olivia, and this is Freddy. You are . . . ?"

"Billy."

"Good to meet you, Billy. So is that private elevator ours?"

Adam squirmed a little at the word *ours*, then pretended to be distracted by something outside, so Billy would be forced to answer.

"Yes, ma'am, that's the one. You have your key, sir?"

Unsure, Adam pulled the key ring from his pocket.

The man looked at the key, then at Adam. "No, I meant the keycard for the elevator." Then he looked harder. "Are you all right, sir?"

"Mr. Adams had an accident. He was pretty banged up, and he's been a little disoriented since. I imagine the keycard is lost for good."

"Why didn't you say so?" The doorman's eyes widened, then he pulled on a ribbon that led to his pocket, and out came several keycards, all clipped together. Fanning them out, he found the one with the P on it and hurried to the elevator, sliding it through the reader.

There was a ping, and the doors opened. Billy stood there holding them open, smiling as Adam, Olivia and Freddy, who looked warily around the car first, stepped inside.

"You just let me know if you need anything, sir. Anything at all. I'm sorry about your accident."

He meant it, Adam realized. "Actually, I don't want anyone to know I'm here."

"Absolutely, sir. You can count on my discretion, as always."

"Thanks. Has anyone been here looking for me. Asking about me?"

"No, sir. No one."

"You let me know if anyone does, okay?"

"Immediately, sir. As always."

Adam nodded and said, "Thanks for going above and beyond," one hand automatically slipping toward his pocket, before he remembered he didn't have any cash there.

But before he could confirm that, Billy was holding up a hand and shaking his head. "No need, sir. You go on, get some rest. I hope you feel like yourself again soon, sir."

"Thanks, Billy."

Billy nodded, reached inside the car and pushed the P button, then backed out again as the doors slid closed.

The car swept them upward at a rapid, nonstop pace that made Freddy tense and whine up at Olivia. Then it stopped smoothly, and the doors opened again to reveal a foyer of sorts. A couple of claw-legged, brocade-covered chairs flanked a sofa table with no sofa. A huge arrangement of fresh flowers took up most of the table-top, reflected in the high mirror behind it.

Freddy bounded out of the elevator, spun to look back at it and released a small woof, as if telling it off. Adam stepped out more slowly and stood for a moment staring at the door to his home. It wasn't as ornate as he'd expected. Just a plain, darkly stained, rich wood grain door with layers of shellac making it shine.

He jumped when the elevator doors slid closed behind him, too intent in his contemplation of the door to have noticed anything else. The doorway to his life. The portal to his past. All of his memories, and the truth about who and what he was, lay beyond that door. And suddenly he was cold to the bone and nauseated to boot.

Olivia's hand slid up his arm to rest on his shoulder. "You're scared, aren't you?"

He looked down at her. "I don't want to walk in there and find out that I'm a piece of shit."

"A piece of shit wouldn't be bothered by finding out he was one," she said.

He frowned. "You're going to need to translate that."

"I mean, if you were a piece of shit, you wouldn't be worried about it. You wouldn't care. The fact that you want to be a good person tells me that you *are* one."

"Maybe I am now. Maybe I wasn't before."

"I don't think people really change all that

much. You are who you are, memory or not."

"I don't think that's true. Look at you. Would you be who you are without your memories? Hell, your past has formed your entire life. Even your identity."

She held his eyes. "You're delaying the inevitable."

"Okay." He took out the key and walked right up to the door, feeling as if he were about to unlock a cage that held a deadly beast. He didn't know why he was so unsure about what he was about to find. He already had a pretty good idea, didn't he? Of course, he was hoping there would be a logical explanation for all of it. That he wasn't going to turn out to be a hired thug who killed for money. But he was pretty sure that was exactly what he was. Or what he'd been. And then he would lose her.

And he cared about that, he realized slowly.

He put the key into the lock, turned it, heard the tumblers fall. Closing his hand around the doorknob, he twisted it and pushed. The door opened a few inches. He paused and looked down at her. "Whatever we find in here, Olivia, I want you to know that I . . . I like you."

"You *like* me. Gee, thanks."

"I care about you. I've become really invested in making sure you're safe. And I would never hurt you, not on purpose. Whatever I might have been in the past, whatever I might have done . . . or planned to do . . . those things are true. And they'll remain true. I'm not faking anything here. Okay?"

She frowned deeply at him. "Okay."

He steadied himself, lifted his chin and opened the door.

Olivia tried to calm her nerves as they stepped inside. Part of her expected some gorgeous blonde model with legs up to her neck to come prancing out of a bedroom wearing one of his shirts.

That didn't happen. Thank God.

He walked in ahead of her, and for a moment she was more interested in watching his reactions than in looking around the place herself. Freddy had the opposite notion, quickly moving from room to room to check things out for himself.

Olivia saw that the ceiling opened up via skylights to the building's roof, so sunlight poured in like the cascade from Shadow Falls. The place was decorated entirely in an African tribal theme. Authentic masks and wildlife photography lined the walls.

There was a lioness and her cubs moving through the tall grasses of the Serengeti. There were graceful giraffes bowing to drink from a water hole. The end table was a kettledrum with a sheet of glass over the goatskin drumhead. One entire wall was lined in books. The interior foyer spilled into the living room, where brown leather furniture was draped with orange and green throws, and pillows that added splashes of yellow to the mix. She could see through to the kitchen, which was huge and entirely done in stainless steel and black. Black granite countertops. Stainless-steel double sink and appliances. Recessed lighting. An island delineated the boundary between kitchen and dining room, and a stairway led up between the two rooms.

She wondered where the stairs led. Onto the roof? She looked at him, half expecting him to tell her, but his expression stopped her. He was standing still, his gaze moving slowly over everything around him, his eyes wide at the power of the emotions surging through him.

She moved closer, sliding her hands up his broad chest. "Adam?"

"It's coming back. It's just . . . so much." He didn't meet her eyes. His own were jumping from one thing to the next. "That kitchen has state-of-the-art everything because I cook. I'm a gourmet cook, in fact. I love it. It relaxes me."

She smiled broadly. "That's fantastic, Adam!"

He shot her a quick look, nearly beaming. "Yes, Adam. That's my name, I'm sure of it now. Adam Selkirk, but I don't give it out. Everyone here knows me as Mr. Adams."

"And why is that?"

"My work — if people knew where to find me, I'd end up . . . dead." He frowned. "But why?"

"Just take it slow. Come on, show me around." She closed her hand on his upper arm and walked him into the kitchen, admiring the rack with the cookware dangling from it, the well-filled spice rack, the brick oven in the wall and the flat-topped range built right into the counter.

"Where do these stairs go?" she asked.

"Breakfast nook."

"Breakfast . . ." She looked curiously at him, then went up the stairs to a landing closed off by a steel door. She unlocked the bolt and pushed it open, Adam right behind her.

A warm, heavily scented breeze gusted right by her face as she blinked into the sunlight. She was on the roof. Potted plants stood around a tiny square table and two chairs. A red-and-white striped umbrella for shade lay furled nearby. Flowering plants were everywhere, spilling their fragrance into the warm air.

"You have your own little haven up here," she said.

"Yeah."

She went back down the stairs, sensing he needed a moment alone to process the myriad thoughts that must be racing through his mind, and looked around the kitchen, then headed back into the living room and through a door on the far right wall. It opened into what looked like a small den, with an archway at the far end and a bedroom just beyond that. The den held bookshelves, a spotless desk and a computer. More wildlife photos in here, though she had yet to see any dead creatures, mounted on the walls. Thank goodness.

She walked far enough inside to peek into the bedroom. His bed was a California King, neatly made up as if waiting for his return. The bedding was a tribal art pattern of lines and angles in vivid colors. The curtains were white, the walls sky-blue. And the dog was lying right in the middle of his mattress.

"Freddy, get down," she told him.

He sighed but obeyed, front legs first, hind ones splayed as he slowly dragged his body to the very edge, lowering those big back feet to the floor only when he had to. Then he lay down on the plush carpet and looked up at her with long-suffering eyes.

She could see a door that must lead to the bathroom. But she was more interested in the den. She moved behind the desk just as Adam, having finished his inspection of the rooftop paradise he'd created, came in.

"Remember anything else?"

"It's like a flash flood." He sounded distracted. "Almost more than I can . . ." He held up a hand as his voice trailed off, and wandered through into the bedroom.

Olivia rifled through the desk drawers, finding ordinary items like paperclips and staples, printer cartridges and paper. She flipped on the computer, then crossed the room while waiting for it to fire up and went to check out the closet.

"The bathroom has two doors. One leads back into the living room," he called.

"This is a really nice place, Adam."

She opened one of the closet's double doors and looked inside. It was deeper than it was wide, with shelves and clothes bars on both sides, and a lone hook right in the center of the back wall, which held a single bathrobe. Not two, one. And no women's clothes, either. In fact, she hadn't seen a single sign of a female presence in the entire place.

She frowned. There was something wrong with the closet, though. It was odd enough to have a clothes closet in the den, but that bathrobe? It belonged in the bedroom, or maybe the bathroom.

"Where did you go, Liv?" he called. She heard his footsteps coming toward her. "Olivia? Wait up, don't —"

She spun to face him, lost her balance and grabbed the robe to steady herself. The hook gave at the pressure, and the wall swung away.

"What the —"

"Olivia, don't!" He sounded almost panicked.

But she was already moving into the newly revealed opening, and as soon as she stepped through, lights came on. A motion sensor?

She stared around her. The room was small, maybe four by six or so. But it wasn't the size or the motion-sensitive light or the hidden entrance that made her jaw drop. It was the racks upon racks of weapons. Shotguns, rifles, handguns. There were small guns that would fit into a pocket, and one so big she didn't know what it was even intended to kill. And ammunition. Boxes and boxes of ammunition.

Adam was standing in the doorway now. "Olivia, please come back out here."

"No." Her eyes widened and slid to the only spot that was clear of weaponry: a small desk, with a chair in front of it. On the desktop was an eight-by-ten color photograph of her. A large sheet of paper, its edges torn unevenly, lay beside it. Across her face, in silver marker, was this mathematical problem:

$500,000 up front
+ $500,000 when it's done
= $1,000,000

She felt everything inside her go icy cold. There was no way to misunderstand what she was seeing. This was the arsenal of a professional killer. A killer who had been offered a million dollars to murder her. A killer who had apparently been paid half already.

Adam had been sent to Shadow Falls to murder her. And as she stared unseeingly at that desk with tears of fury burning in her eyes, she spotted a small stack of what looked like old mail fanned out on a corner of the desk. Recognition burned through her, along with humiliation. She was staring at the letters she had written to Aaron Westhaven.

He'd never even received them. This . . . this fraud, this hired *killer,* had intercepted them somehow and used them against her. Used her love of Westhaven's work to get close to her.

She turned around slowly, stared straight into his eyes and whispered, "Who hired you, Adam?"

"I don't know," he said.

"Was it Tommy? He's known where I was all along, he said. And those letters! Some of them are years old. How on earth did you get them?"

"I don't remember."

"You don't remember? You don't fucking remember?"

He shook his head slowly, then pressed his hands to either side of it. "Dammit, I'm trying."

"Not hard enough, you aren't." She spun again, snatched the pile of envelopes, yanking the paper out of one at random and shaking it at him. "Look at this! It's practically coming apart at the folds. How many times did you read this, Adam? How many times? And did you psychoanalyze me, figure out just what kind of man would appeal to me most? Or did you just intuitively know what to do, what to say, to get me to trust you? To sleep with you? To fall in love with you?"

"Olivia, I didn't —"

"So what's it going to be, Adam? You going to finish the job? Collect the other half of that money? What did you do with the first half, anyway?"

"It's —" He turned his head to look back into the bedroom, and she saw the satchel lying on the bed. He must have just found it. It was unzipped, banded piles of green bills spilling out of it.

"So pick a weapon and let's get this over with," she said. Tears were pouring from her eyes like water from a fountain. "Or do you want me to pick one? Here, how about this?" She yanked a gun off the wall without even looking at it and handed it to him. "Go ahead, do your job, Adam."

16

He didn't answer. He didn't know what to say. He couldn't believe he was a killer. It wasn't fitting together in his head the way everything else had done. It didn't make any sense. There wasn't that feeling of, "Of course! I should have known!" hitting him.

He couldn't be a killer.

And even if he had been once, he wasn't anymore.

Olivia pushed past him, stomping through the office into the bedroom, where, pausing, she bent over the bed. "I'm taking enough to cover what we've spent on this asinine wild-goose chase. I should take it all," she said, picking up a stack of bills. "It's my life it paid to have snuffed out."

"Don't take any of it."

She shot him a hate-filled look.

"I'll have to give it back to have any hope of calling off the hit . . . once I figure out where it came from, that is."

"Good luck with that." She threw the money she'd picked up onto the bed, turned and strode past him to the front door. "Come on, Freddy! Goodbye, Adam."

Freddy got up and loped to her side, then stood there looking miserable at the thought of leaving again when they'd only just arrived.

"Olivia, dammit, whatever I was, it's not what I am now. Whatever I intended to do —" He reached her, gripped her shoulders and turned her around to face him. "I'm not going to hurt you. I could *never* hurt you, Liv."

She stared through her burning tears into his beautiful eyes and wondered how a lying thug could seem so damn sincere. "You've known for a while now, haven't you, Adam?"

He lowered his thick lashes. Despite everything, her belly knotted with need. And then he gave a jerky nod. "I've suspected, yes. And I tried to tell you that."

"You did tell me. I just didn't want to believe you."

"I didn't, either. I *couldn't* believe it. I thought — I thought there must be some other explanation."

She sniffled, blinking back a fresh rush of tears. "How can I believe you now? How can I know for sure that this entire amnesia thing was anything but an act, some elaborate trap I was stupid enough to walk right into?"

He shook his head slowly. "What would be the point? If I was going to kill you, why wait? Why not just sneak up on you and do it?"

"I don't know. And I can't afford to stick around long enough to find out. Goodbye, Adam."

She pulled free, but he pulled back. He jerked her hard against him, bent his head and kissed her mouth. Tears rolled so thickly that she tasted them on her lips, and on his, as well. He fed from her, cupped her cheeks, and finally, finally, lifted his head slowly, staring through unfocused eyes into hers. "There's something between us, Olivia. You were right about that."

"Desperate times call for desperate measures, don't they, Adam? I can't believe you'd say that now, just to keep me here."

"That's not what this is, and you know it."

"I don't think I know anything anymore." She pulled free of him, half-blinded now by the flood of her tears, and felt for the knob. "I'm taking the Lincoln." She held out her hand for the keys, and after one look at her adamant expression, he handed them over. "Freddy, come!" she commanded, and her dog loped along beside her as she ran for the elevator. No keycard necessary to go down, luckily. She hit the button, and the doors opened instantly. She stepped inside, and Freddy sat down beside her, patient and loyal to a fault. She punched another button and waited for the doors to slide closed, slowly shutting out the blurred image of Adam's face, the regret and the unspoken plea in his eyes, as he stood there in the doorway.

Adam didn't chase after her, and he didn't beg her to stay. He just stood there and watched her go. What could he do, after all? What could he say? He couldn't even deny that her conclusions were correct. It was all falling into place in his mind, clicking in like the pieces of a jigsaw puzzle. He'd been hired to kill Sarah Quinlan. He'd been provided with mail that had been intercepted from her for years, apparently, though by whom, he didn't know. Probably Skinner, no matter what the man had said. He'd been paid half his fee up front. He'd studied the letters she had written to Aaron Westhaven with the intent of posing as the man in order to get close to her. He knew the plan. There was no denying it. He'd apparently intended to do it — to take money for murdering an innocent woman.

He turned and walked back into his apartment, hating himself with every breath he drew. He wondered what other foul secrets his past life was waiting to reveal. And systematically, he began searching every nook and cranny of the place. He found a locked drawer full of phony driver's licenses and passports. Every one of them bore his face, or some version of it, above an alias. In some he was heavier. In some he wore eyeglasses. In some he sported a beard or sideburns, or a moustache or goatee, or some combination thereof. In some his hair was long; in others his head was shaved. The names had nothing in common. They didn't rhyme or begin with the same letter. Adam was closer to Aaron than to any of the others, but that was clearly only coincidental.

He slammed the drawer closed to keep himself from obsessively examining the stamps on the various passports to see where he'd been. No time. He had to figure out who'd hired him and try to call off the hit. If it wasn't already too late. Someone had tried to kill him, too, after all. And a second man had been dispatched to Olivia's right after that. He no longer had any doubt what that man had been intending to do that night.

But who had hired him? And how were things connected? If he'd been hired to murder Olivia, why would the man who hired him then have decided to kill him? To keep him from being able to tell anyone who'd paid him, maybe? Hell, it made as much sense as anything else. If only he could remember now who his employer had been.

He went through his bedroom, through his closets and drawers. But he didn't find a hell of a lot that would tell him anything about who he was. Who he'd been. No journals or diaries. No photo albums. No notes.

He had no idea what the hell to do next. The memories were returning, but not fast enough, and not in any logical order.

And then he noticed that his phone machine was blinking.

He hit the button, then grabbed paper and a pen so he could write down anything that seemed important or might provide a clue.

There was only one message, but it was a stunner.

"Adam, it's Bruce. I've been in touch with the authorities in Shadow Falls, so I know

what happened. You're probably very confused right now, but don't believe anything
until you've spoken to me. I'm the only
person in the world who knows as much
about you as you know about yourself. I'm
the only one who can answer the questions
you have right now. You've got to come in,
Adam. You've got to come in. Call me. If I
tell you the number, you'll never know it's
for real, but you'll be able to figure it out.
I'm counting on that. Don't do another
damn thing until you call me."

Olivia couldn't believe she'd been such a
fool. She'd known it was a mistake to trust
a man she didn't know anything about.
She'd spent the past sixteen years not trusting anyone with the truth about herself. And
then she'd broken her own most important
rule, the one she'd lived by, and given her
secrets away to a killer.

He wasn't Aaron Westhaven. Aaron Westhaven had never even received her letters.
God, when she thought back on the things
she'd written . . . The way she'd talked
about his work and how much it had meant
to her, the way she had connected with it.

And she *had* connected with it. Westhaven's interpretation of human nature rang
truer than ever to her now. He knew love

was false and fickle and downright self-destructive. Every time Harvey let himself fall, he wound up paying a terrible price for it. And she knew that, dammit. She *knew* that was how it was in real life, because it had been exactly that way for her. She'd loved, or thought she had, and she'd nearly died because of it. She'd paid with her own identity, her own name, in exchange for her freedom. She'd learned that lesson the hard way, dammit, and there was no reason why she should have had to learn it all over again.

Except for her own stupidity.

She'd let herself fall, and fall hard.

And the results were just the same the second time.

She got out of the elevator and strode through the lobby, her dog keeping pace at her side. Poor Freddy, looking up at her as if to ask what was wrong. She must be vibrating with pent-up frustration, humiliation and hurt.

Mostly hurt.

She'd actually let herself believe the man might feel something for her, too. What an idiot.

She nodded to the doorman but didn't answer any of his friendly questions as she passed. No, everything wasn't okay, but that wasn't any of his business. No, there was nothing he could do to help her. There wasn't anything anyone could do. She just needed to go home.

God, she wanted to go home.

She wondered if she would be able to stay in Shadow Falls, or if the new life she had built for herself would be lost to her forever, just like the old one had been. Would she have to start again somewhere else? A new name, a new career, another new life? Where was she going to find another conveniently dead woman, someone with no family or friends to ask questions, whose identity she could steal?

She got to the car and opened the back, though her hands were trembling. Thankfully, Freddy obeyed her command to get inside, even though he must be so sick of cars by now that he could hardly bear it.

"I promise, I won't drive you anywhere again for a week, boy," she told him. Then she leaned in and stroked his face. "I love you, Freddy."

He licked her cheek. And she let the tears flow into his fur as she buried her face against his neck. "Never again. Never again, boy. It's just me and you for good. I mean it."

She closed the hatch and moved around

to get behind the wheel, started up the engine, fastened her seat belt, then laid her head on the steering wheel and cried as if her heart were broken.

In fact, she thought it was.

Come in, the message had said. *You have to come in.* How the hell was he supposed to come in when he didn't know where *in* was? Or who the hell Bruce was?

And then something occurred to him, and he started digging though desk drawers, moving from one room to the next. He already knew he didn't have a phone book or appointment book anywhere. But he did find a drawer full of cell phones in the weapons room. All of them untraceable, he bet.

He flipped one open, and searched the directory. And just as he'd hoped, he found a listing for Bruce. Just that, nothing more.

Saying a small, quick prayer, he put the call through.

A man answered on ring number three. "Yes?"

"I'm, uh . . . calling for Bruce."

"Adam? Adam, is that you?"

"Yes."

"Thank freaking God. You have no idea how worried I've been. Where are you?"

"I . . . Look, I don't know if I'm comfortable telling you that."

The other man was quiet for a moment. "You still don't know who you are, do you?"

"I have . . . some idea."

"I doubt that. What phone are you calling from?"

"A cell. I seemed to have a supply of them around."

"Of course you do. You need them. It's safe to assume it's secure. So listen, and listen carefully. I don't have time to go into a lot of detail here. But I can tell you what you need to know most, and that's this. You work for the FBI, Adam. Same as I do. I'm your boss."

He frowned. "The FB—"

"You're an undercover operative. You pose as a hit man, get hired, then fake the job and relocate the supposedly dead victim someplace where they can start a new life. You're the best there is."

He blinked as the meaning of the man's words sank in. "Then I wasn't going to kill Olivia Dupree?"

"No! Hell no. You were going to fake her death and get her safely relocated."

"Who wanted her dead? Who hired me?"

"Part of the job was trying to find out. It was all done through third parties. You've been playing along, hoping to figure out who was the money behind the job. But getting her safe in the meantime was the main goal."

Adam nodded. "And something went wrong?"

"Yeah, something went wrong. Your cover was blown before you ever got to her. The bastard who hired you must have found out you were a Fed and sent someone to take you out before you could get to Olivia and tell her that she was in danger. The shooter was supposed to take her out once you were out of the way."

"And that someone is still after me?" Adam said. "And Olivia? "

"Exactly."

Adam nodded, but his eyes shifted toward the door. "I have to go after her. I have to —"

"Not alone, not on your own. No more of that. You've nearly gotten the both of you killed trying to play it solo, my friend. You come in. Meet with me, and we'll make sure you're safe and pick her up, too. It'll be fine. Just come in."

"What if this asshole gets to her before we do?"

"Where is she now?" Bruce asked.

"She's on her way back to Shadow Falls."

"That's where I am. Been trying to steer the local yokels away from too much info. What's she driving?"

Adam hesitated.

"I'll have some of our guys catch up with her, make sure she's safe until we can get all this cleared up. So what's she driving."

Adam lowered his eyes. "Black Lincoln."

"Okay. We'll intercept her. Where's she coming from?"

Adam blinked. "You don't know where I live?"

"Hell, you don't tell anyone where you live. You've got the landline jumping through so many hoops it's untraceable. God, I can't believe you've really forgotten everything."

So he didn't even tell his boss where he lived? That seemed off. As if maybe he didn't trust the man.

"Look, I don't know you, okay? I'm not telling you anything more until I'm sure. Let's meet. You need to show me some proof that what you're telling me is true, and I need to get this clear in my head, all right?"

"All right. All right. Let's meet. How fast can you get back here?"

Adam drew a breath and sighed. "I don't have a car."

"What, you get rid of the Porsche?"

"Porsche?" And as soon as he said it, he spotted the key ring, complete with the rearing stallion logo, hanging near the door. "Maybe I *do* have a car."

"So how soon can you be here?"

"Nightfall," he said.

"Good. I'll see you then. Be careful, Adam, and don't talk to anyone else about any of this. No one. Understand?"

"Yeah. Yeah, I understand."

"Call me when you get in, and I'll let you know where we can meet."

"All right. See you then."

"Make sure you come alone. I can't emphasize that enough, Adam. You can't say a word to anyone. Not even the mark."

"Yeah, all right."

"I mean it."

"I told you, I've got it."

"Good."

Olivia drove all day long, stopping only when Freddy's whining or the vehicle's gas gauge let her know there was no other option. By nightfall the Lincoln's high beams were spilling onto the fan-shaped windows of her garage door and shining onto the pristine vinyl siding of her home sweet home. She'd never been happier to see it.

She shut off the engine and sat there for a

moment. God, she felt as if she were returning home from a war. As if she'd just spent months fighting for her life in a battle that had been as much mental as physical. Her brain had been bent and twisted by deceit, and fooled by her own desires. She'd seen what she wanted to see, rather than what really was. She'd been a fool. And it remained to be seen just what the cost of her foolishness would be.

Until then, though, she was home.

"Mrrrrph," said Fred.

"I know. I know, boy." She opened the door, removed the keys and dropped them into her pocket, silently thanking Tommy for the new ride, even while worrying about the Expedition she'd abandoned. It wasn't even her own. She was going to have to take it somewhere to have it cleaned and detailed — not to mention get the interior repaired where Freddy had clawed it up trying to get to her during the shootout. She shuddered to think what might have happened if her beloved dog had managed to escape the SUV that night.

Just add it to the list of things to worry about, she thought, as she went to free Freddy, who bounded out, butted her in the thigh with his head in a gesture of playful affection and then turned and ran for the front door. He was, she thought, even happier to be home than she was. When he reached the front door, he sat down, his tail swiping back and forth over the stoop as he waited impatiently to be let inside.

Sighing, she dug out her house keys, unlocked the door and let the dog in.

And then she let him do his thing. Whenever they'd been away, even for a few hours, Freddy performed the same routine upon returning. He went from room to room throughout the entire house, as if performing some kind of inspection. She never knew exactly what he was looking for, but he always looked. And when he finished, he would go to the patio doors off the kitchen and sit there until she let him outside, so he could complete the job by inspecting the fenced-in backyard.

She watched him wander into the bedroom as she sank onto the sofa, exhausted and wondering what she should do first. Calling Bryan seemed like a logical choice. And it would put off the inevitable — continuing to think about her broken heart. And about what she had done to her perfect, false little life.

Freddy emerged from the bedroom, wandered farther down the hall and went into the guest room.

Olivia picked up the phone and dialed Bryan's number.

He answered with, "You're home!"

Clearly he'd seen the caller ID. "I'm home."

"It's about damn time."

She smiled at the phone, even though her eyes were welling up a little. "Yeah, I'm sorry about taking off like that. I just — I had to."

"With him? Who is he really, Olivia?"

She lowered her head. "He's the guy who was hired to kill me."

"And how did you find that out?"

"First I got your message. Then —" She bit her lip there. If Adam really had changed, maybe he deserved a chance to start his life over again with a clean slate. Maybe he really wasn't the man he'd been before the bullet in his skull. If Bryan didn't already know his real name, then who was she to tell him?

God, listen to her. What was she, stupid? Was she actually *still* unsure? *Hey, lady, your boyfriend's a hit man.*

Yeah, I know, but he's a nice *hit man.*

Was she really that lame? Was she so naive that she would play this out the way so many victims did, right to their own bloody ends?

No. She wasn't. She was intelligent, with the degrees to prove it. And she wasn't buying into this crap.

"Olivia?"

"I need to know if Tommy's still behind bars."

"Absolutely. No bail. Every weapon on him was illegal. He left the state while on parole. He had cocaine in his pocket. And if all that weren't enough, let's not forget that he did have a gun to your head in front of a dozen cops — cops he and his thugs shot at. He's not going anywhere for a long time. And I convinced the judge that he was a danger to you, so there's no bail."

"That won't stop him from sending more killers to my door."

"His assets have been frozen until this is all sorted out. They're raiding his house. He won't be able to burp without the authorities knowing about it. Now that you're home, I can send patrols by to check on you. Hourly, if you want. We'll set you up with a panic button tomorrow. And . . . hell, I never thought I'd hear myself say this to anyone, but maybe you should consider getting a gun."

"I'm way ahead of you on that." She pulled the gun from her handbag.

"Just make sure you're ready to use it.

Never pull a gun unless you're sure you can fire it. And don't hesitate when you do."

"Don't worry. I'm pretty much through fucking around with men who only want to do me harm. I'm done letting them take the first shot."

"Good."

"How's Sam?"

"He's fine. Bullet went in and out the fleshy part of his shoulder. His mom bandaged him up in the E.R. and took him home."

"Thank God."

"You can say that again."

"How did you know, Bryan?" she asked at length. "That he wasn't really Westhaven, I mean?"

"Oh, that. I'm sworn to secrecy."

"But you're going to tell me anyway."

She heard his soft laugh. "Yeah, I am. But don't repeat it. No sense ruining your favorite author's career. Not that I really believe it would, but . . . Westhaven is a woman."

"No!"

"Mmm-hmm. Erin, with an *E*. She changed it to Aaron with an *A* because she felt her work would be taken less seriously if her gender were known."

"Do you think that's true?"

"No, but what do I know about the lite-
rati? But that's what she thought, and so
the recluse story was born."

"I never would have guessed. Not in a million years," she said softly. "God, I couldn't
have been more wrong, could I?"

"Did he hurt you, Olivia?"

"No."

"Did he try to hurt you?"

"No. Not in any way. Even when he found
out that he used to be . . . what he was . . .
even when he knew that he'd been hired to
kill me, he insisted that wasn't who he is
now. He says he could never hurt me, can't
believe he was ever the kind who could."

"Ah, hell, Olivia."

"What? I didn't say I believe him."

"But you do."

"I'm home. Alone. If I believed him —"

"You believe him."

She closed her eyes, and her tears spilled
over. "I want to."

"Did you fall for him? Is that it?"

"How'd you know?"

He was silent for a long moment. "I don't
know. Maybe because you sound like I
sound when I'm away from Dawn too long.
Dammit, Olivia . . ."

"The FBI is looking for him, you said."
She changed the subject, knowing he would

let her get away with it.

"Yeah. They're being very tight-lipped about it, though. That trace on his skull plate, though . . . I think that was legit. The serial number links up to an Adam Selkirk. Sledding accident when he was ten earned him the fractured skull and the steel plate. An Iraqi IED cost him his life in Desert Storm. He got a medal — posthumously, of course. At least that's what the records show. The Feds won't say one word about how that's possible. But I imagine a hit man would need a fake identity. Faking his death as a war hero is the height of hypocrisy, but a hit man is soulless anyway, so to him, it was probably no big deal."

She opened her mouth, instinctively ready to defend him. Adam wasn't like that. He wasn't soulless. He wasn't a hypocrite. He wouldn't do those things.

But he had, hadn't he?

God, she didn't know him at all.

"I'm really sorry to have to tell you all this," he said. "I just think you ought to know. And I don't think whitewashing it, or playing it down even a little bit, would do you any good. You need the truth."

"Yes, I do. It's overdue."

"Hang in there, okay? You're tough enough to get through this."

"How?" she asked. "God, how, Bryan? Tommy's going to trial, and that means he's going to talk. He's going to tell the world who I really am."

"Who you were, not who you are," Bryan said. "You've changed."

That was right, she had changed. She'd changed completely and utterly. And that meant change was possible. So why couldn't Adam have changed, too?

She decided not to say that out loud. It would only make Bryan worry more about her state of mind. And of heart. Instead, she continued with her earlier train of thought. "I'll lose my job. My career. Maybe even my degree. Not because of who I was, but because I've been lying about who I am. False name. Fraud. There's no way they'll let me keep my tenure."

He sighed.

"And Professor Mallory's SUV! I'll probably be charged with stealing it."

"We found the SUV. It's safe."

She felt only slightly relieved. "I drove home in Tommy's Lincoln."

"He hasn't said a word about a vehicle. I don't imagine he came by it legally, or he would have. Anyway, I'll have a car parked outside your house tonight, if you want, and for as long as you want, until I can be sure

Tommy hasn't sent anyone else out looking for you. Okay?"

"Okay."

"All right. Now I need you to tell me something."

"Of course, Bryan."

"These disks Tommy was talking about, the night you met with him. What are those about?"

She thinned her lips, lowered her head. "It's a long story. Can we talk about it tomorrow?"

"The Feds will be asking. If they find out you're back, you'd better believe they're going to want to question you from daylight till dark."

"I can't handle that right now, Bryan. I'll talk to you, but not them. I mean it. I'm not dealing with them."

He sighed. "Then don't tell them you were with their boy at all. Say you ran off on your own after the shootout, afraid Tommy was going to find you. Say you didn't even know 'Westhaven' was missing. Deny any knowledge of anything to do with this case until and unless they let on that they know otherwise."

"Do they? Know otherwise?" she asked.

"I don't know."

"I'd just as soon avoid them altogether

394

until you do."

"I don't blame you."

She sighed. "Do I need a lawyer?"

"I think that might be a good idea. Get one lined up in advance, just in case. And above all else, Olivia, if Aaron-Adam tries to contact you again —"

"Don't worry. I won't talk to him."

"Good girl. I'm sending a car to watch over you. Try to get some sleep, okay?"

"Okay, Bryan. Thanks. You're a good friend."

"You're welcome."

The other end of the line went silent. Olivia sighed and replaced the receiver in its cradle, then stared at it for a long moment until she realized that she was willing it to ring. Wishing for Adam to call her.

He wouldn't, of course. If he were an ordinary man who was as attracted to her as he'd pretended to be, if he were feeling the same kind of unfamiliar and overpowering force pulling him toward her that she felt pulling her toward him, then he would have phoned five times by now.

But he wasn't any of those things.

He was just a liar. He'd been faking every bit of it. The friendliness. The attraction. The sex. All make-believe, just to mess with her head before he finished the job.

That's not true, and you know it.

She closed her eyes to block out the little voice of her heart. She wasn't going to listen to her heart. She was going to listen to her head, to her experience, because she'd learned from her past, and she wasn't going to waste those expensive lessons now. She wasn't going to chuck everything she knew and waste herself on another man who would only hurt her in the end, just because her foolish, gullible, hopeful heart wanted her to.

She wasn't.

She looked at the phone again.

God, why didn't he call?

17

"Do you recognize me?"

Adam stood in a long-since-abandoned cinder-block building with fading letters painted on the front that spelled out Cheese Factory. He was face-to-face with Bruce, and he knew him. He felt a familiarity. All of the pieces weren't yet in place, but he knew this man. That much was certain.

"I do. I do know you. Bruce . . . Modine. My boss."

"Yeah. I'm your contact and your confidant. And we're tight, even though I just took over the position last year, when your former boss retired."

"Earl Baker," Adam said slowly. "I trusted him with my life."

Bruce clapped Adam on the shoulder. "I'm glad to see it's coming back to you. Glad you came in. First things first. About your mission . . . ?"

"I failed. Olivia is still in danger, and she's

still on her own. At least our efforts weren't wasted the other night. I gather the cops managed to put Tommy Skinner behind bars."

"I figured you were the 'unidentified male' who was with her at that shootout. Damn local cops kept us in the dark or we'd have been there for you, Adam."

"Still, at least Skinner's out of the picture."

"It wasn't Skinner who ordered the hit."

He lifted his brows, not entirely surprised, but bruisingly disappointed. He'd hoped so much that Olivia would be safe now that her former abuser was behind bars. "Skinner wasn't the client who hired me to kill her?"

"No."

"But you said we didn't know who it was."

"But we know who it wasn't. And it wasn't Skinner."

"Then who — ?"

"Undoubtedly someone whose name and likeness appeared on those disks the good professor's been keeping all these years. Apparently Skinner told people they existed, then extorted exorbitant amounts of money from them to learn where the disks were."

"I know all that. They paid him, and in exchange he told them about Olivia."

"Where she lived, what she did, her current name. He even provided recent photographs. As far as we can tell, he's been watching her for years. She's a target for I don't know how many people who have good reason to want the information on those disks buried, and her buried with them."

Adam nodded. "The only solution is to take them public."

"Excuse me?" Bruce asked.

"Make them public. Publish them on the Net or send them to the media, so there's no more motivation to keep them quiet. I mean, once it's public knowledge, what good is it going to do to kill her? Once *everyone* knows, then no one wins by silencing her."

"But everyone loses. Everyone whose face appears on those disks, at least. For buying weed sixteen years ago, Adam. Do you really think that's a solution?"

"It makes Olivia a worthless target. It takes away any reason anyone might have to want her dead."

"Unless that reason is vengeance," Bruce said. He shook his head slowly.

Adam frowned, trying to work through it in his mind.

"It's okay, pal. You're still trying to unlock your memory. Your skills are all still in there.

The rest will come back. But you're thinking like a rookie now. So why don't you just relax and let me call the shots until we can close the book on this one, okay?"

Adam nodded slowly. "I guess so." But for some reason, he wasn't entirely comfortable ignoring his own judgment in favor of his boss's. It didn't feel like the kind of thing he'd been accustomed to doing.

"So, what do we do now?" he asked.

"First we need to get our hands on those disks. And any and all copies you or Olivia might have made of them. That's the priority." Bruce looked at Adam as if waiting.

Adam said nothing. He felt a little queasy. Shouldn't saving Olivia's life be the priority here?

"So? Did you make any copies?"

Adam shook his head. "No," he said. "We didn't see the need. Our plan was to trade the disks back to Skinner in exchange for his promise to leave her alone and keep his mouth shut about her true identity."

"And you didn't think he might break that promise? That you might need some kind of ammunition to use against him in case he did?"

"Those disks wouldn't hurt him," Adam said. "He only wanted to use them to blackmail people. Not to protect himself.

He's already done time for dealing way back then. They can't charge him with that again."

"So what did you think was going to make him keep his promise?"

Adam shrugged. "I wanted to put a bullet in him and end it. Liv said no to that, said she could tell by looking him in the eye if he was going to keep his word or not." He sighed, let his head fall forward. "But she had another plan she didn't tell me about. Notified her friend the cop and got Tommy thrown into jail, where he can't hurt her."

Bruce nodded slowly. "So where are the disks?"

Adam averted his eyes. "I can get them."

"Olivia still has them, doesn't she?"

"I can get them. Give me until tomorrow, and I'll —"

"I thought we just established that I'm the boss." Bruce ran a hand over his bald head, letting out a frustrated sigh as he did. "This isn't like you, Adam. I need to know the facts here, despite what are admittedly extenuating circumstances."

Adam lifted his head, swallowed hard. "Look, I'll get the disks for you by tomorrow. That's the best I can do. Fire me if you have to."

"Fire you? All I'm asking is for you to

trust me. You used to trust me with your life, Adam."

"Maybe. But I don't have any right to trust you with hers."

"So she *does* have them."

Adam shook his head, turned around and headed for the door. "I'll meet you back here first thing in the morning with the disks. We'll take it from there."

"I'm afraid that's not going to be good enough, Adam."

A gun barrel was pressed to the back of his head. There was no mistaking the shape of it, or the sound of Bruce working the action.

"Sorry, but I want those disks tonight, because I can't risk her showing them to anyone else. Once they're destroyed and the only two people who know what's on them — namely you and Olivia Dupree — are feeding leeches in the bottom of the nearest swamp, my job will be done."

"We're not the only two people who know," Adam countered.

"Tommy Skinner's gonna die in prison. And aside from him, no one else has seen the disks."

"What about you?"

"What?"

"You. You'll have them, along with the opportunity to look at them. Is whoever you're working for going to be okay with that, do you think? Or do you think offing your ass will be his way of closing the final loophole?"

Bruce laughed deep in his chest, softly, dangerously. "That's a nice try, but you don't know shit, and it isn't going to work."

"So who are you working for?"

"Shut up and walk."

"To where?"

"To your car. We're going to pay the good professor a midnight visit."

"She doesn't have the disks, Bruce, and you're not going to get them by taking me there."

"We'll soon find out, won't we?"

"You think the cops aren't watching her house? You think she didn't call her pal on the P.D. the second she got back into town?" He said whatever he could think of to keep this bastard from going near Olivia. And it seemed to work.

Bruce went still, apparently thinking. "You're right. We'll have her bring the disks here."

"She doesn't know where they are."

"Then you'll fucking tell her. Or you'll fucking die, and then I'll go hunt her down myself." He slammed Adam into a straight-backed chair and handed him a pair of handcuffs. "Snap these on your right wrist."

Adam took the handcuffs, but he hesitated.

Bruce jammed the barrel harder into his head. "Do it!"

"All right, all right." Adam slipped the handcuff around his right wrist, but he didn't snap it all the way shut, hoping to slide his hand free as soon as Bruce wasn't looking.

Bruce was smarter than that, though. He snapped it shut himself, then looped the chain through the back of the chair and snapped the other cuff around Adam's left wrist. Now Adam found himself bound to the chair, hands behind his back, feeling more vulnerable than he'd ever felt in his life.

"How much of what you told me was true?" he asked.

The other man sneered, then flipped open a cell phone and dialed a number. He held the phone to Adam's ear. "Talk," he said. "Tell your girlfriend what we need her to do."

Adam heard the phone ringing, but finally Olivia picked up. Her voice was rough, as if she'd been sleeping — or maybe crying.

"Hello?"

Adam pursed his lips, steeling himself

404

against her voice.

"Adam, is it you?"

Still he said nothing.

Then the gun barrel cracked against the side of his head. "I said talk to her, damn you."

"What the hell is going on?" Olivia demanded. "Who is this?"

"No matter what he says to you, don't do it, Liv. Don't do it. Stay as far —"

Bruce yanked the phone away and clubbed him again. This time the chair went over sideways, and he went with it. His head pounded like a bass drum for about two and a half seconds, and then it swam and he thought he would throw up. Fortunately, he passed out before that could happen.

Olivia stared at the telephone in shock, wondering just what the hell she was supposed to make of all this. She'd heard Adam's voice briefly, and then some other man, followed by a blow, a grunt of pain, a crash.

"Adam?" she whispered. "Adam, are you still there? What's going on?"

"Adam's . . . tied up at the moment. This is . . . well, hell, you don't have to know who this is. Just bring the disks. And bring them now."

She frowned at the phone, shifting higher in her bed and pulling the covers with her. From his nest at the foot, Freddy lifted his head, ears perked forward, sensing her distress, she knew. He was alert and ready for action.

"Who are you?"

The caller sighed, and his anger was palpable. "Bring the disks to the old cheese factory."

"I don't have a clue where that is." It was a bald-faced lie, but she was trying to buy time.

"Upham Road. Use your GPS, sweetie. Three miles up on the right, big cinder-block building with barely any glass left in the windows. Bring the disks, and any copies you made of them."

Her throat was so dry she could barely speak. "We didn't make any copies," she lied.

"Yeah, so I've been told. I was just making sure. I'm an hour away from you. That's how long you have to get them here."

"I'm not even dressed."

There was a pause then, "You can't see it, but I'm smiling. Because you didn't say the disks were somewhere else. I guess he lied about that part. I'll give you five minutes to get dressed, and another five in case you get lost. So an hour and ten, total. And then I'll put a bullet in your friend Adam's head. The front of it, this time."

She swallowed hard. The man didn't wait for her to reply. He just hung up the phone. Olivia licked her lips and reached for the phone again. She needed to call Bryan.

Or not. What if the guy had tapped her phone?

But that wasn't the biggest "what if" that was plaguing her mind right then. What if this was just the endgame in Adam's twisted plan? What if he was luring her out so he could finish the job and collect the other half of his million bucks? What if she was walking straight into a trap that could cost her her life?

Okay, okay, worst-case scenario — she would get killed.

But what if this was for real? And she didn't go? Worst-case scenario, Adam would get killed. Because of her.

And as sad as it was, she would rather risk her own life than his. Just how sick and twisted did that make her? Especially when this bastard might decide to kill them both anyway, once he had what he wanted.

She looked at Freddy. "I know I promised, but I need you with me. You up for one more drive?"

He tilted his head to one side as if to ask if she'd lost her mind. But she knew he would do whatever she asked of him. He loved her. And if he got hurt during all of this, she would never forgive herself. But she knew she would be a lot safer with him by her side than she would be alone. And she knew that the three of them together would stand an even better chance. If Adam was indeed on her side.

She didn't feel confident trusting anyone else to come with her and not end up getting Adam killed, even accidentally. Not even Bryan.

She slid out of bed with a glance at the clock. Two minutes had passed, but she wasn't worried. She knew exactly where the old cheese factory was. And it wasn't an hour from her. She could make it in half that time, taking the back roads she'd been traveling for years.

She dressed for action. Running shoes, comfortable jeans, sports bra, tank top and a denim jacket despite the warmth of the night. She took the .38, loading it fully and wishing it was an automatic with a clip instead of a revolver that only held six bullets at a time. But she put more bullets in various pockets, and then, as an afterthought, she yanked her pants leg up high enough to duct-tape a small paring knife to her inner calf.

She was as ready as she could be.

She grabbed her flashlight from the wine rack, went outside and turned to call Freddy, but he was already there. His eyes met hers, and they were solemn.

"I know," she said. "I miss him, too. Let's go get him back, okay?"

She opened the back of the Lincoln, and Freddy leaped in all by himself. Then she looked around. The car Bryan was sending hadn't yet arrived. Thank goodness.

"You're wasting your time, you know. She's not going to risk her life coming here."

"She risked her life to spend the last several days with you," Bruce said.

"Yeah, but she left me when she found out I was sent to kill her."

"But you weren't. What I told you before was the truth. I *am* your boss at the Bureau, and you *weren't* sent to kill her."

"She doesn't know that."

Bruce shrugged. "Women are strange creatures, Adam. They tend to believe what they want to believe about a man. Especially one they've fucked a few times. You *have* fucked her, haven't you?"

Adam didn't answer, but he hoped the

man could read the warning in his gaze.

"Yeah, you've fucked her. You make it good for her? The way females confuse orgasms with undying love could really work to your benefit here. So did you get her off a few times? Go down on her?"

"You're over the line, pal."

"What are you gonna do? Hit me? You're bound for glory, buddy." Then Bruce rolled his eyes. "I don't need you to answer. If you did her right, she'll be here." Then he smiled. "Hell, if you went down on her, she'll be here loaded for bear."

"It's a shame you kept on running your mouth, Bruce," Adam said. "Up until just now I was considering letting you walk away from this alive. But now — hell, you're a dead man. You just don't know it yet."

"You're the dead man, my friend. And it's a crying shame." Bruce sighed, shaking his head slowly. "Frankly, you should have been in the ground by now. Why the hell didn't I know you had a freaking steel plate in your head?"

Adam shrugged as best he could, considering he was handcuffed to the chair. "Guess you didn't read my file thoroughly enough. It's in there."

"You're right. I didn't read it very well at all. Boring shit, most of it. Desert Storm.

All the fucking medals and accolades. And then your *tragic* death in battle. Not enough left of your body to send home for burial."

"I never should have gone along with it."

"Why not? You've saved a lot of lives, Adam. Done a lot of good for your country. You should be proud, if you're into that sort of thing. Me, I'm out for number one. Always have been. Took the job because there was no limit to the money I could make. But enough of that. I'm not going to be one of those eggheads who confesses everything to the condemned prisoner, only to have it come back and bite him in the ass later on."

"Maybe you're just realizing that you've been underestimating me all along and I'm the one who's going to come out of this in one piece. Not you."

Bruce seemed to pause, to freeze and to pale, but it was all so subtle and so quick — like the flicker of a lightning bug in the night, there and gone in a heartbeat — that Adam couldn't be certain he had reacted at all.

"You know that already, don't you, Bruce?"

"I've got the guns. You're trussed up like a Christmas goose. I'm not worried."

"You're a desk jockey. I'm in the field. You

don't stand a chance here, and you really should have figured that out before you got involved." He shrugged. "So who is it, hmm? Who's paying you to get the disks and take Olivia and me out?"

"None of your business."

"Come on, I want to know who's killing me before I check out for good. Is it Senator Gainsboro?" And he saw it. A quick blink, nothing more. "That's it, isn't it? It's the senator."

"Afraid not," said a female voice from the other side of the room. Heels clicked as she moved forward, out of the shadows and into the meager light offered by the battery-powered lamps Bruce had brought.

She was a leggy brunette with a body to die for and a face so perfect it seemed almost false. Like the kind of face you would see in a wax museum or on a department-store mannequin. Hair in a knot, not one strand out of place, suit tailored to fit like a second skin, with its pencil-straight skirt skimming her knees and the short jacket nipped in at the waist. Black suit. Black shoes. Black hose. She looked as if she'd just come from a funeral.

"Corinne, what the hell are you doing here?"

She shot Bruce a look that would have

wilted lettuce. "You want to say my name again, or do you think he got it the first time?"

Adam said, "No need. I got it. Fascinating to meet you, Mrs. Gainsboro. You're the only aspiring first lady I've ever met." Then he shrugged. "At least that I remember. Not that you'll ever get beyond the aspiring stage. I mean, really, your husband's fat and bald. They don't elect unattractive men to the White House anymore, or hadn't you noticed?"

She shot him a scowl. "You let me worry about that."

"Right, I'm sure you've got it covered. Obviously you have a great plastic surgeon on retainer."

"The best," she said with a lift of her brows. "All I need are those disks."

"All you need is a good divorce lawyer — or you will soon. Unless the senator is in on this?"

She ignored him, turning to face Bruce. And Adam saw something else then. The way Bruce's face changed when he looked at her. The man was hot for her. Maybe more than that, given the way she responded to that look with a secretive little smile.

"You're banging her, aren't you?" Adam demanded.

Bruce gaped, and "Corinne" went white, her eyes widening.

"Wait, I just got another snippet of my memory back, Bruce. You told me you were Secret Service before you joined the Bureau. You must have met on the job, right? What were you doing? Working for her husband? That's certainly playing with fire."

The other man smiled just a little. "You can say that again."

She smiled, too, and the two of them met in the middle of the room with a steamy embrace and an even steamier kiss that left Adam almost embarrassed for them. Ruthless, that was what she was. And far more dangerous than Bruce at his worst. Adam sensed it right to his gut. He'd thought he had a shot before. Now, though . . . now he might just be in trouble here.

18

Olivia made the trip in twenty minutes. She was proud that she'd become so familiar with the back roads of her chosen home-town.

Hometown. The word stopped her, because she'd never thought of Shadow Falls that way before. It had been her haven, and sometimes her prison, but she'd never thought of it as her home. And yet that was what it had become.

It felt good to have a home.

Freddy nuzzled her neck from behind, reminding her of her mission, and she nodded and stroked his nose. "Yeah, we're here. Now you're going to be a very good dog for me, Freddy. You're going to listen to me and obey without hesitation. Right?"

Not waiting for an answer, because she already knew what it would be, she wrenched open the door and climbed down to the grassy ground. She'd pulled the SUV off the road fifty yards from the abandoned cheese factory, in a small tangle of woods. She tucked the keys into the lowest crotch of the tree nearest the driver's-side headlight, making a mental note so she could find them again quickly, and kept on walking. Freddy trotted close beside her, keeping pace, his entire body tense and alert. He knew something was up. The dog was damn near psychic, and he wouldn't have missed the adrenaline surge in his favorite person. She was pumped. Scared shitless, but feeling strong. Empowered. She was taking her life into her own hands, living it on her own terms, for the very first time since she'd escaped Tommy. For once she was doing what she wanted to do, rather than making the choice less likely to expose her secret past. To hell with her secret past. And she wasn't doing this for Adam, either. To hell with him, too. She was doing this to put the past behind her, to cut through the chains that had bound her to it for so long. Forget Prince Charming.

She was rescuing herself.

And so she picked her way through the tangles and the briars until the cinder-block building came into sight. Rusted metal tic-tac-toe frames hung in the window openings, all of them devoid of glass. Faint traces

416

of red paint that had once spelled out the unimaginative name of the one-time business now clung in bits that would soon be too faded to make out. Weeds had overtaken what had once been a driveway and small parking lot.

It took several moments of crouching contemplation for her to pick out the faint light emanating from one of the windows near the back. She decided to approach from the front, instead. Ducking back into the woods, Freddy at her side, she took a path that gave the factory a wide berth until it angled around to the front of the building and a hatchway door set into the ground like a storm cellar door in an old farmhouse.

Inside, a set of stairs would lead from the basement up to the main part of the factory. And that was where she was going. She clutched the soft furry nape of Freddy's neck. "You ready, boy?"

She glanced down and saw his stance, and she nearly jumped in surprise. He was rigid, leaning slightly forward, making his chest seem wider than it had ever looked before. His ears were cocked, and the fur along the ridge of his spine was standing stiff and erect, like a razorback's. She'd *never* seen his fur do that before.

"Just take it easy, Freddy. Listen to me. Listen."

He looked up at her, and even she was amazed at the intelligence and understanding she saw in those brown eyes.

"Listen to me, okay?" She gave him a squeeze. "We're going to run, Freddy. Run!" And she dashed toward the angled door, her only cover the night itself, unlike Freddy, whose brindle markings made him nearly invisible in the dark as he loped along beside her.

They reached the hatchway door, and she stopped, crouching low and whispering, "Freddy, sit," as she gave him the matching hand signal.

He sat right at her side almost before she'd finished telling him to. She hugged his neck and whispered, "Good dog. *Good dog,* Freddy. Now *stay,*" accompanied by another hand signal. She looked for a lock and saw none, so she clasped the edge of the wooden door and pulled upward.

The door swung open, hinges creaking and moaning in protest so loudly that Olivia flinched in a knee-jerk reaction. She crouched in the shadows, one arm around Freddy as she scanned the darkness, listening so hard her ears would have perked up like his if they could.

418

Crickets sang in chaotic harmony. The wind whispered through the leaves and young graceful limbs, still green enough to bend in greeting. A creature of some kind, a raccoon maybe, rustled in the brush nearby. But there was no sound of human footsteps. No muttering male voices, no guns being readied. Nothing.

Sighing in relief, she moved to the top of the dark opening and tugged the tiny flashlight from her pants' pocket, flicked it on and pointed it ahead of her. The beam illuminated a curtain of cobwebs, draping low over crumbling concrete steps that led down into a cinder-block basement. She patted her thigh, and Freddy leaped to her side, then sat at the top to let her go on ahead, as was his custom when they negotiated any staircase together.

Waving her hands to knock down cobwebs, then rubbing them together to wipe the sticky things away, she proceeded down the steps. When she reached the bottom, Freddy picked his way down to join her.

The cellar was huge, the same size as the factory floor above, and musty, as if it had been holding the same air for a hundred years. It had a broken concrete floor, stacks of wooden crates filled with objects too dusty to identify, some pipes and knobs and not much else. But there was an ancient-looking wooden staircase at the far end, leading upward.

She crossed the basement, gesturing for Freddy to come with her and using her light to be sure nothing dangerous to either of them lay in their path — like broken glass or hairy spiders.

None appeared. She reached the foot of the staircase and paused, looking up. More cobwebs, but they'd been swept away recently, opening a clear path to the warped wooden door at the top. The top step was a small landing of sorts.

She shone her light on the wooden planks that served as stairs. Yes. The tread of a large shoe marred the dust on every one of them.

Turning, she caught Freddy's eye and signaled him to sit and stay. He obeyed the sit part. There was no telling how long the stay command would stick, she thought, as she made her way slowly, silently, up the stairs.

Every step was deliberate, careful. She lowered her weight onto each board gradually, bracing for a tell-tale creak that would give her away.

None did. And every few seconds she glanced back and repeated the stay signal, trying to keep Freddy where he was. He would be fine until she reached the top. But once she got there, she didn't know what would happen.

It was time to find out. She took the final step, onto the platform at the top, right in front of the door, which looked in even worse shape up close than she'd thought from below. The landing squeaked a little as she stepped down onto it, and she froze, eyes widening, breath stopping in her chest, as she listened, waiting.

Nothing. No . . . wait, there was something. She leaned forward, pressing her ear against the door.

Voices. Male . . . and female, too? What the hell?

Swallowing hard, she put her hand on the doorknob, then turned it carefully and pushed the door slowly open. Just a bit. Just enough to peer through . . . and to realize she'd found the source of the light she'd seen from outside.

Adam's chair had been unceremoniously dragged into a small room off what had once been the main factory floor. He was surrounded by cinder-block walls, and the only door had a rusting old padlock on his side and a shiny new one on the other. He'd seen it in Bruce's hands, heard it snap closed after he'd been shoved inside.

The senator's faithless wife had wrapped a strip of duct tape around his head, covering his mouth and damn near over his nose, too. He'd had a moment of panic, but he could still breathe, thank God.

He humped and bumped the chair closer to the door, then managed to hunker down enough to try peering through the keyhole, but he couldn't get the angle right. There was light shining under the door, though, so he tipped his chair over sideways, bracing for impact on the way. His shoulder hit hard, driving a grunt of pain out of him — pain that eased considerably as his mind processed the accompanying loud cracking sound as having come from the chair, not his arm.

Good. He shuffled his body, chair and all, until he could get his head up tight to the crack underneath the door. And then he could see, more or less. Bruce and his whore, from the hips down, at least, were moving around, always close. Then they stopped, and she whispered, "Bruce, get a load of this."

Frowning, Adam shifted his attention in the direction both sets of feet were pointing. And then he saw it. A door, opening slowly *away* from them. Way too slowly for it just to be swinging in an errant breeze. Someone was clearly on the other side, getting ready to sneak in.

Olivia!

The two killers stood silently, probably smugly, watching and waiting. He saw Bruce move, twisting, his arm rising out of sight. When he lowered it again, there was a gun in his hand. And as Adam watched the door open farther, he saw Bruce raise that gun.

Adam tried to shout from behind the duct tape, but all that emerged were sounds too muffled to be heard. He strained aching muscles and thumped his head hard against the door. Three big bangs, and it hurt, but it made them turn. He pressed his eye to the crack again and saw them turning his way.

"Dammit," Bruce whispered. He must have signaled the woman to deal with it, because she strode toward the door, her pumps and black stockings blocking Adam's view of what was going on in the other room.

"Be quiet, Adam," she whispered near the door. "It'll go better for her if you do as you're told. Trust me on this."

He thumped the door again, pleased to see her jump. Then she moved to one side, as if she thought he might somehow be able to reach through that door and hurt her as badly as she deserved to be hurt.

"I mean it, Adam."

He wasn't listening. He could see again, and what he saw had his full attention. The door opened a little more. Bruce had moved to stand directly behind it, one hand on the doorknob. Backing up a few steps, he lifted the gun, then yanked the door wide open.

Olivia came flying through, tripping on the doorsill. She slammed to the floor, the gun she'd been holding skidding away. She quickly kicked the door closed, making it look like an aftereffect of her fall, but Adam knew damn well it wasn't.

Freddy must be down there.

And then Bruce was on her, a knee in the middle of her back, a gun to her head. "Don't even think about moving," he said.

"Who the hell are you? What do you want?"

"None of your business." He gripped her by the hair and got up, pulling her up backward, and she whimpered at the pain in her scalp and gripped his hand with both of hers until she could get her feet underneath her and find her footing.

He must have released her hair then,

because she stumbled a few steps away from him.

"Who are you?" Olivia demanded again. "Where is Adam?"

"Adam didn't think you'd come. I'm glad to see he was wrong. Did you bring the disks?"

"Of course I did. And I also left copies with my lawyer, who'll be forwarding them to the U.S. attorney general and the press if anything happens to me."

"You didn't have time to do that."

"I've had plenty of time to do that. I've had the disks for days, after all, while I've been running around with Adam."

"And you copied them without him knowing?"

"You don't think I *trusted* him, do you?"

"You wouldn't be here if you didn't."

"Bullshit. I'm here for me, not him. I want this over with — for myself. Understand?"

"Fine." Corinne walked away from the closed door, her heels clicking on the concrete floor. "So we'll let you go and kill Adam, then. Leave the disks on your way out."

Her bluff must have worked, because he heard Olivia gasp. She collected herself quickly and said, "I didn't come here to leave without him."

"I didn't think so." Corinne shifted to face Bruce. "Kill them both."

"That's what I said from the beginning," he reminded her. Then he turned to Olivia. "The disks?"

She must have handed them over, Adam thought, judging from what he heard. Then she spoke.

"Go ahead and kill us," she said. "The press and the attorney general will get every name and face in those files. Go ahead. The discs go out the minute I'm reported missing."

"That gives me a good day, maybe even two, to go to your house, rifle through your papers until I find out who your lawyer is, go to *his* house, and shoot him between the eyes," Bruce said. "Hell, even a desk jockey like me could do that in a couple of hours. You're making this too damn easy."

He took her by the arm and marched her across the room toward Adam's door. Corinne hurried ahead of them, and he heard her playing with the padlock. He twisted and writhed, snaking his chair away from the door to save himself from being clocked in the chin with it.

He made it just in time. The door swung open, Olivia was shoved inside so hard she stumbled and fell, and then it slammed closed again. No one had even noticed him lying on the floor.

Olivia pushed herself up off the concrete and lifted her head, so her hair curtained her face. Then, slowly, she looked to the side and spotted him lying there, staring at her.

He met her eyes, which filled with tears the second she looked back.

"Oh, my God, they beat the hell out of you." She helped him right the chair. And then she smiled. She actually smiled. "Thank God, Adam. Thank God they beat the hell out of you." She pressed her palms to either side of his face and kissed him square in the middle of the duct tape.

Then she found the edge and started peeling it away. Several strands of his hair came with it, roots and all, and he thought maybe his jawline lost some of its day's growth of whiskers. But that was nothing compared to the layers of skin he lost from his lips as she yanked the tape away.

But then she was kissing them again, so he decided he really didn't mind.

He was confused as hell about why she'd done an about-face toward him, and hoped to God the two of them were going to live long enough for him to figure her out.

And . . . then he stopped thinking and just felt the tide of relief mingled with desire that rushed through him at the pressure of her mouth against his. God, it was good, and he had been craving this and not even realizing it — not until right now. Now every muscle relaxed as she whispered soft things against his lips, things he couldn't hear and didn't need to.

Finally she backed away just a little, her eyes closed, as if she were feeling too much emotion to look at him just then. He felt her trembling as she moved around behind him and began tugging at the handcuffs.

"What the hell are you doing here, Olivia?" he asked, craning his neck to try to see her as he spoke, so he could read her face. Or maybe just so he could keep drinking it in. God, he was glad to see her. And yet he wasn't, because it meant she was going to die with him. And of all the many things he'd fantasized about her doing with him, dying was not one of them.

"That bastard said he was going to kill you."

"Yeah, and for all you know, I was sent to kill you. So why did you come?"

She stopped working on the cuffs and leaned closer, her breath near his ear. "I had to make a decision, Adam. I had to decide whether to believe what the evidence in your apartment was telling me, what Bryan was telling me, what even *you* seemed to believe — or to believe what my own heart and soul were telling me about you."

"Bryan knows who I am, then?"

"He thinks he does. But he's wrong. *I* know you, though." She gave up on the cuffs and came back around to the front, where she knelt on the floor, her palms pressed to his thighs, then looked up at him and leaned forward. "The man I've been getting to know these past few days is a good man. He's not a murderer. There is something down deep inside every person, something very basic, at their core. It's what determines how someone acts when the chips are down and choices have to be made. It's the heart of every human being, and it's either good or bad. I've seen your heart, Adam. I've felt it, and I know it, and you are good. You *are.* That's what I choose to believe."

"That's a pretty big leap of faith. A pretty big risk."

"If I'm wrong, it'll be a devastating one. But if I'm right, then this decision to believe in you despite all the evidence is the most important leap of faith I will ever take. I've weighed my options, and I've decided that I'd rather risk heartache for a shot at the best thing I'll ever find than protect my heart and never know love."

His throat went dry.

"And that's what this is, you know," she said, holding his eyes. "You do know that, right? I'm choosing to believe in you because I love you. And I'd rather be in love with a good guy than a killer. So I'm choosing to believe that's what you are, and I'm hoping to God I'm not making a huge mistake."

He stared at her, stunned right to his soul. He knew she was waiting for an answer, a sign, something. And yet he was speechless.

Her eyes started to moisten, and she looked away fast, scurrying behind the chair to begin yanking on the wood, trying to free him, talking way too quickly. "I know it's a lot to take in all at once," she said. "But it would do me a world of good if you'd give me some kind of answer."

"I'm just . . . I'm stunned, and I'm —"

He gave up on speech and stood up, chair and all. Then he moved away from her and swung the chair into the nearest wall. It crashed to bits on the floor around him.

Quickly Olivia wrested the broken piece of it from the cuffs. Free of the chair, he sat on the floor and slid his cuffed hands over the backs of his legs, then his feet, until his hands were in front of him.

"Are you all right?" she asked.

"I'll be okay."

"So?" She sat on the floor and looked at him. "Don't you have anything at all to say to me?"

"Thank you seems like way too little."

The frown that marred her face let him know that she thought so, too, but he was damned if he could form words. The enormity of what she had done for him was so overwhelming that he was all but speechless. He didn't know where to begin.

She lowered her eyes then. "You're right. It is." And then she appeared to be trying to dislodge a large lump from her throat. "Well, let's see about getting out of this mess, then."

She got to her feet and, turning away from him, moved to the door, testing the knob, running her hands up and down its surface, feeling the hinges.

Adam's legs had fallen asleep from being still for so long, and they prickled now with a thousand unseen needles. He stomped, shook one leg, then the other, even while noticing how she was keeping her face averted, avoiding his eyes as she pretended to be busy.

He moved closer, but she still kept feeling

431

up the door, like some secret escape hatch was going to open if she just looked hard enough.

"I'm not a hit man," he told her. "I want you to know that right now, before anything else happens. I was only posing as one."

That got her to turn and face him again. She searched his eyes.

"I know this is going to sound farfetched, but since you believe in me without any reason to, maybe you'll be willing to take my word for this part of it, too, until I can show you the proof — and I will be able to show you proof, Olivia. Assuming we make it out of here alive, anyway."

"I want to believe you," she whispered.

"I'm an undercover FBI agent," he said. "A very specialized one."

Her brow creased. "Posing as a hit man?" she asked.

"I know how it sounds. Believe me. I know. But it's the truth. I pose as a hit man known as Mr. Adams. And Adams has a great reputation in the underworld by now. So I get hired on to take people out, but instead I stage the hit, fake the mark's death, then hustle them into a government relocation program."

"So someone *did* hire you to . . . to murder me?"

"That's what I was told."

"Who?"

He nodded at the doorway. "Didn't you recognize her? That's the wife of the good senator. She wants to be first lady one day, and nobody is going to tolerate a president and first lady who are on film buying marijuana, much less toking their brains out — in her case from a five-foot bong."

"I *thought* the woman in that photo looked familiar. But who's the man with her?"

"My boss."

Her eyes widened as they met his.

"Bruce Modine. He and Corinne met when he was with the Secret Service."

"And they're lovers?" she asked.

He nodded. "I don't know the rest. But I can put at least some of it together."

"So can I," she said. "My lovely ex must have tried to blackmail her or her husband."

"And she turned to her lover for advice on how to handle it," Adam elaborated.

"If you're banging someone in the FBI, you'd definitely run a blackmail attempt by them," she agreed. "So then she paid Tommy the hush money he demanded, and in exchange, he told her where she could find the disks with the evidence on them. He told her about *me*. He was telling us the truth about that."

Nodding, Adam went on. "Bruce wouldn't have had any trouble at all finding a legitimate hit man to do the job for his lady friend. But something must have gone wrong. Probably a leak. Someone else in the Bureau must have learned there was a hit being taken out on you and informed him. If he hadn't sent me in to fake your death and relocate you, it would have looked fishy. That was his job. So he did it. But he told the real hit man about it, or had her tell him. His job was to kill us both and get those disks, clearing her husband's path to the White House."

"And his wife's path to being first lady. My God."

She nodded slowly and met his eyes. It seemed there was more she was waiting to hear from him. But he could see she'd accepted what he'd told her so far. He could see it, he just couldn't quite believe it.

"You look like you believe me."

"I'm choosing to believe you. I'm not being stupid, I want that clear. If you're playing me, I'll find out soon enough, but dammit, Adam, I want to believe you."

"I swear to God, Olivia —"

"You don't have to swear. But dammit, Adam, it would be nice if you'd —" She bit her lip to cut herself off, shook her head hard.

"What?"

"Never mind. Let's just get out of here, okay?"

"How do you suggest we do that?"

"First we need to get out of this room," she said. "Then I have a secret weapon. All I have to do is, uh, unleash it. So to speak."

He met her eyes and felt hope for the first time. "Freddy?"

She nodded.

"Where?"

"Basement. He's being quiet and staying still, just like I told him, but that won't last forever. And if they find him . . ."

Adam felt the blood rush from his face to his feet, and went to the door, pounding on it. "We want to make a deal! Do you hear? We'll get all the copies for you."

No answer. He pounded again. "Corinne, come on. You don't even know about the copies that are being mailed to the opposing party's leaders tomorrow."

Staccato clicks came closer, and Corinne said, "What the fuck are you talking about now, Adam?"

"Open the door. We can do this like adults. Look, I've got secrets in my past, too. So does Olivia, as I'm sure you know.

435

You smoked some weed. So what? It's not that big a deal. Not like murder. We can come to an understanding here."

There was a sigh. "I'd be an idiot to let you live."

"You'd be an idiot to murder two people, only to have the truth come out anyway, getting you twenty to life or worse for your trouble."

"Ignore them, Corinne," Bruce said.

"Yeah, ignore him," Olivia shouted. "I'll be laughing in my grave when you go down in a public train wreck tomorrow afternoon, taking your unsuspecting husband with you."

"They're bluffing," Bruce said.

"He doesn't even know those disks exist, does he, Corinne? What do you think he'll do when he finds out what you've been up to?" Olivia went on.

The lock turned, and the door opened. Corinne was standing there with a gun pointed at Adam's chest.

Sighing so loudly it was almost a growl, Bruce stomped past her into the room, gun drawn. "Back up, Adam," he said, aiming the gun at his forehead.

Adam took two steps back. No need to make waves at this point.

"You," Bruce said to Olivia. "Come here."

She stepped forward. Bruce grabbed her, twisted her around and pulled her back against him, one arm around her chest and his gun to her temple.

"*Now* we can talk."

"I don't know," Olivia said. "I don't really feel like talking now. I feel like screaming." And then she cut loose with a shriek that should have had Bruce's ears bleeding.

He quickly clamped a hand over her mouth, cussing at her while ordering her to shut the hell up, but she bit him hard. And when he jerked his hand away in response, she screamed again.

"What the hell is *wrong* with you?" Bruce demanded, even as Corinne marched right up to Olivia and slapped her hard across the face.

She stopped screaming, but it didn't matter. The message had been delivered. And it took all of three seconds before they all jumped, startled by a sound that could only be compared to a wrecking ball demolishing a condemned building with its first and only blow.

Wood cracked and splinted. The already rickety basement door didn't fly open — it exploded into a thousand bits, some the size of toothpicks. And then, from the midst of

the splinter-starburst, came what looked like
a rampaging bear.

19

Bruce spun around, still holding Olivia to him. The skinny brunette shoved past them and leveled her gun at Freddy. But Olivia reacted instinctively. Leaning back into Bruce, she drew both knees up, then kicked out for all she was worth, landing a double-barrel blow to the small of Corinne's back and putting her on her knees. She never got a shot off before her gun was on the floor.

"Call him off! Call him —" Bruce didn't get to finish, because he'd turned his weapon away from Olivia's head, attempting to aim it at her best friend instead, and the instant he did, Adam hit him like a speeding semi, taking him down, and Olivia along with him, even as a shot rang out.

There was a horrible cry, a yelp that tore at Olivia's insides as she fought to disentangle herself from Bruce's grip. He tried to hold on to her — she was peripherally aware of him pointing the gun at her again and re-

439

alized that he was speaking, probably something threatening. It had no impact. She was flailing her arms, kicking her legs, twisting her body, and there was nothing he could do to stop her. She knew she landed at least a blow or two before getting free, and then she scrambled to her feet, racing to where Freddy had fallen.

Adam and Bruce were entangled in deadly combat as she fell to her knees beside the dog. There was an ominous hole in his chest, right between his front shoulders, and blood pumped from it in time with his heartbeat.

"No, no, no," she moaned, pressing a palm to the wound to stanch the bleeding. "Hold on, boy, just —"

She broke off with a grunt of pain, as a pair of hands gripped her by the hair and jerked her backward. She landed on her ass but bounded to her feet, swinging at the woman who'd attacked her. She hit Corinne hard, barely seeing her, reacting purely to the surge of adrenaline.

A fist connected, then another, then a foot, and then she was straddling Corinne, pounding the woman's head repeatedly into the floor.

"Hey. *Hey!*" Adam said. "Enough. You're gonna kill her."

Olivia only glanced at him long enough to see that he was now standing, holding a gun on the prone and badly beaten Bruce. She looked back at Corinne just long enough to see that she was no longer conscious. And then she was scrambling on all fours across the floor and pressing her hands to Freddy's wound again.

"He's bleeding, Adam! Do something!"

"Already am."

Another sideways glance told her that he was on a cell phone — calling for help, she hoped.

"There's been a shooting. A federal officer is down. Shooters have been disarmed. We need police and an ambulance. And the name of an emergency vet. We're at . . ." He shot her a look. "Damn, what's the address here?"

"The old cheese factory building," she told him. "They'll know it. Everyone in Shadow Falls knows where it is."

He repeated the information into the phone, then hung up even while the dispatcher was advising him to stay on the line. Moving toward Bruce, he waggled the gun. "Handcuff keys. Now."

"Go to hell," Bruce said.

"You hurt my woman, and you shot my dog, pal, and it's taking everything I have not to put a bullet in you for that. Just give me a reason."

Bruce got the keys from a pocket and offered them to Adam. Rather than take them, Adam held out his arms, pressing the gun to the man's forehead. "Unlock them."

Bruce obeyed, and the minute they sprang open, Adam snapped them around Bruce's wrists instead. Then, moving quickly to Corinne, he assured himself that she was out cold before he tucked the gun into his pants and joined Olivia on the floor beside Freddy.

Freddy's eyes were open, but they kept closing, staying closed a little bit longer each time. His breath was coming rapidly.

"We're going to lose him," she said through her tears. "Freddy, please, baby, hang on . . ."

"No, no way are we losing him. No way, babe. I'm telling you, he's going to be okay." But his voice held no conviction, and she knew as well as he must that Freddy had been hit in the worst possible place, with the possible exception of a head shot. Her dog's massive heart lay right between his shoulders. It would have been a tough target to miss.

Sobs that had been caught in her throat suddenly broke loose, and she burst into a crying jag that rivaled the worst any woman had ever had.

"Keep the pressure on him, Liv. Keep it on. It's okay. You're doing great."

"H-h-he's sh-shivering."

"So are you." Adam looked around the room, spotted a tarp stretched over some ancient piece of equipment and went to get it. He gave it a solid shake, sending a cloud of dust into the air, and then he brought it back and draped it over the dog, leaving room for Olivia to keep the pressure on his chest.

He put a hand on her shoulder. "I'm so sorry. I'm so sorry."

"I never should have brought him."

"He saved your life. Mine, too."

The dog heaved a broken, pain-wracked sigh.

"Oh, baby, I'm so, so sorry. Please hold on. Freddy, please hold on."

But he only looked at her, his soft brown eyes more full of love and need than she'd ever seen them — and then they rolled back, flashing their whites in a brief, horrifying display, before those heavy lids fell closed.

Collapsing on top of her dog, and ignoring the sounds of sirens and the strobe lights coming through the windows, she sobbed as if her heart were broken. Because it was.

"What about Carrie?"

She lifted her head slowly and whispered, "What?"

"Where does she live?" Adam asked.

Her eyes widened as she realized what he was getting at. "Two miles, maybe less."

"Okay." He got to his feet, took the gun from his jeans and laid it on a table. Then he held his hands up, and faced the door just as it burst open and Bryan Kendall lunged into the room, his .45 leading the way.

"We're not armed," Adam said quickly. "They aren't, either. But we need to get help for Freddy or we're going to lose him."

"They shot him, Bryan!" Olivia yelled. "They shot my dog!"

"Shit. Okay, okay." Bryan checked out the scene for himself before holstering his sidearm. Then, as his men swarmed into the building, he helped Adam pick up Freddy. The men grunted with the effort, and Olivia joined them to help bear the dog's weight.

As they loaded Freddy into the backseat of the nearest police car, Bryan shouted to his men, "Secure the scene, take those two into custody and — Holy shit." He looked at Corinne, who was being lifted to her feet, her hands now in handcuffs, her face bruised to hell and her hair in her eyes. "Is that who I think it is?"

"Yeah," Adam said. "And the other one's my former boss."

"Boss? Wait, he's FBI!"

"So am I," Adam said. "Difference is, I'm clean and he's dirty."

"I knew that prick was no good," Bryan muttered. Then he tossed Adam the keys and said, "I've got to stay here. But I'll need a statement from you, ASAP."

"Just as soon as Freddy's in good hands, I'm all yours." Adam jumped behind the wheel, started up the engine and drove away without a moment's hesitation.

In the back, her knees on the floor, her body wrapped around Freddy's, Olivia wept into warm, soft fur, even while trying to keep the pressure on the hole still pumping out his precious blood. "Left at the main road, Adam, then the second right. Hurry!"

It was Sam who opened the front door in response to Olivia's frantic pounding. He was dressed in pajama bottoms, no shirt, and his hair was tousled. But he took one look at her tear-streaked face, then darted his gaze past her to where Adam was single-handedly trying to lift a seemingly lifeless canine from the back of a police car.

"Mom!" Sam shouted. "Mom, get your bag! It's Freddy!"

And then he was racing toward the vehicle to help. Seconds later Carrie, in a terry bathrobe, was there, and she and Olivia ran to help the men. The four of them managed to get Fred inside, where, with a sweep of her arm, Carrie cleared the kitchen table so they could lay him on top of it.

The table groaned beneath his weight, but it held. And then Carrie was shouting orders, and Sam was shooting back and forth, assisting his mother as if he were a seasoned medic himself. In a few minutes their frantic efforts slowed, then stopped.

Carrie sighed, leaning over the dog, one bloody hand covering her eyes and leaving red streaks on her forehead.

Olivia whispered, "Carrie? God, Carrie, is he . . . ?"

"No. God, no," the other woman said, her head snapping up fast. "But I've done all I can. He needs blood, and he needs surgery, Olivia, and I can't do that here. But I think I've got him stabilized enough to make it to the animal hospital." She patted Olivia's arm. "You were smart to bring him here. As mad as I am at you for getting my kid shot, I'm glad you came to me. He would never have made it across town. But now . . . well, he's got a chance." She glanced across the room to where Sam was speaking softly to someone on the phone.

"We're on our way now. Ten minutes or so," he was saying.

When he hung up, Olivia went over and hugged him hard. "You saved my life, you know."

He went red. "It was no big deal.'

"Thank you, Sam."

"So what are you driving?" Carrie asked Adam.

"Police cruiser. You coming along?"

"He's my patient. I go where he goes until I can hand him off to another doctor. I only wish it were as easy to keep tabs on *all* my patients."

She sent him a wink, then looked at herself. "Let's get him to the car. Put the heat on full blast, and drive as fast as you can. We'll throw on some clothes, and then we'll be right behind you."

At the animal hospital, Olivia paced and waited. Bryan came by with a tape recorder and spent a long time in a small room talking to Adam, and then it was her turn. For the moment there were no Feds impeding his investigation. Bruce had been the only one to come to town, and he'd been working off the books. There would be others now, though.

She told Bryan everything that had happened, everything she had learned about Adam. And the whole time she was talking, her eyes were still glued to the mesh-lined glass in the door, beyond which she could see the waiting area and the double doors through which the vet would emerge when the surgery was complete.

Adam, Sam and Carrie were out there, along with Bryan's fiancée, Dawn, a friend of Olivia's and, more important, of Freddy's.

"I'm sorry to make you go through all this tonight," Bryan said.

She nodded. "Maybe it made the waiting go a little faster. He must still be alive, though. I mean, if he'd died in there, they would have said so. So he must still be alive."

"That would be my guess."

She nodded hard, and dragged her gaze from the door to meet Bryan's. "Is it true, what Adam told me, Bryan? Is he really some kind of . . . undercover agent?"

"Yeah. And his agency is sending his former boss in to debrief him, and you along with him. That's why I wanted to talk to you now, before they get here and take over and tell me I'm not allowed."

She frowned. "If you're not allowed, what good did it do you to talk to me at all?"

He shrugged. "I just wanted to make sure I knew everything, so I can help you later on."

She lowered her eyes. "That's right. I'm going to have to face up to sixteen years of lying about who I am, aren't I? Did I break any laws, I wonder?"

"I don't know."

She thinned her lips. "What about Adam?"

"What about him?"

She shrugged. "Do you think he'll go back to his old job, now that this is all over? I mean, would they let him, do you think?"

He sighed, lowered his head. "I have no idea. You're going to have to ask him that yourself."

The double doors opened then, and she saw everyone in the waiting room rise as one. The vet, still wearing surgical scrubs, walked in. Olivia rose and shot out of the room all in one motion. "How is he?"

The vet looked solemn, and Olivia felt her vision beginning to go dark around the edges, felt the horrible approach of a dead faint closing in on her. And then Adam was beside her, his strong arms holding her, supporting her, and the humming in her ears faded, allowing her to hear what the doctor — Dr. Lassiter, who was pretty and female and relatively new in town — was saying.

"We've done all we can. He'll either wake up from the surgery or he won't. Every hour he lives from here on will increase his chances of a full recovery. He just needs to hang on long enough to get some of his strength back. If he makes it until morning, he'll make it."

Olivia released an openmouthed sigh that was only slightly relieved.

"He's made it this far, Liv," Adam told her. His arms tightened around her, and he pulled her closer to his side. "He'll make it."

"Can I stay with him?" she asked the vet.

"You can see him. But be very quiet and calm, and keep it brief. We don't want to put any strain on his heart right now. And besides, he's still unconscious, and we hope to keep him that way until morning. Afterward, you might as well go home and try to get some sleep."

"I can't leave him!"

"Someone will be watching over him constantly, Professor Dupree," Dr. Lassiter said. "I promise, he won't be alone, and if he even starts to wake up, I'll call you so you can be here. Okay?"

Olivia blinked. "I'm so afraid to leave him."

"You don't have to," Adam whispered in her ear. "Go on in and see him now, hon. I'll be in shortly, okay?"

She nodded, sniffling and wiping at her eyes. Adam handed her off to Sam, who put a strong hand on her shoulder and walked with her and the vet through the double doors toward the recovery room.

The vet opened the door, and Olivia looked in to see Freddy lying still on a stainless-steel table, with a tube in his mouth. He was covered in a blanket, and his eyes were slightly open, mere slits in his face, which seemed worse than if they had been closed. She moved closer and carefully, softly, stroked his neck.

"It's okay, boy. You're a good dog. You're a good, *good* dog, Freddy."

Tears burned in her eyes. She felt it when the door opened, whispers were exchanged, and Sam slipped out of the room as Adam replaced him. She knew it was him without even looking. She felt him there, felt him moving closer to her, felt his hand slide over hers in the dog's gorgeous brindle fur.

"Adam's here, Freddy. We're both here. We're fine. You made sure of that. Now you just need to rest." She spoke very softly but cheerfully, so her dog would know that all was well. "I love you, Freddy. You're *such* a good boy."

A thump, followed by another, weak but unmistakable, drew her eyes to his tail. He wagged it again, thumping the table twice more.

She smiled, and tears streamed down both cheeks. "Did you see that?" she whispered.

"I sure did."

"He's going to be okay. I know he is. God, what a dog. He's going to be just fine."

"I believe you. But how about his owner?"

She blinked, finally turning to meet his eyes. "I just don't want to leave him."

"You don't have to. I promised the clinic a hefty donation."

She gaped at him.

"Well, I had this half mil lying around that no one else knew about. Considering what it was supposed to buy, I thought the best thing it could be used for would be this."

The tears returned. Grateful ones, this time. "Thank you. You didn't have to do that."

"After all I've put you through? Yeah, I kinda did." He put his hands on her shoulders, looked her squarely in the eyes. "I want you to know something, Olivia."

She lifted her brows in question.

"I've got my memory back. There are a few spotty places, but it's pretty much intact."

She smiled. "That's great news, Adam. I'm so glad for you."

He nodded. "Me, too. Did you know you were my last job?"

She frowned. "I was?"

"Yeah. I planned to quit after this one. Find something boring to do for a while."

She smiled softly. "Boring sounds pretty good to me right now."

"Me, too. Another thing I know is something I've kind of suspected right along. There's no woman in my life. No wife, no fiancée, no girlfriend. Never has been anyone serious."

She felt goose bumps rise on her arms and had to avert her eyes. "No?"

"No. No one who's ever made me feel . . . the way I've been feeling since I looked up from that blank slate that was my mind and straight into your brown eyes."

She did look at him then. "Adam . . . ?"

"Look, I don't know if you're going to have charges to answer. If you do, I expect the system to be lenient. You've been through enough. But either way . . . either way, I'd kind of like to be there."

"Be . . . where?"

This time he was the one to lower his eyes.

"Back at the cheese factory," she said, "when everything was going down, you called me your woman and Freddy your dog. Do you really feel that way about us?"

He looked at the giant animal lying so still on the table and said, "I love that oversize mutt so much I can't even believe it. I mean, he's a dog, for cryin' out loud."

"Shhh," she whispered. "He'll hear you."

"Yeah. Well, even so . . . it's nothing like the way I feel about you."

"Oh?"

"Yeah."

"So how *do* you feel?"

"Oh, well, my head's taken a few too many hits, and my wrists are raw from those cuffs, but aside from that —"

She punched him lightly in the arm. "About me," she said.

He smiled slowly, turning her to face him, his arms around her waist. "I'm madly in love with you."

"You are?"

"I was given those letters to read — the ones you'd written to Aaron Westhaven. Bryan says Corinne got them from Skinner, who'd been intercepting pieces of your mail that interested him ever since he found out

454

you were alive. He sold them to Corinne as a way to get to you. She gave them to Bruce, and he gave them to me as part of my research on you, to prepare for the job. Accepting the speaking gig, pretending to be Aaron, that was just to get close enough to you to tell you what was really going on."

"Uh-huh. Could we get back to the part where you're in love with me?" she asked.

He smiled and kissed her forehead. "I kept reading them. Over and over, until I knew them by heart. The way you bared your soul, talked about your losses — no specifics, but I could feel that you'd been through hell. And that you didn't believe in love or happiness anymore. And I wanted you to. I wanted to meet you and talk to you, and make you believe you could be happy again. I wanted to take away all the pain I felt in those words you had written." He looked over at the dog, sleeping on the table. "Instead, I only brought you more."

"None of this was your fault, Adam. You came here to help me. You couldn't have known you were being used to set me up."

He studied her face, waiting, she knew, for more.

Her smile was tremulous and weak. "You already know I love you, too. And I don't want to be alone tonight."

"Then I'll stay with you."

She blinked and looked at her dog. "For how long?"

"Until Freddy wakes up, at least. And beyond that — well, beyond that, for as long as you'll have me, I guess." His fingers caught her chin, turned her face toward his, and then he bent and kissed her.

Olivia gave herself over to the rush of relief provided by a pair of strong male arms and a solid, warm chest. She let go of her worry, of her grief, knowing he could carry it for her until and unless she needed it again. For the first time in sixteen years she trusted a man enough to let her guard down completely, to lean on him, to reveal her own vulnerability in his presence without fear that he would use it against her.

She relaxed. She breathed. She loved.

Oh, God, it had taken so very long.

When he broke the kiss and she relaxed her head on his chest, nestled safe and warm in his arms, she whispered, "Westhaven's full of shit, as it turns out. Love *is* real. It *does* exist. And it's the most beautiful thing there is."

"Third most beautiful," he whispered. "You're second." And then he clasped her shoulders and turned her bodily around. "*That's* the *most* beautiful."

Freddy lay on the table with his brown eyes open, knowing and aware, looking right at them.

They moved to his side as one, arm in arm, then touched him and spoke softly to him, and told him everything was going to be all right.

And for the first time in sixteen long years Olivia actually believed it was true.

EPILOGUE

They were in Carrie's backyard with a huge crowd of friends and relatives, celebrating Sam's Citizen of the Year Award from the Shadow Falls P.D. for his act of selfless heroism. The in-ground pool was perfect on the hot summer day. Some of the people in it were less than thrilled to be sharing the water with a fit and healthy Old English mastiff, but most seemed to think it added to the fun.

Freddy certainly did.

The barbecue grill was being co-manned by Adam and Bryan. Everyone in town had turned out. Once the press got wind of the story, Sam became the hero of the hour, and everyone wanted to celebrate his award with him.

A federal judge had reviewed the potential case against Olivia and dismissed it. The university had been huffy, at first — and Professor Mallory had been one of the chief instigators against her. Even though she'd reimbursed him for the Expedition that was sitting in her driveway alongside the unclaimed Lincoln, as well as her own Escape Hybrid — it was beginning to look like a used SUV lot — Mallory had still been furious and tried to get her fired. That had spurred Carrie to dump his ass — a very good thing, in Olivia's opinion. Best of all, when word came down that she might be terminated, her students had organized a noisy protest rally that had gone on for three days and nights, nonstop, until the board relented.

Her only "punishment" was that the nameplate on her office door had been changed to read Professor Sarah Quinlan.

There had been a couple of weeks where she'd barely been able to leave her house, due to all the press coverage. That she'd taken on the identity of a dead woman and lived under her name for so many years was the stuff of media madness, and they'd been true to form. But things were finally dying down now.

The real Olivia Dupree might finally be able to rest in peace. And the real Sarah Quinlan had been resurrected and was living life for the very first time.

Ironic, that.

"He's gorgeous," Dawn said softly. "You gonna keep him?"

"For ever and ever," Olivia told her friend as they watched the two men bonding over burgers at the grill.

Carrie nudged her with an elbow. "We'll be planning *your* wedding next."

Olivia smiled, loving that idea, even as Dawn said, "Don't get ahead of yourself. We haven't finished planning mine yet — and it's next month!"

"Okay, okay," Carrie conceded. "Come on, Olivia — Sarah — God, I'll never get used to that. We need to help serve."

"If it's okay, I'd like to give your son a thank-you present first."

Carrie closed her eyes. "I can't believe you're doing this. But I'm not gonna say no." She waved an arm in a "go for it" gesture.

Olivia spotted Sam trying to wrest a deflated beach ball from Freddy's jaws, and called out to him. He got out of the pool, calling Freddy behind him.

"Would you walk out front with me, Sam? I want to talk to you about something."

"Sure."

He fell into step beside her, and she said, "You know, with everything going on, I never got a chance to thank you for what you did that night."

"You did so. You said thanks the night Freddy got shot." He shook his head. "Man, that was scary."

"It was. But it wasn't a proper thank-you. And you saved Adam's life, too, before you got around to saving mine. We figured we'd get you a really special present to show you how grateful we both are. Think of it as a birthday present, if you want."

"My birthday was six weeks ago."

She held up a set of keys. "Better late than never."

Sam's jaw dropped. "What — what do you — what are you —"

She pointed, and Sam turned, staring at the red-and-black SUV.

"I thought you might like a slightly used —" she cleared her throat "— Funkmaster Flex Edition Ford Expedition. *Phew!* Do you know how often I had to practice saying that?"

He just stared. Then he shook his head. "No way."

"Um, yes. Way."

And then he smiled and turned and hugged her neck *while* bouncing up and down, as a round of applause broke out from all the people who'd quietly followed them around the side of the house.

"I can't believe it! I can't! Oh, God, I can't believe it! No way! For real?"

"Yeah, for real. I broke it, I bought it. And I don't really need another SUV. You seemed to like this one, and really, it's hardly a fair trade for saving our lives."

"I can't believe it."

"Believe it. I wouldn't have missed out on the life I'm living right now for anything in the world," she said softly, as Adam came up beside her and slid an arm around her shoulders. "It took a long time for me to start living again, Sam. Without you, I wouldn't have had the chance."

"You're awesome, Prof," he said. "God, I don't even know what to say."

"Say you'll be careful with it. Now go check it out already."

"All right!" He took the keys and ran, a dozen other almost-juniors stampeding behind him.

Smiling, she turned into Adam's waiting arms. "That felt great. Just what I needed today."

He frowned. "Why today?"

She lowered her head. "Today's the day the real Olivia Dupree was murdered. I used to think of it as my birthday. My *new* birthday. The day a cop I didn't know was actually a killer helped me be reborn."

462

She closed her eyes. "Let's drink a toast to her tonight. In a way, she helped me, too."

"Okay, it's a deal. And from now on, we'll remember this date and drink a toast to her every year."

"That would be nice," she said softly.

"And it won't even be hard to remember," he said. "Six weeks after Sam's birthday."

"Yeah, six weeks after . . ." She stopped speaking. She turned and stared at Sam, out there with his friends, admiring his new wheels. She looked at him.

Really looked at him.

And she realized for the first time that he had his mother's eyes.

"Hey. Where'd you go?" Adam said.

She blinked and brought herself back to the present. Back to Adam, to her life, a life without secrets. She wished all the people she cared about could have the same.

"Nowhere," she said softly. "I'm right here."

"Right where I like you — by my side."

"It's where I'll always be."

Freddy chose that moment to force his head, followed by his big wet body, right between them, and they both laughed out loud. "Well, where I'll always be if we can get around our dog," she said.

"Yeah, he can be a bit of an obstacle.

463

Luckily he approves of us."

"I wouldn't be with you otherwise," she joked.

He kissed her, then kissed her again. "So how are we getting home now that you've given away our wheels?"

"It's a nice day for a walk," she suggested.

He slid his arm around her again, patted his thigh for Freddy to fall in beside him, and they walked away arm in arm, turning briefly to wave to their friends.

She leaned her head on his shoulder. "I really didn't believe in it, you know."

"In what?" he asked.

"In this." She drew a breath, closed her eyes and felt a warm bliss in every part of her being. "In loving this much. In being this happy. But it's real. It's *real,* and it's actually mine. It's my life. This wonderful, unbelievable, can't-wait-to-get-out-of-bed-and-start-every-new-day, can't-wait-to-fall-back-into-bed-with-you-every-night, life is *mine.*"

She felt as if she were glowing, alive, beaming with joy and still barely able to conceive of herself feeling that way. And yet she did. "I love you."

"I love you, too." He bent to the grassy roadside and plucked a little blue flower, then held it toward her.

She frowned.

"It's a forget-me-not," he said. "Better hold on to it, just in case." He tucked it into her hair, and they laughed while they kissed, and Olivia would have sworn Freddy was laughing right along with them.

PERFORMANCE-BASED INSTRUCTION